A Trace of Smoke

REBECCA CANTRELL

A Trace of Smoke

A TOM DOHERTY ASSOCIATES BOOK
NEW YORK

A TRACE OF SMOKE

Copyright © 2009 by Rebecca Cantrell

All rights reserved.

A Forge Book
Published by Tom Doherty Associates, LLC
175 Fifth Avenue
New York, NY 10010

www.tor-forge.com

Forge® is a registered trademark of Tom Doherty Associates, LLC.

The Library of Congress has catalogued the hardcover edition as follows:

Cantrell, Rebecca.
   A trace of smoke / Rebecca Cantrell.—1st ed.
      p. cm.
   "A Tom Doherty Associates book."
   ISBN 978-0-7653-2044-5
   1. Crime and the press—Fiction.   2. Germany—History—1918–1933—Fiction.
I. Title.
   PS3603.A599T73 2009
   813'.6—dc22

                                                            2008050421

   ISBN 978-0-7653-2690-4

First Hardcover Edition: May 2009
First Trade Paperback Edition: January 2010

Printed in the United States of America

0 9 8 7 6 5 4 3 2 1

To my father, my husband, and my son

Acknowledgments

So many people helped me create *A Trace of Smoke* that I don't have space to list them all, but I will do my best.

Thank you to my attentive and clever editors, Kristin Sevick and Claire Eddy, for making Hannah's emotions shine through, catching those niggling details, and in general making this a better book.

Thank you to my steadfast and talented agent at Reece Halsey North, Elizabeth Evans, for never giving up, not even for a second, and likewise to the delightful Kimberley Cameron for taking a chance on me at Maui.

To those who gave me historical, technical, and fashion advice: Mysti Rubert, Michael Palmieri, Chris Keane, Brigitte Goldstein, James Bisso (for finding a war booty copy of Ernst Röhm's 1928 autobiography), Richard Friedman, Richard Gorey (for the wonderful book trailer), James Rollins, David Lang, Karen Joy Fowler, Norah Charles, Angela Marklew, Jeannie Bollet, and John and Carl McCormick. Any errors I managed to introduce in spite of all that help are my own stubborn fault. Also a special thanks to Anthony Stallone for guiding me through an unknown world. I hope you can see where the path ended. Thank you to Stephen Spittler, my high school English teacher in Berlin. May I use sentence fragments now? Thanks to the incredibly generous Carroll family for letting me live in Boris's house in Berlin, long before I knew that's what it was. *Vielen Dank* to

Mirna Stefanovic Derfel and Jörg Derfel, for giving me a tour of the modern geography of my book, and the Berlin edition of the Duden.

I owe a special debt of gratitude to Kona Ink. These wonderful writers helped me keep track of my language, my props, my plot, and my characters, over many Diet Cokes. Thank you David Deardorff, Judith Heath, Karen Hollinger, and Kathryn Wadsworth. I can't wait to see your books in print soon.

But none of that happens without the support of those close to home. Special thanks to those who gave the most. To my nephew Frank and Elsbeth and Mom for holding things together while I ran off to plot books. To my husband, Toby, for giving me the time, space, and financial security to finish the book, and for listening to me read every word without once complaining, even when I stopped reading to mutter and cross things out. To my son, Max, who waited so patiently for me to finish writing and get on with my most important job, being his mother. To my father, Ralph Edward Cantrell, for always knowing that I would be a writer. I wish you were here to see it.

A Trace of Smoke

1

Echoes of my footfalls faded into the damp air of the Hall of the Unnamed Dead as I paused to stare at the framed photograph of a man. He was laid out against a riverbank, dark slime wrapped around his sculpted arms and legs. Even through the paleness and rigidity of death, his face was beautiful. A small, dark mole graced the left side of his cleft chin. His dark eyebrows arched across his forehead like bird wings, and his long hair, dark now with water, streamed out behind him.

Watery morning light from high windows illuminated the neat grid of black-and-white photographs lining the walls of the Alexanderplatz police station. One hundred frames displayed the faces and postures of Berlin's most recent unclaimed dead. Every Monday the police changed out the oldest photographs to make room for the latest editions of those who carried no identification, as was too often the case in Berlin since the Great War.

My eyes darted to the words under the photograph that had called to me. Fished from the water by a sightseeing boat the morning of Saturday, May 30, 1931—the day before yesterday. Apparent cause of death: stab wound to the heart. Under distinguishing characteristics they listed a heart-shaped tattoo on his lower back that said "Father." No identification present.

I needed none. I knew the face as well as my own, or my sister

Ursula's, with our square jaws and cleft chins. I wore my dark blond hair cut short into a bob, but he wore his long, like our mother, like any woman of a certain age, although he was neither a woman nor of a certain age. He was my baby brother, Ernst.

My fingers touched the cool glass that covered the image, aching to touch the young man himself. I had not seen him naked since I'd bathed him as a child. I pulled my peacock-green silk scarf from my neck to cover him, realizing instantly how crazy that was. Instead, I clenched the scarf in my hand. A gift from him.

I knew standard procedure dictated that the body be buried within three days. It might already be in an unmarked grave, wrapped in a coarse linen shroud. After Ernst left home and started earning his own money, he swore that only silk and cashmere would touch his body. I flattened my palm on the glass. The picture could not be real.

"Hannah!" called a booming voice. Without turning, I recognized the baritone of Fritz Waldheim, a policeman at Alexanderplatz. A voice that had never before frightened me. "Here for the reports?"

I drew my hand back from the photograph and cleared my throat. "Of course," I called. My damp skirt brushed my calves as I trudged down the hall to his office in the Criminal Investigations Department, struggling to bring my emotions under control. Feel nothing now, I told myself. You can feel it later, but not until after you leave the police station.

Fritz held the door open, and I nodded my thanks. He was the kindly husband of my oldest friend, and I feared that he would recognize the photograph too, if he studied it closely. He must not suspect that Ernst was dead. My identity papers, and Ernst's, were on a ship to America with my friend Sarah and her son Tobias.

Sarah, a prominent Zionist troublemaker, was forbidden to travel by order of the German government. We'd loaned them our identity papers so they could masquerade as Hannah and Ernst Vogel, a German brother and sister on vacation. Their ship would dock soon, and our papers would be returned, but until that happened no one could notice anything that Hannah and Ernst Vogel did in Berlin without placing their lives in danger. Even though Ernst had acted distant with me for the past six months, he had agreed to the plan.

"Still raining, I see." Fritz pointed to my dripping umbrella. I'd forgotten I still held it. He closed the office door.

"Washes the dog shit off the sidewalks." I forced a laugh that tore my lungs. The weather remained our favorite joke, Fritz and mine. We jested about that and his Alsatian dog, Caramel. "How are Bettina and the children?" I tried to always keep it light with him. To make him enjoy handing me the police reports so much it did not cross his mind that he did not need to do it.

"Are you crying?" he asked, concern in his gray eyes. No getting past Fritz, the experienced detective.

"A cold." I wiped my wet face with my wet hand. I hated to lie to him, but Fritz ran everything by the book. He would neither understand, nor forgive, passing off my papers, even to save Sarah. "A cold and the rain."

He took a clean, white handkerchief out of his uniform pocket and handed it to me. It smelled of starch from Bettina's wifely care. "Thank you," I said, wiping my cheeks. "Anything interesting?"

Like every Monday, I had come to the police station to sift through the weekend's crime reports in search of a story for the *Berliner Tageblatt,* looking for a tale of horror to titillate our readers. Mondays were the best times for fresh reports. People got up to more trouble on weekends, and at the full moon. Ernst's photograph flashed through my head. He too, had got up to more trouble on the weekend. I swallowed my grief and handed Fritz his handkerchief.

Fritz shook his head. "We found a few floaters last weekend." He walked behind the wooden counter that separated his work area from the public area. "Mostly vagrants, I think. Probably a few from a new power struggle between criminal rings, but we'll not prove it."

I held my face stiff, using the polite smile I'd mastered as a child. I was grateful for the beatings, slappings, and pinchings I'd received from my parents. They had taught me to hold this face no matter what my real thoughts and feelings. Ernst had mocked me for it. Everything he thought or felt showed on his face the instant it entered his head. And now he was dead. I gulped, once more fighting for control. Fritz furrowed his brow. He suspected something was wrong, in spite of my best efforts.

"Anything worth my time?" I said to Fritz, because that is what I would have said on any other day.

"A group of Nazis beat a Communist almost to death, but that's not news."

"Not news," I said. "But newsworthy, even though the *Tageblatt* will not run it. Someone should care what the Nazis are doing."

"We care," Fritz said. "But the courts let them go faster than we can arrest them."

He turned and walked to a large oak file cabinet. As he sorted through folders I took a few steadying breaths.

"Here we go." He pulled out a stack of papers.

I leaned against the counter and tried to look composed.

Fritz passed me the incident reports with his short, blunt fingers. "Not much, I'm afraid."

"Hey!" called a high-pitched male voice behind Fritz. "You must not give her those reports." A small man with erect military bearing rushed over to us and snatched the papers from my hand. "Who are you?"

Fritz looked worried. "She's Hannah Vogel, with the *Berliner Tageblatt*."

"You have identification?" He stared at me with dark crow's eyes. His thick black hair was perfectly in order, his suit meticulously pressed.

"Of course," I said. My identification rested in Sarah's purse on a boat in the middle of the ocean. I rummaged through my satchel for show, grief replaced again by fear.

"I've known her since she was seventeen years old," Fritz said.

The man ignored him and snapped his fingers at me. "Papers, please."

"They must be here somewhere." My knees threatened to collapse.

I took things out of my satchel: a green notebook, a clean handker-chief, a jade-colored fountain pen that Ernst bought for me after he left home.

"What do you do at the *Tageblatt*?" His tone sounded accusatory. He leaned closer to me. I yearned to back away, but forced myself to remain still, like someone with nothing to hide.

"Crime reporter," I answered, looking up. "Under the name of Peter Weill."

"*The* Peter Weill?" His tone shifted. He was a fan.

"For the past several years," I said. "I have worked closely with the police all that time."

I pulled my press pass out of my satchel and handed it to him, then flipped open my sketchbook to a courtroom sketch published in the paper a week ago.

His face creased in a smile. "I remember that picture. Your line work is quite accomplished." He returned my press pass, and I tucked it into my satchel.

"Thank you," I said. "It's so rare that anyone notices. You have a discerning eye."

Fritz suppressed a smile when the man stood up even straighter and held out his hand.

"Kommissar Lang."

I wiped my palm on my skirt before shaking his hand. "Good to meet you."

"The pleasure is mine." He rocked back on the heels of his highly polished shoes. "Your articles have astute insight into the criminal mind. And the measures we must take in order to protect good German people from the wrong elements."

"I try to do a good, fair job by getting my information from the source." I glanced at the reports in his hand.

He bowed and handed them to me. "So many reporters these days speak only to victims. Or criminals."

"They are important sources as well." I took the reports with a hand that trembled only slightly. "One must be thorough."

"You have such insight into the male mind. You and your husband must be very close."

"She's never been married," Fritz said. The corners of his mouth twitched with a suppressed smile.

"Might you autograph an article for me?" Kommissar Lang clasped his hands behind his back and leaned forward. "Do you have an article in today's paper?"

I had not yet read today's paper. "I am not certain."

"Yesterday's," Fritz said. "Front page."

"I will procure a copy." Kommissar Lang hastened out of the room. Fritz returned to his desk without saying a word. His shoulders twitched with laughter, but he kept a serious face. It cost me, but I gave him the expected warning smile.

When I glanced down at the reports, I saw gibberish. Lines of black type ran along the paper, but my mind could not turn them into words. My hand shook as I pretended to take notes, but I hoped Fritz could not see that from his desk. I willed myself to think of nothing but numbers and stared at the second hand of my watch, silently counting each tick. When three minutes elapsed, I put the unread reports down on the counter. "You are correct, Fritz," I said. "Not much there."

I would find no report of a sensational murder or string of robberies for Peter Weill's byline today. And the murder I most wanted to research I could not ask a single question about. No attention dared fall on Ernst or me. If Sarah and her son were still underway, they might be arrested. Because of her political activism, she had been denied immigration to the United States three times. But it was becoming harder for even apolitical Jews to leave Germany. If the National Socialists, the Nazis, were to gain the majority in the Reichstag, I shuddered to think what would happen. Anti-Semitic scapegoating ran deep everywhere in Europe. As disgusting as I found it, I had to admit that Hitler was far too clever at using it for his political ends. Things would get worse before they got better.

I turned and marched back down the hall, willing myself not to glance at the photograph. If I did not look, perhaps it would not be true.

"Fraulein Vogel," called Kommissar Lang. I heard him sprinting after me.

Something was amiss. Would he demand to see my papers again, papers I still did not have? I envisioned bolting through the front door of the police station, but instead I turned to him, ready to concoct a story of lost papers.

"You forgot my autograph," he panted.

"I do apologize." Relief flooded over me. "It slipped my mind. I am so late for the Becker trial."

Kommissar Lang nodded. "The rapist who targeted schoolgirls in the park?"

"That one." Any other day I would have asked him about his involvement in the case, but today I needed to get away before I broke down.

He thrust the paper at me.

"I apologize in advance if there's anything inaccurate. My editor has a leaden touch."

He handed me a pen. "Come to my office and sign it." He gestured back down the hallway, past the photograph of Ernst. If I followed him, I knew that he would regale me with tales of his arrests and later be offended that I did not write each one for the *Tageblatt*. I had been through that with countless police officers, and afterward they were never much use as sources.

I placed his newspaper against the wall and signed it. "I must be at the courthouse early. It is best to watch the accused come in and sit down. One learns so much."

He nodded. "One can determine a great deal from watching someone walk."

I handed him back the newspaper and walked out the front door, trying not to let the wobble in my knees betray me.

Outside, a gust of wind tried to rip the umbrella out of my hands, but I held on, cursing and half-crying as I stumbled across cobblestones to the subway. I pushed my way down concrete stairs, against the crush of people going to work. They chattered and laughed together, gleeful in the mundane details of their lives. I wanted only to go home and be alone.

Pictures of Ernst flashed by in my head. The most painful images were from his childhood. He'd been a wonderful child and, later, a great friend. I leaned against the wall of the subway station, face turned toward the tile, and sobbed, safely alone in the crowd. When I could stand and walk again, I did.

Once aboard the train I collapsed on the wooden seat and drew a deep breath. I ran my fingers over the oak slats of the bench. The wood was blond, like Ernst's hair. Across from me, their faces hidden behind twin newspapers, sat two men in black fedoras. One man read the *Berliner Tageblatt*, the other the *Völkische Beobachter*, that Nazi rag.

2

A burst of humid air hit my face as two teenage boys pried open the doors of the moving train. The train had entered a tunnel, and the boys were daring each other to stick their arms into the darkness, never knowing when they would draw back a bloody stump. Their parents thought they were safe in school. I closed my eyes and did not open them until I sensed the subway car had reentered the light.

The train stopped at Kaiserhof station. I had missed my connection at Friedrichstadt. I should have climbed out and taken a bus to Moabit for the trial, but instead I rode west toward the more expensive borough of Wilmersdorf. Eventually this subway would take me to the Berlin Zoological Garden, only a few blocks from Ernst's apartment building. I stayed on, unable to do anything else.

When I got out at Bahnhof Zoo, I climbed the stairs like an old woman, hesitating on every step. Fewer passengers jostled me now. I wound my way through fashionable buildings, barely sparing a glance at the neo-Gothic spires of the Kaiser Wilhelm Memorial Church.

As I wavered in front of Ernst's apartment building, Rudolf von Reiche burst out—tall, lean, and aristocratic in a gray three-piece suit and a shirt so white it cut my eyes. He carried a cardboard box the size of a child's schoolbag and almost knocked me off the stoop. "Ah, Hannah, Queen of the Bourgeoisie," he said in a frosty tone, tipping his gray bowler at me.

"Hello, Rudolf, Defiler of Children." I leaned backward to look at him. Thirty centimeters taller than me, and he always stood too close. He never forgave me for despising him, and I never forgave him for seducing my sixteen-year-old brother out of my home and into his decadent life. Inside a week of meeting Rudolf, Ernst left school, moved out of the apartment, and started singing at the new El Dorado, a queer club on Motz Strasse. I barely saw him after that. Rudolf had turned him from a serious student into a chanteuse.

"He's not a child anymore," Rudolf said. The front door swung shut behind his back. "In fact, he's turned to defiling them himself."

"What are you doing here, visiting Ernst?" I knew he was not, but a lie from him might be illuminating.

"He's not here." Rudolf pursed his thin lips. "You look pasty in that horrible coat, Hannah. It is the color of a paper bag. And the cut is all wrong. Are you dressing out of the dustbin?"

"Where is he?" A cold weight lodged in my stomach.

"Cavorting with that Nazi boy he's seeing no doubt." Rudolf scanned the street.

"Nazi boy?" I stuttered.

"Someone more his own age. A luscious youth." Rudolf hefted the box against his narrow hip. "Someone of whom you would approve."

"When did you last see Ernst?" I tried to remember the date under the photograph. The body was found Saturday.

"Friday night." Rudolf sniffed. "Not that it concerns you. Or me, since he abandoned me for that youth."

"You let him leave the bar with a stranger?" I felt like a hopeless old maid as soon as the words left my mouth.

Rudolf laughed, a sound like a horse's whinny. He walked down the street. "Your brother does what he wants."

"What is in the box?" I followed him. I cast a glance over my shoulder at Ernst's front steps, imagining him sweeping down them, admonishing Rudolf and me for arguing over him like two dogs over a bone. A delectable bone, he would add, arching his eyebrows. I bit my lip. He would never come down those stairs again.

"The box has only trinkets I gave your brother to show my feelings. Back when he shared them." Rudolf tossed his head like a horse without upsetting his thick gray hair. I suppressed a smile at the feminine gesture. He certainly did not do that around his rich law clients.

"May I see these trinkets?" I hurried to keep pace with Rudolf's long-legged stride.

"Why?" Rudolf asked. "They do not belong to you."

"Nor are they yours," I said. "If you gave them to Ernst."

Rudolf narrowed his eyes and stopped walking. A crowd of workmen in caps and open-necked shirts pushed by us on their way from the subway station.

"Are you stealing them, Rudolf?"

Rudolf sighed, and his pockmarked face sagged, caving in under the weight of his fifty years. As angry as he was, he was hurt too. "He might cast them out on the street," he said. "If they mean nothing to him now, I should have them."

"Perhaps they have financial meaning?"

"I have no need to stoop to petty thievery," he said. "Take them. Pass them along when you see him." He thrust the cardboard box into my hands.

A tiny scrap of red silk stuck out from under the flap of the box, and I stroked it with my fingers. One of Ernst's handkerchiefs. I'd taught him to sew. We'd hemmed many handkerchiefs together, always red and always, when he could afford it, silk.

A cold wind brushed my face and I turned up the collar of my coat. I tucked the corner of red silk out of sight. "Do you know the Nazi boy's name or address?" I asked Rudolf.

"Certainly not." Rudolf sniffed again.

I wondered if he'd been sniffing cocaine in Ernst's apartment.

"I do not associate with that lot," he said.

"Your nose is bleeding." I dug for a handkerchief in my satchel.

Rudolf pulled a lace-edged handkerchief out of his pocket and held it to his nose. A red stain bloomed through the white linen. "Damn allergies," he said. "I must be on my way. Inform Ernst that we have much to resolve." He raised his hand to hail a taxi. "Make sure he knows the consequences."

"Which are?"

"Very unpleasant." Immediately a taxi stopped in front of him, as taxis must have done all of his life. He climbed in without a backward glance, and the taxi trundled off like a giant black beetle.

My mind filled with thoughts of Ernst and the Nazi boy. I had always wanted him to date a boy nearer his own age. But not a Nazi. I was a Socialist and despised Nazis for many things, including wanting to force women back into the home—children, kitchen, and church were to be our only realms. A particularly bad set of choices for those of us who neither had nor wanted a husband or children. And I did not want to think what would happen to the Jews and Communists if the Nazis gained power. I suspected that children, kitchen, and church were far better alternatives than what the Nazis would give them.

Still, Ernst thought those brown shirts and chocolate-colored shorts quite fetching. He'd only dated much older men. I had hoped that he would end up with a nice girl, in the end. Loving men was dangerous, and I would have shielded him from that danger if I could, or I would have had him not choose to go down that path. But I knew that he had no choice. He had been exactly who he was from his earliest days. Still, he could have chosen a man less predatory than Rudolf. Perhaps this boy had been an improvement for him. I stifled a sob. Too little, too late. At least he'd been alive while dating Rudolf. I rubbed my hands over my face, trying not to think of Ernst as dead.

Would Ernst have left a good provider like Rudolf for a youth? He cared so much about his own comfort. When he betrayed Rudolf in the past (as he had often done), he'd been careful to conceal his affairs. Rudolf was a jealous and powerful man.

The bell for the Kaiser Wilhelm Memorial Church rang ten. I was late for the trial. If I did not go, I might lose my job, lose everything. I thought about trying to convince Ernst's landlady to let me into his apartment, but did not think I could face his rooms after all, with his dresses and his scent.

I plodded back toward the subway station. A sign with a white *U* against a dark blue background marked the entrance. Ernst called those signs empty smiles. He had preferred the confines of a taxi with a rich partner to the crush and noise of a subway car. And now he was to be buried alone, without the pomp he loved. I clutched Rudolf's box and walked to the platform.

Waiting for the train, I tapped the box, anxious to know what it contained, but I dared not pull anything out here. What if Rudolf had stuffed expensive jewelry in there? Or cocaine? Or a bizarre sexual instrument?

I took the subway back toward the courthouse, staring at my reflection in the window glass while the train careened through darkness.

I climbed endless courthouse steps and pushed open the absurdly tall doors designed to make us feel that law was a grand process and justice about more than the skill of your lawyer. The trial had started. The judge gave me a censorious look from his carved bench, a relic of richer times before the war. Any other day I would have cared, but today I returned his stare without apology.

About one hundred spectators stuffed the courtroom, but I slipped past them and crammed myself onto the press bench, next to Philip Henker from the *Berlin Börsen Courier*. He nodded a greeting, his jowls drooping like a mastiff's.

The trial was wrapping up, so the curious were here to find out the verdict. Luckily it was less full than the Kürten trial I'd recently covered in Düsseldorf. For that one, people overflowed into the halls outside.

I put the box on my lap and automatically got my sketchbook ready, paging through sketches of the suspected rapist I'd drawn at the beginning of the trial. Fat and round like a ball, he seemed more pathetic than sinister, but I'd tried to find a menacing angle for him. He looked like a self-indulgent old shopkeeper. Nothing worth running in the paper. I wiped sweat off my forehead with the back of my hand, careful not to smudge charcoal on myself. All of the people packed into the courtroom kept it warm and comfortable during the winter, but in summer the heat was oppressive.

I scanned the spectators, looking for Boris and his daughter Trudi. I had met them at the courthouse last Friday, when my life still traveled on familiar tracks. The next day, Boris and I had gone out on a date. He'd given me a small but electrifying kiss after delivering me to my doorstep. Hard to believe that kiss had been only two days ago. It seemed like part of a different lifetime now.

As if he sensed my gaze, Boris turned to look at me. His eyes narrowed, and he shot me a look of such venom that I rocked back in my seat. It was the same furious expression he'd had when the rapist was brought into the courtroom Friday.

3

On Friday, before I met him, I had sketched Boris in the courtroom. At first he had looked tender as he'd bent to talk to Trudi. His look had been so touching that I had turned to a blank page. I sketched broad strokes with my charcoal pencil, trying to capture the protective arc of his arm as it went around her shoulders, the tilt of his head toward her. His tailored navy-blue suit sat on him like a second skin. I guessed he worked as a banker or a lawyer. Someone used to money. Someone who expected the system to pay attention to his problems.

I remembered how, when the suspect marched in, Boris had glared at him with such loathing I turned again to a fresh page and sketched his fury. I wondered what he would do if the suspect were acquitted. He'd looked ready to hunt him down and mete out his own justice.

At the end of the day I had hurried out of the courthouse, anxious to get to the paper and make my deadline. I'd slipped on the wet stairs and pitched forward. A strong hand shot out and caught my elbow. My sketchbook flew out of my hands.

"Careful," said a concerned voice.

"Thank you," I said, steadying myself on an arm clad in navy blue. I gazed into Boris's eyes for the first time. They were brown, flecked with gold. Up close he was even more handsome. I jumped back and tripped again.

"You seem intent on hurling yourself down the stairs." He caught me easily and pushed his beautiful lips into a slow smile. "Surely things cannot be so bad, young lady."

No one had called me a young lady since before the war. "Easy to say from inside such an expensive suit." I smiled back.

He retrieved my tattered sketchbook, open to the picture I'd drawn of him glaring at the rapist. "A masterful likeness," he said. "Yet I am at a loss as to why you would sketch me."

"I do courtroom sketches," I said to allay his suspicions. "For the newspaper."

"Do I look so . . ." He paused, staring at the sketch. "So hateful?"

"I draw what I see," I said. "But it's understandable. . . ."

He raised his eyebrows, and my voice trailed off.

"Why would it be understandable?" His voice was cool and controlled.

"Most people hate a man who commits those crimes."

"Not all?" He closed the sketchbook. "There are those who would not hate someone who takes a child and defiles her, hurts her, damages her on a whim?"

His daughter climbed down the steps to us. "Is everything in order, Vati?"

He smiled and gently touched her arm. "Of course."

He turned to me. "Fraulein . . ." He paused expectantly.

"Vogel. Hannah Vogel." I was grateful that I wrote under a pseudonym and he did not know I was also a reporter. He might be a good source, and if not, he was a very attractive man. Most men did not desire a woman who did my job: interviewing criminals, fostering connections in the criminal world, investigating crimes, and using all of that to write up stories as a man. No need for him to know that I was a reporter just yet.

"Fraulein Vogel was just standing here when I almost knocked her off her feet. She's quite a talented artist." He handed me the sketchbook. "Come along," he said to his daughter, and they started down the stairs.

I turned to go, but my journalistic impulses triumphed over my good manners. Perhaps they knew more about the case. The best stories required the most digging. Or perhaps I fooled myself and wanted more contact with a handsome man who did not wear a wedding ring. Whatever the reason, I called to the girl. "I have a lovely drawing of you, Fraulein."

When she turned I leafed through my sketchbook and pulled out the drawing I'd done of her. She looked young and lost and beautiful, sitting in the courtroom next to her father. She faced the windows behind the judge, and light suffused her face. I'd drawn her large, widely spaced eyes and the luxurious long hair that she would probably cut soon. I guessed her to be fourteen, almost old enough to demand a bob.

"I look so beautiful," she said, in a surprised tone.

"You are beautiful," her father said. "It's an amazing likeness."

"Please keep it," I said.

She took the drawing slowly from my hands. "Could we pay you something for this?"

"No payment is required."

"But of course it is," said the father. "I'm Boris Krause, and this is my daughter, Trudi. Would you care to join us for dinner?"

He extended his hand. His palm and long fingers were warm, and I held his hand a second too long. "I would love to," I said.

Boris chose a busy café half a block from the courthouse. The three of us crossed the street together, dodging a bus and a horse and buggy. I could not remember the last time I ate in a restaurant. The smells were luscious: wurst, potato salad, beer, and herring. Usually I had a roll for dinner and, if I felt wealthy, an apple or a banana. My stomach grumbled, reminding me that I had not eaten since a scanty lunch.

In front of the restaurant a wizened organ grinder pumped away, his monkey capering at the end of a long chain. When Trudi dropped a few coins in the monkey's cup, the organ grinder smiled his thanks without slowing his rhythm. His monkey tipped his tiny purple fez at Trudi, and she waved to him.

We sat at an outdoor table, encircled by a simple cast-iron railing that followed the arc of the sidewalk and separated us from passers-by. A draft horse in the street chewed his way through a nosebag of oats, his docked tail twitching in a futile attempt to shoo flies.

We ordered wurst and fried potatoes from an efficient waitress in a starched white cap. Boris and I chose Schultheiss pilsner, a little stronger than I liked, but better than mineral water with the wurst. When Trudi requested a lemonade, I noticed dark rings under her eyes. Was she one of the rapist's victims? Their names had been withheld from the press.

"What brought you two to the trial?" I asked.

Trudi started, and Boris laid his hand over hers. "We came to help a friend," he said. "And you?"

"As I said, I work in the courthouse," I answered, which was not a complete lie. Much of my workday was spent in the courthouse, after all. "And what do you do, Herr Krause?"

"I am a banker for the Dresdner Bank."

"Steady work."

"So far."

The waitress came with our food. It was served on simple ceramic plates with a sprig of parsley. The meaty smell of bratwurst made my mouth water. I concentrated on eating in a ladylike manner, instead of gulping it down the way my hunger demanded.

"Where do you go to school?" I asked Trudi, taking a sip of bitter beer.

"At the Bülow Gymnasium." Trudi pushed her wurst around on her plate with her fork. "But I want to quit and become a hatmaker. I want to learn a real skill instead of trigonometry."

"Why not go to university and meet a nice man?" her father asked.

"Vati," she said. "No smart girl wants to do that anymore."

"My friend, Sarah, is a hatmaker," I said. "She loves the design work and all the colored felt and feathers."

"See, Vati," Trudi said, smiling for the first time. She had beautiful brown eyes, like her father. "It's a wonderful occupation."

She looked so thrilled that I cast around in my mind for something to sustain that excitement. I described films for which Sarah had made hats: *Hocus Pocus*, *Three from the Gas Station*, even *Storm Over Mont Blanc* with Leni Riefenstahl.

"I do want to be a hatmaker," Trudi told her father. "Especially now that feathers and birds are coming back in fashion on hats."

"The hours are very long." I did not want to be the cause of this girl dropping out of school to spend a lifetime bent over hat forms and feathers. "She works until late at night."

"Does this Sarah have a husband?" Boris popped the last bite of bratwurst into his mouth and smiled. "One who puts up with the long hours?"

"He died in the war," I said. "Along with my fiancé. So now we both must work."

"I'm sorry for your loss," Boris said, serious again. "I lost Trudi's mother in childbirth. She was a wonderful woman. Strong, like Trudi. Beautiful like her too." Trudi smiled. A tiny smile, but it promised to be radiant when she was happy again.

"It's not easy to lose a loved one," I said.

Boris nodded. "And to that war. It was a terrible war. I am lucky that I survived, quite by chance, while so many others did not."

We sat through a long, uncomfortable silence. A double-decker bus roared by, full of workers heading home. I needed to get to the paper to write up the trial, but I did not stand.

"How many hats does your friend make in a day?" Trudi asked finally.

"For that, you must ask her employer, Frau Charmain."

Trudi gasped. "But she is a famous designer!"

"And a good woman. She kept Sarah on when some of her largest department store clients demanded that she employ only German workers, not Jews."

"It makes me ashamed to be German," said Boris. "That kind of nonsense."

Handsome and no Nazi. I smiled at him. "Indeed it should."

Trudi looked from Boris to me. "I must powder my nose."

"Should I come with you?" I asked.

"I can find the way," she said tartly. "I am fourteen years old, for goodness sake."

"Practically an old maid." Boris winked at her.

She walked confidently, with her shoulders back and her head held high, but she flinched away from tables occupied by men.

"Thank you for coming," Boris said. He too, watched Trudi. "You are good with her."

"Perhaps she is the one being good with me," I said, turning back to him, knowing that she had left us alone on purpose.

The waitress came to clear our plates, glaring at Trudi's untouched meal.

"Would you care for another wurst?" Boris asked, noticing my empty plate.

"No, thank you," I said, embarrassed that I'd eaten so quickly.

The waitress gathered our plates and hurried back along the route Trudi had chosen, taking no special notice of the tables of men.

"Trudi does not eat much."

"You know how young girls are," he said. "Starving one day and eating only confections the next."

"I only know about young boys," I said. "Boys are different."

"Do you have children?" Boris asked.

"I've never been married," I answered. "I raised my brother, but that did not turn out as well as I'd hoped."

He raised one eyebrow. "Why?"

"The path he was given to walk is one I would not have chosen for him. One that I would choose for no one." I thought of the boys who had attacked him at school, sensing his difference even then.

"That's a shame." Boris reached across the table and covered my hand with his. I barely knew him, but it felt safe and right. "We cannot protect our children from everything, no matter how much we want to."

"Why not?"

Boris sighed. "Because we do not run all the world."

I forced myself to smile. "You are correct, of course."

Light glinted off the gold flecks in his eyes, like a painting. The warmth of his hand sent a current of electricity up my arm, a reaction I had not felt so strongly since I was with my fiancé, Walter, many years ago. "Perhaps we could meet for dinner sometime?" Boris asked.

"Perhaps." My heart fluttered, actually fluttered, like in a romance novel. I bit the inside of my cheek to keep from smiling at the thought.

"Let me give you my telephone number." He fished a card out of a silver case. Already, I missed the feeling of his hand on mine. He wrote a number on the back of his card, his tapered fingers producing elegant handwriting. "The front is my number at the bank. The back is my number at home."

I barely heard his words, because I watched his lips while he said them. I tucked the card in my satchel. "I—"

He laughed. "Do not say no immediately. Give yourself some time to consider it."

I tore my eyes away from his lips and sipped my beer. I had a rule about not dating men I met at the courthouse, but Boris seemed like a man of high character, someone I could get involved with. Then I reminded myself that Peter Kürten, the Vampire of Düsseldorf, had character witnesses too, and they were every one wrong. "Now is a difficult time for me."

"Now is not always the best time for anyone." He glanced to where Trudi emerged from the door. "Sometimes the worst times are exactly when you need to reach out to other people."

There was truth in that.

"Tomorrow?" he said. "I could pick you up at seven."

Before I could think better of it, I wrote down my address on a sheet of paper in my notebook. I tore it out and passed it to him, my heart pounding.

"Hello," Trudi said, sitting back down.

"I apologize," I said. "But I must go."

Boris rose as I stood to leave. "I will see you soon." He leaned forward and kissed my hand. Tingles ran up my arm to my stomach and I, the hardened reporter, blushed right there in the café, in front of a roomful of hungry diners.

"It was delightful talking with you, Trudi," I said. "And with you as well, Herr Krause."

I hurried out of the restaurant, my heart racing, my kissed hand wrapped safely around my sketchpad.

I arrived at the paper late that night, having dawdled too long at the restaurant with Boris and Trudi. On the bus, I'd compared Boris to Walter, the man I would have married if he had lived through the Great War. I wondered what kind of parent Walter would have been and rode right by my stop on Koch Strasse. Walter had loved children. He'd been wonderful with Ernst, although Ernst had been only six when Walter died. But the war had brought out an angry side of Walter, one that sometimes spilled over into violence. What would Walter have done if he'd seen Ernst singing at the El Dorado? I would never know.

I walked back the two blocks, admiring the modern façade of my office building, the Mosse House, when it came into sight. Faced with shiny black tile and sensuous curving windows, the building arced to follow the street and stood tall and plain, like an elegant modern cake. After the original building was damaged during the Spartacus uprising at the end of the war, old Herr Mosse hired noted Expressionist architect Erich Mendelsohn to remodel it. The Mosse House was not as curvaceous and provocative as the tower he built for Albert Einstein, but still shocking enough to annoy the other newspaper owners.

I hurried across the expansive lobby to the elevator. "Good day, Xavier," I said to the elevator operator.

He held the door open with one gloved hand. "Fraulein Vogel."

"Five, please."

The fifth floor was a letdown after the beautiful façade and posh elevator. Mosse had decided we did not deserve new furniture and had brought furniture from the old building. Battered wooden desks paired with creaky chairs. The office teemed with people. Conversations rumbled under the clattering of typewriters.

I hurried to open the window and let out the thick clouds of cigarette smoke.

I stole a chair from an empty desk, then rolled a piece of clean paper into the heavy black typewriter, enjoying my favorite part of being a reporter: the moment when the white page stood open to receive all possibilities. I'd worked here long enough now that no one dared to disturb me this close to deadline. I savored the moment, forming the story in my mind.

The rapist looked guilty to me, so I chose a headline that started with "Guilty Verdict Assured." They had eyewitnesses who had seen the man disappear with the girls, written testimony from the girls, and hair ribbons found at his apartment. I would look a fool Monday afternoon if they acquitted him, but by the end of the week no one would remember.

I started my story evoking the innocence and trust of the Berlin schoolgirls, walking home in the bright sunshine. Open and friendly, willing to look for a lost puppy. None of them could bear the thought of a little dog wandering alone in the park, not with all of those automobiles. Like Little Red Riding Hood, they stepped off the path, away from the street with its safe stone sidewalks, and into the shadows of the woods. There they lost their innocence, figuratively and literally. Would any of them enjoy a sunny day again?

I sighed. It was a good story, but this time I felt a connection to Trudi and her father. Was Trudi one of the victims, or just the friend of one, as her father had implied? When I wrote about how the girls were unable to eat, I remembered Trudi pushing the uneaten wurst around on her plate. How she sat with her face upturned to the tall windows, bathed in the sunlight that had not protected her after all. Bogeymen did not always live in the shadows.

I had typed feverishly. The piece flowed well. I had pulled out the final sheet of paper, and run it down to printing. I missed my deadline, and the story would not run until Sunday morning.

And I had met Boris Saturday. We had a delightful time. He was charming, witty, and the attraction between us was undeniable. I had promised to go sailing with him and Trudi soon. Then we had shared that wonderful kiss on my stoop.

I remembered stealing a glance at him before I closed my door. He had looked at me in a tender way that no man had for a very long time.

4

Now, in the courtroom, Boris's eyes were no longer tender. I shifted on the bench, bumping Philip with Rudolf's box. Philip rolled his eyes, and I smiled apologetically. Out of the corner of my eye, I saw Boris still watching me. He must be angry about the story, angry that I'd put in details about Trudi and her loss of appetite.

To keep from facing Boris's angry eyes, I outlined the two possibilities for today: "Man Acquitted in Travesty of Justice" and "Rapist Convicted." Both stories were pat, boring. Luckily, I'd written each a hundred times before, as my mind did not seem to be working well. As much as I tried not to, my thoughts returned to the photograph I saw in the Hall of the Unnamed Dead that morning.

I closed my eyes and tried to listen, but I did not hear much until the verdict came down.

Not guilty.

A gasp traveled through the courtroom.

I glanced at Trudi. She looked stunned, like a child after she falls down and before she begins to cry, disbelieving that the world could have provided the hurt. I remembered that expression from Ernst's childhood. Boris wrapped his arm around her shoulder and pulled her to him.

I rushed out to claim the pay telephone and to get away from Boris. Hopefully Maria, the fastest writer at the newspaper, would be waiting for the news. The telephone booth was occupied, and I paced in front of the glass door, wanting to be done with the story and on my way home, away from everything, shut up alone in my apartment. I hefted Rudolf's box on my hip.

"Hello, Herr Weill," said a voice behind me. Boris.

I winced and turned. He stood close enough to touch. I felt heat emanating off his body. Even furious, he was incredibly sexy.

"Herr Weill," he repeated.

There was no point in denying that I was Peter Weill. He must have read my article, the bit about the girls being unable to eat. "Hello, Herr Krause."

"You have a good story now," he said. " 'Poor Wolf Wronged by Little Red Riding Hood.' "

"People want to know how the case came out." It grated to be third to phone in the news, but I stepped to the side to let Philip use the now empty telephone booth ahead of me.

"People—want—to know." Boris talked at a normal volume, although any fool could see that he wanted to shout. He leaned closer to me. His cologne smelled of limes and cedar trees with a hint of musk. "Is it just a bedtime story to you?"

"It's not my fault he was acquitted." I glared into his brown eyes, angry that he accused me, angry that he leaned close because he hated me, and angry that he smelled so good. "What have I done?"

"Lied to me." His lips compressed to a thin line. "Exploited the sorrow of his victims to sell papers. And glamorized him."

I was incredulous. "I was in no way sympathetic to him."

"He didn't need your sympathy. He needed your voice," he said. "And you gave him that. You have a gift, you know, and you are squandering it."

"What are you talking about?" My eyes strayed to Philip chattering in the telephone booth, phoning in his story. He flailed with his free hand as if the person on the other end of the line could see him.

"He was talking about your story this morning, as they brought him in. Did you not hear? He is your biggest fan."

My stomach dropped to my feet. I was horrified, but I tried not to show it. "I am not responsible—"

"You have the public's ear, and you are filling it with stories of evil, poison." He lowered his voice and leaned closer. "Poison that will infect us all."

"My job is to report to the public what happens."

"Why not make it your job to show justice? To show wholesome things?"

"I have to eat," I said, feeling like an ass. But I certainly would not let him intimidate me. My job was to write the news in a way that sold papers. "No one pays for wholesome."

"But—"

"And while we are on the subject, you are not campaigning for justice. You are a banker. Banks might dispense money, but they do not dispense it justly." I shifted my satchel to my left arm.

"People withdraw what they deposit," he said, shaking his head. "Which is more than I can say for the criminal justice system."

"Rich people put money in," I said. "And they draw it out. Usually that's how the criminal justice system works too. Just not this time."

"Of all the—"

"Vati." Trudi approached and put her gloved hand on his arm. "Let's go."

"Soon." He placed his hand over hers. "I have a few more things to say to Herr Weill."

Trudi looked confused. "That's Fraulein Vogel," she said. "You went out to dinner last weekend, remember?"

Boris looked at me, as if seeing me for the first time. He narrowed his eyes as if he disliked what he saw. "I remember," he said. Trudi led him away.

I blinked back tears, pacing in front of the telephone booth, waiting to do my job. Boris was only a man I'd dated once. I should not care what he thought. Except, I did. Today, of all days, I wanted to fall into someone's arms and be comforted. Philip hung up the telephone.

I shook my head. I would get no comfort from Boris, today or any other day. As always, I was on my own.

Philip stepped out of the booth in front of me. He held the door open. "Nice piece on Sunday." I nodded, avoiding his eyes.

I stepped into the telephone booth, dropped my coins in the slot, and dialed the familiar number. The switchboard put me right through to Maria, which was a blessing. She wrote well and fast.

"How'd it come out?" she asked. Typewriters clacked in the background.

"Not guilty." I stared out the glass door at the front of the courthouse. The defendant walked down the stairs and hugged his discomfited lawyer. I turned so I faced the telephone box.

"Really?" She sounded surprised. "He seemed guilty in your last piece."

"I think he was." I twined the rough cord of the telephone around my finger.

"Give me a headline," she said, and I dictated the story to her, dwelling on the antics of the defense lawyer, playing up how he had snatched victory only through a spirited defense. His impassioned pacing and spitting had made all of the difference.

"I'll have to tone that down." The sound of keys clattering in the background reminded me that she sat at a battered desk, in a cloud of smoke. "What if that lawyer has some pull? You know how much Neumann loves those angry telephone calls."

"Heaven forbid we write anything that makes Neumann's job difficult." The defense lawyer sprinted down the street and hailed a taxi. He ran like a man escaping from prison.

"He does write our checks," Maria said. "And I remember being unemployed quite vividly, even if it seems remote to you. Do you know the unemployment figures right now?"

"Five million or so, I think. I know, Maria. Everywhere qualified men are willing to do my job for less money."

"Why is this one so personal to you?" Maria asked. "You've been through worse without blinking before."

"I am not blinking now," I said. "I am fine."

"Your last piece was great," she said. "But it was not Peter Weill. It was a softer, kinder writer. Someone who won't be keeping her job if she writes more like it."

"Neumann ran it on the front page."

"Because it was news, not because he liked it." She inhaled, probably sucking in a lungful of smoke from her cigarette.

"Then why didn't he change it?"

Maria sneezed. "People like to see a soft stance sometimes, but mostly they want gory details."

"There is a balance," I said. I suddenly felt very hungry and missed the lunch I might have had with Boris, if things had been different. He was the first man in a long time to whom I'd felt a connection. And, like Ernst, he was gone.

"Well, lean back to the other side," Maria said.

"But people should be outraged that this rapist is going free."

"You're a reporter," she said. "Not an executioner."

"But does anyone care that he's going free? Besides the victims? And who cares about them?" The memory of Boris's hurt and angry eyes swam across my vision.

"Hannah," she said, speaking slowly. "You might feel that way, but people don't want Peter Weill to be a pansy. He's supposed to be streetwise and tough."

"You seem to have been studying his persona carefully," I said. "Should I be worried?"

"Oh, for heaven's sake." She hung up the telephone.

I slumped against the side of the booth like a puppet whose strings had been cut. I had made it through the day, and my time belonged to me again.

A reporter I did not recognize knocked on the glass, and I slid out, apologizing without meeting his eyes. He was under deadline too.

I rounded a corner, wanting only to get home. A couple that looked so much alike they must have been brother and sister walked toward me. He said something and smiled devilishly. Her merry laugh cut across me. That. That was what I would never have again. In my mind's eye I saw the photograph of Ernst, spread out on a riverbank, alone.

Some time later I found myself in front of my door, staring at its shiny black surface as if I'd never seen it before. My body had brought me here when my brain had failed.

I unlocked the door, but froze on the threshold, afraid to enter. What should have been familiar now looked foreign. A strong morning light poured between blue-checked curtains into the kitchen. The worn but clean furniture was placed just so. My eyes rested on the white tile stove beside two square-backed chairs and a tiny well-used table. I could not believe there was a time when I had calmly wiped crumbs from the smooth oak, pushed the chairs in straight. And yet I must have done it this very morning before I left for the police station.

A door slammed upstairs, and I started. I stepped into my kitchen and pulled the door closed behind me. The door lock clicked into place. I was alone. Hot tears wet my cheeks. I set Rudolf's box on the kitchen table, dropped my damp umbrella into the hall tree, and peeled off my overcoat.

I turned into my bedroom and collapsed face-first on my narrow childhood bed. When we were children, Ernst used to run to me in this bed, afraid of monsters and Father's drunken rages. This bed was the only piece of furniture our sister Ursula left unclaimed when our parents died.

She took Mother's bed. "I was born in it," Ursula said, conveniently forgetting that I had been born there as well, as had Ernst. In fact, our mother had been born there too. The family bed now stood proudly in our sister's small bedroom in Schöneberg, crowding the other furniture, waiting in vain for another child to be born in it.

Our family name will die with this generation. We are all childless: I unmarried at thirty-two, Ursula married but childless at thirty-eight, and Ernst dead at twenty. Father's name was all but gone, and for that I was grateful. Father did not deserve a legacy, not after all he'd done to me, and to Ernst.

I ran my hand over the threadbare linen duvet. Fourteen years ago, these linens were part of my trousseau. Ernst and I had embroidered red roses along the edges of the cream-colored pillows and the top of the duvet. Over time the roses had faded to pale pink.

I'd had a whole trunkful of such frippery when I dutifully became engaged to Walter, an officer in the German army. I knew I'd need these things in my married life, that I would be measured by the other soldiers' wives on the fabric of my sheets and the skill of my needlework. I had cared about such things then, as had Walter, and we talked often of the house we would set up together when the Great War ended.

After Walter died in the trenches, I felt discharged of my duty to Father and never married. Instead I moved out of my parents' house and took up a life as a journalist. None of my work colleagues knew that I could beat meringues to perfect stiffness, tighten my sheets so that you could bounce a one mark piece off them, or shine a soldier's boots until they looked like glass. I did not do these things anymore.

I traced the pale roses of the duvet with my index finger. The duvet fit a double bed and so drooped to the floor on both sides. Mother would have shaken her head in disapproval. She had worked hard to prepare me for life as a housewife, a life that I had never led. Father had worked even harder to prepare Ernst for a soldier's life, a life that he could never have led; would never lead now. My finger stopped on the uneven stitches of the one rose I had let Ernst embroider. He longed to add one, but I did not want it to stand out against my own careful stitching, so I made him work it into the corner. I stroked each precious uneven stitch.

I sold the rest of my trousseau in 1923, the worst year of the inflation. I made millions, billions, and then trillions of Papiermarks each week writing poetry and occasionally filling in for the original Peter Weill at the newspaper, but it was no longer enough to buy food. It cost fifty-six billion marks to take the subway.

Ernst and I lived on eggs and boiled fish soup. I collected fish heads and entrails at the fish market and boiled them and strained out the pieces through Mother's old silk stockings. The stench was terrible. On lucky days we also had turnips and bread. Ernst carved elaborate boats out of stale bread, and we sailed them on our fish broth to England and America and places where they had fine things to eat. Even as a twelve-year-old boy, Ernst made every meal a party, somehow. He was so funny and dear.

Luckily, I soon got a job writing love letters for an American businessman named Jim O'Donnell who was in love with Greta Hansi, the stage actress. Ernst and I quoted Goethe and Rilke like mad, and he paid us in American dollars. Each letter bought two good meals: meat, potatoes, chocolates, and dry goods like split peas and flour. We wrote Greta every other week, when Jim O'Donnell traveled to Hamburg for business.

We needed food because Ernst ate and ate. He grew a half meter those first few years and became tall and gangly. He worked hard at his studies at the gymnasium. He was on his way to his Abitur and then university when he met Rudolf von Reiche.

I clenched the rose inside my fist. I had sources through my experiences with the paper. I was no helpless woman, fit only for motherhood, the kitchen, or prayer. I would find who had done this. If Rudolf had murdered Ernst, he would pay.

5

I rubbed my sticky eyelids. It was Tuesday morning.

An old woman stared back at me from the bathroom mirror. My face was swollen and pale, my bloodshot eyes squinted in the light. I shuddered. I looked like Father when he was hungover. I washed my face, smoothed my blond bob with wet hands, and hoped for the best. I could not face that woman in the mirror again.

Move on with the day. Breakfast was next. I straightened my spine and marched into the kitchen. What did I have? A few rolls, a hunk of cheese, a pair of eggs, an onion, and a liter of milk, the most food I'd had in the kitchen in ages. I grabbed a stale roll from the corner of the breadbox. I cut it in half and scooped the crumbs into a teacup. They could be added to soups.

I scraped butter across the roll with a silver knife Ernst had pilfered from Ursula. Her favorite lecture rang in my ears. "Let Father beat it out of him," she always said, with a deep sigh. "If he carries on this way, he will end up dead in a gutter someday. They all do. You will see." Still I had tried to protect him. And failed.

My appetite lost, I wrapped the buttered roll for lunch. My stomach did not want it, but I added it to my satchel with my sketchpad, notebook, and pens. I gathered a few coins from the sugar bowl. Little enough, but it would have to do for the day's expenses.

Pausing on the stoop, I glanced around at the sooty buildings that surrounded my home. My neighborhood was not the kind of place where I felt safe walking after dark. The kindest description for it was working class, and I remembered how Ursula shuddered at the mere mention of my address. Middle-class ladies did not visit Hallesches Tor, let alone live there. I had lived in my apartment for more than a decade and my sister had never visited.

During the day I felt quite safe as I strolled down to the newsstand. Schmidt sat in his tiny stand, balanced on a stool, stumps of his legs pointing to the side.

"Morning, Fraulein Vogel." He touched his workman's cap respectfully. I'd seen him almost every day since he opened the stand after returning from the Great War without his legs.

"Good morning, Schmidt." I pulled four different newspapers from his selection and handed him a few pfennigs.

"It'll be a fine day." He dropped my coins into a metal can with a *clink*. "Just see if it isn't."

I nodded in return and hurried to my bus. Schmidt was convinced that every day not in a trench was a fine day. I imagined Walter and the ten million other men who died in the trenches would have agreed with him. So many young lives wasted. Just like Ernst, with no trace left of what they might have become. Were there traces of Ernst left in the world? Were there traces left of my life? Who would mourn me if I died tomorrow? Certainly not Boris. Not my sister Ursula. Sarah was far away. Fritz and Bettina Waldheim would mourn. And Paul, a trusted friend who worked at the paper.

I listened to the rough Berlin accents of workmen in caps and coarse cotton clothes, off to factory work they were grateful to get. How many of them would be mourned?

I pulled my thoughts away from such a morbid track, trying to think of something practical. What if Maria was correct about Herr Neumann's opinion of the new Peter Weill stories? He might fire me. Then it would be back to eating fish-entrail soup.

I had to come up with a story for today, but first I had to return to the police station to see Ernst's file and find out what I could about the last minutes of his life.

Bright June sun mocked me as I walked to the police station, head down, studying the sidewalk. I dreaded it, but I needed to see him again, to make my head convince my heart that he was dead. I plodded through the Hall of the Unnamed Dead. The day was starting for many of the workers; a flock of typists, colorful as parrots, chattered around me. They were young, most not more than twenty. I felt old and dowdy.

I reached the spot where I had seen the photograph. I could not raise my head. I stared at the golden oak floor as the hall emptied out.

When I finally looked at the photograph, even my heart could not deny it. The picture recorded cold fact. Tears ran down my cheeks. It was a waste. A terrible waste of life, love, laughter. His beautiful voice stilled. Hundreds of songs unsung. Hours of conversation unspoken. I closed my eyes and leaned my forehead against Ernst's photograph. He was gone. Forever.

I straightened and wiped away my tears. I would find the man who did this. He could not kill my brother with impunity. Perhaps I would turn him over to justice, as Boris had done, or perhaps I would settle it myself. But even as I pictured myself shooting a shadowy man, I drew back. Ernst would not want me to become a killer.

"Fraulein Vogel," said a familiar high-pitched voice. "Are you well?"

I turned. Kommissar Lang's diminutive form stood in front of me, concern in his boot-black eyes. At a loss for words, I stood between him and the picture of Ernst. It was plain that I was crying. How long had he been watching me?

He handed me his spotless handkerchief and took my elbow, his eyes looking past my head at the photographs. "Did you recognize someone on these walls? A friend, perhaps?"

"No." I cursed myself for not being able to respond cleverly. I needed a story. An answer that he would believe. "I just heard terrible news."

"Come to my office." He steered me through the empty hallway as if we were dancing. With each step away from the photograph, I relaxed a little.

"You do not need to go to so much trouble on my account," I said, after he closed his office door. "It is only weakness on my part. I'd hoped to take a shortcut through the building and get home sooner, before I made a fool of myself and started to cry. Obviously I am a bigger fool than I thought."

"What news have you heard?" he asked, in a gentle voice, pulling back his guest chair for me to sit. I sat, and he knelt next to me, once again too close for my comfort. I did not move away, to avoid arousing his suspicions.

"I—" Before I knew what I would say I saw the double lightning bolt symbol of the SS, the Schutz Staffel, Hitler's elite army, pinned to his lapel. I must be very careful. I swallowed. "Ran into one of Becker's victims and—"

"You knew the victims?"

"One," I lied, my story gaining strength. "A wonderful young girl. I just saw her, and I tried to be strong for her, but . . ." I bowed my head, unable to meet his eyes, and cried in earnest. I felt like a complete ass, crying in front of a member of the SS, but I could not stop.

"You are a kind soul." He took my hand in his cold one. "To care so for your friends."

I managed a weak smile. "I don't know what is wrong with me, to take it so hard. I am a grown woman."

"Grown women are emotional too." He patted my hand. "Which one was your friend?"

"I cannot give you her name." I longed to pull my hand back from his.

"But I have a list of all the names," he said. "I probably spoke to her."

Was this a test? Did he suspect my story? "She has been violated enough," I said, trying to sound determined without provoking him. "Do not make me violate her trust further."

"It wasn't the Jewish one, was it?" he asked. "I never trusted her statement. You know how they are."

I pulled my hand back. "I must go, Kommissar Lang. Thank you for your kindness."

"Let me walk you to the front door," he said, rising.

"You are too kind." I rose too, glancing around his orderly office.

As we walked down the hall, I steeled myself to neither look nor slow as we passed Ernst's photograph. But Kommissar Lang slowed, and his eyes darted to that set of pictures.

I put my hand on his arm, hating what I was about to do, but needing to distract him. "Thank you for your thoughtfulness." I looked into his dark eyes. "It was kind of you to indulge my foolish outburst."

Kommissar Lang's eyes left the photographs to meet mine. We walked to the doors together.

"Fraulein Vogel." He moved closer to me, and I kept my hand on his arm, although I wanted to snatch it away and strike him. Why was I so angry at him? He had made a simple anti-Semitic comment. I heard worse all the time. "It is wonderful to see a reporter who cares so for her subjects."

"Good writing must come from the heart."

He reached up and tucked a strand of hair behind my ear. "Then you must have an extraordinary heart."

I looked down demurely to hide my disgust. I wanted to run through the front door and wash my hair. I did not want the touch of an SS man on me. "Kommissar Lang, I—"

"Perhaps you might be free for dinner?"

"I must hurry to the paper," I said. "Another time, perhaps."

"Thank you." He inclined his head forward and opened the front door. I escaped into the sunlight.

I had received only anger from Boris, a man I thought I could have opened up to. Yet the one who had tried to comfort me was Kommissar Lang, a member of the SS, an organization that was not supposed to have feelings. And my brother was buried in an un-marked grave. Nothing made sense.

At the paper, I poured a cup of coffee, then pushed my way through the smoke-filled room to a window and opened it. It never helped much, but I did it every day.

"Our air not fresh enough for you?" Maria asked, a cigarette between her fingers. She tossed her head so that her brunette bob swayed around her severe face.

I plastered on a polite smile. Maria never forgave me for getting the Peter Weill writing job, and I loathed the way she treated my friend Paul. Still, she was good at writing up breaking stories when I phoned them in, so I tried to get along with her. "Are you certain there is any air left in here?"

"Not air for those who do not smoke," said Paul, the peacemaker, coming up behind Maria. "Your tender lungs are not as tough as ours."

Paul helped me get my first job at the paper and was more than just a shoulder to cry on after Walter died, at least for a time. Currently, he was dating Maria, and it was ending badly.

"Excuse me." I walked toward an empty desk. "Under deadline."

A shape blocked the light from the window. "Hello," I said. I turned. There stood Herr Neumann, my editor. He was tall and thin, with fingers like a skeleton.

"Good piece Sunday, about the trial." He shook his brown cigarette at me with nicotine-stained fingers.

This kind of flattery from Herr Neumann was extraordinary. I waited for the other shoe to drop.

"Thank you." I took a sip of coffee and tried not to make a face. Herr Neumann was the only one in the office who liked the coffee.

"But you missed the deadline." He blew a cloud of smoke at my face, smiling when I coughed.

"I'm sorry, Herr Neumann." Usually he wanted an abject apology, but I could not seem to get the tone today.

"You don't sound sorry."

I clenched my jaw and dropped my eyes. I wanted to throw coffee in his face. "I have a cold."

"I can find other writers to be Peter Weill," he said, running his fingers through his thinning hair. "It's time you remembered that."

He dropped his cigarette in my coffee cup and walked off, tweed jacket flaring behind him like a bird's tail.

"That's the best thing that could happen to that coffee," said Paul, suddenly next to me.

I laughed and dumped it in the sink, then removed the soggy cigarette butt so it did not clog the drain.

"Does he have any other way to make a point?" Maria slid her hand possessively through Paul's arm.

"It's very Freudian," Paul said, as I tossed the flaccid cigarette into the garbage and washed my hands.

"It's all Freudian to you," said Maria, with a snicker. "Freud is just some Jewish crackpot."

I wondered how she reconciled her anti-Semitism with the fact that, although Paul had a Christian father, his mother was Jewish. "Maybe you'd best reread his sections on the ego," I said.

Maria shot me a quizzical glance, and a smile flitted across Paul's face.

"Paul!" called a voice from across the room.

"In a moment." Paul nodded to us both and limped off. His leg had been wounded in the Great War, and it pained him more than he let on. I sometimes wished that I'd been ready for him when he was ready for me, but I had been too grieved by Walter's death when Sarah introduced us. It had never worked out. I shook my head. All of that was years ago.

"You'd better have a good story today." Maria broke into my reverie. "If you miss another deadline, he may find another Peter Weill." She bared her teeth in a satisfied-looking grin.

Back at my desk I typed up a desultory analysis of the Becker trial. Not brilliant, but it would do. I straightened the typing paper and tried to read through the story again, but none of it made sense.

Paul strolled over, without Maria. "Is something wrong?"

I looked at him, calculating. He knew that Sarah had my papers. Perhaps I could tell him the truth.

Paul cocked his head to one side, waiting.

I opened my mouth to tell him everything, but changed my mind. Once I started talking to him, where would I stop? And the newsroom was no place to discuss personal secrets. "Could you read through this story?" I asked instead. "See if it makes sense."

He took the story, but I could tell from his disappointed expression that he knew I was withholding the truth from him. He skimmed the pages.

"Not your best work," he said, slowly. "But coherent."

"Today, coherent will have to do." I took the story back.

"I found a letter in your box." He drew an envelope out of the inner breast pocket of his tweed jacket. "For Peter Weill/Hannah Vogel."

We both hoped the letter came from Sarah, but we pretended not to care so as not to arouse any curiosity in the newsroom.

"Thank you." I took the envelope. "I'll open it right now. Would you like to wait and read it when I finish?"

"I'd like that," Paul said.

I pulled a bronze letter opener from the top desk drawer and slit the envelope open. It was not Sarah's careful handwriting, but perhaps she'd hired someone to write it for her.

My dear Fraulein Vogel,
Sincerest apologies for my beastly behavior at the courthouse.

"Oh," I said, flustered.

Paul cleared his throat.

"It's not from Sarah," I said quickly.

Paul raised his eyebrows. "Is it Boris?"

I blushed. I had run into Paul and Maria while on my date with Boris on Saturday. Now the entire newsroom probably knew. "Perhaps."

"I liked him," Paul said. "He seemed very strong, but also charming. Exactly the kind of man you need to be seeing."

"I do not imagine I will see him again."

"Because?"

"I met him at the Becker trial. His daughter—"

"He's a source?" Paul's tone was incredulous. "You meet a man like that, and you can't think of anything better to do with him than to use him as a source?"

"It was one hell of a story," I said. Paul, of course, was correct.

Maria waved from across the room. Paul nodded and ambled to her.

I hurried downstairs to be alone while reading Boris's letter. Boris's handwriting was firm and masculine, the product of a strict teacher in his past, no doubt.

I was very emotional about the acquittal. Although I certainly did not behave as such at the time, I realize that it was not your fault. You and Trudi got along so famously at lunch, and I enjoyed our time on Saturday. Please do meet us at the Wannsee on Friday. We will be at the Potsdam Yacht Club at 13:30.

With kind regards, Boris

I folded the letter and placed it back in the envelope. How curious. Boris wanted to see me again.

I flipped to the drawing I'd sketched of him during the trial, before I'd met him. His jaw muscles stood out like ropes on his finely sculptured face. He looked like a film actor, but not so effete. Gold streaked his wavy dark hair, his jaw was firm and square, his eyes large and expressive, and his lower lip was full and sensual; kissing lips, we'd called them in school.

My heart beat faster. I wanted to see him, of course. He was the most attractive man I'd met in years. I had no idea what he wanted. But I did not think that I would go. I had to find out who killed Ernst. I could not let myself be distracted by a pair of brown eyes.

6

That night I pulled the only evening gown I owned out of my tall oak wardrobe. Ernst gave it to me after he had moved out, so that I could watch him sing without embarrassing him by wearing "some sack or other."

Chiffon whispered against my ears as I pulled the dress over my head. I smoothed my hands over my hips, careful not to dislodge the interlocking circles of silver beads. The dress fell straight from my shoulders to right below my knees, a style all the rage in the twenties. Ernst told me that the thin flapper look was good for someone with small breasts and a small bottom like me. He harrumphed when I pointed out that my slender appearance was an economic statement, not a fashion choice.

I caressed the smooth glass beads. When I had exclaimed that the beads reminded me of chain mail, Ernst huffed that I had lost contact with my femininity. I insisted that chain mail looked beautiful, but he refused to believe that it was a compliment.

I rolled my Elbeo stockings up to my thigh and clipped them on. I smoothed the dress down again. Even I had to admit that the dress made me look younger, flirtatious, and sophisticated.

I regretted that Boris would never see me in it. He would always remember my practical shoes and my sensible brown coat. What was it about Boris? He was not the only man in the world. Yet something drew me to him. The tenderness he displayed toward his daughter was beautiful, and there were those amazing lips and eyes, but that did not explain my feelings. There had been a connection there.

Forget Boris's lips, I told myself sternly. There are other attractive men in Berlin. Paul had quite nice lips, but I did not long to kiss them every time I was near him. I ran a comb through my straight blond hair. A bob looks the same all of the time, which is a relief.

It wasn't as if Boris was the only man I'd ever been attracted to. I had been intimate with Walter, and a few other men since he died, in spite of what Ernst always said about me being the last nun outside of a convent in Berlin. But none of them generated heat and electric current with a single glance as Boris did. I put on powder and pink lipstick, almost ready to go.

Kommissar Lang generated strong emotions in me too. He made my heart race, but with anger and disgust. Did he suspect something? Would he take the photographs from where I had stood into Fritz? I hoped not. Fritz would identify Ernst.

Enough about men.

I took one last glance in the mirror. Ernst would have been proud.

I gathered my few coins from the sugar bowl. Drinks at the El Dorado would be expensive. I'd have to skip dinner for a week to afford it. But then I would not have to waste time cooking.

I donned my brown coat, remembering how Ernst cringed at that coat touching his dress. I pinned on my brown hat, a gift from Sarah. Practical and built to last, it matched the coat, not the dress. Ernst had never understood that I was safer on the street looking poor rather than wealthy.

Mitzi was not on the stoop when I reached the front door. I missed her. She appeared when Ernst moved in, right after our father was killed in 1923, a year after Mother's death. I could not afford to feed Mitzi back then, but she seemed to do fine on the rats outside. Now I gave her milk every evening, and she slept on my pillow. If a mouse crept in, she caught it and left the tail and feet on the bathroom floor. We were growing old together, companionably.

I called her Mitzi, but Ernst had called her Mademoiselle Zee and claimed she embodied the spirit of a gypsy fortune-teller. For a while he made her a series of purple collars out of a pair of Mother's old shoes. Each day she lost a collar, and each night he made a new one. He claimed that she traded them for the freedom of her kittens from the gypsies. Eventually he ran out of leather for collars and proclaimed that all of her children were free. Lucky timing all around.

I watched from the doorway before stepping onto the stoop. Automobiles cruised by with the men's faces hidden under fedora brims behind rolled up windows. The baker's son leaned against the side of the store, smoke curling past his narrow shoulders. I stood as tall as I could and stepped into the street. I hated being out alone at night. I'd read too many reports of rapes and murders, sat through too many trials, to believe I had any safety.

I hurried the last block from Nollendorfplatz station to El Dorado. Ernst had been proud to work in the Schöneberg borough, the area where the newly famous Marlene Dietrich was born. A safer area than my apartment, but not around the nightclubs.

When I arrived at the corner of Motz Strasse, I paused. A giant mural covered the outside wall of the club. It started with a woman in a long formal dress dancing with a man in a tuxedo and monocle. Next to them were two men in tuxedos dancing together, one with a feminine birthmark and red lips, but unmistakably male shoulders and hair. A few centimeters away, two women danced cheek-to-cheek, their backs to a roguish man in a tuxedo dancing with another man and a laughing woman.

The mural told you that entering El Dorado was stepping through the looking glass. I remembered my first visit, not long after Ernst started working there.

"Hello, old bird," Ernst had said, whisking me past the coat-check girl, through a thick set of velvet curtains, and into the smoky air of the club. "It's simply divine to see you."

Fringe on his red flapper dress swished with each step. He kept his hair short then, and he wore it in a bob with a wave, like all flappers. His lips glowed scarlet and his breasts looked bigger than mine.

"Hello, Ernst." I took a deep breath. I'd never seen him with breasts before, but I was determined not to be shocked.

"Come meet my confidant. Oliver the bartender." Ernst minced to the bar, holding my elbow in one red-gloved hand. "He takes such care of us, don't you, Oliver?"

Oliver smiled from behind the bar. With his carefully trimmed black beard and well-padded frame, he looked like a panda bear. "I do my best, little one."

"I'll have an absinthe," Ernst said. "And Hannah will have one too."

I opened my mouth to protest, but he cut me off. "Don't say you want a Berliner weisse. That's so passé."

I closed my mouth and glanced around the room. A dozen round tables ringed the oak dance floor. Each was set in a shallow alcove painted with a stylized scene from a Chinese opium den. Between each table hung a red curtain or a large tarnished brass gong. Every so often someone rang a gong with a bottle of Champagne, and the band stopped playing and started a different song.

"Here you go, Fraulein." Oliver sat a glass of emerald-green liquid, a carafe of water, a slotted spoon, and a sugar cube on the bar in front of me.

I placed the sugar cube on the spoon, then set the spoon on top of the glass and dripped cold water over the sugar cube. As water dripped through the sugar, the green liquid turned cloudy white. I had tried absinthe with Walter, back when it was still legal. Absinthe had been made illegal in Germany years ago because the distilled wormwood it contained was said to cause insanity. But it was still served at El Dorado, where the clientele was obviously unconcerned about the law or sanity.

"Sip it if you're not accustomed to it," Oliver recommended.

I nodded to him and took a sip of the milky liquid. Just as I remembered, it tasted like licorice with an aftertaste of shoe polish and it left my mouth numb. I clenched my teeth to keep from gagging from the bitterness. Ernst drank his in one swallow, the rings he wore over his gloves clacking against the glass. "Another," he said.

"How are you?" I asked. "Ready to come home?"

He giggled in a high-pitched affected way that I'd never heard from him before. "And give up all this?" When he gestured around the room, light sparkled on his rings.

I took another sip of absinthe. It still tasted terrible. Farther down the bar, a fat, badly shaved man in a white beaded gown winked at Ernst.

"Oh, Lola." Ernst waved two fingers at him. "Isn't he lovely?"

"That is not the first word that comes to mind."

"You must try some cocaine." Ernst whipped out Mother's silver powder compact. "It's divine."

"No," I said, losing the battle to remain unshocked. "Just, no."

He slid the compact back into his tiny beaded purse and pouted.

"How is Herr von Reiche?" I asked.

"Around somewhere." Ernst glanced at the stage, where a dark-skinned boy who looked twelve years old sang a jazzy dance song. "I must dash to my show." He kissed the air near my cheek and hurried off, skirting the dance floor and vanishing through a side door.

I pushed the absinthe across the bar to Oliver. "Do you want a Berliner weisse?" he asked.

I shook my head. "I heard it's passé."

On the last downbeat the dark boy opened his tuxedo front to reveal decidedly female breasts. The boy, or girl, left the stage to scattered applause.

The stage went dark, and for a moment there was no music. The pianist began to play a slow love song. A dazzling spotlight pierced the darkness of the club. In the middle of the circle of light, Ernst's pale leg stuck through the curtain, and he kicked his high heel straight toward the ceiling. He slid sinuously through the curtain and onto the stage. Every hand in the room applauded.

Ernst's red dress glowed like embers in the spotlight. He wore so much jewelry that when he moved he flashed like a chandelier. After the applause subsided, he raised one gloved hand above his head and began to sing a throaty love song. All of the pain in the world flowed out of his body through his voice. All talking stopped. All drinking stopped. The audience sat, mesmerized.

I stared at Ernst, singing so beautifully in that red dress. I did not realize I held my breath until he stopped singing and applause washed over him like rain. He sang only two more songs, then curtsied and blew dramatic kisses to the applauding crowd before prancing off stage.

A few minutes later, he returned to the bar, fighting his way through admirers.

"And?" he asked.

"Amazing!" I remembered the times my singing teacher and I had let him take my place in my voice lessons. "Truly. Frau Witte would be proud of that voice."

"If not the costume," he said with an impish grin. "Now tell me everything. Is Greta still spurning Jim? How's Mademoiselle Zee? Does she miss me?"

"The cat is inconsolable," I lied.

Oliver placed a tray of Champagne glasses in front of us. "All for you, my lovely," he told Ernst. "I can list the name of each admirer if you would like."

Ernst giggled. "No need. I cannot possibly keep them all straight."

He turned back to me. "The cat is not inconsolable. But what about the love letters? And all that crazy poetry for the paper?"

"I have been promoted," I said. "I am writing full time as Peter—"

"Hello, liebchen," interrupted a voice behind my shoulder. Ernst's eyes flicked to the man who spoke. He widened his eyes as if he'd been given a Christmas gift, then dropped his eyelashes like a professional coquette. His playacting skills had certainly improved.

"Rudolf," he said. "You missed my act, you naughty boy."

"I never miss your act." Rudolf draped his arm over Ernst's shoulder. "I couldn't beat my way through the throng of admirers ogling you."

"Try harder, darling." Ernst pouted.

"Your wish is my command." Rudolf slid his arm around Ernst's waist and led him to the dance floor. They danced together, plastered so close that I feared the fringe on Ernst's dress would rub off. Rudolf massaged Ernst's bottom with both hands. I won, Rudolf's eyes seemed to say to me. And you lost.

When I turned back to the bar, a Berliner weisse appeared in front of me.

"On the house," Oliver said. "You should be able to finish it before they're done dancing."

I finished that beer, and another, before Ernst came back and kissed me on the cheek, his lips touching me this time. "I must dash," he said. "Come again tomorrow."

When he and Rudolf strolled out of the club, hand-in-hand, Oliver's eyes followed them. Ernst turned before he left the room to wave to his many admirers and to me, sweeping his blond hair back out of his eyes with a graceful gesture so much like our mother's that tears stung my eyes.

7

I shivered, still standing outside in front of the mural. I walked to the end scene—a man and a poodle with long lashes and a pink tutu did the foxtrot. I saluted the coquettish poodle, straightened my shoulders, and stepped through the looking glass.

Inside, the coat-check girl wore a short black skirt that showed well-turned ankles, but the hands that took my coat were large.

"The tables are through the curtains, madame," said a deep, sultry voice.

"Thank you, mademoiselle," I rejoined, and he flashed me a coy smile. Fooling me was his job, after all, and I could not let on that he had not fooled me.

I pushed through deep red curtains, inhaling their musty, smoky smell. They kept noise from filtering into the street and trapped heat in the winter.

Half of the tables contained groups of revelers sitting around a festive silver bucket holding a green bottle of Champagne. White El Dorado balloons floated above the buckets, anchored by the handles. Most of the guests were dressed as women, but how many were actually female was anyone's guess.

I headed to the corner of the long teak bar, near the sink, the place where bartenders can stand a minute and talk while they wash glasses. Oliver kept everything spotless. He spent a good deal of his

time at the sink. I'd only been here a few times, but Oliver might remember me.

The smoke thickened, and I stifled a cough as I climbed onto a bar
stool designed to hold someone a few centimeters taller than me, so
that men could perch on them without wrinkling their evening dresses.
Oliver sauntered over in his dapper bartender's jacket. He might look
like a panda bear with his black beard and white jacket, but Ernst said
he was an accomplished street fighter who threw out the most unruly
drunks himself. He'd once ejected an entire gang of Nazi hooligans
who'd tried to destroy the place.

"Fraulein?" he asked.

"A Berliner weisse with a shot," I said. "Green."

He poured a quick flash of woodruff syrup into a glass, then flipped
the top off a bottle of wheat beer and added the beer to the glass with
the syrup. It was beer for children and tourists, but I loved it anyway.

I slipped his payment across the counter with a hefty tip. "It's
good," I said when he tried to hand me change. "I am looking for my
brother."

"Aren't we all?" he said, with a booming laugh. He poured a clear
liquid into ten shot glasses lined up on a tray.

"His name is Ernst Vogel, and he sings here."

"The little songbird?" He wiped down the spotless bar. "You are
sister to the Nightingale?"

"Hannah Vogel." I reached my hand out to him. Ernst had loved it
when people called him the Nightingale.

"Hannah," he said, shaking it. His grip was firm and damp from
the towel. "I remember you now. Haven't seen you in a long time."

I nodded. "Is Ernst here tonight?"

Oliver shook his head. "And Winnie is furious. Excuse me."

Oliver carried the tray of full shot glasses to a table of businessmen.
At least they looked like men. Oliver bowed and handed out drinks.
Although each glass was filled to the brim, he did not spill a drop.

I stirred green syrup into my golden beer.

Oliver returned with a tray of empty glasses and began washing them in the sink. Steam rose off the water.

"When did you see him last?"

"After his performance Friday." Oliver wiped the back of his hand across his brow. "He missed all his weekend performances."

I choked on a lump in my throat and pretended that was the reason for my sudden tears.

"Are you well?" Oliver asked with concern.

I coughed a few more times and then said, "Perfectly. What was Ernst doing Friday?"

"He and Rudolf argued about the little Nazi boy."

"Nazi boy?" I took a sip of my beer. I loved the way that the bitter beer mixed with the sweet tang of the woodruff syrup, turning the adult brew into candy.

Oliver pointed with his sudsy thumb. I turned to see a teenage boy with blond hair sitting at a table next to the stage. His carefully pressed Nazi uniform was the brown of fallen autumn leaves. "Rudolf and Ernst argued about it, but Ernst left with the boy in the end. The boy is smitten with your brother. He walked right over to him when he came off stage, and they kissed as if they'd been separated for years."

"What's his name?"

"Wilhelm."

"What's his last name?" He looked familiar.

"Don't know his last name." Oliver looked down at the glasses he washed. "Don't know anybody's last name."

"Mine's Vogel."

"Forgotten it already." He rinsed off glasses and dried them with a snowy white towel.

I dropped a few coins onto the bar with a clatter. "Buy the boy a drink from me."

"Not your type, sweetie," Oliver said with a smile. "But he's all the rage here. He's almost as big as Ernst was, once upon a time. Before he got old."

"Ernst is only twenty!"

"Don't look so shocked. The men who come here like them young."

I remembered when Ernst had visited me a year ago. He'd come to my apartment at seven that morning and had not been to bed yet. He still wore his dress, and his eye makeup was smudged at the corners.

I was dressed and ready to leave, but I'd made him tea while he complained about work.

"I'm positively ancient." He pulled at the corners of his fresh young eyes, studying them in his compact mirror.

I'd laughed. "You are not even twenty. I am in my thirties and even I am not truly old yet."

"Maybe for your world," he said, his crimson lips pursed. "But now all those rich beautiful men have turned their attention to the next big thing. Or rather the next little thing with a big thing, if you know what I mean."

"What about all that lovely jewelry? Isn't that from admirers?"

"It's not real," he said. "No one gives me real stuff anymore."

I had shaken my head and hurried out the door to catch my bus, telling him that he was exaggerating. But he had been correct.

Oliver cleared his throat, and I dropped my eyes down to my beer. "Please buy the boy a drink from me."

I pretended to study an El Dorado beer coaster while Oliver carried a shot of whiskey to the boy. The coaster was creamy white and had "Here, it is right!" printed on it in a flowery script.

After Oliver took Wilhelm the drink, I walked to his table and sat down without being invited. Wilhelm lifted his tortoiseshell cigarette holder to his sensuous lips and took a drag of the cigarette. Atikah, Turkish tobacco. Ernst had smoked it once too.

"Good evening," I said. He turned startled blue eyes to me. Had he mistaken me for a man from across the room?

"Hello." He tapped his cigarette ashes into the silver ashtray. "Thank you for the whiskey."

"I'm looking for someone," I began.

"I am not interested," he interrupted, without meeting my eyes. "I don't do girls, not even for money, no matter how much."

"I'm looking for Ernst Vogel," I continued, wondering why he would not look at me.

The boy sat ramrod straight in his chair. I saw his Nazi bearing, was aware now of his youth and strength, and knew I must be careful. "I'm looking for him too. He said he'd stop by but he never did, so I've been here every night since Saturday, waiting." His words tumbled over each other. "And waiting."

"When did you see him last?" Before he could answer, someone struck a gong, and the band launched into "Yes, We Have No Bananas," an old favorite. Wilhelm clapped time. His hands were too large for his body and finely formed, like Michelangelo's David.

I let him sing for a few moments, then picked up the closed bottle of Champagne from the center of the table and used it to strike the gong. The band immediately stopped and started playing a different song. Wilhelm stopped clapping and turned to me.

"Saturday morning early," he said. "He climbed out my window so my father wouldn't see, and he said he'd meet me that night at the club, but he wasn't here. I waited all night."

Oh God, Ernst, I thought. Wilhelm still lives with his parents. Just as you lived with me until you met Rudolf. I took a deep swallow of beer and steadied my voice. "You waited here all Saturday night?"

"And Sunday and Monday," he said. "Over three days, in case you're counting, which I am."

Behind his head, Rudolf entered the room, alone in his trademark gray suit. He strode to the bar without looking right or left. I turned my back to him. I did not want him to know that I was asking around about Ernst, verifying what Rudolf had told me. What if he was the killer? I watched his reflection in the Champagne bucket, and hoped he would not recognize the back of my head.

"How old are you?" I asked Wilhelm, keeping my voice level with great effort.

"Seventeen. How old are you?" He took another puff of his cigarette and stuck out his chin.

"Thirty-two." I ran my finger along the cool edge of my beer glass and watched Rudolf's reflection check his watch.

Wilhelm blew out his smoke in surprise. "That old?"

In spite of my worry about Rudolf, I smiled. "My name is Hannah Vogel." I held out my hand.

"Wilhelm," he said, shaking it firmly. "Wilhelm Lehmann."

"The little boy from school?" I asked, surprised. More than five years ago, Ernst had brought an awkward twelve-year-old boy to our apartment. Now that I knew what to look for, I saw the ghost of the boy in the young man's face. Obviously thrilled by the attention, Ernst claimed that Wilhelm followed him around like a puppy. I bet Ernst had been even more flattered now that Wilhelm was all grown-up and filled out.

Wilhelm nodded. "Back then he always tried to talk me out of loving him."

"He did?" I'd not seen this side of Ernst. I'd never known him to turn down love or adoration. He never got enough of it.

"He said to find a nice girl. Said I was too young. But not last Friday when I showed up at the club. That night he knew I was a man. They all knew." Wilhelm knocked back his whiskey like Tom Mix, the western star. He clunked his shot glass back on the table. "I could have had any of them. I picked Ernst, because I thought he cared."

"Oh," I said, my usual comment when at a loss for words. Wilhelm was now a man, and a Nazi. He'd been a gentle boy, good with Mitzi. Now his mission was to beat up Communists and Jews.

"But then Ernst vanished. Without a single word to me. He didn't come to work." Wilhelm slumped in his chair, and his lower lip stuck out ever so slightly. He did not look manly anymore. "I don't know, but I think he ran off with that rich soldier he was talking about."

"A soldier?" I leaned forward. "What was his name?"

"Somebody famous. Somebody more important than me."

I suppressed an impatient sigh. "Do you know anything else about him?"

Wilhelm furrowed his brow. "Ernst said that he was scared of him, but he liked it."

I'd never known Ernst to be afraid of anyone, even when he should have been. "Why was he scared?"

"He said it like it was a big joke, but I think he meant it." He glared at me. "But who knows what he means when he says things."

"And you have heard nothing from him since?" I stole a quick glance toward the bar. Rudolf leaned toward Oliver, who shrugged and pointed to the stage door. Was Rudolf asking about Ernst? If so, Oliver was not telling him Ernst wasn't there.

"No, but I am not the only one looking for him either. A pair of SA officers came to the bar yesterday. I told them I had not seen him in days, but they just kept asking and asking."

Why were members of the Sturm Abteilung, Hitler's burgeoning private army of storm troopers, interested in Ernst? Rudolf stalked to the backstage door, and I turned my chair so that Wilhelm sat between me and the stage. It was the best I could do without running away. "Did they say why they wanted to find him?"

Wilhelm shook his head. "Maybe he is hiding from them. Or maybe he's hiding from me," Wilhelm said, suddenly sad. He pulled a red silk handkerchief out of his pocket and dabbed his eyes. The kind of dabbing expressly forbidden under the Code of Manliness, a series of rules I'd invented for Ernst, to protect him.

Wilhelm ran his hand absently along his cheek. He tucked the red silk neatly into the pocket of his brown shirt so that not the tiniest glimpse was visible. "Do you think Ernst couldn't bring himself to tell me that he hates me after all? That he's hiding so he doesn't have to face me?"

Ernst was not hiding from Wilhelm, but I was hiding from Rudolf. What if he found me here? If he'd killed Ernst, whom he'd loved, he'd have no trouble dispatching me, whom he loathed. The hair raised on the back of my neck.

"I do not think he would hide from you," I told Wilhelm, trying to be reassuring.

"Only cowards hide," Wilhelm said angrily. "Papi says . . ." His voice trailed off.

"What does your father think of your new friends?" Ernst had long ago told me that Wilhelm and his father did not get along.

"Papi?" Wilhelm took a long drag of his cigarette. "He fixes me up with girls. He hates what I am."

"What are you?"

"Queer. He doesn't like queer men. Says we're a blight on the race. He says Hitler thinks it too. That one day Hitler will round us all up and kill us. But he's wrong about that. Isn't Hitler's best friend Röhm? Röhm is as queer as me, and nobody's rounding him up."

"What if something happened to Röhm?" I took the last sip of beer, sweeter than the others, mostly syrup. I placed my glass softly on the wooden table.

"Hitler can't afford to lose him. They'll protect him all right. He's the only one who can handle the storm troopers. That's why Hitler begged him to come back from Bolivia."

I raised my eyebrows. Hitler was not the begging type.

"Röhm is much tougher than Hitler. Men followed him into battle in the war, paid with their lives in Verdun, and still more followed him." Wilhelm's eyes shone, and he ran his index finger across his lips.

"Does that say more about him, or the men who followed him?"

Wilhelm shook his blond head. "Röhm's a hero. Once he marched sixty-five French prisoners back from the front lines. He had been shot in the chest. It grazed his lung. But he took them back to the base, stumbling along with three other wounded German soldiers. His authority was so strong that none of the prisoners ran, even though Röhm and his men had only Röhm's service revolver, with only six shots."

"And how do you know about this feat of valor?" Behind Wilhelm the musicians took a break, putting down their shiny instruments and waddling up to the bar like penguins.

"My father told me and he should know because he's Röhm's top lieutenant in Berlin."

"Does it bother him that Röhm's queer?"

Wilhelm laughed incredulously. "He worships Röhm. It's fine for Röhm to do whatever he wants. It's just not fine for me. Plus I don't act manly enough."

"What does that mean?"

"Ernst used to coach me on ways to act manly around my father."

I winced. Ernst certainly had experience in that.

"He called it the Code of Manliness. You should know all about it. He said you made it up."

"I did, to keep him safe from our father."

"The tyrant."

"Is that what Ernst called him?"

"That was the nicest thing Ernst called him." Wilhelm laughed. "I'd have to apologize to say what he said in front of a lady."

"That sounds like Ernst," I said, smiling.

A tall, overweight man dressed in a badly tailored flapper dress with black fringe wobbled over to our table. He looked like a circus tent about to unravel. "Hi, darling," he said, to Wilhelm. I remembered him from my previous visit to El Dorado. Lola.

Wilhelm pulled out a chair and watched the man with calculating eyes.

"Nice falsies," the man said to me, through his garish coral lipstick. "You're a convincing woman."

"And you are a convincing man," I said, "which I'm guessing was not your intention."

He blushed and gave me a genuine smile. I smelled the floral odor of Vasenol body powder. "I'm sorry, esteemed lady," he said. "My vision isn't so good and I thought you were, well, you know."

I laughed. "Hannah." I stuck out my hand.

He took my hand in his moist hairy one. "I'm Lovely Lola."

"Please, sit down." I gestured to the empty chair.

The man shook his head, and the black hair in his wig swung from side to side. "I came to invite your friend . . ." He pointed one coral fingernail at three small doors along the back wall. The wall, and the doors, were painted with a mural of a Chinese harbor. The doors were invisible, unless you knew what to look for.

Wilhelm started to shake his head, but then looked over at me defiantly. "I'd love to go into the dark room with you. And you, Hannah, be sure to tell Ernst that when you see him."

Wilhelm stood and shook my hand. His grip was firm and dry; the grip of a young man afraid of nothing. "It was wonderful seeing you, Hannah. If you see Ernst, please tell him I'm looking for him. I miss him so and I want to make it right, whatever he's upset about. I can do anything that soldier will do, and better."

Lovely Lola smiled.

I turned over one of the El Dorado beer coasters and wrote my name and the telephone number at the newspaper on the back using my jade-green fountain pen. "Call me if you see him."

He wrote an address on his own beer coaster and handed it me. "We don't have a telephone, but here's our address. It's by the bottle factory."

"Thank you." I glanced at his messy handwriting before tucking the coaster into my purse.

"Tell him to stop by and say hello. Or anything. Anytime. And that I'm not waiting for him. Not really."

Wilhelm took Lovely Lola's hand and led him back to the door on the far left. From Ernst, I knew that those doors contained little rooms with only a wooden bench in them, for bracing oneself against while . . . while one was intimate with a companion. If one could call it that. I shuddered and left the table. I knew I was a dreadful prude, but I could not bear to think of fresh-faced Wilhelm and that old transvestite in that little room. I did not want to see them again when they came out, flushed and sweaty like the men I'd seen emerge from those rooms in the past.

It did not help to know that Ernst had also had Lola, or that Wilhelm was only doing this to make a point to Ernst. Without me there as a witness, none of this would be happening. I swallowed a ball of nausea and headed back to the bar.

8

On the way back to the bar an excited female voice trilled in Dutch. Out of the corner of my eye I saw two couples. The women looked like women as they giggled and tried not to point at "women" at the other tables. The men looked dazed.

"Thank you, Oliver." I set my empty glass on the bar and climbed onto a bar stool. "Do you know about a rich soldier Ernst might have mentioned? Wilhelm thinks they're away on a trip."

Oliver shook his bushy head and looked away. "Your brother mentions many men, including soldiers. But I never heard him mention a particular one." He polished a glass and set it in the row behind him.

"Oh." Was this part of Oliver's selective forgetfulness? Like last names, and dalliances? The perfect bartender.

"Don't worry. He'll show up soon. He's missed a show or two before you know."

"He has?" I asked, surprised. Ernst was responsible about his act.

"When Rudolf left to see a sick relative to make sure he was still in the will, your brother disappeared for a week." Oliver pulled six shot glasses down and expertly filled them. "And he wasn't with Rudolf."

"Do you know where he went?" I leaned my elbows on the smooth teak bar.

"Could have been anywhere." He placed glasses on a round red tray. "Your brother never lacks for offers."

"Thank you for the information," I said. In my experience, a source only gave this much information if they wanted something in return. What did Oliver want? "Was that Rudolf?"

Oliver's lips smiled, but his eyes were blank. "He was asking after your brother too."

"Did you tell him he's not here?"

"I told him to check backstage. Right now he's probably listening to a long tirade from Winnie." Oliver glanced back toward the stage door. A customer raised one hand with his fingers outstretched, and the thumb and forefinger of his other hand. Seven.

"He seemed in a hurry."

"Winnie will slow him down." Oliver took down another shot glass, filled it, and added it to the tray.

I stood to go. It would be well to get out of the El Dorado before Rudolf noticed me.

"Not sticking around for the show?" Oliver asked. "They've been using Francis instead of your brother. Quite an opportunity for an ambitious man. He's a gifted dancer, and at the end of the act he's wearing nothing but a fez and a loincloth."

"Who's Francis?"

"I need to deliver these." He cut across the dance floor to a group of mustached men sharing a table in the corner. They looked so much like men that I suspected they were women.

Oliver returned and dropped a few coins into an empty beer stein behind the bar. "You never heard of your brother's archrival?" he continued. "Francis has been trying to get into Ernst's act, and his pants, for over a year. Ernst's vacation is the best thing to happen to him since he got here."

"Where is Francis?"

Oliver pointed to a petite, curly-haired man sipping absinthe at the other end of the bar. His black hair and dark eyes and skin made him look exotic. He wore filmy harem pants, a black harem vest that seemed to cover pert breasts, a fez, and golden slippers with long curling toes. He looked too small to take down Ernst, but I walked over anyway. If he got close enough, he could have killed him.

"Can I buy you a drink?" I asked.

"Please," he sneered, glaring up at me with bloodshot eyes. The smell of alcohol from his breath was overpowering. "I know you spent hours getting those hips right, but you're still not my type."

"Hannah," I said, sticking out my hand.

"A real woman." He ignored my hand. "As I suspected. A transvestite would never wear those shoes with that dress. They're a train wreck. Your dress, by the way, is four years out of style."

"Give or take." I gestured to Oliver to refill Francis's glass, but Oliver shook his head.

"I don't take drinks from women." Francis wagged his long, lacquered fingernail at me drunkenly. "It gives them the wrong idea."

"What idea is that?" I asked.

"Do I know you?"

"I'm looking for my brother," I said. "Ernst Vogel."

"When you find him," he said, trying to push himself off the bar to a standing position. "Tell him to get back here."

"Why?"

"Listen, Anna," he said. "This glamour business is wearing me out."

He turned and lurched off toward the bathrooms. I was still trying to decide whether to go after him when Oliver came over. "He'll sober up before he has to perform. He always does."

"He said my shoes were terrible," I said. "But he liked my hips."

"You have very womanly hips," Oliver said. "Most men in here would kill to have those hips."

I laughed. "Would Francis?"

Oliver shook his head. "His hips aren't bad either."

"Is he always so drunk?"

Oliver polished the bar with a spotless white towel. "He's always a little drunk, but not too much."

"He looked bad to me."

"He's been drinking since the weekend."

"I wonder why," I said aloud. Perhaps he had done something he regretted on Friday. He had the anger to do it.

"I think his lover left him." Oliver folded the towel neatly in half. He excused himself to attend two figures in tailored tuxedos who looked suspiciously feminine, but I did not care to guess. The game had lost its appeal.

I glanced at the bathroom door. Francis was still in there. Would Ernst have trusted him enough to let him get close with a knife?

Wilhelm came out of the dark room, tucking in his brown shirt. A large man in a well-pressed SA uniform marched up and grabbed his arm. The man was strong and square. His neck was thick, like a bull's, and short, light blond hair covered his bullet-shaped head.

Wilhelm struggled against him, his face flushed.

The man casually drew his arm back and slapped Wilhelm across the face. I gasped.

The man stepped close and spoke slow and quiet in his ear. Wilhelm hung his head like a whipped dog as the man growled at him, his close-shaven scalp flushed red with anger.

Finally, Wilhelm nodded. The man gripped Wilhelm's elbow and frog-marched him out the front door. Lola stepped out of the dark room, straightening the strap of his gown. He watched them go, his face expressionless.

"Oliver," I hissed when he returned. "Did you see that man hit Wilhelm?"

Oliver avoided my eyes. "I did. That man is his father. He does not want Wilhelm in here. What father would?"

Before I could reply, Francis stumbled out of the bathroom, looking pale but more coherent than when I'd talked to him. Ernst would not have thought him a threat, but Ernst never did take hatred into account.

Rudolf slammed open the backstage door and hurried across the floor, knocking Francis over in his haste. He helped Francis up and brushed him off solicitously, bending his head to murmur something to him. At first I thought it was an apology, but Francis went white so I assumed it was something nasty instead. I turned my face toward the bar. When I peeked over my shoulder again a few minutes later, Rudolf's gray coattails were slipping through the red curtains on the way to the coat check.

What had he found out backstage that put him in such a hurry? Perhaps something about Ernst? I hurried after Rudolf, eager to see where he went. I tried to be patient while the coat-check boy pranced back to the coats.

"It's the brown one," I said. "The only brown one."

I slid into my coat and turned up the collar. I pushed my hat down so that the brim covered my face and slunk toward the front door. Not much of a disguise, but it was all I had. Hopefully, Rudolf would not be looking in my direction.

Bright moonlight glinted off the water-glazed street. I took a deep breath, savoring the clean air. The street looked safe. A well-dressed couple climbed out of a Hanomag automobile. Halfway down the block a young man vomited in the gutter. Two women entered a building across the street. Nobody looked like a killer or rapist.

Rudolf climbed into a taxi and slammed the door. I watched helplessly as it roared off. I'd lost him. How would I ever find out why he was so angry? I walked toward Nollendorfplatz to catch the subway home. I had only walked a few steps when El Dorado's front door closed with a *thud*. I flattened myself against the wall and turned.

Francis swayed on the steps, his curly hair outlined in the light. He walked past me without a glance in my direction. Why was he leaving the club? He had a show to do soon. I followed him. Of the men in the bar, Francis benefited most from Ernst's death. Now he was the star.

But what if the killer was a stranger? Ernst had left Wilhelm's alive, if Wilhelm could be believed. That left my brother wandering around the streets at who knows what early hour, probably dressed in his party clothes. An easy mark for the bands of Nazis that swept through the streets, putting up posters and harassing anyone who did not look Aryan.

If the Nazis killed him, I would never know. They moved in on victims, beat them to death, and disappeared. Witnesses rarely came forward. Even if they did, Nazi gangs would not do much time in jail. I thought about *Four Years of Political Murder*, a book published by the statistician Emil Gumbel in 1922. Gumbel's analysis of court records showed how judges supported right-wing political violence. Gumbel pointed out that average prison sentences for left-wing murderers were fifteen years or execution, but right-wing murderers' sentences averaged four months. And it had gotten worse since 1922.

But Ernst was a great fighter and a quick runner. After he left home he'd signed up for boxing lessons. Father would turn over in his grave if he knew that Ernst practiced such a low-class sport, but Ernst could defend himself. If he'd been attacked by a band of Nazis, he would have bruises on his body. His face and body were unmarked in the photograph.

Francis covered the few blocks to Wittenbergplatz in record time. He was more fit than he looked and walked with a self-assured grace. He was probably a wonderful dancer. I limped after him, wishing I'd worn more sensible shoes.

Wittenbergplatz was deserted, except for prostitutes standing under the lampposts that illuminated the traffic circle around the subway station. A few lights shone in the tall apartment buildings, but most were dark. It was late, after all. Off to the west loomed the spires of the Kaiser Wilhelm Memorial Church, barely visible in the darkness, but comforting nevertheless.

Francis slowed and approached an emaciated woman. Even leaning against the lamppost she was taller than he. Her hair was black as pitch, and her eyes were heavily made-up. Her shiny boots were laced up to her knees. I could not make out the color of her boots from so far away, but I knew that they would signal her niche in the Berlin prostitute industry. There were guides that detailed the perversions indicated by boots and shoelaces, but I'd never read them.

I ducked into a doorway, pressing my back against the cold surface uncomfortably. I must remain unseen. I did not want anyone to know I had been here. As a reporter, I had learned that it was always best to know more than the source thought you did.

An automobile drove by, and I lost sight of them. How could I get close enough to hear what they were saying? The automobile stopped, and someone shouted to Francis and the woman. She laughed and shook her head, pointing at her arm as if she had a watch there.

She stood upright next to the pole and folded her arms across her chest. She loomed over Francis. Undaunted, he waved his finger at her imperiously. I heard urgency in the tone of his voice, but could not make out a single word.

She tucked her long hair behind her ears and shook her head. Her arms were ghostly pale in the streetlight, but they moved with confidence. She did not fear Francis.

He reached out and caught her arm, his gold shoes flashing in the light. He drew back his other arm as if to strike her. She pushed him away with the palm of her hand, and he fell on his bottom, probably getting dirt on his expensive harem pants. She put one booted foot on his legs. What did Francis want her to do?

He handed her a small packet. Money? She walked away from him without a backward glance, and Francis hailed a passing taxi that sped with a screeching of tires back the way we'd come.

I could not follow him, so I followed the woman. She hurried down the sidewalk, eyes forward. When she turned right into a dark alley I hung back, afraid to follow. This street belonged to drug dealers, prostitutes, and their feuds at night. Buildings loomed on both sides, windows dark behind tiny square balconies.

She emerged with a man more skeletal than she. Despite the evening chill, he wore only a thin, stained undershirt and tight-fitting pants. After he glanced furtively up and down the street, he held out a dirty hand. She gave him the packet she'd received from Francis, and he spent a few seconds fingering the contents, his lips moving. I guessed that the packet contained money, and he was counting it.

He nodded and held out a fat envelope. She snatched it from his hand and sprinted toward the subway station. I hurried behind her, watching as she slipped through the door to the public toilets.

I wished again that I'd worn older shoes. The toilets at Wittenbergplatz were none too clean even during the day. I was reaching for the metal door handle when a large, hairy hand smashed me against the side of the building.

"What's it cost?" a voice slurred.

I tried to talk, but the breath was knocked out of me. I shook my head and struggled in his hold. Once again, I needed to lie myself out of this. Or fight him if I got a chance.

"Not." I shoved myself away from the wall. "For sale."

"Too proud to do a cripple?" He leered at me. He had no right ear. It was a shame he was not really crippled. That would have given me an advantage.

"Too ill to do anyone," I said. "I have the clap."

"That don't stop me." His beery breath scalded my face as he thrust his groin against me.

I ran through a list of actions I could try and picked the one that seemed most likely to get him to let his guard down. I smiled seductively and said, "A dollar for a blow job. American."

He stepped back a pace and reached for his back pocket, still holding my arm.

I rammed my knee into his groin as hard as I could. He folded in half, releasing me as he dropped moaning to the ground.

I sprinted toward the bright white *U* shining in the streetlights, thoughts of Francis's prostitute forgotten. I raced down the stairs. I ran onto the nearest train. I ducked below the level of the windows until it pulled away.

My back ached, and a bruise already encircled my arm where he grabbed me. But I knew how fortunate I was. If he'd been any less drunk or stupid, I would still be back there with him. I clenched my teeth together because they started to chatter. Glad to be alone in the car, I wrapped my arms around myself.

When the train emerged from a tunnel, a movie poster of an out-stretched arm with a red letter *M* in its palm flashed by my vision. It was the poster for the latest Fritz Lang film. A drama about a child murderer loose on the streets of Berlin, starring Peter Lorre as the killer who cannot stop himself from committing heinous crimes. I was on the Kurfürstendamm, passing the neoclassic façade of the Theater des Westens, and heading the wrong way.

9

I limped up the dark stairs to my apartment, nursing the blisters that my dress shoes raised on my heels. Mitzi yowled behind me, angry over the lateness of her dinner. It was after midnight. A time ridiculously late for me and ridiculously early for Ernst.

I fumbled with the key, grateful for the tiny bulb in the hall.

"Indian greetings," said a tiny voice. "The brave has a message."

I whirled, one arm raised defensively, legs wide apart, ready to fight or flee.

A small blond boy stood in front of me holding an envelope. He was the size of a three-year-old, but looked older. Perhaps five. I glanced around for an adult, but saw no one else. What was he doing out by himself at this time of night?

"For you, ma'am," he said in a precise voice. His grimy fingers held a soot-streaked white envelope.

"Why aren't you home?" I took the envelope without thinking. "Who takes care of you?"

"Sweetie," he said, without a hint of sarcasm. "Sweetie Pie."

"I have the envelope now," I said. "You can go home."

He did not move. Was he waiting for a reply to whatever was in the envelope?

I slit the envelope with the point of my house key. It held two pieces of paper. I took out a note written on faded yellow paper with ink the dark green color of bile. I struggled to decipher the poor handwriting in the dim light. I read silently.

My dearest Ernst,
I am finished. You did not pay this week, not even in food. So Anton is yours. Keep him. You won't find me to give him back. With love, Sweetie.

I turned over the note. Nothing else.

I pulled out the other piece of paper. A birth certificate. It stated that Anton Vogel had been born at Steglitz Hospital on June 10, 1925, which made him almost six years old now. His father's name was Ernst Vogel. I read it twice to be certain. Had Ernst fathered a child at the age of fourteen? That was impossible. But perhaps he experimented more than I knew.

I stared at the part of the form that listed the mother. What woman had Ernst dallied with at fourteen? I remembered a few girls, but he never seemed interested in them. I shook my head. No matter. I would find her and return this child to her. She was probably already worried that he was gone.

I read the mother's name twice. My eyes could not focus on the words. They danced in front of me. The mother's name was Hannah Vogel—my name. That could not be. It must mean another Hannah Vogel.

The address listed was my address. Someone had lied. Someone had forged my name on this birth certificate. My knees collapsed, and I slid down the wall. Beads from my evening gown dropped on the dirty floor of the hall. Mitzi hissed and backed away.

"Are you ill?" the little boy asked. "If you open the door, I can fetch firewater. That helps my aunt."

"I am fine." I used the wall for support and stood. "Thank you."

He nodded his head. His matted hair flopped against his shoulders.

"Are you Anton?" I looked at his pointy chin. Ursula, Ernst, and

I inherited a square chin from our mother. Anton looked nothing like us.

"That is my white man name," he said. "My Indian name is Little Eagle."

"I see," I said, although I didn't see a thing. I unlocked my front door and turned on the light. "Let's go inside."

Anton picked up a battered stuffed bear and walked through the front door behind Mitzi. She twitched her long white tail in annoyance at his presence. He had no bag with him, no clothes of any kind. And he smelled of unwashed hair and stale urine.

"Tell me about your mother." I refolded the note and counterfeit birth certificate and placed them back in the envelope.

"You are my mother." He said it so matter-of-factly that my head spun.

"Oh." I closed the door.

"Sweetie said you will take care of me. That you are my mother. She always said she will bring me to my mother someday. And here I am."

"Here you are." I had trouble breathing. "Where do you live?"

"In a tall wigwam," he said. "With Auntie Sweetie."

I felt like I was talking to Flying Deer from the Kästner book, *Emil and the Detectives*. He too, spoke as if he'd ridden out of a cowboy movie from America. I tried to ignore the sense of unreality and focused on my most important objective: returning him to his real mother. "What is Sweetie's full name?"

"Sweetie," he said slowly. "Pie."

"Where does Sweetie Pie work?" I stepped out of my shoes and lined them up next to the front door. Slipping off my coat, I folded it carefully in half and hung it over the back of a kitchen chair. Order seemed important all of a sudden.

"She works under the moon," he said. "She locks me and Winnetou in the wardrobe. We do not come out or make noise until morning."

"Oh," I said.

"No matter what we hear," he recited in a singsong voice. "We

never come out or make a sound. The brave understands the importance of silence."

"Who is Winnetou?"

He held up the bear by one greasy paw.

I decided to ask only questions that led to finding his mother and
getting him safely out of my apartment. "What does your aunt look
like?"

"Her eyes are blue and she makes her hair black. Like a raven. She
wears tall green boots to work. With golden shoelaces."

A boot girl, like the one I'd seen with Francis. I did not know
what the green boots meant, but I knew it was shorthand for a
horrible perversion I did not want to think about. Had Ernst slept
with a prostitute when he was fourteen? He had threatened to once,
to make himself into more of a man. He'd said it after a ferocious
beating at school. Perhaps the boy was his child, from some ill-fated
and probably short assignation.

Did the prostitute I saw with Francis know her? There were many
places to buy a boot girl in Berlin. Prostitution was rampant since
the Great War. I had middle-class friends who turned tricks for food
money in 1923. I had been lucky to have avoided it, grateful for the
newspaper and the American's love letters.

His mother must have a pimp. "Do you have an uncle?"

"No." He hugged his bear close. "Thomas has an uncle, but I
don't. His uncle hits his mother."

"Do you know how to get home?"

He looked down at his dirty shoes and shook his head. "We took
many trains."

He was so small and pale and drawn. Ernst had never been so thin.
I relented, even though I knew that I would regret it, and probably
soon. "Have you eaten today?"

"I ate yesterday." He bit his lip, but stared bravely into my eyes.

"You can have a bite to eat." But then I will have to send you out
again, I thought. Surely your mother will come for you. If not, how

do I find her? How do I find a woman my brother might have slept with six years before?

I led him to the sink and instructed him to wash his hands. He wet his hands with cold water and vigorously rubbed my Elida Queen soap between them, occasionally lifting his hands to his mouth and blowing lather into the sink. He squirted the soap from one hand to the other, smiling.

I lit a fire in the stove. While the stove warmed I slipped into the bedroom and changed out of my evening gown and into a worn housedress. As raggedy as it looked, I felt worse.

I poured Mitzi and Anton milk and cooked the boy an omelet with the onion, cheese, and eggs from my pantry. I'd hoped to get two or three meals out of them for myself. I put the omelet and a roll on a plate and fetched the scrap of butter from where I kept it cooling on the windowsill.

"Are you done washing your hands?" I asked.

He dropped the soap in the soap dish with a *thud* and dried his hands. He had a high-water mark of clean white skin halfway to his elbow that contrasted with the filth on the rest of his arm. "Yes, ma'am."

I gestured toward the table. "Sit and eat."

Staring at me with anxious eyes, he gulped his food as if I might snatch it away from him. His thin hands trembled. My heart went out to him. So many children were malnourished in Berlin. He looked like a Käthe Kollwitz lithograph, from the series she'd done of starving children and mothers.

"The food is only for you, Anton," I told him gently. "Eat more slowly or you will be ill."

He ate with exaggerated slowness.

I wanted to hold him in my arms and tell him he was safe. Instead, I pulled my old wooden laundry tub from the corner and filled it with warm water and fetched a washcloth and my bar of soap, which had shrunk from his handwashing session.

He stared at me with big round eyes.

"Time for a bath," I said.

"In the bowl?" He pointed at the laundry tub on the floor. I'd put it close to the stove, so he would not get a chill.

"It's called a tub," I said. "Please get undressed and climb in."

"Will I slip under and die? The brave can't swim."

"No," I said. "The tub is very small, and I will hold your head until you feel safe."

He took off his filthy shirt and pants. Angry red flea bites peppered his arms and legs. His clothes must be infested too. "I will have to burn your clothes."

He seemed unconcerned as he squirted the soap from one hand to the other. "Do you have new skins for me to wear?"

"We will find something."

He climbed in the tub, and I scrubbed the grime caked on his wrists, elbows, and knees. When I ran my fingers through his greasy hair, I saw nits. He had lice. "Soak here," I said. "You have lice biting your head."

After I dropped his clothes in the stove, I washed his head with kerosene kept for my emergency lamp. "Keep your eyes closed, Anton," I said. "This will burn, but it will kill the lice."

I knew that it burnt his head, but he did not struggle or protest.

I rinsed his hair again and again, lifted him out of the water, and wrapped him in a towel warming next to the stove, reminded of Ernst's days as a little boy. I pursed my lips. I was not his mother. All I could do was fix him up and send him back to her. That was all I had the right to do.

I sat him on a chair and cut his hair as close to his scalp as I could, then carried the clippings to the stove and burned them.

"Can I hold Winnetou?" he asked. "Please."

"He must have a bath too." I dunked him in the laundry tub. I saturated him with kerosene and let him soak, then rinsed him thoroughly. When the harsh kerosene smell dissipated a bit, I set him next to the stove to dry.

"He will dry tonight," I said. "And be fresh and clean for tomor-row."

"But how will I sleep?" he asked.

"In the bed."

"I can't sleep without Winnetou." He sniffled. "He protects me."

I lifted his light bony body and set him on my lap. "We will wait for him to dry, Anton," I said. "Right here."

He turned his face to my dress and sobbed. "Thank you," he said between sniffs. "I don't want to be a rude boy. Please don't hit me."

I pulled him back to see his tear-streaked face. "I will not hit you," I said. "Ever. I do not hit children."

His eyes widened in disbelief.

I told him the story of Little Red Riding Hood while combing nits out of his hair. He fell asleep before Little Red Riding Hood reached the grandmother's house. I combed out all of the nits and carried him to my bed. I dressed his limp, sleeping form in an old shirt of Ernst's from my sewing bag. Ridiculously long, it flopped down below his knees, but it smelled clean.

I wanted no more surprises, but the time had come to open the box Rudolf had given me Monday afternoon. I rubbed my gritty eyes. I longed for sleep.

Instead, I pulled back the cardboard flaps. Inside was Mother's black lacquer Chinese jewelry case. When I opened it, I found a long, red-beaded necklace, the kind that flappers tie around their necks. Ernst had made it himself, stringing and then crocheting the string of beads. It was different shades of red, from deep burgundy to pale pink. I pulled out a choker of what looked like large diamonds set in square onyx beads. Very Art Deco. There were four small bracelets, one with large diamonds and onyx, the others all simple diamonds. If they were real, they could have fed Ernst for years. Any one piece would have paid for Sarah and Tobias's tickets to America. They looked sumptuous, but I suspected they were fake. As much as he loved pre-cious things, Ernst always lost them.

Underneath the lacquer case was a neatly folded red silk dress, a pair of burgundy women's underwear, and a red handkerchief. I brought the handkerchief to my nose and breathed in the scent of lavender orange Kölnisch Wasser. The scent Ernst sprinkled on his handkerchiefs to smell fresh. A tiny lead soldier fell out of the corner of the handkerchief.

I held the cold captain in my palm. It was part of his lady battalion, although I'd not known he kept this one. Ernst had painted it when he was seven and glued on scraps of cloth to make a dress. The Kaiser's soldier wore a purple dress over his proper uniform and a wide-brimmed straw hat covered his Prussian helmet. Ernst showed amazing artistry, even then.

I remembered what had happened when Father found the soldiers, so long ago. I had moved out of the house when Walter died, taking my unused trousseau and my parents' disapproval with me. Back then I still came home every Sunday night to cook dinner for the family and to try and keep Mother sober enough to eat it.

From the kitchen I heard Father roar, "What have you done?"

I busied myself dropping dumplings into boiling water. Father had the right to yell at Ernst, to beat him as he had Ursula and me.

"Soldiers should not be defiled," he bellowed, and I wondered what could have gone wrong. Ernst had no interest in soldiers.

I listened to the slap of Father's belt striking Ernst until I could bear it no longer and ran down the hall, not certain what I would do when I reached the room.

Father had Ernst bent over the bed and struck his bare bottom with a belt. Ernst lay silent and stoic. He had learned early to take his punishments in silence, although if Father had ever looked at him, he would have seen the rage that blazed in his eyes.

"General Heinrich called," I lied. "You are to report to him at once."

Father put his belt on and walked out the front door without a backward glance. He could not ignore a direct order from his general.

I gathered Ernst in Mother's smelly bedclothes and carried him back to my tiny apartment. He never made a sound. When I tucked him into my bed, I noticed that he clutched three painted lead soldiers. Later, he told me that the one in the purple dress was named Mirabelle.

Until Father came to retrieve him the next week, he spent most days on his stomach in my apartment wearing an old pair of my underpants, cutting movie stars out of *Film Woche* magazine. His bottom was so swollen that he could not wear pants or go to school. While he cut out pictures I read him his Karl May books. May wrote about the American Wild West, and Father loved his Winnetou character. Winnetou was an Apache brave, a strong and faithful warrior. Until Father died, he gave Ernst a leather-bound Karl May book every year for his birthday and for Christmas. They were very popular books for German boys, and he had hoped, in vain, that reading them would teach Ernst how to be a man.

I invented the Code of Manliness and drilled Ernst on it every day. I tried to list everything that he should and should not do in order to avoid Father's wrath. I taught him how to play with soldiers like a boy. He learned it all, but he believed none of it.

I turned Mirabelle over in my hand, wondering how long it had taken Ernst to transform her from Prussian soldier to proper lady. I imagined his chubby fingers cutting purple cloth for her dress, wondered where he had found such a tiny straw hat. I set Mirabelle on the table. He had kept her for a dozen years, until the little lead soldier had outlasted him. I had outlasted him too. But I was the elder sister, the one who was supposed to be first in everything, but most especially in death. I missed him, and that was all I would ever have: his absence. I wept into the silk handkerchief, inhaling my brother's comforting scent.

But eventually I had to stand up, tidy the kitchen, and stumble off to bed. Holding Anton's tiny sleeping body reminded me of the times I'd held Ernst in this same bed after he cried himself to sleep on nights Father came home drunk and angry.

I tightened my arms around Anton. I knew he should not stay with me. Look how Ernst turned out. Dead in a gutter. I had failed to protect him from Father, and I had failed to protect him from his killer. Perhaps Anton's real mother missed him, would come back for him anyway. Perhaps this was a scam to extort money from Ernst, who surely was no more the father than I was the mother. Watching Anton eat, I did not know how I could afford to feed him. When I dropped my chin to the top of his head, I smelled kerosene. I had no claim on this child. But I wanted one.

Father had often reproached my sister and me when we were children. "You will never carry on my name. All that I am will die with me."

But when I was eleven, Mother became pregnant for the third time, and Father felt hope again. He pampered her with her favorite foods and watered the sherry. "It will be a son," he said in the bellow he used to shout commands across the parade ground. "I've waited long enough."

I hoped for a younger sister, but I did not contradict him. Later I followed Mother into the tiny patch of a garden that she created no matter where the army posted Father. The sun gleamed, and she wore a broad-brimmed straw hat with a blue ribbon to match her new maternity dress. She trimmed a branch from her favorite red rosebush. "You must always cut off the first blooms before they become full blown," she said. "Or the bush will not make more."

I nodded and gingerly took the thorny stem from her hand.

"How does Father know the baby is a boy?" I smelled the heavy fragrance of the rose and the lighter, green scent of the cut stem.

She laughed, a musical sound that I rarely heard. She stood and caressed her belly with one graceful white hand. "He doesn't know," she said. "He only hopes. He said the same when I carried Ursula and you. As if his loins could only produce male children."

I looked at her in shock. "So Father is wrong?"

"About everything," she said, not laughing now. She tucked her beautiful golden curls behind her ears and turned back to her roses. "Everything of consequence."

Mother's belly ballooned, and Father strutted around like a rooster, trying out boys' names. Ernst, Konrad, Hans, Adolf.

I could not wait for my new sister, as I was convinced the baby would be. I wanted to usher her into a world not wholly determined by Father, but when the day arrived Father sent me to my friend Bettina's house. Ursula was allowed to stay home with our parents, and our grandmother came from Heidelberg to help. I loved Bettina and her quiet, happy family and had secretly always longed to live with her, but now I yearned to be home. Every day at school I quizzed my sister for news of the baby.

Father had been correct. I wanted to meet my new brother, but I was not allowed home for a full month, not until after our grandmother left to take care of our sickly and querulous grandfather.

I dashed to our parents' bedroom, my feet skimming the polished oak floors. The green velvet curtains were drawn, and it took a moment for my eyes to adjust to the darkness. I could not yet see Ernst, but I could hear him. He squalled so loudly I could not believe such a huge sound came from that tiny bundle of blue flannel held so loosely by Mother.

I lifted him out of her outstretched arms and held him close to my face to see him in the dim light. I fell irretrievably in love in that first instant. Ernst was the most beautiful creature I had ever seen. He had long blond hair, even then, and mysterious blue eyes that later darkened to a soft brown, like a pony's. He knew I loved him more than anyone else did. He quieted, clutching my little finger and staring into my eyes with complete trust.

Mother looked pale, drawn, and drunk. Another one of her bad spells, probably brought on by some cruel action of Father's. "Take him away." She rolled over and went to sleep.

I bore him out of that room, away from the smell of sweat and sherry. "Father," I said. "He must have a nurse for when Ursula and I are in school."

Father looked surprised, because I did not demand things, but only said, "Of course."

I knew he would find one and pay her well. He could see that Ernst must be protected from Mother's carelessness, in a way that did not matter for us girls. We had only to learn to run a household and marry well. We were to marry officers if we could, shopkeepers otherwise. It was a simple plan, and we needed little caretaking to achieve it. Ernst had a grander future—follow in Father's footsteps. He was to join the army, distinguish himself in battle, conduct himself with honor, and carry on Father's name. Father had such high hopes for Ernst, in the beginning.

10

The bed was empty. My heart raced. The mother had come. The child was gone.

"Anton," I called, standing.

"I'm here," he answered from the kitchen. "Being quiet."

I pulled on Walter's old bathrobe, a gift from his mother after he died, and walked into the kitchen. Anton sat cross-legged on a kitchen chair, holding his bear. His well-scrubbed face was pale and his just-trimmed hair stuck out in all directions, like down on a newly dried chick.

"Good morning," I said.

"Indian good morning," he answered, looking serious.

"Did you eat any breakfast?" I asked.

"I never touch food without permission." He hugged his bear. "That's stealing. The brave never steals."

"You can eat anything in this apartment whenever you want. Do you understand?" I said, trying to keep my voice calm, to conceal my anger at a life that had kept him from food.

I set the table with two plates, two knives, my last two rolls, honey, milk, and two cups. I even found napkins. I heated water for my honey tea and milk for Anton.

"There we are," I said. "A party for Anton, Hannah, and bear."

"Winnetou," he said.

Anton gulped breakfast more quickly than his dinner the night before. He ate his roll without seeming to chew.

"I am full." I handed him the rest of my roll. If I had not seen Ernst eat as a child I never would have believed Anton could hold it in his tiny stomach.

"Thank you, ma'am."

"When is your aunt coming to get you?" I asked.

"Never," he said. "She said that my real father and mother would take care of me from now on. Forever."

Big fat tears plopped onto the half-eaten roll. "Auntie Sweetie said she was finished with me. No matter what I wanted."

I reached across and stroked his fine, soft hair. "Such foolishness. We will find her."

He held up his hand, his palm facing me. "Stop," he said. "She said she would beat me if I came home. She said she was moving to Munich to get away from Thomas's uncle."

I sighed. I had no time to get into a complicated discussion about his mother and her whereabouts. If Herr Neumann did not get a story I would lose my job. But what would I do with Anton? "I have to go to work today."

He scrutinized me as I stood there in my old scruffy bathrobe and bare feet. "Where are your boots?"

"There are many kinds of work," I said. "I write stories for my job."

"Like Little Red Riding Hood?"

I thought of the stories of serial rapes, murders, and beatings I cranked out for my newspaper. "A little."

He stood and walked into my bedroom. The wardrobe door creaked open and closed.

I opened the door. There he sat on the bottom of the wardrobe, holding his bear. My black dress shoes and winter boots were pushed neatly to one side.

"We're ready," he said.

"For what?"

"For you to go to work," he said. "We will be very quiet."

"I will never lock you in a wardrobe," I said. "I will take you to a friend's house. She has other children for you to play with."

We cleaned the kitchen and got dressed. I wore a long-sleeved gray dress, too warm for the weather, but it covered the bruises on my arm. Anton looked pathetic in the too large shirt, a pair of Ernst's childhood lederhosen, and his own dirty shoes with no socks.

We hurried down the stairs to catch a bus to Bettina's apartment. I felt the eyes of Schmidt the news seller on me as we ran to the bus stop. He'd never seen me with a child.

Bettina lived on the ground floor of her apartment building. Built about ten years ago, it had elegant, clean lines, unlike the sooty brick of my own building. A young mother dressed in a fashionable short gown rolled a pram by and nodded politely.

I lifted the polished brass knocker and rapped on the front door.

"Hannah," Bettina said, answering the door at once. She wore an immaculately pressed blue dress and a white apron. "It's wonderful to see you. Come in, there's tea."

"Thank you," I said.

Anton clung to me with one hand and to his bear with the other.

"This is Anton," I said. "Anton, this is Aunt Bettina."

Bettina raised her perfect brown eyebrows. "Nice to meet you, Anton. Please do come in."

We stepped through the front door into the hall. Her apartment was bigger than mine and much more homey. The furniture was new and comfortable, and the open curtains let friendly morning light stream in. I took a deep breath. Bettina's apartment always smelled good enough to eat. Today it smelled of cinnamon and vanilla.

"Sophia," she called. "Aunt Hannah brought you a playmate."

Bettina had three children. Her youngest, Sophia, was four. She appeared, perfectly dressed and brushed, like a doll in a shop window, with long brown curls and round blue eyes in a porcelain face. Underneath her charming exterior she was impish and strong-willed.

"I have a tea party." She held out her plump pink hand. "You and your bear can join. My doll Claudette is pouring."

Anton took her hand in his bony white one and followed her out of the room, his pointy chin held high.

"Well?" Bettina said. "Feeling better? Fritz said you were ill on Monday at the station."

"I'm fine," I said. "Except for this." I waved my hand in the direction that Anton had gone.

"Yes." She led me to her tiny kitchen and poured me a cup of tea. "Tell me."

I smiled. We'd been friends since childhood. Her father was in the army too, but at a higher rank than my father's. He was not a screamer, or a beater, or a drinker. Bettina's husband, Fritz, was funny and thoughtful. She had always lived the life I wanted.

"He may be Ernst's son," I said.

"Ernst?" she said, shocked. "But wouldn't that mean that at one point he had to . . . with a woman?"

I nodded. "That would be my understanding."

"But that boy looks four," Bettina said. "Ernst would have been sixteen!"

"Biology and mathematics," I said. "You are a genius. But Anton is five, almost six, which means Ernst would have been fourteen when he was conceived."

Bettina smiled. "You'd better ask Ernst." She placed a warm scone onto a plate and handed it to me.

I took the scone. I wanted to tell Bettina everything, but I knew that she might tell Fritz. And Fritz, being Fritz, would start an investigation immediately, before Sarah and Tobias reached safety. I could not ask Bettina to lie to her husband for me.

"Is little Anton visiting his aunt Hannah for long?"

"I have no idea." I handed her the note and birth certificate and ate the sweet raisin scone. It was warm from the oven, and I was hungry from my half breakfast. "His mother left him on my doorstep yesterday."

She gasped when she read the birth certificate. "Is he yours?" She looked at me with wide eyes.

"Of course not," I said impatiently, taking a sip of strong black tea to clear my throat. "You have known me all this time. You would not have noticed a pregnancy and child?"

Bettina laughed. "You've always been such a slender little thing."

"I'm grateful that you remember."

She ignored me. "My goodness. What are you going to do? Drop him on Ernst? He can't raise a child. He's up all hours. And the people he associates with—"

"I cannot raise a child either." I sat the teacup down in its delicate saucer with a *clink*. "I am an unfit mother."

"Nonsense. Where did you get that idea? You are not an unfit mother."

"Of course I am. Look how Ernst turned out." I wanted to add, "Dead in a gutter."

"He's a fine boy, Hannah." Her eyes snapped in anger. This was a familiar argument. "He loves you, and he takes care of himself."

"Does he?" I thought back to his photograph in the Hall of the Unnamed Dead. He did not take care of himself. And I had not helped him.

"Of course he does. He's a headline singer at El Dorado. That's a good job, and he lives in a wonderful apartment and he never has to ask you for money."

"Rudolf pays for the apartment."

"And? Fritz pays for this apartment, my dear."

I laughed. "You're married."

Bettina shook her head. "Well, maybe Ernst would be married too, if it were allowed."

"I cannot raise this child, Bettina," I repeated.

"What about his mother?"

"She's a prostitute," I said, and told her everything I learned from Anton.

"I can't believe Ernst impregnated a prostitute when he was fourteen. He was always precocious, but not in that way."

"There was one time"—I cleared my throat—"he said he was going to go find a female prostitute and try . . . try to be normal."

"Oh, that poor boy," Bettina said. "You didn't let him go, did you?"

I shot her an angry look. "Certainly not. But I also did not follow him every second of his life. If he had wanted to go, he could have done so without my knowledge."

We ate scones in silence.

"Well, no matter who his father is, you can't send him back to live with some prostitute." She began to clear the table. Bettina never sat still for long.

"I cannot find her to send him back," I said. "But there are orphanages."

"My God, Hannah." She took another tray of scones out of the oven. I inhaled the comforting scent. "Those places are terrible. Let Ernst raise him before you do that."

"Ernst is missing," I said.

"He's always somewhere." She scooped each perfect triangle onto the counter to cool. "He'll turn up before long."

I dared not trust even Bettina, but oh how I wanted to. I bit my lip. Who knew what she might let slip to Fritz?

"May I leave Anton here today?" I said. "I may need to leave him here off and on until I get a few things sorted out."

"He needs continuity," she said. "Not shuttling around between houses."

"I will only have him for a few days. Perhaps a week. By then I should find some place for him to go."

"And if you don't?"

I looked down at my hands, my fingers interlocked, as if in prayer. "I will."

She sighed and shook her head. "You can't promise something like that."

"Will you take him today?"

"To keep the wee one from being dragged around to Peter Weill's favorite haunts?" She smiled. "I will."

"Thank you." I headed for the front door. "I must be going."

"Oh no, you don't," Bettina said. "That boy has been through too much already. You are not abandoning him."

"I think it will be easier if I leave quietly."

"Easier for you, perhaps. Now go tell him good-bye and promise you'll be back." She put her hands on her rounded hips and glared at me.

I opened my mouth to argue, but Bettina folded her arms across her chest and gave me her stubborn look. "Hannah," she said, sounding like her mother.

"I'll do it." I followed her to Sophia's room, tucking Sweetie's note and the birth certificate into my satchel.

Anton sat in a tiny white chair in Sophia's room, turning her doll over and over in his hands. I think he'd never seen one before. Winnetou sat on the floor by his feet. Caramel, the dog, stretched out near the door, keeping watch. He stood when we entered and wagged his tail. I petted his thick brown fur, comparing his calm demeanor now to his ebullient puppyhood. Anton had none of that ebullience.

"Anton," I said, and he dropped the doll and jumped to his feet, looking sheepish. He picked up his bear. "I am going out for a while, but I will be back before dark to pick you up."

His eyes filled with tears, and he hugged his bear so hard I thought the stuffing would come out.

I leaned down to give him a hug. He dropped his bear and wrapped both arms around my neck. He held me so tightly I could barely breathe.

Bettina peeled him off me gently and held him in her arms instead, rubbing his back with one strong hand.

"I will see you soon," I said.

He looked at me with his big eyes and shook his head.

"You do not believe me?" I asked, surprised.

He shook his head again.

I looked at Bettina for help.

"She will be back, darling," Bettina crooned, rocking from side to side as if he were an infant. "She would never let me keep a sweet thing like you all to myself. And she'll want some cookies."

"Cookies?" Anton looked at her suspiciously.

"The cookies we are going to bake right now." Bettina ran her hand through his hair, straightening it out. "Butter cookies. Hannah's favorite. She stops by to get them every time I bake them."

"You will come for the cookies?" Anton asked me.

"I will come for you," I said. "And the cookies."

Anton relaxed against Bettina, and I glanced at her. Her face was chalk white, and her chin was set. "Kiss him," she mouthed.

I kissed Anton's soft cheek. "I promise," I said. "I will see you later, Anton, Bettina, and Sophia."

"And Winnetou," Anton said.

"Winnetou too."

As I walked out, Sophia said, "Aunt Hannah keeps her promises, even if she is strange sometimes."

I stifled a laugh. It was the nicest thing anyone had said about me in a long time.

11

Ernst knew only one person who could have faked that birth certificate, and I was going to visit him. Then I had to make up some kind of story to satisfy Herr Neumann before deadline.

I gripped the cold brass handrail as the elevator lifted me to Rudolf's fourth-story office. The elevator operator in his navy-blue uniform was better dressed than I and stony-faced. He'd probably seen all manner of people come up here. I ran my hand over my hair and clutched my satchel.

Who was Anton's mother? I tried to remember Ernst's school friends. Many girls visited him, both at our apartment and, before that, at our parents' house. Father held out hope that this was proof of Ernst's virile nature, but I'd always assumed that girls were friends with him precisely because he was not masculine. He was playful and exciting, and there was no need to worry about sexual advances. Although obviously one girl should have worried. Or perhaps it had been a prostitute, and I would never know who it was.

If Rudolf knew, would he tell me? He'd never been forthcoming with information before. Yet I had proof that he had broken the law. He had put his career on the line to help Ernst by forging the birth certificate. I had thought him incapable of doing something so altruistic. That meant there was more to his actions than I knew. If I dug deeply enough, I expected to find a darker motive.

The elevator opened onto a sumptuous waiting room as unlike the bullpen at the paper as I could imagine. The large room had a golden oak parquet floor inlaid with a basket-weave pattern, and a thick burgundy Persian rug. A man in his twenties wearing a pressed suit one shade lighter than the gray that Rudolf favored sat behind an imposing desk.

"May I help you?" He smiled, showing perfect white teeth.

"I am here to see Herr von Reiche," I said. "On a matter of some urgency."

He raised his eyebrows toward his pomaded blond hair. "Herr von Reiche the first or Herr von Reiche the second?"

"The second," I said, remembering that Rudolf's father still worked here. I took small pleasure in realizing that Rudolf would always be second.

"And when is your appointment?" He glanced meaningfully at the inlaid clock on the wall.

"I have no appointment," I said. "But he will see me."

"Name?" he asked.

"Hannah Vogel."

If he recognized the name from Ernst, he gave no sign. "Please sit," he said. "May I fetch you a cup of coffee, perhaps?"

"That would be delightful." I knew that etiquette dictated I refuse the offer, but I needed to make the frosty little man wait on me, if only for a while.

"Wait right here," he said, and disappeared through a thick wooden door. I darted behind his desk and paged through Rudolf's appointment book, but it only had initials in it. Right now he met with a J. L., whoever that was. The appointments went forward from today, so I could not find out what he'd been doing around the time Ernst died.

When the secretary returned, I sat innocently in my leather chair, reading Anton's identity papers. They looked completely authentic.

"Herr von Reiche will see you in a few minutes," he said, sounding surprised.

"Of course," I answered, trying not to look shocked. I'd expected a battle.

He handed me a porcelain cup with a blue Chinese scene painted on it and a delicate saucer so thin it was translucent. The cup cost more than my rent. The coffee itself tasted excellent, rich and strong. I sipped it, happy to be costing Rudolf something.

Rudolf made me wait for half an hour. I drank his rich coffee and admired the oil paintings of his esteemed ancestors on the walls. A stiff and starchy lot. I paced the expensive rug and looked out the spotless windows. Rudolf had a large inheritance to come, I suspected. I thought of my own: my childhood bed. At last the thick mahogany door swung open, and Rudolf strode through.

"Good day, Hannah," he said with an outstretched hand. We had not shaken hands since Ernst moved out.

"Herr von Reiche." I nodded my head fractionally. I did not take his hand. I would not pretend I liked him in front of his secretary or anyone else.

"This way, please." He led me through the door and down a hall with dark wainscoting. When we stepped into his office, it smelled of coffee.

Another huge Persian rug covered the floor, anchored by a massive desk and a collection of chairs. The desk was suspiciously free of papers, as if he thought I would snoop if given a chance, which, of course, I would.

"Please seat yourself." He gestured to an uncomfortable-looking wooden chair across from his desk. It was every bit as unpleasant as I expected, like Rudolf himself.

"What a large desk," I said with a smile. "Compensating for something?"

Rudolf snorted and steepled his fingers, his onyx cuff links clacking against the mahogany desktop.

I handed him Anton's identity papers. "Where is his mother?"

Rudolf skimmed the papers, straightened them out, and tapped them square on his desk. He handed them back, his face expressionless.

"His mother is sitting across from me. And what an ugly little drama it is."

"Are these forgeries your handiwork? Or were they done by someone in your employ?" I tried to keep my voice level.

"Tut-tut, Hannah." The corners of his lips twitched into a smug smile. "They are fully genuine, I assure you. Obtained when the boy was age two with all of the requisite legal documents, including the mother's legal papers and a very good signature too, I might add." He chuckled.

"Except that I am not his mother." I felt a flush rise in my face.

"A triviality." He steepled his fingers again. "That would be harder to disprove than to prove."

"Rudolf," I began. He had control of the conversation, and I did not like it. I wanted only to find Anton's mother. "You broke the law. Who were his real parents?"

He cocked his head to one side. "The certificate says Ernst and Hannah Vogel."

"Which you and I know to be untrue, perhaps on both counts."

He gave me his tight-lipped, thin smile. "Think so?"

"How long have you known about the boy?"

"Since I met Ernst." His eyes darkened with what looked like sadness, although I did not believe it of him. "He once trusted me with everything. Even with this delicate matter."

"Why?"

"He needed papers for the boy, and the boy was already two years old." Rudolf fished a lace handkerchief out of his jacket pocket. "And he needed money to support him."

"He supported Anton?" I said in surprise. "Why?"

"Because he was a fatherless little boy." Rudolf wiped his nose. "And your brother is a kind soul, underneath it all."

"Have you met the boy?" I shifted on the uncomfortable chair.

"Once or twice." Rudolf folded the handkerchief in fourths and stuck it back in his pocket. "How is the little tyke dealing with the death?"

I stared at him, open-mouthed. He knew Ernst was dead. He'd been pretending all along. My eyes darted to the closed door. Did he plan to kill me in his office?

"Don't look so astonished," he said. "Weren't you aware that his mother was dead? She died last night."

"I— I—," I stuttered out the words. I knew nothing, apparently. But I did know enough to lie. "I never met her. Or the boy."

"She was a prostitute," he said. "I identified her body at the morgue only this morning."

"Why you?"

"She had my card on her person when she died."

Last night I had seen Francis give a package to a prostitute. Perhaps she was the one who had died. Would Rudolf have been so careless as to include a calling card in Francis's package? "Why is that?" I asked. "Did you give her one?"

Rudolf ignored me. "Could have been a scandal, but I was having dinner with Count Nessler and friends last night, so my alibi is impeccable."

"Indeed," I said, grateful that he had not seen me at the El Dorado last night. So he lied to me, although I would not have known it from his demeanor. I studied him. Sometimes you learned more about a source from the lies they told than from the truth that they hid. Why was he lying? Had Francis been running an errand for him, or acting on his own? Was the woman I saw last night Anton's mother?

"Frequenting female prostitutes does my reputation good. My father would approve." The corners of his thin lips curled.

"How did she die?" Francis had left her alive, but he could have returned.

"Cocaine overdose, they believe." He glanced at the door. "I did not tell the police about the boy. That helps no one. Has someone delivered him to Ernst?"

"No. Ernst hasn't seen the boy in days." Or longer.

"They will. Her friends know that's where the money is." He paused. "How did you get the birth certificate?"

"From a source," I said, shading the truth. I would not give Rudolf a scrap of information I did not have to.

"Your brother, you mean." Rudolf shrugged. "Tell Ernst to bring him to me immediately, and we can talk. Now," he said, standing. I stood as well. "Where is your brother? Did he send you in here to blackmail me about these papers?"

I smiled. "Why Herr von Reiche, how could you think such a thing?"

"I won't pay him for this." He took out his gold pocket watch. "I'll drag your name through the mud with his. An incestuous child. Is that what you want your friends at the paper to hear?"

I kept my voice light when I answered, waving my hand around the office that his father's money provided. "I think you have more to lose than I."

"Not as much as you might think." He shut his watch with a *click*. "Do not tempt me. And instruct Ernst to come in person for these little exchanges. Or is he afraid to see me?"

"Why would he be afraid of you, Rudolf?" I placed my palms flat on his cool, smooth desk and leaned toward him. "Is there any danger?"

"There is always danger, my little treasure." He leaned close enough to kiss me. "As Ernst well knows."

A chill went down my spine, but I smiled at Rudolf and walked out of his office with my head held high.

12

I kept my brave façade until I was out on the street, out of Rudolf's sight. There I leaned against the cool stone wall and took a few deep breaths. Rudolf was a powerful man to anger.

I combed my fingers through my hair as I walked to the subway station. So, according to Rudolf, Ernst had fathered a child with Sweetie Pie. But why had Rudolf helped to give the child a legitimate mother, even if it was me? Why would Anton need a fake birth certificate at all?

Perhaps Anton's mother was still alive. I owed it to the boy to find out. Rudolf was too accomplished a liar for me to accept what he said at face value.

I boarded a subway bound for Alexanderplatz where, only the day before yesterday, I had started this nightmare.

When I arrived at the police station, I raced down the long Hall of the Unnamed Dead, never looking at the spot where I'd seen Ernst's photograph, hoping that I would not see Kommissar Lang. He would surely want to follow up on his refused dinner invitation. I focused in front of me, seeing the door at the end, the polished floor.

Today, I would not ask about the pictures, but after I had my identification back and Ernst's killer was found, I would do a piece on the Hall of the Unnamed Dead for the paper. Fritz was not responsible for posting the pictures, but he would know who was. The people of Berlin needed to be reminded about this hall, how it worked, and why it was needed. Perhaps a few would come and find a lost loved one. Perhaps a few would try to change a world that allowed so many people to die alone and unclaimed.

I paused in front of the sturdy oak door to Fritz's office. It would not do to barge in looking as if I'd just finished the Six Day Bicycle Races. I smoothed my hair, patted perspiration off my forehead with a plain handkerchief, and waited until my breathing returned to normal. I straightened my shoulders and walked in, my polite smile ready.

Behind the tall counter that ran along the front of the room sat a row of desks and typewriters, with men pecking out reports. It looked like the newsroom, except that the typists were all men. And they wore newer suits. Bureaucrats earn more than reporters.

I checked each one. Kommissar Lang was not there. I breathed a sigh of relief.

"Hannah," Fritz called when I caught his eye. "Back so soon?"

He closed a file cabinet and walked to the counter. His smelly cigar hung from the corner of his mouth. Bettina hated his cigars, so he only smoked them at work. I wondered how he would react when he got home tonight and discovered I had dropped an unclaimed child off at his house for a day of play with his daughter. But I dared not mention it to him. I was unsure I could lie to him, not if he started asking the right questions. So I told him nothing, even though I knew he would never fully trust me again.

"You know I can't keep away from you, Fritz."

Fritz shook his large, close-cropped head and studied me. "Feeling better, are you?"

"Much," I said, glad that I'd caught my breath outside the door. "I needed rest."

"And chicken soup," he said. "Bettina makes a wonderful chicken soup with dumplings. Puts you right back on your feet."

"I am a terrible cook," I lied. Bettina used my chicken soup recipe, but I would keep her secrets. "I have to stay on my feet without the soup."

"Pity." He took out his cigar and shook it at me. "Stop by and have some of Bettina's. She'd like to fatten you up and pair you off."

"Like a lamb to slaughter." I smiled my first real smile since I'd entered the building.

"So far, you've gotten away every time, lambkin." He chuckled, his gray eyes twinkling.

"I am a fast runner."

"But do you always have to run?" He put his cigar between his lips and puffed. The smoke smelled stronger than cigarettes, and I could see why Bettina hated it. "Kommissar Lang asked me about you. He's a good man. Perhaps even a little lovestruck."

"He's a member of the SS," I said, louder than I intended.

"Many men are." He chewed on the cigar end. "And more join every day. Soon you'll have no one to date if you don't date Nazis."

"I'd rather be alone."

He shook his head. "What's the real reason you're here, besides my irresistible nature? Or perhaps a chance to see Kommissar Lang?"

"I am doing a piece on drug overdoses and prostitutes," I said. "Any recents?"

"Other girls come in here asking about family and friends," he said. "With you, always the story."

"A girl has to eat."

"Chicken soup if she can get it." He ambled back to the file cabinets. He retrieved a few gray folders. Fritz had an amazing knack for finding the right cases for me. When he went on vacation I never got anything useful out of the office.

"Some of these are old." He slapped folders down on the counter in front of me. "But I never know which one will have the best details for you."

"You are a born newspaperman, Fritz." I opened the first folder, aware of his eyes on me. It was about a fourteen-year-old girl named Gretel who overdosed on heroin. I sighed and skimmed through the details. I had to look interested in all of them, but I also wanted to get out of there before Kommissar Lang came in. Lovestruck or no, he was no fool. He might have matched up Ernst's folder with the picture I'd been standing near.

Four folders in, I found her. Alias: Sweetie Pie. Name: Unknown. She looked like the woman I saw with Francis last night, but I could not be certain. It had been dark.

I sat the folder on the counter and took out my notebook. I skimmed the rest of the report. Age: early twenties. That made her anywhere from fourteen to eighteen when she gave birth to Anton. Cause of death: cocaine overdose. Her body had been found in the public toilets at Wittenbergplatz. My knees weakened, and I clutched the counter. I had been one of the last people to see her alive.

There were no coincidences, Paul used to say. Only reporters who were not smart enough to see the whole picture. Francis had seen her last night. He had given her money to buy the drugs that had killed her. But why?

Occupation: prostitute. The police had no name, they had no origin, no next of kin, and no address. How had she managed to practice her trade for all these years without anyone knowing her real name? If Rudolf had known more about her, he had kept it from the police. Nowhere did the report mention that she'd been identified by Rudolf von Reiche, so I assumed that must have cost him a bit for a bribe. She was listed as single with no children.

And, like that, Anton became an orphan. An invisible one.

I turned the folder upside down so Fritz could read it. "Tell me about this one."

Fritz glanced at the report. "Nasty piece of work, that one," he said. "I was here when they brought her in this morning. Chockfull of diseases, I imagine. Sores everywhere. Bone thin too."

I nodded and massaged my temples. Anton had no mother and no father. Anton's only relatives were me and Ursula, assuming that the dead Sweetie Pie was his real mother and Ernst his real father. I looked down at the photograph. What kind of childhood had Anton experienced so far?

Fritz lifted the picture. "I never look at these," he said. "Luckily, it's not my job."

I took it out of his hands and studied it. The woman lay on the white tile floor of a bathroom stall, trapped between the toilet and wall. Her black hair pillowed her head. She wore knee-high lace-up leather boots and thigh-high dark stockings with a rip above the knee. The rip was so sad that I stared at it instead of her pale face, turned artificially toward the camera. I was grateful to see no resemblance between her and Anton.

"There's not much information on her."

Fritz nodded. "Maybe not from around here. And not all of the local girls have a history with us."

"She looks so old to be in her early twenties."

"That kind of life burns them out young." Fritz looked down at the picture. "I don't think she got much chicken soup either."

"Or gave out any," I said, without thinking.

"You think she had children?" Fritz asked. "Her kind gets them cut out before they are ever born."

True. Pregnancy was bad for business and a child such a burden. Why did she carry him full term? Perhaps it was before her life on the street? Perhaps her parents cast her out because she was pregnant? Poor Anton, losing both parents within a few days of each other. A coincidence, or something more sinister? Was he in danger? Was I?

I slid the report back into the file with shaking fingers.

"You're taking this one a bit seriously," said Fritz. "I've seen you look at worse than this before. Did you know her?"

"No," I said, glad that I did not have to try and lie to Fritz when he asked a direct question. "Getting soft in my old age."

"You have a long way to go to get soft," Fritz said. "But you're softening. I read your story on the little girls in that rape case. It was refreshing to see someone writing about the victims instead of analyzing the poor, sad perpetrator."

"Thank you." I skimmed the rest of the files to disguise my interest in Sweetie Pie. I'd never concentrated on prostitutes before, unless they

were murdered. They died many other ways as well: malnutrition, tu-
berculosis, syphilis. Most had names, real names, next of kin, and real
addresses. But Sweetie Pie was not the only one cut off from everyone
and everything.

I tried to take notes for Anton, but there was nothing I wanted to
tell him about how his mother had lived and died.

"Useful bits?" Fritz asked.

I handed Fritz back the folders with a smile. "Not many. But perhaps I can turn them into a story."

"Need anything else?"

I took a deep breath and willed my voice to sound calm. "How
about those floaters you told me about the other day? How many of
those do you have, say over the last two weeks?" Ernst was sure to be
included in that group. I concentrated on keeping calm, but my heart
raced, and my breath was short and quick. It hurt to call Ernst a
floater.

Fritz turned and headed to the file cabinets. "I'll take a look."

I pretended to take notes in my notebook about the prostitute files
I'd seen, trying to distract myself while Fritz opened cabinets and
shuffled through folders.

"Here you go." Fritz set a few more folders in front of me. "More
light reading."

"Thank you." I forced my hands to slow down and open each stiff
folder in turn, eyes darting to the photograph. The first one was not
Ernst.

"I'll leave you to your work," Fritz said. "I have reports to type.
Let me know when you're done. And, Hannah, take a day off. You
don't look well."

He walked across the room to the shiny black typewriter. He was
so relaxed and solid, I felt suddenly bereft.

The next folder was Ernst's. I placed my green notebook on top of
it, as if taking notes, and slid the picture between the pages. I hoped
Fritz would not notice that the picture was missing. It was not his

job. I copied details from the report to my notebook mechanically, trying not to read them.

But I did read them. I became Peter Weill, the detached reporter. Ernst had been killed by a single stab to the chest. It's rare for a person to die of a single stab wound. A murderer with military training, perhaps? Or a doctor? A policeman? Or a very lucky stroke? It seemed most likely that the person had military training, but that was no help. Almost every man over thirty-five had received military training for the war.

Hard to believe he'd let an armed man get so close to him. Ernst was no fool. But there were no bruises on his body to indicate that he'd fought back. No bruises, no cuts to his hands. Except for the stab wound, there were no marks on his body. Did he know his murderer?

He'd been found naked, so the murderer must have stripped him before dumping him into the river. Why? Ernst wore distinctive, hand-tailored dresses for his shows. They would have led the police right to the tailor, and then to the man who paid the bills, Rudolf von Reiche. I shivered. Even if the killer had been a stranger to Ernst, he must have known that one did not buy evening dresses for a man two meters tall at Wertheim Department Store.

He'd been in the water for a few hours at most when a Berolina tour boat fished him out. The tourists got to see a side of Berlin they had not paid for.

The taste of blood in my mouth startled me. I was biting the inside of my cheek. I willed my jaw muscles to relax. After closing Ernst's folder, I paged through the others without reading them.

I stuck Ernst's folder back in the pile and tapped it on the counter. "Thank you, Fritz," I called.

"Always glad to be of service." The hall teemed with people hurrying to lost-and-found or the passport office. I pushed my way upstream against the human tide. My eyes filled with tears. Tears for Ernst. Tears for Anton. Tears for myself. Tears for a prostitute I'd never met.

Two dead. Two cast adrift. Anton's only safe harbor was me, and I was drowning too. I would sort out what to do with him. I cleared my throat and swallowed. The time for tears had gone. It was time to act. I would find out who killed Ernst, and I would bring him to justice.

13

An unusually small man dressed in riding clothes stood near the pictures in the Hall of the Unnamed Dead, scanning each one. He looked familiar, with curly hair and exotic skin. As he neared Ernst's picture, I realized who he was.

"Francis!" I called.

Without turning, he ran. He darted up the hall and slipped through a crowd of people. I had never seen anyone move so swiftly.

I walked as quickly as I could without attracting attention, but when I reached the back door he was gone. What was he doing here?

Still thinking about Francis, I strolled the few blocks down to the newspaper, wondering if my eyes had deceived me.

Inside the newsroom, the clack of keys greeted me, the sounds of writers typing furiously, proud each time a bell dinged at the end of a line. I hurried to pour a cup of the vile coffee. Even that would be better than the taste of blood in my mouth.

Cup in hand, I walked through swirling smoke to open the windows. I inhaled the outside air, which smelled only of manure and automobile exhaust; a bouquet compared to cigarette smoke. I sat at an empty desk and looked for Paul or Maria. They were nowhere to be found. Unusual for both to be gone so early in the day. Had they resumed their romance? In their heyday, they'd barely come to work.

Back then I was happy that Paul had found someone, but now I wished it had been anyone but Maria.

I sat down at a battered typewriter and rolled in my paper, savoring the familiar clicking sound as I turned the drum. I had no new sensational trial. The rape story had finished early. For the first time in years, Peter Weill had nothing to say. I'd spent my research time fencing with Rudolf and verifying his story. Good for my curiosity, bad for my journalism.

Still, I had a typewriter and paper. No sense in letting that go to waste.

Dear Fritz,
I know that this seems fantastic, but you would only be receiving this letter if my suspicions had some truth.

I then typed details of my conversation with Rudolf, my suspicions that he had killed my brother, that he had killed Anton's mother, and that he would kill me. Even to me, it sounded foolish. Although I understood Rudolf's anger at Ernst's infidelity and believed him capable of a quick crime of passion, I had trouble believing he could have killed Ernst with one blow. He had no military training, and I doubted he picked up anything heavier than a fountain pen most days. Even if he had killed Ernst, why kill Sweetie Pie? That was no crime of passion.

I typed up everything I knew, adding a note asking that Anton be delivered to my sister Ursula. Bad news for him. She was no one's idea of a nurturing mother, but she was his only living relative. As difficult as she was, living with her was preferable to an orphanage. Then I signed my name. I sealed the documents in an office envelope and wrote "In the event of my death, deliver to Fritz Waldheim at the Berlin Alexanderplatz Police Station." I felt paranoid, but Ernst was dead, Sweetie Pie was dead. And I was the only one who had made a link between their deaths. So far.

The smell of cigarette smoke and burnt coffee was all but forgotten as I moved into the world of my story. I wrote of a woman visible only in the brief moment when a man picked her off the street. Then she became desirable and earned money and notice, until she returned to the street again. In death, Sweetie Pie lay alone, nameless, clutching the card of an aristocratic lover, a man who identified her body at the police station but stayed out of official reports, a man with an important name, a rich man.

I hoped Herr Neumann would have no time to read through the story. He'd pull that line as slander, although I knew better than to use Rudolf's name. I did "accidentally" capitalize the word *Reich,* matching as it does von Reiche. Only a lazy typesetter would miss it, but I could always hope.

Perhaps it would trigger an investigation, if Fritz read it in conjunction with my letter. If I were killed. I snorted. Now all I had to do was die, then Rudolf would be sorry. I felt like a twelve-year-old, mentally viewing the attendees of my imaginary funeral, thinking they were sorry that they had treated me badly.

"You're looking rather odd," Paul said. I looked around for Maria, but she was gone. He handed me a cup of warm coffee. Mine had long since gone cold.

"I try." I sipped the coffee and made a face. "Will you hold this for me?" I handed the envelope to Paul.

He leaned against my desk, his long elegant legs angled toward the window. He shifted to the right, putting his weight on the leg that had never been wounded.

"What is this?" Paul asked, reading the outside. " 'In the event of my death'?"

"Probably nothing," I said. "Paranoia."

"You're not the paranoid type." Paul scrutinized my face. He stood and came around to the back of my desk.

"Everyone can be, under the right circumstances." I stood as well.

"Not Peter Weill," he said.

"I have to go."

Paul put his hand on my arm, over the bruises concealed by my long sleeves. "Hannah?"

"Stay out of it, Paul," I said. "It's the only way you can be of use to me."

He took his hand off my arm and bowed slightly. "I'd rather be of use to you while you're still alive."

"We do not always get what we want, do we?"

Hurt flickered across his face, but was replaced by a studied politeness. "Indeed."

"You are a great friend," I said. "But—"

"Paul!" shouted a reporter from across the room. "I need you over here."

Paul held up one long finger. "Just a second."

"I cannot explain," I said.

"Does this have to do with the rape case?" he asked. "And that new man you are seeing?"

I shook my head. "First, I am not seeing him anymore. Second, it has nothing to do with him." I thought about his Friday invitation. I would not go out on a boat with him. Not at all. I had no time for frivolous pursuits.

Paul lowered his voice to a whisper. "With Sarah?"

"Only indirectly," I said. "And that's all the information you will get from me."

"Paul!" called the other reporter. "It will just take one second."

"That's all I'm getting so far," Paul said. "Don't think I'm giving up."

He slipped the envelope in his jacket pocket and walked across the room to the other reporter. Before he came back, I sneaked out the side door of the newsroom.

I had to pick up Anton before Fritz got home from work.

Before I finished knocking on Bettina's door, Anton opened it.

"You returned from the hunt." Dropping his bear, he threw himself at my legs. "The brave is pleased."

I bent and hugged him. Bettina had trimmed his hair properly and dressed him in a pair of short pants and a singlet. He looked like an

ordinary boy. Small and pale, perhaps, but nothing like the dirty raga-
muffin I'd seen at my door the night before.

"Return of the chief," Bettina said, with a smile from the doorway. "Quite a greeting."

"Usually no one notices when I come home except the cat." I
scooped Anton in my arms. "We must be off," I said. I did not want
to meet Fritz after he found out about Anton. He would ask hard
questions about Ernst. He would know the birth certificate was a
fake, and he would want answers. He would not be as easy to put off
as Paul.

"Please can we take the cache of cookies?" Anton gripped my
hand. "I made them all by myself. Didn't I, Auntie Bettina?"

She smiled and led the way to the kitchen. "You certainly did, Little Eagle."

She slipped a glass jar filled with soup into a canvas bag and added
a loaf of her special bread and two apples. Finally, she wrapped a
handful of cookies in a warm dish towel and placed them on top.
"You can take this home for a big supper, in case you forgot lunch,"
she said. "Anton loves it."

"I do," Anton said. "Auntie Bettina said it's like the stew the Indians used to make."

"I had no idea." My stomach growled, reminding me of my
missed lunch. I'd had nothing but coffee since Bettina's scone that
morning.

"Chicken and dumplings," Bettina said, winking at me. "A staple
on the prairie."

"Thank you, Bettina," I said. "I don't know what I'd do without
you."

"Nor I without you, Hannah." She gave me a hug. "And now I
don't know what I'd do without you either, Anton."

She stroked his hair and stuck a small picture book in his hands.
"For bedtime," she said. "In case Hannah has no good books."

Anton fell asleep on the bus, holding his bear and his picture
book. He had insisted that a brave carries his own supplies. I watched

the neighborhoods change from the neo-baroque Wilhelminian apartments in Bettina's world, to the newspaper district with its assortment of modern and humble buildings, and finally to the sooty brick tenements crammed together in a mishmash around Hallesches Tor, and home.

I pulled the cord to signal the bus to stop and gathered everything up, including the sleeping boy. It was heavier than I wanted, and Mitzi did her best to get in my way as I entered the house, but I could not bring myself to wake Anton. He was an orphan now, the same as me.

When I turned to close the door with my foot, I glanced outside. A small figure slid gracefully into the doorway across the street. Francis? I slammed the front door and hurried upstairs, locking my apartment door carefully.

I carried Anton in and put him down on the bed. He did not stir so I held my fingers under his nose, to make certain he was breathing, as I used to do with Ernst when he was an infant.

I stared out the window in my dark kitchen for several minutes. No one waited in the street below. Mitzi twined around my ankles, yowling for her milk. I had been imagining things, I decided firmly, turning on the light and feeding her.

I stroked Mitzi while she drank her milk, her fur warm and soft under my fingers. Her throaty purr was the only sound in the kitchen. Hungry myself, I sliced Bettina's bread and opened the jar of her treasured dumplings. The soup was still warm, and the smell of onions and chicken wafted up. Mmm. Treasure was right.

Treasure.

Mother's jewelry case. She'd called it her secret treasure chest, because of its special compartment. Mother kept her most valuable pieces there. I set the case on the table, thinking back to the secret compartment Mother showed me when I was a small girl. How had it worked? The case had a false bottom that could only be opened when you closed the case, tilted it forward, rapped it on the left side, opened it back up, and pulled a tiny gold loop in the left corner.

I went through the steps, tugged at the gold loop, and lifted out the red velvet false bottom. Brightly colored feathers filled the hidden compartment. Clever. That would muffle the sound if anyone shook it. What did Ernst have worth hiding there?

I picked out the feathers. First I found two of Mother's necklaces: a diamond pendant and a heavy gold locket. He must have stolen these pieces before Ursula could get to them. I felt a thrill of fierce pride. Well done, Ernst. It was wonderful to see them again after I'd given them up for lost.

But Ernst was more clever than I. He'd hidden the necklaces in the bottom of the case. A bottom Ursula had never noticed, perhaps because she had no interest in Mother, wanting only to be Father's chosen one.

I sprang the locket open with my thumb. It contained a picture of Ernst at two years old and a lock of fine blond hair. He'd been so beautiful as a child. I remembered the sunny day I'd taken him to the photographer and the way he'd sat, serious about his picture, wanting to look just right, even then. I kissed the locket and tears welled in my eyes. I took a deep, shaky breath. I needed to be clear-headed in case something here gave me a clue that would help me find Ernst's murderer.

Both necklaces were valuable and could be sold in a pinch for food, though I would be loathe to do so. I weighed the locket in my hand. I hated to part with it again, but food for a hungry child is more important than sentiment. I set the jewelry on my battered kitchen table and withdrew more feathers.

Hidden in the far left corner was a masculine-looking ring. I lifted it out and gaped. It was gorgeous. Two golden snakes with tails intertwined formed the back of the ring. In their fangs they held a giant square ruby that glistered in the light. The red light hypnotized. Power emanated from the stone. I shook my head. Ridiculous.

It could not be real. I had never seen a stone that large except on a movie screen. I laughed aloud. I was uncertain that I'd seen a stone that large on a movie screen either. Its size was absurd. Only royalty could flaunt something like this. But it was exactly the kind of ring that a status seeker like Ernst would wear, even if fake. Mitzi jumped onto my lap and kneaded my dress. I stroked her snowy head absently.

Where did the ring come from? It was not Rudolf's style. I bet that he gave Ernst the more decorous onyx-and-diamond pieces. Modern and almost masculine, but not quite. Besides, if he gave it to Ernst, why would Ernst hide it?

Who else could have given it to him? His rich soldier? If it was real, no wonder he hid it. But it fell beyond a soldier's budget. I wondered what other admirers he had. My hands became ice. What if he had stolen it? I pictured him sneaking out of the bedroom of some rich man, helping himself to the contents of the night table on his way.

I shook myself, set Mitzi on the floor, and stood. The ring was fake. It was too large to be real. And yet I turned it over and over in my fingers. An inscription inside was too tiny to read. Tomorrow I would take it to a jeweler, a friend of mine and Sarah's. I might also take the onyx-and-diamond ones that were outside of the secret compartment. I'd like to see what he could make of them, where they came from. Perhaps I could trace the man or men who had given him the more valuable pieces.

But if they were valuable, why had Rudolf given me the case? He must not have known about the secret compartment. I could think of no sinister reason he would have knowingly given me expensive jewelry.

Pulling out more feathers, I found a diamond-and-ruby bracelet, and a golden cross set with rubies on a fine gold chain. If they were real, they would be worth enough to keep Anton and me for months. I angled the jewels to and fro, watching them catch the light. I felt like a child playing pirates, except that I'd uncovered a real treasure chest. Such beautiful things, jewels. Never in my life had a man given me a jewel. Walter had only given me a simple gold engagement ring, promising to replace it with something nicer after the war. He never had the chance. Yet Ernst had several pieces. He'd probably owned and pawned more.

Diamonds and rubies were perfect for him. He loved the luxury of diamonds, and red was his signature color. He'd always wanted red clothes as a child. He ate red food, if he could—apples, rare steaks, beets, red potatoes instead of white ones, strawberry ice cream. The color mattered more than the flavor.

Luckily Father approved of red. After all, the piping on his uniform was red. What if Ernst had fancied pink? Wishing for a magnifying glass, I picked up the large ruby ring and tried again to make out the inscription.

"That is my father's snake ring," piped a tiny voice from the bedroom doorway.

I turned. "It is?"

"I saw it on his finger," he said, walking sleepily into the kitchen. "I'm hungry."

"What do you know about your father?" I filled a bowl with warm soup for him.

"His name is Ernst," Anton said.

So Anton thought that Ernst was his father. That seemed to make it true then. Why would Ernst act as father to Anton otherwise?

"And he will take care of me." Anton climbed onto a kitchen chair. "He is rich."

I'd never thought of Ernst as rich before, but from Anton's perspective I guessed he was.

"What about your mother?" I set a spoon next to the bowl.

"You are my mother." He sat at the table and picked up his spoon. "Auntie Sweetie said that someday she would take me to my mother and she did."

I opened my mouth to deny the relationship, but no words came. "Let me get you some bread," I said and spread a slice of bread thickly with butter. I watched him eat, twirling the ring around my finger. I was as close to a mother as he had now, poor child.

What if Sweetie Pie was not his mother either? Perhaps she told the truth when she said that she was only his aunt. Perhaps he had a real mother somewhere.

After I tucked Anton back in bed, I returned to the kitchen, stuffed the jewelry among the feathers and closed the secret compartment. Even if only the pieces from Mother were real, they were valuable. I placed the jewelry case back in the bottom of the box and piled old newspapers on top. My treasure buried, I, too, went to bed. It had been a long time since I'd had valuables in the house, and I tossed and turned with worry. I must learn the value of the jewelry, to see if it needed more safeguarding than I could provide. I fell asleep thinking of sinister figures creeping nearer, one doorway at a time.

14

"Indian good morning," Anton said when I walked into the kitchen the next day. Oily crumbs from the last of Bettina's cookies dropped from his fingers onto the bare table.

"Good morning. I am happy you found your own breakfast today."

"A brave learns a lesson with one showing."

"We should all be that wise." I cut Bettina's apples into wedges and gave one set to Anton. The other I ate myself, along with a fat slice of fragrant bread.

After breakfast, I dressed in a simple dark green dress and moved Ernst's jewelry to my satchel. I did not have to turn in a story today, so I could retrieve my paycheck and run errands, like finding out more about the jewelry and perhaps buying Anton a set of used clothing from a street vendor. For now, I dressed him in the clothes Bettina had given him yesterday.

On the way to Bettina's, Anton regaled me with tales of Indian derring-do. He talked of riding fast horses over the prairie, yet the only horses in sight pulled carts and wore blinders. We rode a bus in the shadows of tall stone buildings as he told me about teepees and the harsh sun in the land of the Apache.

He chattered away until we reached Bettina's house and knocked.

"Good morning," said Bettina when she answered the door. "You missed Fritz."

"Give him my regards."

She raised one eyebrow. "Come in, Anton. I have fresh oatmeal with apples."

"He had breakfast already," I said, as we entered Bettina's cinnamon-scented front hall.

Anton squeezed past us and streaked toward the kitchen.

"He's a growing boy," she said, laughing. "He can eat two break-fasts. Maybe three. Don't worry, I'll keep him fed."

How would I ever pay for his food? It was wrong for me to de-pend on Bettina's charity. If he was like Ernst, he would eat more than an adult. Before I left home, I'd often slipped Ernst bits of my dinner, breaking Father's strict rules about portion control. "Thank you, Bettina," I said. "I won't need to bring him this weekend so you can have a break."

"I don't need a break from him, Hannah." She reached over and straightened the collar of my dress with one efficient gesture. "But I think it's good if you spend the weekend with him."

"I can give you something for his food—"

"Nonsense." She raised her finger warningly. "One more foolish comment like that and I'll turn you over to Fritz."

"Turn me over to Fritz?" I kept my voice carefully neutral.

"He is very interested in Anton and how he came to be here." Her eyes twinkled. "He wonders why you didn't mention it when you went to the station yesterday."

"I forgot."

"I told him you did not want to explain it in a police station, which I think is closer to the truth." Bettina shook her head. "So early in the day, and you're already lying to your old friend."

"When is he coming home tonight?"

"So you can avoid him?" Bettina tilted her head to one side and flashed her impish smile. "Around six."

When I arrived at the paper for my paycheck, Rudolf stood in the lobby looking at his watch. People parted around him like water around a stone in a stream. Too late, I turned to leave.

"Hannah." He strode across the room. "We have something to discuss."

"We have nothing to discuss." I hurried toward the elevators.

He grabbed my upper arm; his fingers pinched me cruelly. In the five years of our acquaintance, it was the first time he'd ever touched me. "Listen to me now, or you will deeply regret it later."

I stopped. "Release my arm," I said in a loud voice. Xavier, the elevator operator, looked curiously in our direction. Rudolf let go, but stayed too close for my comfort. I resisted the temptation to rub where his fingers had been. I would not let him see that he had hurt me.

"Tell your brother that he must deliver the package we talked about the other day." His voice was low and urgent.

People hurried past us, crossing the elegant lobby on their way to the elevator, but I saw no familiar faces. It was as if we were standing outside Rudolf's office and not mine.

"I have no idea what you mean." Was it the ring? If Rudolf knew about it, Ernst would not have hidden it from him in the secret compartment.

"I think you do, but even if you do not, Ernst does. He knows the stakes for withholding it." Rudolf leaned into me. He smelled like stale sweat. Whatever startled Rudolf out of his careful grooming could not be good.

I stood my ground. I would not be intimidated. "Does he?"

Rudolf gripped my elbow and marched me to the corner of the lobby, away from the crowds by the elevator. I was afraid to go too far from other people, but I wanted to know why Rudolf sought me out. I kept quiet.

Rudolf lowered his voice. "They will kill first him, then me. Finally, probably, even you. He knows they are skilled in torture, and they will find what they need. Tell him to take the easy way."

My hands shook. I clasped them together so that Rudolf would not see. Could he smell my fear, like a dog? "What should he return? And where?"

"He knows. And he knows the place. Sunday at his apartment. In three days."

"Return it to whom?" When the elevator bell dinged I turned toward it, ready to get away.

"If he hasn't told you whom he is dealing with, Hannah, I will not either," Rudolf said, leaning down to whisper in my ear. "Ask him."

I said nothing. Rudolf straightened again. "You are good at asking questions, aren't you? And reporting the answers to others," he said in his normal voice. "I read that story in the paper last night. The one written by your friend, Peter Weill."

Rudolf did not know I wrote as Peter Weill. He thought I made a living selling poems and sketches. His previous indifference to my existence was useful after all. I struggled to keep my expression neutral. "Indeed."

He sniffed and ran his hand over through his thick hair. "I had a pertinent conversation with the editor of the paper. He will take care of Herr Weill."

"How nice for him."

"He is fired, Hannah." Rudolf clucked his tongue. "Poor man. Maybe you can find him and tell him before your editor does. The editor wouldn't tell me his name, but he promised that Peter Weill will be written by a new hand."

"Peter's a big boy," I said, although a cold chill settled in my stomach. "He can take care of himself."

"Would you like to tell him more?" Rudolf asked. "Would you like to tell him how Sweetie Pie died? How I paid her to procure something for me? How instead of delivering it she spent the money on drugs?"

"What did you need her to procure?"

"My messenger paid her too much, I see that now. She spent it all in one place, against the old caution. She bought enough cocaine to kill a cow."

"Why are you telling me this?" Rudolf would not give me information without a goal.

"So you can tell your Weill friend where he got it wrong."

"If he got it wrong."

Rudolf waved his hand. "She is no good to me dead. Alive, she had one function to perform. One I can't get from the boys."

"How lucky for her."

"Tell Ernst he can't trust his Nazi boy to bail him out of this."

He turned and strode out of the building, his soft leather shoes silent on the marble floor.

I rode the elevator to the newsroom in a daze. Peter Weill had been my identity for so long. Herr Neumann would keep his word to Rudolf and fire me. I was amazed that he had not given Rudolf my name. He had a shred more integrity than I'd expected.

Peter Weill had provided me with food when I was hungry. The fan mail that I received for him made me feel like a real writer. Now I was just one of five million other unemployed workers in Germany. And I had no identity papers to show when I applied for jobs. At least I had jewelry to sell. Even without the ring, the jewelry would feed us for a time.

Plus, there were other newspapers. Peter Weill was not the only crime reporter in Berlin. And I would get my papers back soon enough. I hoped.

"Your floor, Fraulein Vogel," said Xavier. "Is that where you're going . . . today?"

"Yes, thank you, Xavier." I stepped out of the elevator and took a deep breath to steady myself. From force of long years of habit, I walked through the newsroom and opened the window. Smoke drifted out into the sunny morning.

"Hannah," called Maria from across the room. "I need to talk to you." Her happy tone told me that she knew I was fired.

"Good day, Maria." I turned to face her. I left one hand on the wet windowsill.

"Herr Neumann will tell you officially, but I wanted to break it to you sooner." She placed her hand next to mine on the windowsill, not quite touching. "So that you wouldn't cry in front of him."

"I can think of nothing you or Herr Neumann can say to make me cry," I said in an icy voice. I wiped my damp hand on my skirt and crossed my arms across my chest, glad that Rudolf had warned me.

"I'm so sorry," she said, not sounding sorry, "but you are fired from the paper."

"So I gathered."

Her perfectly plucked eyebrows shot up in surprise. I'd stolen her scoop. "Someone is threatening to sue about your prostitute piece, someone with power."

"Rudolf von Reiche, the lawyer."

"Really?" She looked ready to pull out a notebook and interview me. "Is he the rich man from the article?"

"What good would it do you to know?" I asked. "Really?"

A shadow crossed her face. "None at all."

"I can see by your barely disguised glee that you are the new Peter Weill." I reached out and closed the window with a *clunk*. Let them suffocate in their own smoke, after all. "Congratulations."

"I didn't want it this way," she said, sounding almost genuine. "But I'd be a fool not to take it."

"And you, Maria, are no fool," I said. "Ask Paul to pick up my mail for me."

Herr Neumann's bony finger tapped my shoulder. When I turned to face him he smiled.

"You're lucky I don't sue you," he said. "For exposing the paper."

"To what? The truth?"

"To a lawsuit." Herr Neumann puffed himself up like a toad. "Why—"

"So firing me is as bad as it gets?" I interrupted.

Herr Neumann looked surprised by my tone. "Well. Yes."

"Thank God for that." I left the newspaper office for the last time, stopping in accounting to pick up my final paycheck. For the first time in my adult life, I had no job. I wondered how I would feed myself, and Anton. Then I laughed. The way things were going, I would be lucky to stay alive long enough to go hungry.

15

I took the bus to Alexanderplatz, then walked past the police station to the heart of the Jewish quarter. Sarah used to live here, as did our jeweler friend, Mordecai Klein. Like Sarah, he had dark suspicions of what would become of the Jews if the Nazi party gained power.

An old woman, her body bent double with age and the weight of her display case, tried to sell me shoelaces. I shook my head as she first entreated me in guttural Polish, which I did not understand, and then in Yiddish, which I did because it's close to German. But I had no use for shoelaces in any language and could ill afford to buy something I did not need. Eventually she walked away, her black head scarf fluttering in the breeze.

A young Orthodox Jew stood on the sidewalk, dark forelocks bouncing as he chatted with a man in modern business clothes. Ignoring automobiles and the occasional horse, a man pushed a handcart full of green apples down the street. I smelled the apples' wholesome scent through the poisonous automobile exhaust. Haggling agreeably before handing over a few of my last remaining pfennigs, I bought an apple for Anton. It might be a long time before Anton got apples again. I tucked it into my satchel.

In the Jewish quarter I blended in. I'd been coming for years with Sarah, and people trusted me. Nowadays, that was a huge gift. Many of them had been through much, losing homes and families in Russia and Poland. Now they waited for a chance to leave Berlin and settle somewhere permanent, somewhere safe. I feared for them. Sarah was right to leave. If the Nazis came into power there was no telling what they would do.

I stopped at Herr Klein's shop. Wrought-iron bars clad the gleaming windows. I knocked on the thick wooden door and waited while someone opened a hinged peephole and studied my face. Heavy bolts rasped as they were drawn back.

"Hannah!" Herr Klein pulled me in and closed the door in one swift movement. "I haven't seen you in weeks." He pushed the bolts into place before turning to me. "Are you well?"

It was such a delight to see him whole and healthy that I almost forgot my own troubles. "I am, thank you," I answered, smiling into his wrinkled old face, pleased that he had not yet emigrated. "How is that cough?"

"Coming along," he said. "I expect it will be strong enough to break windows soon."

I glanced around the tiny room. Two pine stools stood next to an old pine table. The table held a single black velvet display board and a powerful lamp. He had removed the cases of jewels the previous September, after the election made the Nazis the second largest party in the Reichstag.

A thick oak door almost disappeared into the back wall. Behind it lay the room where Herr Klein cut precious stones. Although I'd been visiting him for over ten years, I had never seen behind the door.

"I have something for you," I said, glad the shop was empty. "Questions."

"Maybe I have answers, although it's hard to say." He gestured to the simple stools and perched on one himself, like a friendly black crow. "How are Sarah and Tobias?"

"I expect they are very busy," I said, not meeting his eyes. With their lives, I did not trust even Herr Klein. I had refused to let Sarah tell me her final destination. If anything went wrong, I had nothing to reveal to the police.

"I expect they are." Herr Klein looked at me over the tops of his round, rimless spectacles and cleared his throat. "What are your questions?"

"I have many," I said and took the jewelry, except the ruby ring, out of my satchel and set it on the table. The onyx looked dull in the light, but the diamonds and rubies flashed. "Can you tell me what these are worth?"

Herr Klein picked up each piece and examined it with his loupe, his hands swift and confident, tilting each piece to and fro to watch the light glint on them. He quickly made two piles. "This pile." He pointed to the pile that had been in the top of the jewelry case, the ones I assumed came from Rudolf: the onyx-and-diamond choker, the onyx-and-diamond bracelet, and the diamond bracelets. "Is all fake, as I told your brother the first time he brought them in."

"Ernst came here with them?" So Rudolf thought he was stealing back his worthless jewelry. Perhaps he was more sentimental than I'd thought.

"Many times." Herr Klein laughed. "He wants me to bring glamour into this room." He gestured at the bare wooden walls. "He says it looks like a poor old peddler's house. Tells me I need to buy a leather club chair, an antique table, and a silver tea service."

"But then everyone walking by outside would know that you have items of value in here. Your tea service if nothing else."

Herr Klein nodded his grizzled head. "That is what I told him, and he said, 'A brave understands the value of camouflage' like someone out of a Karl May book."

I smiled. That sounded like something Anton would say. I was glad to know that he and Ernst had spent time together. "So he asked you to authenticate the pieces?"

"Your brother learned to spot fakes himself, my dear," he said.

"We spent time with these pieces, and real ones too, learning how to establish authenticity. They are quite good fakes. And worth some amount of money."

I smiled, surprised and proud of Ernst. He'd known that Rudolf's pieces were fake, and he'd known to identify and hide the real ones.

"These." He pointed to the other pile, the pile Ernst hid. It included pieces from Mother and the pieces with diamonds and rubies. "All real. We can go over the value of each of them, separately."

He pulled out a pad of paper and wrote a brief description of each piece. I fingered the red handkerchief wrapped around the ruby ring.

"Here we are," he said. "Now we can talk about the value of the pieces."

"Before we do that, I have one more thing." I pulled Ernst's ruby ring out of my satchel and placed it on the spotless table with a *clunk*. "What can you tell me about this ring?"

"Oh, a mystery!" He held the ring where the tails intertwined on the back and examined it with his jeweler's loupe. "I love the unexplained."

"Always glad to be of service." I glanced around the room while he studied the ring. The room was dark, but immaculately clean. Even Ursula would be unable to find dust.

Herr Klein coughed, spitting into a fine linen handkerchief. He took a moment to catch his breath.

"Is this from one of your stories?" he wheezed.

"Perhaps," I answered. "You know I cannot tell you that."

He gazed at the ring in silence for several minutes. Did he know I still stood there? It must be a clever fake, and he wondered at its artifice.

"Hannah," he said. "This ring is priceless."

"It is?" I searched his face for a sign that he jested, but I found only openness and a hint of fear.

"It is Ernst's?"

"I cannot tell you," I said. "How do you know it's priceless?"

"See the color? That deep, rich red is unusually rare. It's called pigeon's blood."

"Can you tell where it came from?"

He turned the golden ring over and over in his hands as if shocked by its authenticity. Light glinted off the snakes' fangs, poised to pump venom into the ruby.

"Rubies of this size and quality are almost unheard of. I've never held one this size in all my life, and I've been cutting precious gems longer than you have been alive." The rumble of automobiles passing by made me suddenly grateful for the thick bars on the windows.

My heartbeat sounded loud in my ears. "Where did it come from?"

"It came from Burma." He smiled grimly. "But I'm sure that doesn't interest you. It's an old stone. See how it's cut? It's called a native cut. They cut them to get the biggest possible stone, without regard for the optic properties."

"Do you know who it belongs to?"

"How could I not?" he asked, pausing dramatically. "This stone is famous. It's called the Burmese Python. The setting was designed with the name in mind."

"The stone has a name?"

"All rubies of this size have a name." He coughed again. "They're profoundly rare. How did you come upon it?"

"I cannot tell you that."

He shook his head. The corners of his eyes tightened into a worried squint. "Hannah, this ring belongs to Count von Heinberg from Bavaria. Have you heard of him?"

"Of course." He was one of the richest men in Germany. Nobility for hundreds of years. His family lived in a fairy-tale castle that had been featured in the *Berliner Illustrierte Zeitung* a few months ago. Of course I knew who he was. What did that have to do with Ernst? He did not know the von Heinbergs. As far as I knew, he'd never been to Bavaria. But there was the ring.

"The inscription reads 'To Bootsie, from Ernst, with love.' And there's a tiny swastika next to it. Do you know what that means?"

"No." Was Ernst a Nazi? That I could not believe.

Herr Klein sighed, a wheezy exhalation that I worried would set off another coughing fit. "You are in some kind of trouble, Hannah? Give it back to Ernst. Tell him to hide the ring. Drop it off at the Pergammon Museum. Get rid of it."

"Why? Is it stolen?"

"I would have heard if something like this went missing." He held it to the lamp again. "The count would have filed for his insurance. I believe it's insured for one million American dollars."

In spite of my journalistic cynicism, my mouth fell open. "That cannot be possible."

It was not possible that Ernst had a million-dollar ring in the bottom of Mother's jewelry case. That a million-dollar ring had been lying in my shabby apartment for days. Herr Klein must be making a joke.

"It is true, Hannah," he said, with such an air of conviction that I did not doubt him. "The count is a powerful Nazi. You won't tell me how you came in contact with it. Something illegal going on, perhaps?"

"That cannot be possible," I repeated, like a fool.

"Let me get you some tea," Herr Klein said.

He placed the ring on the table and knocked on the back door. He used a complicated rhythm. Seconds later the bolts pulled back, and Herr Klein scooted through sideways. The door shut soundlessly.

I held the ring in my palm. The stone was deep red, like a pool of blood. Had someone killed Ernst to get the ring back? I placed the ring in the center of the table and wiped my hand on my dress.

Herr Klein emerged from his back room carrying a fine china cup full of strong tea sweetened with honey, the way I liked it. "Thank you." I took the cup with a hand that trembled.

He nodded and said nothing while I sipped the tea. We both stared at the ring lying, sinister, on the old wooden table. A king's ransom. Or a queen's.

"Ernst must get rid of it," he said, speaking like a schoolteacher.

"If he is found with it, he must prove its provenance. And he cannot, is that correct?"

I nodded my head and took another sip of sweet tea.

"There are a few things you can do."

"What?"

He ticked off my choices on his gnarled fingers. "Give it to a museum."

"No." It was not mine to give away.

He held up a second finger. "Mail it back to the von Heinbergs anonymously. Put a return address such as Hotel Adlon on it. Pack it tightly and send it off. I'm sure you can find the address at your paper."

"I do not want to get rid of it yet," I said, although he had succeeded in frightening me. This must be the package that Rudolf wanted back so desperately.

Herr Klein sighed and stared out the window for a long time. I watched dust motes dance in the light. Finally he spoke again. "If it will keep you and your brother safe, I can take it and cut it down to two smaller rubies." He shook his head. "It would be defacing a treasure."

"A Nazi treasure," I said.

"But even so, a treasure." He held the ruby ring between his finger and thumb. "I can sell them for you. You won't get one million dollars, but you will get hundreds of thousands of dollars. You could leave Germany, join Sarah. And be rich forever."

I wondered how he knew about Sarah, but I was not surprised. Although he rarely left his shop, Herr Klein knew everything.

"I do not want to leave Berlin," I said. "It is my home." Berlin was the one place I'd been able to sink roots after moving from base to base throughout my early childhood. So many people here came from somewhere else. They did not care about your past, your parents, infractions you had committed as a child. It was a place of beginnings, a place to test yourself. Here I had established myself as a writer. The world came to Berlin, there was no need to go into the world. Anywhere else I would be alone, starting over.

"It is my home too," Herr Klein said softly. He cleared his throat with a rheumy cough. "My family has lived here for over two hundred years. But I will be leaving soon. I have one more shipment of stones to cut before I go." He smiled. "Naturally, you can tell no one."

"I have nothing to tell."

"I have contacts in the gem industry. Places where I can go."

New York. Or Belgium. "Far from here?"

"Far enough," he said, "to never fear for my life because I am a Jew."

"Can you keep the stone here?"

He pressed the cold ring into my hand. "That, my dearest Hannah, I cannot do. It is too dangerous." A horn tooted outside, and we both jumped, then laughed. I took the ring.

"How about these pieces?" I gestured to the pile of real jewelry. "How much are they worth?"

"Some are worth much." Herr Klein wrote an amount for each of them next to its description on his white pad of paper. "Sell them soon," he said. "The price for jewelry is dropping and, if Hitler becomes chancellor, everyone will be selling their jewelry to escape. Prices will fall through the floor. I have heard of such things in Russia after the fall of the czar."

I sold one necklace to him. During the inflation, I'd learned to sell precious objects slowly, because the money you got for them became worthless so quickly. I left him the rest of the real jewelry, to hold in his safe. Herr Klein had a reputation for having impeccable security.

Herr Klein handed me a receipt with a detailed description of each piece in his safe.

"I trust you." I tossed the fake jewelry from Rudolf into my satchel.

"I may not be here when you claim them," he said. "If you come back."

I dropped a bracelet on the floor with a clatter. "I beg your pardon?"

"That ring is dangerous," he said. "If you are found with it, it's a death sentence."

I blinked. "That seems an extreme—"

Herr Klein shook his head. "Gems like this invite death. Why do you think so many of them have bloody histories? And you do not know where it came from, should anyone, including the police, ever ask."

I stared at him.

"I'm sorry, Hannah, but if you are going to keep it, you must understand these risks."

"I understand," I answered numbly.

He shook his head sadly. "That you do not. But assuming the worst does happen, what should I do with the remaining jewelry?"

I was still thinking about being killed over the ring, but I forced my thoughts back to Herr Klein's question. What should I do with the money from the jewels? I thought of the people he could help with it. And then I thought of one small boy who might be forced to live with my older sister. "Put it in trust, for a boy named Anton Vogel. For a boarding school."

He nodded. "If it comes to that, I know lawyers who can see to it that the money is used for that purpose."

I took his knobby hand in both of mine. "Thank you, Herr Klein."

He shook his head. "There is nothing to thank me for. I have only told you of the burden you carry with you. I have not eased it."

16

I wrapped the ring in Ernst's red handkerchief and stuck it deep in my left coat pocket. I borrowed a safety pin and pinned the pocket closed. It was not enough, of course, but I tried to walk calmly, as if I did not carry a million dollars. As if I could not change my whole future in an instant.

I went to Anton. The weight of the roll of bills in my left pocket, with the ring and the larger heft of gold coins in my other pocket, pulled at my coat. I had not seen this much money since the end of the inflation. Having money again made me feel buoyant, even with my worries about the ring and the fact that, for the first time since I'd left my parents' house, I did not have a job.

Tripping up the steps, I rapped on Bettina's door.

"You're early," Bettina said when she opened the door. "The sun is still up."

I smiled. "I could come back."

She pretended to close the door.

"Hey." I pushed it open again.

"What is that on your face?" she asked as I stepped into her hall.

I glanced at the mirror there. My face looked a little flushed, but ordinary. "Nothing."

"I do believe it's a smile, but it's been so long since I've seen one that I can't be sure." She dried her hands on a striped tea towel. "Try frowning so I know it's you."

I laughed.

"Are you in love?" she asked. "Or did you find a pile of cash lying in the street?"

"You are closer than you think," I answered. "Where is the boy?"

"His name," she said, "is Anton. He's playing with Sophia in the back bedroom. He's an Indian, big surprise, and she's an Indian maiden, which seems to involve bossing him around and making him commit feats of daring that drive me crazy. Earlier, he counted coup by stealing cookies from the top shelf of the kitchen. But he wouldn't let her eat any and he had to return them because stealing is wrong. Quite a drama."

We walked back to Sophia's bedroom. The skirt on Bettina's ample form rustled as she walked down the hall. I glanced at the few framed photographs she kept on the walls. Her children smiled down at me. I thought of the pictures in the Hall of the Unnamed Dead and shivered.

When we opened the back bedroom door, Anton crouched on top of the wardrobe, three meters in the air. I looked around for a chair he might have climbed, but there was nothing there.

Sophia turned to me and said, "Hello, Aunt Hannah, the brave Anton keeps watch from the canyon wall."

"I see that," I said. "Why is he wearing only his underwear?"

"I wear a loincloth," Anton said from the top of the wardrobe, in his best Indian voice. "A brave needs nothing more."

I thought about the state of his clothes—ill-fitting hand-me-downs from Bettina's children. "That's a relief," I said. "Now come down here this instant."

Anton jumped off the wardrobe. His tiny pale limbs flashed through the air. Even as I reached for him, I knew I was too late to catch him. He landed at my feet with a *thump*. Bettina screamed. My heart raced.

I stood, rooted to the ground, but she bent over him immediately. "Are you hurt?" she asked.

He shook his head. I was surprised that I had been so frightened when he jumped.

"That's too far to jump," Bettina lectured.

"The brave can jump great distances," Sophia explained. "He's very tough."

"Don't encourage him." Her mother felt Anton's feet and legs.

"Anton," I said, finally finding my voice. "Please dress like a white man. We are going out on the street."

Anton stood and walked over to his clothes. "A brave understands the value of camouflage."

I smiled, remembering how Ernst had used those exact words while talking to Herr Klein. Ernst had spent time with his son.

"Where do we journey?" Anton struggled into his short pants. Sophia straightened the waistband and handed him his singlet, already a proper mother.

"Wertheim," I answered. "We must buy you clothes."

He stopped. "My auntie Sweetie was thrown out of Wertheim."

"Why?"

"She borrowed boots."

"Ah," I said. "Stealing."

"She meant to return them."

"They won't throw us out," I said. "We will pay for what we take." I felt jaunty, with my million-dollar ring.

Bettina gave me a calculating look. She knew that I could not afford a shopping spree at Wertheim under normal circumstances.

"Something came up, Bettina," I said.

She nodded, unconvinced.

It was only a short bus ride from Bettina's affluent neighborhood to the expensive shopping district on Leipziger Strasse. Wertheim was the largest department store in the world, even the Kaiser shopped there before the war. It had been built before the turn of the century, and the front had been remodeled a few years ago, in 1925.

Anton clutched my hand as we mounted the imposing stairs. Massive pillars supported each of the four arches at the Leipziger Strasse entrance, and I felt as tiny as an ant. I knew I was meant to feel rich and important to shop in such a grand building, but I felt rather sheepish. I'd been once with Bettina, but had no money to buy anything then. Today would be different.

Many department stores were bright, clean, and stocked with more than one would ever need, but I picked Wertheim because Herr Wertheim treated his workers fairly. Also because he was Jewish. I was aware of no formal boycott of the store, but I knew that the strident Nazis and their quieter but no less anti-Semitic supporters voted with their pocketbooks and spurned Jewish-owned businesses.

I pushed the heavy brass-and-glass revolving door. Anton crowded against my knees and walked in tiny steps. We stepped into the noise and bustle of the first floor. The fishy smell of seafood rolled over us, and Anton wrinkled his nose. Cod lined up on a bed of ice shone like silver. Anton clutched my hand and looked around furtively, probably searching for the store detective.

"You have nothing to fear," I told him. "This is a safe place for those who can afford to pay."

"And we can pay?"

"We can. We are safe."

Anton relaxed, but did not let go of my hand, barely glancing at luscious displays of food as we walked toward the escalators in the middle of the store.

After we mounted the escalator to the children's clothing department, he counted the disappearing stairs ahead. "Where do they go?"

"They stack up in the cellar," I answered with a smile.

"Then where do they come from?"

I laughed. "They go back down the other side. It's a giant metal belt of stairs."

We almost reached the top when he backed down the escalator.

I took his bony hand. "We can jump the last step together. One, two, three."

We jumped safely onto the second floor, under the disapproving eye of a matron wearing a loden-green Bavarian hat. I resisted the urge to apologize for our boisterous behavior. We were paying customers and entitled to a little frivolity.

Anton told me he'd never owned any new clothes before. He studied each article after I gave him the responsibility of picking colors and fabrics. I bought three trousers, three shirts, three undershirts, three pairs of underwear, and a nightshirt. Lugging our increasingly heavy bags, we went to the shoe department and bought a pair of leather shoes that he assured me were the same color as moccasins. We'd long since used up my paycheck, but I still had my money from the sale of the necklace.

When we arrived at the café for a late tea, Anton looked at the dessert cart with wide eyes.

"You can order something." I unfolded his stiff linen napkin and put it in his lap. "What would you like?"

"The brave desires . . ." His voice trailed off.

I ordered a glass of milk, a pot of warm tea, and a piece of tart plum cake with a dollop of whipped cream.

He stared at the cart, hypnotized.

"Your father used to love the apple strudel."

"Apple strudel," he said.

I glanced down at the square of plum cake. Red plum crescents covered with a thin layer of clear jelly topped the cake. I had not eaten plum cake in at least two years. The whipped cream next to it was heavy and held its shape. Perfectly whipped, Mother would have said.

"Start eating whenever you wish," I told Anton.

He nibbled his strudel. "It's delicious!" He sounded surprised.

I laughed and took a bite of my own, savoring the tart plums. I took a small forkful of whipped cream, then chased it down with a sip of hot, strong tea with honey. It tasted like the promised land.

Anton and I ate in companionable silence, each of us savoring the luxury of sweets. It felt wonderful being extravagant with him in the way I'd always wanted to be with Ernst. Anton looked splendid in his new finery. I'd bought a new burgundy jacket for myself. Ernst would have admired it. I'd slipped my old coat into the shopping bag, with the ring still pinned in the pocket.

Time got away from me, and it was early evening when, full and lazy, we stepped out of the store with our purchases. The store was closing, and they locked the door behind us.

I looked out from the archway at the dark, overcast sky. Rain pelted down.

Anton squeezed my hand. "Soldiers."

A sea of brown uniforms surrounded the store's entrance. Men's faces shone orange in the flames from their torches. "Not soldiers," I answered, struggling to keep fear from my voice. "Nazis."

I bent down to look into Anton's frightened blue eyes. "Do not let go of my hand unless I fall down. If I fall, run. Take a taxi to Aunt Bettina's. I will come for you."

"A brave does not leave his fallen friends."

"A brave must obey his chief," I said.

"I do not know the way."

I wrote Bettina's address on a twenty Reichsmark bill and tucked it into the pocket of his new trousers. "Give this to the taxi driver and he will know where to go."

Anton nodded, and together we stepped out of the protective shelter of the arch. I pushed forward, the shopping bag with the ring and coins heavy in my hand. Cold rain blew into my face.

At least a hundred Nazis stood between us and the street, carrying signs with carefully printed Nazi slogans, such as "Don't buy from Jews" and "Germans, protect yourselves." Nazi flags, red with a white circle and black swastika in the middle, waved in the wind. I strode through the crowd, head held high.

A round man dressed in a shopkeeper's suit pushed his way to us. "Don't you know that Germans need that money?" Spittle sprayed my face. My shoulder crashed into his, and I slipped on wet cobblestones. I caught my balance, kept going. Anton clutched my sweaty hand.

"Are you a Jew or only a Jew lover?"

We were halfway through the crowd. The only way out was through. The crowd sang the "Horst Wessel Song," the unofficial Nazi anthem. "Hold high the banner" rang out. At least I no longer heard individual jeers. The street was clear ahead. We were almost free.

A strong hand wrenched the shopping bag from my hand. I gasped. The ring was in that bag.

"Anton," I shouted down to him. "Run. I must go back."

I tried to pry my hand out of Anton's grasp, but he would not let go. His round eyes stared at me, and he shook his head.

"Anton," I said. "Let go. Go to Aunt Bettina's."

The crowd closed around us, chanting. Anton would not let go.

"The chief orders it," I yelled above the chants. If he would not go to Bettina's, I had to send him somewhere. "Run to the advertising pillar with the red words."

Anton released my hand and darted between the legs of the men surrounding us. I lost sight of him immediately.

"Prove that you are German," shouted a harsh voice. "Show us papers."

I thought of my identity papers, safely traveling to America.

Had Anton gotten free? A brown wall of men crowded in on me. "Germans protect yourselves," they chanted.

Bettina would see him taken care of, if only he could make it to her. I raised my arms to protect my face.

"Halt," shouted a voice. "She is a German woman, and she is not to be treated that way."

I turned toward the voice, but I could not tell who had said it.

"Hannah," said a different voice at my shoulder. "It's Wilhelm."

Wilhelm, Ernst's friend from El Dorado. Let him bear witness, if nothing else.

He held my shopping bag and wore a Nazi uniform and a reassuring smile. I was dizzy from relief and would have fallen, had there been room. He would get me out of the crowd, back to Anton. Wilhelm hooked his hand under my elbow.

A tall, muscular man with close-cropped blond hair shouted, "Enough."

With a military precision more frightening than their mob behavior moments before, the singers turned away from us. Wilhelm and I walked to the other side of the street unmolested while the mob waited for the next victim to come through the doors.

Anton darted out from behind the pillar and threw his arms around my knees. I bent and held his trembling body, stroking his hair. "We are safe now," I said. His heart thundered against my chest, racing like a bird's.

I glanced over his head at the brawny man who had called off the crowd. He was the same bull-like man who had struck Wilhelm and marched him out of El Dorado.

"We are safe," I repeated and stood, lifting Anton in my arms. He wrapped his arms around my neck and buried his face in my shoulder.

"Of course you are," said Wilhelm. "We don't harm women and children."

"Thank you, Wilhelm," I said. "For helping us. Who spoke?"

"My father," Wilhelm gloated. "He's in charge of the demonstration. He is very highly placed in the SA."

"I am grateful that he let us go." I stroked Anton's hair. His heartbeat slowed. He raised his head and looked at Wilhelm.

"Naturally, Hannah." Wilhelm took the other shopping bag from me. "Please let me see you safely home."

"We'll take a taxi." I never rode in taxis. They were too expensive, but now I had money. Even though it was a few short blocks through elegant shops to the subway station at Potsdamerplatz, I wanted to get away from the Nazis immediately. I scanned the wide street for a black automobile with a familiar checkerboard stripe on the side. A street car rattled by in a flash of red and cream, but otherwise the usually busy street was deserted. No one wanted to get too close to a Nazi protest.

I walked down the street, carrying Anton.

"You have great courage." Wilhelm offered Anton his hand to shake. "I am Wilhelm."

"A brave has the courage he needs." Anton did not take his arms from around my neck to shake Wilhelm's hand.

"But why should he need it?" I asked. "To buy clothes and eat cakes?"

Wilhelm had the good grace to look ashamed. "We don't want to frighten good German citizens."

"Yet you do." I raised my hand for a taxi. Anton tightened his arms on my neck. A taxi drove by without stopping. I swore under my breath.

Wilhelm raised his hand, and a taxi stopped in front of us, its top raised against rain. He climbed into the front seat and turned to face us. I gave my address to the driver and climbed into the back, setting Anton next to me. He squeezed my hand. I glanced out the window at the automobiles passing us. It felt strange to be in an automobile. Decadent.

"You shouldn't buy from the Jews," Wilhelm said. "Not when so many German storekeepers are going hungry."

"And what of the Jewish ones? Do they not need to eat?"

"They will find a way," Wilhelm said. "They always do."

"Are you a warrior?" Anton asked. His grip on my hand loosened.

"Yes," Wilhelm answered with a smile.

"No," I said at the same moment.

"I wear a uniform," Wilhelm explained, ignoring me. "And I am part of a unit. We are trying to restore Germany to greatness."

"Regardless of the cost." I pulled Anton closer to my side.

"There is always a cost."

"And no cost is too great when others are paying it."

Wilhelm turned to Anton. "And I have weapons. Would you like to see my knife? It's an SA dagger. Only special warriors get them." He looked down at his waist.

"Where is it?" Anton asked excitedly, peering over the seat at Wilhelm while still holding on to my hand.

"I can't find it," Wilhelm said, looking back up. "It must be at home."

Anton looked unconvinced, but he sat back down.

"How is your brother?" Wilhelm turned to me. "Still off with his soldier man?"

"I have not seen him today." I glanced at rain-slick streets. Ghostly light reflected from the tall streetlamps, but it was more comforting than orange Nazi torches.

"Do you know where he is?"

"Perhaps you are correct, and he is with the soldier you said he went to meet," I said, thinking of the ring. "Was the soldier a Nazi?"

"Maybe a Nazi. Maybe a member of the regular army." Wilhelm pulled at his too-red lower lip. "Ernst would not give me details. He said it would be too dangerous to tell me."

My heart quickened. "Did you believe him?"

"I think it was a game, but I don't know, and I don't care. Does he miss me?"

"I imagine so." I tousled Anton's hair, and he looked up at me, surprised.

"So he doesn't talk about me?" Wilhelm asked.

"I don't see him often."

"More than I, I bet." He stared out of the window, a muscle twitching in his cheek.

"I am sorry, Wilhelm."

"I thought we were so close in school," he said. "Did he tell you?"

"Not much."

"He used to defend me against the other boys. He is a powerful fighter. Once he even stood up to my father."

"What happened?"

"My father beat—" Wilhelm looked uncertainly at Anton. "Ernst did the best he could, but my father is much stronger than he."

Ernst often came home from school badly beaten. I wondered if one of those beatings came from Wilhelm's father. Ernst never would tell me who was responsible, adhering to the schoolboy honor code.

"Thank you again," I said. "For helping us."

Wilhelm stared at me and shrugged. "You can trust me not to let anything happen to you."

"You are a trustworthy person."

He smiled wryly. "Unlike your brother, I try."

"Choose your friends wisely," I said. "Or you will violate that trust."

We rode the rest of the way home in silence. When we arrived, Wilhelm insisted on paying for the taxi. I let him. Let his Nazi money get us home safe. If the Nazis had not frightened me so, I would have taken the subway.

As Anton and I walked up the stairs to the front door, I felt Wilhelm's eyes on me. Mitzi marched imperiously next to us, flicking her tail and staying one step away from Anton.

"That was an adventure," I said to Anton. "Let's check the mail."

I pried my hand out of Anton's grasp to open the front door.

"We're safe now," I said.

We walked across the lobby to the mailbox. I had not checked my mail for a few days. Sometimes I would receive a check for poems or drawings I had sent to different magazines. When I opened my mailbox a package the size of a brick fell out. Anton picked it up and handed it me.

I had not expected a package. "Thank you." I glanced down at the address written on the simple brown paper. It was addressed to me in Ernst's flowery handwriting. The outside read, "Hold until I arrive."

Oh God. Another package from Ernst. After discovering the ring, I could not stand dealing with one more surprise from him. Still, this package could not possibly be more dangerous than the million-dollar ring. Could it?

17

I had a strong urge to shove the package back in the letter box and walk away. Instead, I dropped it in one of the shopping bags and led Anton and Mitzi upstairs.

I filled the washtub for Anton. While he splashed around, I put away his new things. He was less interested in the soap than the last time, but he had learned how to scrub himself. His flea bites were healing, and he had no nits in his hair. I might not be a perfect mother, but he was at least marginally better off than when he'd arrived.

"A new nightshirt for you," I said, after I'd dried him off and helped him brush his teeth.

"It's so white," Anton said. "Like new snow."

"It will keep you warm too."

We read the "The Ugly Duckling" from Bettina's storybook. I wanted to stop after a few minutes and open Ernst's package, but Anton was still frightened so I stayed by the side of his bed, reading until he fell asleep. I wanted to talk about the incident at Wertheim, to tell him again that we were safe now—but were we? I had no job. The Nazis grew stronger every day. And both of his parents were dead.

I pulled the coat out of the shopping bag and unpinned the ring and money from the pocket. I'd come close to losing them. For the first time I wondered if Wilhelm had pulled the bag from my hands or rescued it from someone else who had. I wrapped the ring and money in a shabby tea towel and hid them in an iron cook pot before I allowed myself to look at the package.

If Ernst were alive, I never would have opened it, as he must have known. I would have held it until he arrived, as instructed. I looked at the postmark: May 29, 1931. Mailed the day before he was murdered. It must hold something he wanted to keep secret. It could be harmless love letters he'd exchanged with Wilhelm back in school, or perhaps it was a gift for me and he had wanted to watch my face while I opened it. In my heart I knew it was neither. It was something that had frightened him so much that he could not keep it in his own home.

I stared at the package, afraid to know what was inside. Ernst had left the million-dollar ring at his apartment, but had been frightened enough about the contents of this package to mail it to me. I slit the twine with an old kitchen knife.

A heavy, musky scent wafted out of the package. I pulled out a packet of envelopes, tied with a red silk ribbon. The bow was flattened. My shoulders dropped with relief. Love letters.

I glanced at the return address: E. Röhm. I dropped the letters on the table in shock.

Ernst Röhm was the head of the Sturm Abteilung, indispensable to Hitler and, if rumors could be believed, his best friend. Hitler's right-hand man had been writing to my brother.

I touched the letters again with a trembling hand. Röhm held the hearts and souls of more than one hundred thousand men. He was known for his militarism, his brutality, and his flagrant homosexuality. My Ernst must have known him. And known him well. A fling with a teenage boy wearing a Nazi uniform like Wilhelm was one thing, but an affair with one of the most powerful Nazis in the party was another thing entirely. How could Ernst have given himself to such an evil man?

I picked up the top letter. Röhm must want these letters back. If he did, his men would stop at nothing to get them. They roamed the streets at will, beating and killing Hitler's opponents. They would not think twice about destroying my apartment and killing me. Perhaps even Anton. I dropped the letter back onto the pile.

I thought about burning them unread, but what if Röhm was looking for them? Had Röhm quarreled with Ernst? It would be so like Ernst to anger the leader of the most powerful private army in Germany. He would toss off a rude comment and wait for the result. That's what he learned from Father—how not to fear physical pain or death. Just have a witty retort. Deep in my heart I felt proud of his audacity, but practically I wished he had been more wary. Perhaps then his photograph would not be hanging on the wall in the Hall of the Unnamed Dead. And Anton and I would not be sitting in this shabby apartment, waiting for someone to kill us over the ring, or these far more inflammatory pieces of paper.

I took a deep shuddering breath. I had to read the letters. Part of me said that I needed to know what they said to keep us safe, but another part suspected it was journalistic curiosity. They started early in the year, soon after Röhm returned from Bolivia, and continued right up to two weeks ago. About six months. Around that same time Ernst had become more distant toward me. I ordered the letters by postmark. It seemed important to read them in the same order they'd been mailed. To better understand their story.

Dear Bootsie,

Now I knew where the ring came from. I was even more frightened, if that was possible. Röhm had given my brother a million-dollar ring. They must have been lovers. Close lovers.

How I miss the sight of you marching around in my jackboots, swinging your long hair and your cock back and forth.

I put the letter down. I covered my face with my hands and took a deep breath. I knew that Ernst loved men, but I did not know these details. I picked the letter up again and read. Even my journalistic side did not want to know these details. I skimmed the sexual parts. I gleaned that Röhm had met my brother at the El Dorado and quickly become infatuated with him. One of the letters contained a sonnet entitled "Ode to Bootsie's Cock," which extolled Ernst's unflagging duty to cock and country.

Röhm claimed to love every single thing about Ernst, from his physical appearance, scrutinized down to the smallest detail, to his performances at the club, to his views on politics. I did not know Ernst had views on politics, let alone views that the number-two Nazi would appreciate. I disliked the thought of it, although it sounded as if Ernst had talked about Socialism. Socialism, after all those years of teasing me for being idealistic. He'd listened more closely than I knew.

One letter talked about the ring, the Burmese Python, given to Röhm by a count because he saved his life in the Great War. Röhm actually sent Ernst the ring through the mail. One million American dollars trusted to every postal clerk between Munich and Berlin. The naïveté was staggering. How could he have been so foolish? But perhaps Röhm was unaware of the value of the ring when he sent it. And, of course, it did work out in the end. The ring came through.

Later letters talked about trysts on trains, at cottages, in dark rooms, at party headquarters. They had spent a great deal of time together. Did Rudolf know? I thought not. Röhm was certainly more of a threat to him than Wilhelm.

I hurried to the letters at the end. Röhm listed all of the men in his battalion who did not survive the war and described the manner of their deaths. No one had ever told me what happened on the front, not like this. Men with no faces, men with no heads, blood spurting from friends, from lovers. In spite of his warrior demeanor, these deaths bothered Röhm, even though he kept repeating how important they were for the Fatherland. But even now, thirteen years after the end of the War, he had trouble sleeping and when he could not sleep, he wrote to Ernst.

Mitzi jumped onto the table. I started. "What are you doing?"

I pulled her into my lap and stroked her soft fur, my heart slowing.

I set her back on the floor and crossed to the window. When I peeked through the curtain, the street below seemed deserted. If Röhm's men lurked outside, they were well hidden. There was no going back now. Anton and I were stuck right in the middle of this until it played out.

I stared at the letters spread across my simple wooden table. No letter contained a cross word. They had not quarreled. In the most recent letter, Röhm asked to meet Ernst at his apartment the next Sunday. That was the same day that Rudolf had told me to bring the package to Ernst's apartment. Rudolf and Röhm must be connected. Were these letters the package he wanted?

These letters could imprison Röhm for breaking Paragraph 175 of the penal code. When Ernst was fifteen, I'd read the law to him to impress upon him the seriousness of his choices. "The law forbids an unnatural sex act committed between persons of male sex and is punishable by imprisonment; the loss of civil rights may also be imposed."

Röhm was certainly familiar with the law as well. His war hero background might save him in a trial, but the publicity would be horrendous. Everyone knew he was queer, but flaunting it in such detail! I shuddered. Ernst could have brought down the leader of the storm troopers with these letters.

I pulled the painted lead soldier out of my satchel and unwrapped her from her red silk. "Why did he send these to me?" I asked the soldier, as if she knew the answer. Ernst must have been afraid that someone would find them, perhaps Rudolf or Röhm himself.

A rational person would burn them, of course, but Ernst probably loved to read them. Or maybe he planned to use them to blackmail Röhm, perhaps for money or perhaps for his own safety if the Nazis came to power. Despite what Wilhelm had told me, I knew that the Nazis would eventually destroy queer men. Aryan men had to make more Aryans, just like Aryan women. And Aryan men should not submit, certainly not sexually, even to other Aryan men.

I buried my face in my hands. They smelled like plum tart, from my innocent treat with Anton. What was I to do? If I published the letters, perhaps they could take down Ernst Röhm, perhaps tarnish Hitler. But where should I publish them? Perhaps my friend Ulrich at the *Münchener Post* would do it. They still stood up to the Nazis. Herr Neumann would not risk it. The letters were too damning. Morally, could I destroy Röhm for the crime of loving my brother? For feelings and actions that weren't wrong?

But Röhm was evil. He helped Hitler win elections. His thugs beat Jews and queer men and anyone else they pleased every day. If the paper had allowed it, I could have written a story each week about a Communist or a Jew beaten to death by a group of Nazis. The slim stack of paper in my hands could be the means to expose Röhm. Did the ends justify the means? Bringing down evil before it spread was justified at any price. If the Sturm Abteilung crumbled, could the Nazi party go on? Without them, Hitler was only a shrill, screaming man with a tiny mustache and a fondness for brown. And he knew it. That's why he brought Röhm back from Bolivia—because he could find no one else who could control the SA.

I shuffled the letters on the worn tabletop. But the means were horrible: pillory Röhm for something that should not be a crime. It would destroy our family name. Cause a backlash that might hurt all of the queer men in Germany. Röhm's thugs would kill me when they discovered where the letters came from. Where would that leave Anton? Röhm was not a stupid man. He was a ruthless soldier. When Röhm arrived on Sunday, he would want these letters back.

I stacked the letters carefully and tied them with the broad red ribbon. I laid them in my satchel next to the notebook containing Ernst's death photo, and went to bed. How could these letters be related to Sweetie Pie's death? To Ernst's? There were no coincidences. Ernst must have had a reason to mail me these letters so soon before he was killed.

I had to make a decision, and soon: burn them, publish them, or return them to Röhm. I could send them back to him via party headquarters. My head said to publish them, but my heart was not so certain. I tossed and turned so much that Mitzi gave me a baleful look and stomped to the front door. I let her out, glancing nervously back and forth down the hall before closing the door.

Every creak in the building sounded like jackboots marching up the stairs. I waited for Röhm's men to come murder me in my bed. I watched Anton sleep so peacefully. What would become of him? Would they kill him too? If not, Ursula might not even take him in. Bettina was correct about the orphanages. Too many children died there. But where could I put him where he would be safe? I slept little that night.

18

When the sky turned steel gray with morning, I left Anton asleep in bed and made myself a cup of hot water with honey. I'd gotten used to tea without the tea during the inflation and now preferred it. Or at least that's what I told myself.

I poured the leftover water from the kettle into a basin to wash myself and my hair. I combed the wet strands carefully. Today was Friday, the day Boris had invited me to meet him at the yacht club. I'd never planned to go, but why not? Perhaps I could be a different person today. A person who thought only about an attractive man and his attractive invitation. I knew it was foolish and selfish, but if I was truly threatened with death, I wanted a day to live.

I slid into a light blue cotton dress. Ernst once said that it brought out the washed-out blue color of my eyes. He'd also said that my eyes were the best feature on my face, and I'd do well to highlight them to distract men from my masculine cleft chin. Ernst had often made up his eyes heavily, so that no one would notice his own masculine chin. I buttoned up my dress, wondering what Ernst would think of Boris and what Boris would think of Ernst. Ernst would have been thrilled that I was seeing a man. Any man is better than none, he loved to remind me. How would Boris have reacted to Ernst? He was no Nazi, but he did seem very bourgeois, and Ernst was probably far beyond what he had ever had to deal with in his comfortable banker's life.

I shook my head and quickly finished dressing. I had two days to decide what to do with the letters. Two days before I would confront Ernst Röhm in my dead brother's apartment and make a decision that could change Germany's future. I hoped to find out who had killed Ernst at that meeting, or before, if I could. A step ahead was better than a step behind.

Until then, I had to keep the letters safe. I wrapped them in brown paper and tied them shut with twine. Once again, they resembled an innocuous package. I addressed the package to myself and placed it in the center of the table, holding it by the edges, as if it were a hot loaf of bread. I gathered everything else I had to hide: the ring I pinned in the pocket of my dress and the money and coins I left in my satchel. I finally dropped the letters in the satchel too.

"Indian good morning," said Anton from the doorway.

"Good morning to you," I said. "Ready for breakfast?"

"The brave does not trouble his chief."

I pulled flour and eggs from the cabinets. I chopped the apple I'd bought him yesterday, before I'd visited Herr Klein and found out about the ring. "I am making apple slices. Fried in batter."

"A brave likes to earn his keep."

I turned over an old iron pot and placed it next to the stove. "Stand on this."

Anton climbed on obediently and took the sifter I handed him. "First we sift the flour."

While he sifted I heated the stove and dropped a dollop of butter into the skillet. It was profligate to use so much butter. This was how my life would be if Anton were mine, perhaps with a man like Boris to pay the bills and play the father. Of course, nothing could ever be that simple.

Anton dipped each apple slice in batter, as careful as a banker. He did not spill a drop on the stove. I wondered what the penalty had been for wasting food in Sweetie Pie's household. Something painful, I thought, and reached over to stroke his downy head.

He looked up at me in surprise. "Is my hair in order?"

"It looks very handsome."

I dropped each apple slice in the pan, and together we watched them sizzle. The kitchen smelled heavenly, almost as good as Bettina's. She could not take care of him if I died. Fritz would not allow that. Anton would probably end up with my sister Ursula, the child she could not conceive on her own.

I poured all my sugar and cinnamon onto a plate and let him roll his apple slices in it until there was none left. He ate his fried apple slices quietly, with a look of deep contentment.

After breakfast, I cleaned the apartment, like every other week for as long as I could remember. Anton helped me scrub the floor and wipe down the table. The last time I'd changed the sheets, Ernst had been alive. The time before that, Sarah had been living in Berlin and my identity papers were safe in my pocket. What would my life be like the next time I changed the sheets?

After cleaning, I dressed Anton in one of his bright new outfits, and we took the streetcar to Hirten Strasse. We passed Herr Klein's door and walked farther down the street to Sarah's apartment. I bought things from every poor street vendor we passed. At first Anton feared buying from the Jews, remembering the Nazi protest, but I told him that we must buy from them, to keep the Nazis from winning.

I spent my money because, like in 1923, my money might be worthless by tomorrow. Better to share it now than wait for it to disappear. We arrived at Sarah's apartment with shoelaces and apples and milk and bread. I checked her mail, then let myself in with her spare key, which I'd kept so I could ship her things, if she sent for them.

Sarah's apartment smelled of her; a faint scent of roses and milk that took me back to hugging her good-bye at the train station weeks before. Loaning her my papers had seemed a small risk then, before everything had fallen apart.

"Is this your other teepee?" Anton asked.

"I have only one house," I answered. "This belongs to a friend."

And Sarah was my friend. She was my best friend. Bettina was also a friend, but I had to keep too many things from her, to protect her.

The empty rooms felt so lonely. I had not been here since Sarah and Tobias left. I could not believe I might never see them again. She'd helped me through the worst after Walter's death. Even though marrying him had felt like a duty, I had loved him. He was a gentle man, as unlike Father as another soldier could be. He had offered me kindness and security, and he did not deserve to die in a field of bloody mud, on the bayonet of another man who was perhaps also kind and gentle off the field of battle. Two lives were lost that instant, Walter's and the life I might have led as a wife and mother.

Sarah had helped me raise Ernst, always counseling patience and love. That seemed to be her solution to all problems, except the Nazis.

I looked at the neat table covered with a clean, pressed tablecloth. Sarah could walk in at any moment and hold a dinner party. Each chair was pushed in perfectly straight.

I took Anton's hand and led him into the living room. Morning sun, filtered through lace curtains, shone on the horsehair sofa. "Sit there and touch nothing."

He sat and pulled his feet up to sit Indian style.

"No shoes on the sofa."

I returned to the kitchen and unpacked my foolish purchases. I had no time to take them home. Why had I bought them?

I glanced around the kitchen, trying to decide where to hide Röhm's letters. Surely no one would think to look for them here. But where? I pulled open the drawer to add Sarah's latest mail and saw a package, slightly larger than the one I needed to hide. I smiled.

I carefully untied the twine on the package and slid off the brown paper wrapping. I slid it over the package of Röhm's letters and the envelope of money I'd received for the jewelry. I retied the twine.

I walked into the living room. Anton sat cross-legged on the sofa in his brown ankle socks with his shoes lined up neatly at the end of the elegant coffee table.

"Do you search for something?" he asked. "The brave has sharp eyes."

I walked to the cupboard in the corner and took out a box. It contained sketches of hats Sarah had been working on, scraps of felt, feathers, bird wings, and a hat form. She would not need it again, but I knew someone who might have a use for it.

"Shoes back on," I said. "We're leaving."

Once downstairs, I opened Sarah's mailbox. The lobby was deserted. I put the package into the mailbox. The mailman would recognize it as a package he had delivered, and leave it alone. I hoped no one would think to look in Sarah's mailbox for my valuables.

Free of the letters, we headed over to the Wannsee to meet Boris. I would accept the offer he'd extended to me in his letter. That too, was unexpected. But if I only had a few days left to live, I might as well spend one of them sailing on the lake with a handsome man, whatever his motives.

I stopped by the Berolina office and found the schedule for the boat that had spotted Ernst's body in the river. There were no more tours scheduled for that stretch of water today. That was it then. Today I would relax with Boris on his yacht. Tomorrow I would ride the Berolina boat and see where Ernst had been found. Perhaps something there would lead me to his killer before I met Röhm.

19

I treated Anton and myself to a hot wurst and roll from a stand, as I did not want him to be too hungry when we met Boris. I wanted Boris to know that I fed Anton well, that I was not responsible for his emaciated condition. Anton happily dipped his wurst into a golden pile of mustard. As Mother taught me, I ate the wurst first and the roll last, so that I could wipe my greasy fingertips on the bread. The wurst was savory and firm. It felt good to be eating all I wanted again.

Well fed and happy, we walked to the Potsdam Yacht Club, perched on the edge of the lake like a honeymoon cottage. Sparkling glass and well-polished wood shone when we opened the door.

"Good day." I crossed to the small counter, where a girl not much older than Trudi filed her nails.

"And your name is?" The girl behind the counter was unimpressed by my shabby blue dress and Anton's mustard-smudged shirt.

"Hannah Vogel," I said. "Here to meet Boris Krause."

"I'll see if he is here for you." She looked convinced that he would not be. She exuded health, energy, and money. Her well-muscled tan calves stalked around the corner.

"She didn't like us," Anton said. "Because we're poor."

I bent down and took his hand. "That may be. But what she thinks of us does not matter one drop."

"Does it make you angry?"

"Perhaps yesterday," I said. "But not today. Today I want us to play."

"Hannah," called Boris, walking toward us with his hand outstretched and a charming smile. His face was open and guileless. "And who is this fellow?"

"This is Anton," I said, deciding not to try to describe Anton's relationship to me.

"How do you do?" Boris shook Anton's hand as if he were a grown-up man. Anton beamed. Boris wore a short-sleeved shirt and linen trousers. He looked, if possible, even better than he had in the courtroom. "Trudi's stowing our lunch on the boat. Come along."

Anton and I followed in his wake as he led us to a beautiful wooden sailboat. I knew nothing about boats, but this one looked expensive. The light reflected off brightly polished brass and mahogany. I guessed the boat was over ten meters long.

Trudi emerged from a hatch in the deck. "Fraulein Vogel," she called. "I'm so glad you came."

"As am I, Trudi," I said. "This is Anton. Anton, Trudi."

Anton dropped to one knee on the dock. "The brave is pleased to meet you."

She curtsied with a laugh. "It is I who am honored." She turned to me. "And you brought someone with such excellent manners."

Boris stepped easily onto the boat and held out his hand to help me aboard. His palm felt warm but surprisingly rough, perhaps from sailing. He held my fingers a moment longer than necessary; it was not my imagination. I looked up into those gold-flecked eyes and slowly pulled my hand away.

"Here we go, Anton." Boris turned and held out a hand to Anton, but he leaped from the dock to the boat like a cat.

"I brought something for you, Trudi." I handed her the box. "It's scraps, but I thought they might be interesting to experiment with."

She opened the box and squealed with delight. A purple feather floated toward the deck. Anton caught it and handed it to her.

"What is it?" Boris asked.

"Hatmaking supplies," she said, her eyes shining. "And a form and some drawings of hats."

"My friend the hatmaker thought you might make better use of them than she."

"Thank you," Trudi said. "I will."

She closed the box and carried it toward the back of the boat. Anton followed like a puppy.

"Let's find you something to eat." Trudi and Anton climbed through the hatch and disappeared.

"He just ate," I called down to them.

"He's a growing boy." Boris's full lips curved into a smile. "He'll probably eat his second lunch and yours if you're not careful."

"He needs it more than I do. He's welcome to it." I looked back at the dock, flustered.

"Thank you for the thoughtful gift for Trudi. It will keep her and her friends occupied during the evenings." Boris started the engine.

"I am glad it can be of use."

Boris untied the lines mooring us to the dock. "My behavior at the courthouse was inexcusable," he said. "I apologize."

"I imagine you must have been very upset." Muscles in his forearm tensed and relaxed as he untied lines and coiled them on the deck. Powerful muscles for a banker.

"Which is no excuse for lashing out at you." He straightened and looked into my eyes. He put his warm hand on my bare arm and leaned in close.

"No apologies are necessary." I tried not to stutter, too conscious of how near his body was to mine.

He motored out of the slip and into open water. I caught my breath and watched him out of the corner of my eye. His movements were swift and competent, and he handled the boat with a sure gentleness.

"But they are necessary," he said at last, turning to me.

"Then they are accepted." At that moment I would have forgiven him anything, if he kept standing next to me.

He smiled. "I am grateful."

Anton bumped against my back. "Trudi has a cache of supplies," he said. "We can journey for one whole moon."

"A whole moon?" Boris said. "I will need someone to help steer, while I sleep tonight."

I sat in the bow and felt the sun warm me through and through as Boris explained the mechanics of sailing to Anton. Anton held the tiller while Boris and Trudi raised the sails. It was wonderful to watch how easily he moved, swaying with the boat. When Boris took the tiller again, Trudi showed Anton some complicated thing with the ropes and sails. Anton concentrated with his whole body.

I turned to face the beach. The water was a lovely light blue, and air ruffled through my hair. I could not remember when I'd felt so relaxed. I reminded myself that I was in the eye of the hurricane, but I did not care.

On the golden sand, bathers arranged and rearranged themselves on towels, their bathing costumes and caps black and white in the sun. Cheerful orange-and-white-striped umbrellas shaded mothers with fat, pale infants. A balloon vendor strolled down the beach, on the lookout for indulgent parents, with his colorful orbs bobbing above his head. When an adventurous youngster dashed into the water clutching a shovel and pail in his chubby fists, his diaper drooping, his mother dashed after him, her unfashionably long hair cascading down her back.

I turned to watch the tree-covered islands sliding by. A flock of starlings wheeled and dipped, punctuation marks dancing in the sky.

"Nothing beats the feeling of being on the water." Boris sat next to me.

I tensed. "Who is driving the boat?" I turned around to see Anton at the tiller, Trudi standing next to him.

"Sailing the boat," Boris corrected me. "The children can do it. Trudi could take this boat out on her own if I'd let her."

I was very conscious of his open shirt and the dark hair curling on his chest. I peeked for only a second then resolutely turned my attention to the sun-spangled water in front of us. Other sailboats dotted the lake, their bright sails looking like huge prehistoric birds.

"Still on guard with me?" Boris asked. Out of the corner of my eye I saw his relaxed smile. It looked as if it went right into a peaceful, happy soul.

"Not at all," I lied. He thought I was afraid that he would yell at me again, as he had in front of the courthouse. I was more afraid that I would lean forward and kiss those lips, in front of the children and a few hundred swimmers. I looked away, hoping that Boris would not notice the flush spreading up my neck. What had gotten into me?

"Glad to hear it." Boris pulled his straw hat low over his eyes and gazed at the water.

We sailed along in silence. I heard only the sound of the water rushing under the hull and the occasional *snap* of the sail.

Then we talked about life and politics. Boris, like me, was a social democrat, and I teased him for being the only socialist banker in Germany.

"Banking is my job," he said. "It is not who I am."

"You are a complicated man."

"As are you," he said with a smile. "Peter Weill."

I knew that I should tell him I'd been fired, but I did not want to speak of anything sad today, so I just smiled back. Boris had a wonderful, lazy smile.

We dropped the sails in the middle of the lake and swam. Boris and Trudi swam like otters, sleek and swift. I was a cautious swimmer, having learned when I was tossed off the dock by Father as a child. Anton had never been in the water, but Trudi tied him into a life jacket and he bobbed around like a cork, splashing everyone wildly when Boris dove underwater to tickle his toes.

It was a wonderful day. Anton was sleepy and sunburned a rosy pink when we returned to the dock. He no longer resembled the pale, thin urchin who had arrived at my apartment three nights ago.

When I stepped off the boat, the dock bobbed up and down and I stumbled. Boris caught my elbow.

"I am always falling around you," I said.

"And I keep catching you," he answered, not letting go of my elbow. I blushed scarlet and held out my hand for the large picnic basket that Trudi lugged off the boat.

"I'll take that." Boris released my elbow and relieved her of the basket. "Can we give you a ride home?"

I opened my mouth to decline, but Anton shouted, "Yes. Oh yes. Trudi says your automobile is as fast as the wind."

"There you have it then. How about you two run along ahead?" Boris asked.

Trudi gave him a searching look, then took Anton's hand and headed down the path.

I started after them, but Boris caught my arm. "Let's allow them to get a bit ahead, shall we?"

I turned to him, surprised. And he leaned down and kissed me. He tasted like salt, and wind. I opened up under his mouth. Time seemed to expand, and I could have stood there forever. When Boris pulled away, we were both shaking.

When I had my breathing back under control, I reached up and traced his lips with one finger. "What is it about us?" I asked him.

"I don't know," he said in a husky voice. "But I would very much like to find out."

I leaned closer to him, but he stepped away. "Not here," he said. "I don't think I could stop again."

I smiled. "It would be embarrassing to be arrested for public indecency."

"And marched past the children."

We turned as one and headed back down the path toward the car. I was happier than I'd been in a long time.

"I imagine you do a great deal of research for your stories." Boris's voice sounded strained.

I nodded. "More for some than others, but I try to be thorough."

"How do you do your research?" Boris shifted the picnic basket to his other hand and walked closer to me.

"Ask questions, look things up." I quickened my pace, my shoes crunching in gravel on the path. I needed to behave myself until I got to the automobile. "It's boring mostly."

"I don't imagine it's that boring. I work in a bank. That is boring. Every day the same."

"My days were not exactly the same," I said, looking at his wind-blown, dark hair. "But there was a sameness about them."

"Was?"

"I . . ." I looked at the ground, surprised by my strong feeling of loss. "I do not work for the paper anymore."

"By choice?" He stepped closer, sounding concerned.

I stepped away. "No. I was let go. This Peter Weill is retired now."

"I am sorry to hear that," he said. "After I got over being angry, I liked your piece on that man. And the piece on the dead prostitute, did you write that?"

"My last piece." I cleared my throat.

"I take it the rich man with the card that you mentioned in your article retaliated?"

"How could you know that?" I stopped walking.

"I only guess, Hannah," he said. "I am a powerful man. I know how powerful men think."

"Sadly"—I hurried toward the automobile—"So do I."

"What will you do with your research?" He lengthened his stride to keep up. His legs were long and powerful. "Write a book, perhaps?"

I had not thought of that. "Interesting idea," I began, slowing.

He leaned forward eagerly. "I could help you. I know some publishers."

"My notes are at the paper," I lied. I was unsure why, but I wanted to tell him no more. "All of my research is confidential."

"Even information about the rapist?" He stopped in front of me on the path, blocking my way. "You would protect him?"

"For you," I said. "That information is especially confidential."

His gold-flecked eyes narrowed. "What do you mean?"

"Are you going to hunt for him, Boris?" I asked. "Bring about your own justice?"

"What an obscene idea," he snapped. And I knew that I was correct.

"I won't help you become a murderer."

"For a man, there are worse things. During the war—"

"Killing in war is not the same." I knew immediately that I should have said nothing.

"Do you know this?" he asked, his voice deadly quiet. He grasped my arms. "How many men have you killed?"

"None," I whispered, thinking of the murderous rage I'd felt when looking at Ernst's picture the second time. "How many have you killed?"

He smiled grimly, not answering my question. He released my arms. "Besides, there are worse things you can do to a man than kill him."

I shuddered and moved away from him on the path.

Boris stepped close to me again. His face was closed and hard. No trace of relaxed sailor in him now. "If you won't part with them for justice, how about money?"

"You cannot buy me." I fought to keep my voice level, to conceal my fear. I was alone on the path with a man I barely knew.

"It wasn't you I wanted to buy." Boris turned and strode away, his white shirt bright in the shade of the trees.

I lingered on the way back to the car. If I did not have to pick up Anton, I would have doubled back and taken the subway home. But I had responsibilities.

Boris was leaning against his automobile when I arrived. It was, predictably, a Mercedes. Anton turned somersaults on the grass to impress Trudi. His new shirt was ruined.

"He's a fine boy," Trudi said as I walked up. "But he says the oddest things."

"He's had a strange life," I answered.

"That isn't good for a child," Boris said, coldly.

I looked into his angry eyes. "It has not been."

"Vati," Trudi interrupted our strained silence, "look at Anton's somersaults. He can do three in a row."

On the drive to my apartment, Boris and I spoke only to the children. As I turned to climb out, he caught my arm.

"I didn't mean to imply that you, or your information, were for sale," he said in a low voice, so that the children couldn't hear. "I am very sorry."

"You did not imply it." I pulled my arm free. "You said it outright."

He pulled a card out of his glove box. "Call me if you need me, or if you change your mind about anything."

I looked at the card. Boris Krause, bank director. "I won't change my mind." But I tucked it into my satchel all the same before climbing out of the car. "Thank you. Anton had a wonderful time."

I gritted my teeth and waved until they drove out of sight, then wheeled around and stalked to my apartment building. "Come along, Anton," I called.

Anton sprinted up to me, chattering about the boat trip. He said it was the best day of his life and recited facts about sailing.

I nodded without listening. Before Boris had tried to bribe me into giving him information, I'd had a lovely day too. Boris was much like Walter—strong, thoughtful, and gentle. He was a wonderful father to Trudi, the kind of man Bettina would marry. Anton would miss him. I shook my head. I would miss him.

I increased my pace. I could not miss a man who wanted to use me to hurt or kill someone the courts set free. A man who tried to trick and bribe me. I fumbled for my keys.

At least he had not seduced the information out of me. My judgment for men was getting worse by the day. I had thought that I had a connection to Boris. Instead I'd been wasting time sailing on boats instead of searching for Ernst's killer.

Mitzi yowled on the stoop next to me.

"I hear you," I said. "I almost have the key."

"And then Herr Krause said—" Anton continued talking.

"It's time for bed, Anton."

Anton nodded without stopping his stream of words.

As I poked the key into the lock and opened the door, a rough hand shot out from behind me and grabbed my wrist.

It was a man's hand. Someone dressed in Nazi brown.

With my free hand I shoved Anton through the open door. He skidded into the lobby and fell on his knees on the tile floor. He glanced up at me in shock as I slammed the heavy front door so hard it rattled in its hinges. It was locked again. Anton was safe inside. Mitzi disappeared in a streak of white.

20

I whirled to face my assailant, yanking my wrist free. He stepped back in surprise.

"Hannah." It was Wilhelm. He held both his hands up at shoulder level. "What are you doing? It's only me."

I let out a deep breath and leaned against the sturdy door. My knees shook. Wilhelm stepped closer and held out his hands to catch me, as if afraid I might faint. Schmidt the news seller wheeled toward us on his makeshift cart, arms pumping fast. I waved to him. "There is nothing to concern yourself with."

Schmidt rolled to a stop at the bottom of the stairs. I wondered how he could have climbed them to help me. "You sure, Fraulein?"

I nodded. "I was startled, but I know this boy."

Schmidt looked from Wilhelm to me, undecided.

"I am not a boy," Wilhelm said indignantly.

"Thank you for your help, Herr Schmidt," I said. "It is good to know that you are watching out for me."

"Can't let anything happen to my best customer." Schmidt smiled and pushed himself back to his newsstand, his fingerless gloves sliding along the pavement.

I turned to Wilhelm. "Why are you here?"

"I came to warn Ernst," he said. "Let's go inside."

I unlocked the door again and hurried inside. Anton stood ramrod straight, lips pressed together, and blood trickling down his knee.

"I'm sorry." I knelt to look at his skinned knee. I'd pushed him too hard, without thinking. "I did not mean to hurt you." Poor child. He deserved a real mother.

"The brave knows no pain." Anton's eyes brimmed with tears.

"Indeed not." Wilhelm took a handkerchief from his pocket. "Especially a tough warrior like you." He wiped blood off Anton's knee and bandaged it with his handkerchief.

I stood there helplessly. "I was frightened when I pushed you," I said. "I did not mean for you to be hurt."

Anton looked down at the dirty tile floor. I remembered how I had told him that I did not hurt children. Another promise I had broken.

Wilhelm scooped Anton up like a kitten and slung him on his back. "I will carry the brave upstairs."

"The brave can walk in his own moccasins."

"Naturally you can," Wilhelm said. "But a soldier must listen to his medic. The medic says to ride your horse." He trotted up the stairs behind me, neighing like a horse.

Once upstairs, I put on water for tea and warmed milk for Anton. I washed his knee and kissed it. When he shot Wilhelm an embarrassed look, Wilhelm winked and said, "Kisses are magic medicine, Anton, even for soldiers."

Wilhelm took over with Anton. It was a treat to watch them together. Wilhelm pretended that Anton's milk and honey was the ceremonial tea of brotherhood, and they drank it together. He sat Anton on his lap and told him stories of camping in the woods and fighting mock battles with his friends. Wilhelm had read more Karl May cowboy and Indian books than Anton and told him an entire story. Anton listened raptly, but fell asleep in Wilhelm's arms before the story ended. I was reminded that Wilhelm himself was little more than a boy.

Wilhelm carried Anton into bed, and I pulled off his new singlet, socks, and shoes. He looked so innocent lying there with his sunburn and his scraped knee. I covered him with my feather duvet. How many times had I covered Ernst as a little boy? More than I could count, although too few after a long, happy day.

"He likes you," I said, as Wilhelm and I returned to the kitchen. I refilled his tea.

"I like him too," he said. "I always wanted a little brother."

"You have sisters?"

He shook his head. "I am an only child. My mother died in childbirth and my father never remarried."

"I am sorry to hear that."

"I have a gift for Ernst," he said. "From Francis." He handed me a heavy envelope.

I did not want any more surprise envelopes for Ernst. "Are they friends?"

"Yes, but nobody is supposed to know. Ernst told me all about it, but I think it was a secret to most people."

"Why?" If the hostility he showed toward Ernst in our conversation at the El Dorado was an act, it was a convincing one.

"Ernst said that Winnie doesn't like his performers to be friends. He says they don't work as hard. Please give it to him."

I turned over the envelope. It was sealed with gold wax and the outside was blank. I set it down on the table and sipped my tea. "Why didn't you mail the envelope to Ernst?"

"Francis paid me to make sure that Ernst receives it. He said I should put it in his hands myself." Wilhelm shrugged. "I thought putting it in your hands was good enough."

"Why doesn't Francis deliver it himself?"

"Francis left for America."

"Why?"

"Don't know. I didn't open the letter. It's not addressed to me, remember?"

"When did you get the letter?"

"Late yesterday."

Yesterday evening I had thought I saw Francis in front of my front door. "Is the letter why you came?"

"One of the reasons." Wilhelm gripped his cup so tightly I feared that it might break.

I cleared my throat. "Tell me the others."

"Do you know where Ernst is?" Wilhelm looked at me hungrily. His need for Ernst crackled in the air between us.

"Yes." I stood and walked across the kitchen to the sink. His look frightened me, and I did not want to be sitting near him. That kind of need could turn to rage so quickly.

"Is he angry with me?" Wilhelm lost interest in me and stared into his teacup. "Was I not what he expected?"

"Where he is has nothing to do with his feelings for you," I said softly. A part of me longed to pat his back and tell him that everything would be fine, but another part of me wanted to keep some distance between us, just in case. After all, he was a Nazi. I leaned against the cold porcelain sink, waiting.

Wilhelm started to cry. "I've loved him since I was a kid, Hannah. That night together, he said he loved me too. But he disappeared. He never called or sent me a letter. Nothing."

I longed to tell him that Ernst was dead.

"Can you tell me where he is? Can you tell him to come meet me?"

"No . . . I . . . You know he never listens to anyone but himself."

Wilhelm blew his nose on a simple, white cotton handkerchief, different from his red silk one. "I wanted to tell him personally, but I'll tell you. I came to warn him."

"Why didn't you go to his apartment?"

"I've been there," he said. "I staked it out most of the day. He never showed up there. So I decided to come here."

"Warn him of what?"

"Rudolf," he said, not meeting my eyes. "He's very angry at Ernst for disappearing. He's asking everyone where he is."

"He asked you?"

Wilhelm squirmed. "He asked me. Last night, at the Silhouette, after the protest at Wertheim. I have to go to the Silhouette club now, because my father knows about the El Dorado. I met Francis there too, but earlier."

I sat silently. "Did you go home with Rudolf?"

"Yes." Wilhelm looked down at his hands. "He's as close as I can get to Ernst right now."

"Why did Rudolf ask you?"

"He thinks I see Ernst all the time. He thinks I'm lying about it. He said to tell Ernst that he has something they want. That they'll kill him if he doesn't give it to them. By Sunday."

The day that Ernst was scheduled to meet Röhm. Röhm must know that Ernst kept his letters. Were Ernst and Rudolf about to blackmail Röhm over the letters? Would Ernst do something like that? The answer, I knew, was yes. Ernst had no trouble using people that he did not care for. If he felt they were bad people, he would get whatever he could from them. Did he think Röhm a bad person? I did. The letters seemed to indicate otherwise, though.

"What does Ernst have?" I asked, keeping my voice carefully neutral.

Wilhelm shook his head. "Rudolf wouldn't say. But he said that if I didn't tell Ernst to give them what they want, they might kill me too."

I nodded, remembering my own encounter with Rudolf. "He was trying to scare you."

"Do you think so?"

"Yes," I lied. "Rudolf's always doing things like that. It makes him feel important."

Wilhelm looked so relieved that I wondered if I'd done him a favor or not. Should he be on his guard? Being on his guard would not help protect him if Röhm wanted him killed.

"He seemed so serious." He drank the rest of his tea. "If you do see Ernst, will you give him my warning?"

"Of course."

"And will you tell him how I feel about him?"

"He knows, Wilhelm," I said.

"Then I guess he'll find me when he's ready."

I collected our dirty cups.

"I'm sorry I frightened you at the front door," he said.

"After Wertheim, I'm a little on edge." The reason I was frightened had nothing to do with the protest.

"You were like a bear defending her cub."

I sighed. "Does a mother bear wound her cub?"

"If she has to," Wilhelm said. "She does."

He left not long after. When I opened the envelope from Francis it contained a set of gold earrings with tiny horses on them and a letter.

"My dearest," the letter began, not using names. Francis was more cautious than Röhm.

> *I am going to Kentucky! That's right, Kentucky. Where the grass is blue so I don't have to be. Seriously, I've stopped the booze and everything else. You know why? Because of you, my dearest friend. B is the real thing. He owns a farm in Kentucky and he's taking me back with him to race. Another chance to be a jockey! And his horses are beautiful. He showed me pictures and bloodlines. A monkey could ride them to victory. And I'm going to be that monkey. Thank you for introducing us. And thank you for getting me the job at the club and teaching me to sing. I don't know if you ever knew how slim was the edge on which I walked. But now I'm back. Back to the stables and the horses and the smell of manure that you hate so much. I'll write you at your apartment as soon as I get out there. See you later, partner.*

Cynical Francis's letter was unsigned. Ernst had helped him, I thought proudly. Even though Francis was competition for him at the El Dorado.

When I turned the letter over, faint pencil marks caught my eye. I held them to the light. Mirror writing. Ernst and I had often practiced it when he was a boy. I held the letter to the mirror to read it more easily.

I am frightened. O says you are dead, but I don't believe him. I delivered a package to SP for R. The next day she was dead and I don't know what was in the package. Someone followed me there, but I got away in a taxi. Be very careful.

O for Oliver? How did he know that Ernst was dead? It seemed like only the murderer and I could know. I scanned the note again. *SP* for Sweetie Pie. *R* for Rudolf. And Francis had seen me following him. A worse thought entered my mind. What if he hadn't seen me following him? What if someone else there saw us both?

21

Anton's stomach growled as we stood in line to buy tickets for the tour boats at Lake Wannsee early the next morning. It was cold and foggy, and I worried that the riverbank would not be visible from the boat.

"Are you hungry?" I asked.

"A brave can go for days without food."

"Well, I cannot," I said with a smile. "I think they will have pretzels on the boat, perhaps even pastries."

We bought tickets on the first boat of the day. Ernst's police file stated that his body was spotted at 7:45 A.M. by the steward on this very boat. My stomach clenched with anxiety. I did not want to see the bank where he was hauled out of the water. But I had to. I had to stand where he died and pay my respects. He was buried now, and I had not stood at his grave.

Anton's eyes were round as he stared at the huge ship, its flat sides rising out of the water like a house. "It's much bigger than Trudi's boat," he whispered.

"I think we could put Trudi's boat on the deck and barely notice."

Anton eyed the wooden decking as if calculating where Trudi's boat might fit.

"Ahoy," said a crewman dressed in a rough black jersey and pants. He took our tickets as we climbed aboard. "It's a light load we have this Saturday morning."

Only a handful of passengers milled about the deck. I took Anton to the bow where we held the metal railing and peered at the muddy water of the Spree below. It was a couple of meters from the deck to the surface of the water. "Do not lean over the rail," I told him.

I strolled back to the cabin. The steward stood behind a wooden bar serving coffee. Two rows of brass buttons ran down the front of his uniform. Their polished surfaces glittered in the yellow lamplight.

"Coffee and two pretzels," I said. He nodded, holding my eye a second too long.

I sat in one of the tall stools bolted to the deck and sipped my coffee, watching the steward work. He kept glancing back at me. I smiled and waited for other passengers to buy their snacks and leave so I could have him all to myself.

Expensive houses slid by, a few lit windows glowing through the remains of the fog. Anton hurried in to fetch his pretzel and rushed back to the bow.

"Exciting out here on the river?" I unbuttoned my burgundy coat.

"Sometimes," he said with a glint in his eye. "Hopefully not today."

"Why not? Couldn't you stand a little excitement?" I took a sip of coffee and smiled. He was a braggart, my favorite kind of source.

"Last week we had plenty." He puffed out his spindly chest.

"What happened?" I lowered my voice and glanced toward Anton. He stood glued to the front rail, his hair fluttering in the breeze. Probably chilled to the bone in spite of his new jacket.

"Not allowed to talk about it with the tourists." He smiled self-importantly. "Don't want to ruin their impression of Berlin."

"I am no tourist," I said. "I live in Berlin. Taking the nephew out for a ride so his parents can have a morning's peace." I slipped off my coat and draped it over my lap.

"Still bad for the line." He shot a glance around the cabin, to see if any other crew members were within earshot. He clearly wanted to share his adventure with someone.

"Did you run into something? Was anyone injured?" I asked in a worried tone.

"Nothing like that." He shook his head. "Nothing at all."

"What then?"

He came over and wiped at my table with a rag, daring me to ask the next question.

I smiled encouragingly. "I bet it was something you did, something no one else could have done, and you're just too modest to tell me."

He sat on the stool next to me. "I saw a person in the water."

"Did you help with the rescue?"

He shook his head, grandly, tragically. "I would have. But he was dead long before I spotted him."

I gasped. "A dead man was floating down the middle of the river?"

"Not in the middle," he said, irritated. "Anyone could have seen him there. Over on the side, caught in some bushes like."

"You must have eagle eyes"—I looked into his watery gray eyes—"to see something like that."

He leaned closer. "Always have had. My mum used to call me the Hawk."

"How did he get in the water?" I took a sip of my coffee.

"Don't know." We stared at caramel-colored water sliding by outside the cabin window, and I worried that the story was over. "I think he was pushed in dead. Not far from here."

"My goodness. How can you tell something like that?" I widened my eyes, hating myself for worming the information I needed out of him this way. I was no better than Boris. "Did you study medicine?"

He looked embarrassed, but pleased. "Not hardly. But I seen drowned men before. He didn't look drowned. Wasn't in the water long, I could tell that."

"How?"

"The fish usually . . ." He coughed. "Experience."

"Did you tell the police where you think he went in?"

He chuckled. "They never asked."

"Why not?" I asked indignantly. "You probably have more idea of that than some landlubber cop."

"I might." He rubbed his receding chin, watching me, trying to make up his mind to tell me.

"Of course you do. A man of your experience." I leaned forward, hanging on his every word.

"See that factory up ahead? Makes bottles." He pointed toward a set of four smokestacks whose tops disappeared in fog. "I'm guessing he went into the water somewhere past that factory and before where we found him. Not more than a few hundred meters away."

"Why do you think that?"

"There's a pipe upstream of the factory draws in water. He'd a been sucked down into that pipe if he'd dropped in before there."

"Where did you find him?"

"I'll tell you when we get there," he said. A young couple speaking excitedly in Italian tried to order breakfast. My gymnasium Latin told me that they wanted coffee and one of the snail-shaped pastries that looked stale, even this early in the day. The steward reluctantly stepped back behind the bar. I slipped my coat back on.

Leaving him to sort out the order, I walked to the bow and stood next to Anton. I stared at the approaching factory and shivered.

"Are you warm enough, Anton?"

"See how the boat cuts the water?" he said, eyes shining. "I saw two rats and a giant log."

"Interesting," I said. "Keep count for me."

I walked back to the steward as we passed the factory. I cleared my cup from the table and handed it to him. "Are we almost there?"

"See them trees?" He pointed to a small stand of droopy willow branches touching the surface of the water. "That's where he was. Naked as the day he was born. Long hair he had too, like a woman. We dragged him up on shore. I had to wait for the police. The ship had to go on."

"Of course." I marked the stand of willows with my eyes. Somewhere between there and the factory, someone had stripped my baby brother down and thrown him in the water like a sack of garbage.

"Five rats," Anton called from the bow.

"He's got good eyes, your nephew." The steward washed and rinsed my cup, dried it carefully, and added it to the row of clean cups.

When the boat reached the next stop, we disembarked. We would not use the rest of our sightseeing tickets.

"I'm only up to eight rats," Anton said. "The brave wants to find ten."

"Next time," I said.

I hailed a taxi and directed it to the bottle factory. The factory was closed Saturdays and the gate locked. I walked toward the river.

"What are we doing?" Anton scrambled through the mud behind me as I reached the bank.

"We are looking for signs." I searched the wet ground in front of me for evidence of Ernst's presence.

"Like animal spoor?"

"Anything unusual." I thought of Ernst's taste in clothes. "Also anything red."

We walked along the bank, staying as close to the water as possible. I did not know what I looked for as I trudged along, circling away from the bank, staring at the ground. The recent rain had obscured any marks. Mud sucked at our shoes as we squelched along. I would find nothing here.

I walked back to the cobblestone street that ran from the bottle factory along the riverbank. Perhaps I could find something there. I scanned the ground for anything out of place.

We were not far from the willows where the steward had seen the body when Anton called out. "Mother, I found something."

I hurried to his side, too eager to see what he found to explain again that I was not his mother.

He pried an object from between two cobblestones. Probably a bottle cap, I told myself, or part of a dead rat. That would bring his rat count for the day to nine.

"It's a soldier," he said. "But he's wearing a dress."

Resting on his muddy palm was a lead soldier, painted like a woman. Anton's sharp eyes had found what mine could not. My hands began to sweat.

Tears blurred my eyes as I took the soldier from his hand and turned her over and over, thinking back to the day that Ernst had clothed her. The day that I had taken him away from Father for a week and created the Code of Manliness. He had carried this small soldier with him all those years, up until the moment he died with it.

"Soldiers don't wear dresses," Anton said.

"This one does." I reached into my satchel and pulled out the soldier's twin, wrapped in Ernst's silk handkerchief. I smelled lavender orange water perfume, nearly overpowered by the smell of mud and rotting leaves in the alley. "And so does this one."

Anton lost interest and wandered back to the alley.

I stared at the soldiers, fighting the urge to flee from the alley, to run and never look back. Halfway down the alley, Anton poked the cobblestones with a stick he'd found.

I pictured Ernst lying in this alley, bleeding to death. Had he known his killer? I wanted it to be a stranger, an accident, so that he felt only surprise in those last minutes, not betrayal. But the thought of him dying alone, or in front of a stranger who cared nothing for him, not even enough to hate him, felt bleak too.

I drew my new burgundy coat tighter around myself and gritted my teeth to keep them from chattering as I walked to Anton.

"I found something," he said, excitement in his voice. "Under the dustbin."

This was a treasure hunt to him.

His small hands held a dagger. "It's rusty."

I lifted it out of his hands. The dagger had a polished wooden hilt with curves that looked like a woman wearing a long sheath dress. A nickel eagle carrying a wreath encircling a swastika perched right below the curve that looked like a woman's bottom. Blood, not rust, caked the words engraved on the blade: "Everything for Germany." The other side had the initials *W. L.* I thought immediately of Wilhelm, the boy who had seen Ernst on the last night of his life. Wilhelm Lehmann.

"Why are your hands shaking?" Anton asked. "Are you cold?"

"Yes," I said. "Very cold."

A circle at the top of the hilt, where the face would be, if it had been a woman, contained a runic *SA*. A Sturm Abteilung dagger, like the one Wilhelm had said he'd lost. Thousands of men had them; certainly there must be others with the initials *W. L.*, but Wilhelm had told me he lived near a bottle factory. How many other *W. L.*'s with such daggers lived near a bottle factory? And how many of them were with Ernst on the last night of his life?

"But I am warm," Anton said. "I don't need a jacket."

I knelt down and looked in his clear blue eyes. "I feel cold inside," I said. "In my heart."

"Did the knife hurt you?" Anton reached for it.

"It's a dagger." I slipped it into my satchel. I did not want to answer his question.

I took his warm hand, and we walked to the edge of the river together. I hiked all of the way back to the willows where Ernst's body had been found, thinking of Ernst climbing out of Wilhelm's window happy and in love, probably only a few blocks from where we were walking. Did Wilhelm follow him? Perhaps they argued. Or perhaps they never made it to Wilhelm's house. I had only the word of a Nazi boy.

"Are you scared?" Anton asked.

"I am scared, Anton." A dead rat floated down the river. "There's your tenth rat."

"Nine," he said. "Will men hurt you? That happened to Aunt Sweetie."

Of course it had. She'd been paid to let men beat her. "Hopefully not like that."

"I can keep them away," he said. "With that dagger."

"You are very strong and very clever. But so am I," I said. "I am keeping the dagger."

I would have to turn Wilhelm in to Fritz as soon as I recovered my papers. After all my worries about Rudolf, Ernst had been killed by someone he loved and trusted. Someone I had trusted. And I knew that the police would probably let Wilhelm go. They had only my word for all of it. But I knew.

"There's the tenth rat!" Anton shouted.

22

I dragged myself to my feet. The river flowed by as it had all morning, as it would long after my own death. But Anton needed lunch. I decided to make him an omelet and then take a long nap. I hated to believe that Wilhelm was the murderer, not after all his tears and worries. Did Ernst's death have anything to do with the letters, the ring, or the mysterious package that Röhm expected delivered tomorrow? Perhaps Wilhelm too, was involved with Röhm.

I tucked Anton's hand in mine and did not let go all of the way home. Usually he chattered, but today he stayed uncharacteristically silent. My thoughts were on locking myself alone in the bathroom so I could cry without him having to see. As much as I wanted to shield him from it all, I did not think I could keep up a façade of calm much longer.

I checked the mailbox, wondering if Ernst had left me any more unexploded bombs. A letter fell out, unstamped. It must have been hand-delivered. I tensed, but then relaxed when I recognized the handwriting. Boris. I slipped it into my satchel.

Silently we climbed the stairs.

The apartment door stood ajar. A stripe of light ran along the door frame and spilled onto the dirty landing floor. I stopped dead, listening. No sound came from my apartment.

I bent down and slipped a hand over Anton's mouth. "Quiet," I mouthed.

He nodded, and I pulled my hand away. He drew in a quick breath.

"Go up one more flight of stairs," I whispered. "And wait for me. The brave must be silent."

He tiptoed away. I waited until the sound of his footsteps reached the top of the stairs before I pushed open my front door.

Every dish in the kitchen was smashed on the floor. The iron pot where I had once hidden the ruby ring lay on its side. The drawer where I kept my story notes sat on its side on the floor, empty.

I drew the SA dagger from my satchel and stepped inside. Every instinct screamed that entering was a foolish thing to do, but I was furious that someone had destroyed my home. If it was Ernst's killer, I wanted to meet him.

No one was in the kitchen. I tiptoed to my bedroom and opened the door. No one was there, but my clothes were thrown out of the wardrobe and onto the floor.

Someone had slit the mattress and pulled out the stuffing.

I tightened my grip on the dagger and opened my bathroom door. Mitzi's body hung out of the toilet, tail hanging limp down to the floor. I bit back a shriek. Slipping the dagger in my satchel, I ran out of the apartment.

Before I could slam the door, a familiar, high-pitched voice called, "Fraulein Vogel?"

Trembling, I turned to face Kommissar Lang. What was he doing here? Was he responsible?

"What has happened to your apartment?" He pushed past me.

"I don't know," I said. "Someone came when I was out."

I clenched my hands and followed him into my kitchen. He pulled one of the chairs upright and held it for me.

"Where were you going?" he asked.

"To find a policeman," I said. I had only known that I was going away. "Why are you here?" I tried to keep sharp suspicion from my voice, but did not succeed. Had he ransacked my apartment? How did he have my address? I edged away from him.

"I came to call on you," he said. "Perhaps to arrange another meeting."

"It is good that you came." I realized that he was innocent. If he had wanted to attack me, he would have closed the front door. And as an innocent man, he would expect me to be helpless, terrified by what had happened. As if I were innocent myself. "What do I do?"

"Did you go through the house?" he asked.

"I was afraid to," I lied.

"You were correct to be afraid," he said. "Wait here."

He walked quickly through the rooms. I sat, at a loss for what to do.

"There is no one here," he said quietly. "Let us go through the rooms together to see if anything is missing." He helped me out of the chair as if I were old and fragile.

I thought of fleeing, but I would have to go upstairs to get Anton and we would never make it past Kommissar Lang on the way back down. I followed Kommissar Lang into the bedroom.

"I have nothing of value."

"No jewelry?"

At Herr Klein's, fortunately. I shook my head. "1923 was a tough year."

He smiled sympathetically. Everyone in Germany knew that most people had been forced to sell everything to survive through the inflation years. "Especially for a woman alone."

I took in the damage to my bedroom. The slit in the mattress gaped like a wound.

"Whoever did this was angry," he said, looking around. "I think they were threatening you. Are you perhaps involved with a man who—"

"No. There is no one." My heart raced. My vision blurred around the edges, and I sat on the ruined mattress.

"Let me fetch you some water." Kommissar Lang disappeared into the bathroom. I was grateful that I had not been forced to see Mitzi there again.

He came out with my toothbrushing glass full of water. "Do you have a cat?"

I drank the water and nodded. "Why?"

He sat next to me on the bed and put his hand on my knee. "I—"

"Mother?" called Anton, coming in to the room.

"Here, Anton."

Kommissar Lang looked from me to Anton. I could see his mind working. He was remembering that Fritz had told him I never married. And yet I had a son—what must be an illegitimate son. Kommissar Lang yanked his hand off my knee as if it were covered in sewage. He stood and took a few steps back from me.

"I must fetch your local police officer," he said, not meeting my eyes. "Wait for us in your kitchen. Do not leave, Fraulein."

His voice told me that he expected obedience.

I nodded politely, as if his entire attitude toward me hadn't just changed. "Thank you."

I took Anton's hand. He stared at the apartment, and his eyes grew round.

I gave Kommissar Lang a few moments to reach the bottom of my stairs. When the front door to the building slammed, I pulled Anton down the stairs, and we crept through the back door.

All I had was the ring, the letters, and Anton. More than enough.

I hailed a taxi. "Turn around here," I commanded.

The taxi driver swore and pulled the wheel around.

"Now left."

I told him to take more U-turns, then quick turns to the left and right, staring behind us to see if we were being followed. Eventually I sat back in the seat and gave him Ursula's address.

"Mother," said Anton quietly. "Can I talk now?"

I turned to him. "Yes, Anton."

"Why did you make me go upstairs?"

I did not trust the taxi driver. I bent down next to Anton's ear and whispered. "I did not think that the apartment was safe. And it was not."

"Where are we going now?" he whispered.

"To my sister."

"Why are you shaking?"

"I am not—" I looked down at my trembling body.

"You are."

"I am," I said. "And I cannot explain why."

That seemed to satisfy him, and he stared out the window.

I tried to regain control. I certainly could not go see Ursula in this condition. I slowed my breathing and clenched and unclenched my fists. It helped, but I could still see Mitzi hanging out of the toilet.

I ran through a list of suspects in my mind, people who might do such a thing to my apartment. First was Röhm. Perhaps he or his men had destroyed my apartment looking for the letters or the ring. Certainly letters that could destroy his life's ambition and a million-dollar ring could warrant such a search. He would want me to be intimidated, to know that keeping the letters would have serious consequences.

And then there was Wilhelm. He knew where I lived, had been in and out of my apartment days before. He'd been there alone with Anton and with me. It was easy to picture him searching my apartment looking for something that could link him to the murder.

Boris could have been there, searching for information about the rapist. I pictured him as someone who would search carefully, like the banker he was. But who knew what he was capable of, especially in a fury at the man who had wronged Trudi. My story notes were missing.

Rudolf also was anxious to find whatever Ernst was supposed to deliver. Perhaps he was jealous of Ernst's love for the cat. The taxi hit a bump, and I jumped, startled.

Enough, I told myself, glancing at the back of the driver's black hat. This will not solve your immediate problem: how to keep yourself and Anton safe.

The taxi ride to Ursula's took more money than I made in a week of work. I would have to sell the rest of the jewelry to get through this. Get through this how? For now I needed a place to stay and someone to care for Anton.

I rang the bell at Ursula's grand front door. She lived in an expensive apartment building with a wrought-iron fence and a gate. Her apartment was not that large, but, just like Ursula and her husband, it presented a wealthy front.

"Hannah," said Ursula, opening the door. She stepped outside and closed the gate behind her. Her carefully dyed hair formed a golden halo around her head. We had not spoken since her birthday party, six months ago. We had not quarreled any more than usual then, but neither of us tried to keep up a closer relationship.

"Good day, Ursula." I smiled. "May we come in?"

"Who do you have here?" She looked down at Anton as if she smelled something unpleasant.

"Anton, ma'am," he said. He gave a tiny soldier's bow.

"What do you need?" Ursula's glance flicked back to me, her eyes pebble hard.

"A place to stay."

"They have hotels for that." Her voice was cold.

"Ursula," I said in my best shocked tones, although I was not surprised. "We're family."

She drew in a breath. "You ceased being family when you sided with that degenerate."

"Ernst w— is not a degenerate," I said. "And I'd thank you not to—"

"Please." She rolled her eyes. "I watched him prancing around that club of his. He's humiliating all of us."

"In front of whom? Do your friends go to the El Dorado?"

Ursula compressed her lips.

"I am in trouble." I gestured down to Anton. "We are in trouble. And we are family."

"We're all family?" Ursula motioned toward Anton with a sneer.

I nodded, unwilling to reveal more.

"Then I suppose that's his bastard," Ursula said, guessing the truth as she so often did. She was unpleasant, but very smart. "And I won't have you bringing your troubles to my door. I am a respectable woman."

"What's a degenerate?" Anton asked.

Ursula looked down at him. "I think explaining that is your job. You have more experience with it." She turned and walked back to her front door, her back as stiff and straight as Father's on the parade ground.

"A degenerate," I said loudly, "is someone who does not perform her duty."

"I understand," Anton said.

I took Anton's hand, and we began the long walk to the bus stop. I wished she had taken us in, and Nazis had ransacked her house, destroying our parents' china, their antique furniture, and her precious respectability. In fact, I wanted to stomp into her house and do those things myself. If the situation were reversed, I would have helped her because she was all of the family I had in the world. Now I had no family. Except perhaps Anton.

I took a deep breath. Where were we to go?

23

"You're hurting my hand," Anton said, and I loosened my grip.

"I am sorry."

As we waited for the bus, I went over my options. I did not want to be a danger to Bettina and her children, so I could not go there. If the person who killed Mitzi knew where I lived, perhaps he also knew where my family and friends lived. The thought of someone injuring Sophia made me shudder.

A black automobile slowed as it drove by. Pretending to be interested in a ginger cat picking its way across a window box of geraniums, I studied the automobile out of the corner of my eye. The driver wore a homburg with a gray feather in the brim, hat pulled low over his face so that nothing showed but a nondescript chin. He sped up and turned the corner.

"We will walk to the next stop," I told Anton. He jumped uncomplainingly to his feet, and we hurried around the corner away from the automobile.

"Anton." I glanced over my shoulder. No sign of the car. "Bad men came to the apartment today."

"I know."

We walked down the broad sidewalks under leafy linden trees. A squirrel climbed a telephone pole. We stopped to admire him. His long tail was fuzzy. He looked as if he'd escaped from a children's book.

"They wanted to find me and hurt me," I said. It sounded ridiculous, here in this place of peace and calm. "They are very dangerous."

Anton took my hand.

"I think that you need to go somewhere safe." I squeezed his hand.

"Without you?" Anton did not take his eyes off the squirrel, who ran along the telephone wire as nimbly as an acrobat.

"Without me. At least for a while."

His eyes filled with tears. He looked at me and said in a stern little voice. "I won't allow it."

"Anton," I said, just as sternly. "It's for your own good. I will find a nice place."

"An orphanage." His voice was matter-of-fact. He pulled his hand back.

"What makes you say that?"

"Auntie Sweetie put me there sometimes." He drummed his shoes on the ground. "I won't go."

"Anton," I said softly. "You are a child. You must go."

He shook his head. "My name is Anton Vogel. And I know yours too: Hannah Vogel. And I know your address." And he recited it.

I stared at him in shock.

"I will tell them that at the orphanage and they won't let you leave me. The police will find you. I've done it before." He crossed his arms.

"You are a clever little man." I laughed.

"A brave keeps his wits and his arrows sharp."

We walked down the empty street to the next bus stop in silence. Anton drooped with tiredness, but did not complain. He was a brave soldier.

I sighed. He was too young to be a soldier, brave or otherwise, and it was my job to keep him safe. Tomorrow I would deliver the letters or the ring, whichever they wanted. Then they would leave us alone. Or they would kill me. But not Anton. I had to keep him safe.

I took him to Sarah's apartment, the only place I could think of. Röhm or Wilhelm could not link me to this place. I cooked us a late lunch, grateful that I had bought all of that food yesterday. I thought I had been buying it to help out the peddlers, but had I sensed, even then, I would need a hideaway?

More to soothe him and myself than because he needed one, I heated water and gave Anton a bath. He played with the soap and let me scrub his back while he chattered about the three little pigs. Which house was this? I wondered. My house was made of straw. Was Sarah's house the safe, brick house or would the wolf reach in and crush it too?

When I dressed Anton in one of Tobias's old nightshirts, the sleeves hung past the ends of his fingers like a Chinese robe and the hem touched the floor. He looked as tiny and defenseless as an infant.

I tucked him into Sarah's bed. We would sleep in the same bed tonight. At least our fates would be bound together if we were found. I could not bear the thought of Anton frightened or injured without anyone who loved him to comfort him. Ernst died like that. I had not protected him, and now I did not know if I could protect Anton either. I held him so tightly that he stirred in his sleep.

I returned to the kitchen and drank Sarah's excellent tea. I would have to meet with Röhm at Ernst's apartment to trade him the ring or the letters, or both, for my safety and Anton's. The ring I did not mind. It was rightfully his. But the letters I did not want to give up. They might be a key to stopping the evil that had driven Sarah away. Perhaps they were a key to the way out.

I believed that eventually the German people would recognize the evil in the Nazis' anti-Semitism and vote them out. Sarah had always disagreed with me, but looking around her tidy apartment, with everything neatly packed away, it was as if she too, expected to return one day and step back into her old life.

I wanted it to be ready for her. Nervously I paced around, dusting Sarah's possessions. Her ruby cut-glass goblets and her simple dishes. A Hummel figurine of a shepherdess with a tiny sheep that I knew she'd received as a gift from her mother-in-law. Her candleholders, with glass globes and cut-glass crystals hanging down.

Guttural moans cut through the air. I flicked off the light to not cast a silhouette against the front window. Careful not to move the fabric, I peeked between the curtains. Two men kicked a third man crumpled on the ground. The man on the ground moaned again.

"Filthy Jew," shouted a rough voice. Their Nazi uniforms ate up the light cast by a streetlamp.

A board creaked behind me, and I spun around. Anton stood in his oversize nightshirt at the edge of the living room.

"What is making that sound?" He rubbed his eyes with his fists.

"It is nothing we can help." I crossed the room to him. "Bad men doing bad things."

I lifted him to carry him back to bed. He wrapped his warm arms around my neck. "Don't worry," he said. "You will keep me safe."

"If ever I can," I said.

As I was about to drift off to sleep I remembered Boris's letter. I crept out of bed and into the living room.

Dearest Hannah,

I know that what I asked you to do, and how I asked you to do it, goes beyond apologies. But also know that Trudi has not slept a night through for months. And now that he is free and walking the same streets, my housekeeper or I must walk her to and from school. He is free, but she is not.

You know something of traumatized children. Anton is a boy with a past of his own. I know that he is not yours, in spite of him calling you Mother. You took him in, took him away from whatever shaped him, and you are trying to give him something better. I admire that in you, for all that it is unspoken. Would you judge me for wanting to do the same for Trudi?

We are connected, you and I, not only physically, but also through the damage done to our children and all we wish to do to repair it.

If you can move past our disagreement and forgive me, you know how I may be found.

Yours, Boris

I bowed my head over the letter. Boris had seen far more deeply into me than I had thought. I could not give him the address of the rapist, but I could no longer blame him for wanting it. Perhaps after I had dealt with Röhm, Boris and I could start over. I held the letter for a long time before I went to bed.

The metallic *click* of a key in the front lock startled me from an uneasy sleep.

Heart pounding, I leaped to my feet. I needed a weapon. The dagger was in the kitchen. I crept out of the bedroom, silently closing the door. The intruder must not discover Anton.

I slipped into the dark kitchen. I fumbled in my satchel until I found the dagger that had killed my brother. Gripping the smooth handle, I crept across the kitchen floor.

Heavy footsteps walked into the kitchen.

I raised my arm. The kitchen light flicked on. Light flared off the knife as I brought it down.

A hand grabbed my wrist. The dagger clattered to the floor.

"Hannah?"

"Paul?" I heard the shock in both of our voices.

Paul folded me into his arms. "I'm so grateful you're alive."

I pulled back. "I'm grateful I did not stab you."

The reality of the past moment sank in, and I collapsed onto a kitchen chair. For a few seconds Paul and I merely stared at each other in the warm kitchen light.

Paul retrieved the dagger from the floor. "There's blood on this."

"I did not put it there," I said. "Although I probably would have added your blood to it if you had not . . ." My voice trailed off. I hated to even say that I'd almost hurt Paul, but I had come within centimeters of stabbing him.

Paul kept hold of the dagger, probably not trusting me with it. Not that I blamed him.

Thinking of what I'd almost done, I started to shake and stood quickly to cover it. "I'll make tea."

Paul reached out his hand as if to comfort me, but I walked to the sink and turned on the faucet. Neither of us said a word. Water splashed into the kettle, and I managed to stop shaking. Paul kept his eyes politely averted until I did, glancing around Sarah's kitchen, probably remembering happier times we three had spent together here.

"I went to your apartment," he said finally. "It's a mess."

"I know." I'd forgotten that he still had my house key, and Sarah's. Paul, the keeper of the keys. And I had almost stabbed him. I gritted my teeth and tried to think about something else.

"I hoped you might come here. If—" He swallowed and continued. "If you were still alive."

"Oh." If Paul thought I might come here, who else might?

"I opened your letter." Paul placed it on the table. I set the kettle on the stove and lit the flame.

When I turned back to the table, I read the outside of the envelope. "In the event of my death, deliver to Fritz Waldheim at the Berlin Alexanderplatz Police Station." It seemed as if I'd written the letter in more innocent days.

"Why didn't you give it to the cop at the Alex?" I kept anger out of my voice. He'd had no business reading it.

Paul turned the letter over in his elegant hands. "After you were fired, and I saw your apartment, I feared the worst, but I wasn't sure you were dead."

"And I'm not, so it's just as well you kept it." I had thought him more reliable. I turned back to the stove.

Paul rose and stood so close behind me that I felt the warmth of his body. I ached to lean into him, knowing how it would feel to fit myself against him. "I was sorry to hear about your brother."

I longed to turn around into the shelter of his arms and weep, as I had so many times in the past, but I did not. I did not want to involve him in any of this. I knew better than to involve a half-Jewish man in an SA matter. They would kill him without a second thought, and no one would ever question it. And what if he told Maria? With her recent anti-Semitic comments, I sensed that she was being pulled closer to the Nazis herself.

"I am worried about you, Hannah." I heard protectiveness in his tone and bridled at it. I could look after myself.

"It's not your problem." The strong scent of cut black tea wafted up as I scattered tea leaves into Sarah's blue-and-white teapot. Now there was nothing to do but face Paul. I brushed past him and sat back down at the table.

"Who is the child, Anton, you mentioned in the letter? And how did you find out that your brother was dead?" Always the reporter, Paul. He would not let go until I gave him something. I must be careful not to give away too much.

My voice quavering, I told him of finding Ernst's picture and learning he was dead.

The kettle screeched. I went to it and poured steaming water into the teapot, grateful for a distraction and for the distance from Paul.

"What's happened since you wrote the letter?" His voice was quiet, and his eyes full of worry for me. I looked away and poured the tea.

I summarized what I'd learned about Rudolf and Anton. I did not mention Röhm or anything to do with him, the ruby, the letters, and tomorrow's meeting.

After I finished talking, we sipped tea in silence for a few moments. I cradled my warm cup and watched Paul thinking, his dark eyes staring, unfocused, into his teacup.

"Interesting." He took a sip. "Now tell me the rest."

"There is no rest," I said. "Not yet."

Knowing that I was lying, he gave his head a quick impatient shake, as if a mosquito was buzzing in his ear. "Why don't you go to the police?"

"I cannot put Sarah in danger." But that was only part of the truth. If Röhm was involved in this, the police could not keep me safe.

"The price for you helping Sarah was never to be your own life." Paul's voice rose.

"Shh." I glanced toward the bedroom door, worried that he might wake Anton. "I know what I'm doing."

Paul exhaled, making an irritated sound I'd heard a hundred times before. We both laughed.

"I don't know what is worse," he said. "How crazy you sound, or that you really think you know what you're doing."

"You'd best be off," I said, not wanting him to discover that, in fact, I did not know. "Before Maria finds out you've gone."

Paul looked at his watch and swore.

"You will watch for Sarah's letter at the paper?" I walked him to the front door. "And keep it safe for me?"

"Of course," he said. "It appears to be all I can do."

"Are you safe going home this time of night?" I asked, ignoring his hurt feelings.

"I'm safer going home now than explaining to Maria why I was out all night. Or staying here with you if you're armed."

"Take care," I said, and locked the door behind him.

After I washed the cups in the kitchen, I brought the dagger back into the bedroom and set it on the bedside table.

Best to keep it close.

24

The next morning we dressed in ill-fitting clothes from Sarah and Tobias. We looked more like scarecrows than the fine lady and young gentleman we'd been after our Wertheim visit on Friday. Anton seemed unconcerned about the change. I left the dagger and my notebook on Sarah's kitchen table.

I gathered one of Röhm's letters, and a few bills from the envelope of money in Sarah's mailbox, before we went out to prepare for our big day. At a stationery store I deliberated for a long time before purchasing thick bond paper, an expensive Parker pen, and a bottle of royal-purple ink. I bought Anton a tiny toy square with a round silver ball to roll around and try to catch in the holes in the clown's eyes and mouth.

We hurried to a tobacco shop where I added ten packs of Ravenklau cigarettes to our supplies. They cost more than other brands, but they were what I needed. As an afterthought, I bought a few cheaper packs too.

The game kept Anton busy while we rode the streetcar north to Tegel. When the bumps knocked out his little ball, he poked his tongue out of the corner of his mouth and concentrated on maneuvering the ball back in.

My satchel weighed heavy on my shoulder as we climbed off the streetcar and walked toward our destination through the dappled shade cast by the trees lining the sidewalk. A woman with a fruit cart was parked in the strip of grass in the middle of the street. I bought us bananas, a luxury Anton had never eaten before.

Two guards paced in front of a tall brick wall. They wore plain gray uniforms with gray-and-black caps. Behind the wall stood an imposing brick building.

"What is that?" Anton chewed on his banana with a surprised expression on his face. He did not seem to know what he thought of it, but he kept eating.

"Tegel Prison." I savored the smooth texture of the banana. I had not eaten one in a very long time and who knew when I would again.

"Don't leave me." Anton's voice was high and full of fear. "People go in and never come out again. Please, I'll be good."

I stopped walking and picked him up. He trembled, and his muscles were taut under his shirt. "I won't leave you, I promise."

"Then why are we here?" Anton's eyes strayed to the twin spires of the prison church, outlined against the clear blue sky.

"I have to visit a man I know."

Anton nodded. He understood visits to men.

We walked closer to the guards. They should have been pacing in front of the heavy steel gate, but one was telling the other a complicated story about a horse.

"Can I go with you?"

I shook my head. "They don't allow children."

"Will you come back?"

"I will," I said. "Just like I come back when you're at Bettina's."

Anton seemed satisfied with that.

"Good morning, Herr Berndt," I said to the guard on the left.

"Fraulein Vogel." He took off his hat respectfully and held it in his hands. "Haven't seen you in a while. Liked your article about the Düsseldorf trial."

"Thank you."

He called through a tiny barred window and with a screeching sound the gate swung open. Anton and I stepped over the raised metal lip on which the gate rested, and we were through the wall. Leafy elms shaded the wide prison courtyard. Although the high red walls seemed more like part of a castle than a prison, the function of the prison buildings themselves was unmistakable. Soot streaked the thick brick walls and bars crossed each arched window. A few faces peered through the bars, and whistles split the air as I led Anton into the guardhouse next to the gate.

Once inside I persuaded the guard to let Anton sit there until I returned. It cost me a pack of cigarettes, but not the Ravenklaus.

My satchel was searched, but I'd hidden Röhm's letter in my brassiere. Procedure dictated that they pat me down, but they had not in years, and they did not this time either. They did not raise their eyebrows at the cigarettes. Everyone knew what they were for. They assumed that the paper and ink were for me to take notes.

I'd been to the jail often for the newspaper, so I was used to the catcalls of the men in the cells and ignored them as I walked down the long brown hall to the visitors room. The metal chairs were hard and uncomfortable as always, but I managed to trade the remaining cheap cigarettes for a room with a table and uninterrupted privacy with a prisoner. When the guard left to get the prisoner, I slipped Röhm's letter in with the new paper. The room smelled musty and mold grew in the corners. The only window was in the door. It felt oppressive and cold. I straightened and restraightened the papers, waiting.

The guard showed in a man who looked much the worse for wear. He was shorter than I, with perfectly combed brown hair. A coarse cotton shirt had replaced the finely laundered linen he had worn when I first met him. I stood.

"Fraulein Vogel." He took my hand between his ink-stained ones. "Always a delight to see you."

"Thank you, Herr Silbert." I extricated my hand. "You are looking well."

"Would that it were so." His gallant smile was pained.

I looked pointedly at the guard, and he shuffled out, closing the door behind him. If we hurried, we'd have enough time.

"I have something for you," I said. I took out a pack of cigarettes.

"Ravenklau." His brown eyes twinkled. "A lady never forgets a gentleman's favorite cigarettes."

"I have a request," I said. "But those cigarettes are yours to keep regardless, for agreeing to meet me."

"It is always a pleasure to meet with a beautiful lady," he said silkily, slipping the cigarettes into his pocket. "Even for one with a schedule as busy as mine."

I smiled at his sarcasm. Prison bored him. We'd had long conversations about it when I'd interviewed him for a story.

"I have a letter."

"A legal document?" He shook his head, feigning shock. "You know I could do nothing with that."

"It is a personal letter," I said. "From one soldier to another."

"Do I know these gentlemen?" He was brilliant at recognizing handwriting.

"I doubt it."

"Then what do you wish me to do with the letter?"

We both sat down in the uncomfortable chairs. Herr Silbert crossed his legs, sitting like the gentleman he'd been raised to be.

"I would like you to make a copy of it for me, for safekeeping."

"Why me?" Herr Silbert pointed his hand at his chest.

"Your handwriting is so beautiful," I said. "And accurate."

He laughed. His handwriting was the cause of his imprisonment. He'd been arrested for forgery. "I am a calligrapher."

"The letter is one page only," I said. "And I will pay you fifty marks and five packs of your cigarettes."

"If I'm correct about the size of the container, you have nine packs in there." He eyed the paper bag.

"Perhaps some are for myself." He loved haggling, so I should not give in immediately.

"You do not smoke, my dear, as I recall."

"The remaining four packs, then." I shook my head as if I'd been tricked into giving him the cigarettes, although we both knew I must have brought them all for him.

"Let me see the letter." He held out his thin ink-stained hand.

I handed him Röhm's most graphic letter, the paper, and the ink.

"You matched the paper exactly," he said. "And the ink is correct as well. It would be dangerous for the community at large were you to climb from your moral pedestal and take up my former profession."

"Attention to detail is always important."

"Care in everything one does." He began his copy work. He bent over the table, each stroke delicate and precise. It was a treat watching him work. He was an amazing artist. If I had not placed a tiny lipstick mark on the corner of the real letter, I would not have been able to tell the difference. It was only after my shoulders relaxed that I realized how tense they had been. Perhaps this would work.

"Is this about blackmail?" he asked when he had finished. "I don't read much when copying, but there are graphic details in there. Illegal too. The man is besotted. You can see it in his handwriting."

"Indeed." I folded the new letter inside of Röhm's original and slid them in the middle of the blank paper. Herr Silbert had analyzed handwriting for me before. He could divine amazing details from the letters in the simplest note.

"It's nothing to do with me," he said, bowing. "But I think I deserve a piece of the profits."

"There will be no profits," I said. "It's political."

"A politician?" He leaned forward. "A rich one?"

"A poor one," I lied. "But one who owes me a favor, now."

Herr Silbert studied me. "I never know if you are lying or not," he said. "But I can tell that this letter places you in danger. I am in prison, but I still know what is going on outside."

"This is insurance," I said. "To keep me safe."

"Fraulein Vogel." He reached across the table and took my hand. "I know I am no longer a great gentleman, but heed my words: this letter cannot make you safe. Get rid of it and any others you have like it."

He was as correct about the letters as Herr Klein had been about the ring. And I dearly wished that I could follow their advice. But I had no choice. I had to use the tools I'd been given, no matter how dangerous the outcome. I no longer had the luxury of walking away. I thanked him, but knew that I would ignore his warning.

Back at Sarah's apartment, I packed my satchel carefully. I pinned the ring to the bottom, and slid in the letters, the forged one stuffed in the middle. In the outer pocket I slipped Ernst's death photo and Wilhelm's dagger. I hid the original letter that Herr Silbert had copied from in Sarah's mailbox, along with most of my gold and money.

I thought about taking Anton to Paul's, but I knew Anton would refuse. Having no time to argue, I took him with me to Ernst's apartment, hoping Ernst's landlady could be persuaded to watch him. If everything went wrong and I were killed, she would take him to an orphanage. She was a practical sort that way. I shuddered, wishing I did not have to think in such terms.

When we reached Ernst's apartment, the landlady was outside washing the stairs. She tossed a bucket of clean water on the stairs leading to the front door and scrubbed them with a washcloth wrapped around the head of a push broom, as our maids used to. As I mopped my own floors now.

"Frau Müller," I said. "Good day."

"Hannah," she said, delighted. She adored Ernst. "Where is that brother of yours? I haven't seen him in a week or so. He's got a new friend, I'll bet." She smiled mischievously, showing the gap where her front tooth had been. I thought her a spry seventy, but Ernst thought she was a badly preserved fifty.

"I do not know," I said. "But I'd like to see if he's there now, perhaps wait a while for him."

"And who's the little one?" She glanced down at him. "Looks like you. A cousin?"

"His name is Anton," I said.

"Hello, Anton," she said. "Does Ernst expect you two?"

"He does not expect Anton," I said, and strictly speaking that was true.

"Let me get my keys." She limped back to her apartment while we followed impatiently. I knew little about her history. Ernst said she'd never been married, had no children, and no close relatives. She was a good landlady and kept the stairwells and front steps immaculate. She collected rent from most tenants on the first of the month at noon, but Rudolf always paid in advance and paid cash. He wanted no one to trace Ernst to him, I suspected.

"Thank you for letting me in," I said. "Could you mind Anton for me for a few hours? I'd like to have a private conversation."

"In trouble again, your brother?"

"Always," I said. "And little pitchers have big ears."

"The little one can stay with me," she said. "I'll find work for him."

Anton dropped to the ground and wrapped both arms around my legs. "No," he wailed. "Don't abandon me, Mother! I missed you so last time."

Frau Müller looked at me uneasily.

"It's only for a few hours." I peeled his arms off my legs.

"That's what you said last time." He cried real tears. "And you were gone for weeks and weeks."

"Weeks and weeks?" Frau Müller asked.

"He's making it up." I smiled in what I hoped was a reassuring manner.

"Please don't leave," Anton sobbed.

I pulled him to his feet. "You will stay here," I said. "Until I come back."

He hung his head.

"I won't take him if he's going to be difficult," Frau Müller said. "Or if there's any question when you're coming back."

"I'll be back in a few hours."

"She always promises that." Anton sniffled. "But she never comes."

"I'll let you into your brother's place," Frau Müller said. "But I won't take the boy."

Frau Müller hobbled up the stairs ahead of us, her keys jangling.

I gave Anton an angry look, but he smiled smugly back as Frau Müller unlocked the door.

"I will pay you," I said. "I need privacy for this meeting."

Frau Müller looked at me suspiciously. Anton started to cry again.

I handed her ten marks and the salami I'd packed for lunch. She took Anton's hand and dragged him down the stairs.

"You can rake leaves in the back courtyard," she said. "Until she comes for you."

I waited until she was out of sight before opening the door. Ernst's apartment had been ransacked, as mine had, and I hurried through the rooms. Someone had punched a hole in the back of his armoire, torn out his clothes, and skewered a red dress covered with sequins to the bed with a kitchen knife, leaving a long tear in the mattress. A warning, as Mitzi had been. But why would they bother to warn him if they knew he was dead?

They must have visited the apartment after he left it for the last time. Ernst would not go sing at the club, drink, and go home with Wilhelm if his apartment was in this state. He would never leave his clothes lying on the floor to wrinkle.

I cleaned the worst of the mess in the kitchen to make it look as if Ernst had been back. As if he had cleaned it up. I gathered a collection of lacy underthings off the kitchen floor that made my own look like something our grandmother would have worn. My hands worked swiftly, concentrating on cleaning, trying to push my fear away. Soon it would all be decided.

I hid Röhm's ring under ashes in the stove. If he searched me, I did not want to be carrying his treasures. The letters I hid deep in the stuffing of the mattress in the bedroom. I figured that the person who had slit it would not bother to search again. I straightened Ernst's oriental carpet. It was beautiful, probably half a year's pay for me.

Ernst had no tea, so I hurried down to the grocer's to buy the strong green tea that he loved, leaving the front door ajar to get back in without disturbing the landlady. I did not want to face another scene with Anton.

I brewed a pot of tea and sat at a round, marble-topped table that used to stand in the hall of our parents' house. How Ernst had wrangled it from Ursula I could only imagine.

I folded and refolded my hands, jumping up every few seconds to polish a clean pot or sweep the immaculate floor again. I was terrified, but I dared not think about it lest the feeling envelop me and leave me unable to do what must be done to ensure my freedom and my life.

I had to be as ice cold as I'd ever been as Peter Weill to get through this alive. Röhm was a formidable adversary, but he was also only a human being, and I knew a great deal more about what was going on than he did. I could get myself through this. For Anton, I had to.

25

Someone rapped on the apartment door. I smoothed my skirt to calm myself and opened the front door to Ernst Röhm.

He looked every bit the battered war hero. His barrel-shaped body was stocky and strong in his captain's uniform. His immaculate jacket was properly cinched into place by a wide leather belt. Shiny black hair, parted exactly in the middle, topped his square face. But what I noticed, as everyone must have, was his nose. In one of his many war wounds, shrapnel had cut through the bridge of his nose and a pink scar ran across both cheeks. It was a testament to his toughness that he was still alive. He scrutinized the room behind me with wary blue eyes. My mouth went dry. How could I fool this man?

Beside him stood the brawny lieutenant I recognized from the El Dorado and Wertheim—Wilhelm's father. Next to him stood Rudolf von Reiche. So they *were* connected. I had expected Röhm to arrive alone. I had no plan for discussing the letters in front of others.

"Good day, Hannah," said Rudolf. He looked ready to slap me.

I stepped back from the door. Sweat broke out on my palms. I spoke only to Röhm. "Come in and have tea. I am Hannah Vogel, Ernst's sister."

Röhm clicked his heels together and bowed. "You are the very image of him." He took my sweaty hand in his fleshy white one and kissed it like the old soldier he was. "Captain Ernst Röhm. I see that you have already met my lawyer, Rudolf von Reiche. Let me present my assistant, Lieutenant Josef Lehmann."

"Good day, Fraulein Vogel." Lieutenant Lehmann bowed his head in my direction. He did not recognize me, but I had seen him twice before; when he marched Wilhelm out of the El Dorado, and when he called off the Nazi mob in front of Wertheim.

"Is Ernst here?" Rudolf glanced around the hall. "We will not stay long."

"We will stay until that which is mine is restored to me," Röhm said simply. "As you well know."

Rudolf clamped his mouth closed. I might have laughed if the situation had not been so frightening.

"I have made tea." I led them into the kitchen and set out extra cups with trembling hands. "For I think we have much to discuss."

"Where is your brother?" Röhm asked. "I would like to see him. I do not understand why he keeps my own from me, if what Rudolf says is true."

I glanced at Rudolf. "Little of what he says is true."

Rudolf snorted. "An interesting comment, from one such as you."

Röhm held up his hand, and we both fell silent, as if he were our commanding officer.

I poured everyone tea. Röhm and his lieutenant sat, and Rudolf sat next to me.

"This is no game," Rudolf whispered in my ear, too quietly for Röhm to hear. "There are real consequences for us all."

A sharp knock sounded on the front door.

"Excuse me," I said and went to answer it. I expected no one else, but I had expected only Röhm, so what did I know of who would be attending this meeting?

Wilhelm stood outside the doorway, wearing his Nazi uniform. "I came to protect you and Ernst," he whispered. "From Rudolf."

I clutched the door frame. "You want to protect me?"

He nodded. "Both of you."

My first instinct was to tell him to go home, where it was safe. I remembered his bloody dagger found where Ernst had breathed his last.

"To protect us?" I repeated.

"Of course." He looked bewildered. He was an amazing actor.

A red handkerchief peeked out of Wilhelm's pocket. I drew it out and handed it to him. Let him hold it and think of what he'd done. Let him see the consequences today.

"Come in." I bit back my anger. "Let me get you a cup of tea."

He followed me into the kitchen, his shoulders thrown back as if he feared nothing. I smiled bitterly at the foolishness of the young. He had the most to fear from this meeting.

"Wilhelm?" Rudolf's shocked expression was wonderful to see.

"Son," said Lieutenant Lehmann. "This does not concern you. Go home."

Röhm eyed Wilhelm appraisingly, like Mother used to examine meat at the market for flaws. Finally, he smiled. "Sit, little one."

Wilhelm sat. I sat next to him.

Röhm turned his scarred face to me. "Now, Fraulein Vogel. Let me speak to your brother. He will restore that which is mine to me."

I cleared my throat. "What guarantee do I have of my safety once it is returned?" Did he want the ring or the letters?

"Has anyone threatened you?" Röhm's gaze wandered around the table before settling on Rudolf.

"I feel threatened." I clenched my hands under the table. I had never felt more threatened in my life. These men could easily kill me today.

"Why?" Röhm sipped his tea delicately, his eyes never leaving Rudolf.

Muscles in Rudolf's jaw stood out like cords, but he did not say a word. He had not expected me to come to this meeting.

"Yesterday my apartment was destroyed. And my cat killed." I too, looked at Rudolf.

"Mademoiselle Zee?" Röhm asked in a cold voice. "Ernst loves that cat."

"Not anymore," I said, thinking of how Ernst had always complained of Rudolf's jealousy. He once said that Rudolf was jealous of everyone and everything he liked.

Röhm looked at Rudolf, who was shades paler than when he'd arrived. "Explain yourself."

Rudolf smiled unctuously. "I'm not sure what—"

"It will be worse for you if you don't tell me now," Röhm said. "Don't be a fool and force me do something unpleasant."

He cocked his head expectantly and looked at Rudolf, his eyes cold.

"I h-hired it done," Rudolf stammered. He leaned back in his chair, looking at Röhm with terror. "To encourage Hannah and Ernst to find what you are looking for, Captain Röhm. I knew nothing of the cat until this very minute. I swear."

Röhm turned from Rudolf to me. Rudolf slumped in his chair, no expression on his face. Röhm would not let his deed go unpunished. I shivered.

"Bring your brother out of hiding," Röhm ordered. "I personally guarantee his safety, and yours, until this matter is resolved."

When I opened my mouth, no sound came out. I had prepared several speeches for this moment, but my mind was blank. Röhm's power was much more palpable and terrifying than I'd expected. I had never experienced anything like him.

Röhm nodded toward his lieutenant. "Lieutenant Lehmann will go with you to fetch your brother."

Lieutenant Lehmann leaped to his feet. His muscles shifted under his shirt. "Yes, sir."

I remained sitting. I did not trust my legs to support me. This was my cue. I took a deep breath. "He cannot fetch Ernst, as someone at this table well knows."

"Continue," Röhm said.

With icy cold hands, I fished Ernst's death photo out of my satchel and handed it to him.

Röhm dropped it on the table, his face ashen. The scar that ran across his face pulsed an ugly dark pink. A breeze from the open window blew the photograph across the table.

Rudolf snatched the photograph out of the air. Wilhelm looked over his shoulder and cried out.

"Someone murdered him." My voice gained strength. "Eight days ago."

"Who?" Röhm said in a controlled voice. "I will avenge him."

Rudolf stared at the photograph. Wilhelm buried his face in his hands and sobbed. Lieutenant Lehmann stood behind Röhm and made no move to comfort his son. A soldier like my own father, he did not abandon his post to comfort his crying children.

"Who?" Wilhelm sobbed. "Why?"

I looked at Wilhelm cynically. What would Röhm do if I revealed him? Kill him. Then another young life would be wasted.

"I do not know." I could not bring myself to do it. Ernst would not want it. But what was I to do instead?

"Where? When?" Wilhelm's voice was thick with tears.

"Very early the morning of May thirtieth," I said.

"Why would someone do this?" Rudolf asked, his eyes blank. "Ernst was not a threat to anyone." He turned to Röhm. "Did your men do this?"

"My men did no such thing." Röhm rose from the table and stood next to Rudolf. He placed his hands lightly on Rudolf's shoulders. Rudolf flinched. "Did yours, perhaps? The same ones who killed the cat?"

Rudolf shook his head rapidly. "Never. I love . . . loved Ernst. We had our—"

"Where did he die?" Wilhelm's hysterical voice cut above theirs. Did he want to be exposed?

"Near a bottle factory on the Spree." I closed my eyes, thinking of the hard cobblestones where we'd found the lead soldier and dagger. I saw Ernst's blood seep across the stones while a shadowy figure looked down on him in silence.

"But there's one only blocks from my house," Wilhelm cried. "Someone must have killed him right—"

"Someone," I said, opening my eyes. "Must have." Why did I protect him? He was a liar and a murderer. But a liar and a murderer whom Ernst had loved.

Wilhelm dropped his face to the table and sobbed. His shoulders jerked up and down.

His father slapped Wilhelm on the side of the head, and the retort echoed around the room. I jumped. My father had often hit Ernst and me like that.

"Soldiers do not cry like children," Lieutenant Lehmann said through teeth clenched with rage.

Wilhelm continued sobbing as if his father had not touched him. I put my hand on Wilhelm's back, and Lieutenant Lehmann glared at us both. How could he feel such revulsion for his own son? Wilhelm's weakness disgusted him, just as it disgusted him that his son loved men. My own father would have reacted no differently.

A thought chilled my mind to calm. What if Lieutenant Lehmann was there that night when Wilhelm brought Ernst home? What if he heard them, perhaps even saw them? He had access to the dagger. And he had beaten Ernst up once before, when he and Wilhelm were schoolboys.

I pictured him following Ernst after he climbed down the fire escape. Perhaps he walked with him, talked to him about Wilhelm, all the while moving him to a deserted alley. Somewhere they would not be seen. Then he stabbed him and watched him die. He stripped the clothes from my brother's dead body and dumped him in the Spree, thinking that he would be carried away and never found. And he might never have been discovered if I had not walked down the hall and seen his picture.

Wilhelm sobbed.

"You," I croaked, my throat painfully constricted. I pointed at Lieutenant Lehmann. "You."

Röhm's head whipped to face him. "Why is she pointing at you, Lieutenant?"

Lieutenant Lehmann took a step backward, glancing from Röhm to Wilhelm.

"Josef," Röhm roared. "You will answer me."

Lieutenant Lehmann stuttered, "I-I don't know."

"You were there that night," I said. "My brother's last night."

Röhm's voice grew deadly quiet. "Josef."

Lieutenant Lehmann froze, staring at Röhm.

"This boy." Röhm cleared his throat. "This boy had the secret to my future, to the future of the Sturm Abteilung in his hands. Did you know that?"

A flicker of confusion crossed Lieutenant Lehmann's face. "I had to protect my son."

"By leaving his dagger for anyone to find?" I pulled the dagger out of my satchel and slammed it on the table. Wilhelm stared at it, shocked into silence.

Röhm cleared his throat. "This is about something bigger than your son. That boy you killed was key to protecting me from the current allegations. And now he cannot. You have done a disservice to the Reich," Röhm said. "To me. A disservice from which I may never recover. The enemies of the Third Reich gather against me even now, as you well know."

He looked into Lieutenant Lehmann's eyes and continued speaking, "Do you understand that?"

Lieutenant Lehmann looked aghast. He regretted the damage he had caused Röhm, but not taking my brother's life.

Rage rose in me. I leaped toward him. Without turning his head, Röhm caught my wrist and twisted it behind my back. Pain seared through me. I fell to my knees.

"You know what you must do," Röhm spoke only to Lieutenant Lehmann.

Lieutenant Lehmann clicked his heels together, gave the old-fashioned Prussian salute, bowed, and left the room.

Röhm released me, and I climbed to my feet, rubbing my wrist. "I apologize for hurting you, Fraulein Vogel," Röhm said. "I only wished to prevent you from starting an altercation you could not win."

"Where is he going?" Wilhelm asked Röhm.

He should not have had to ask. If my father had been under similar circumstances, there would have been only one honorable way out.

"To do what he must do. What every soldier facing dishonor must do," Röhm said.

Wilhelm bolted toward the front door. My head told me to go after him, to help him save his father. But my heart wanted his father dead. Those were my feelings, and I was not proud of them. I sat at the table and buried my face in my hands, waiting.

Röhm paced, as if thinking about the next problem.

A gunshot cracked near the front door downstairs. Rudolf started. Had Lieutenant Lehmann ended his life like a good soldier? Or had Wilhelm stopped him? I took a step toward the door.

Röhm did not seem to care about the gunshot. He must have given Lieutenant Lehmann up for dead the minute he told him to go.

Röhm put a hand on my arm. "Do you have what I came for?"

"What did you come for?" I asked, numbly. If he would order his trusted lieutenant to take his own life, he would have no scruples about killing me.

"She knows nothing," Rudolf said in a hollow voice. "He wouldn't have known to tell her." He bowed his head and stared at the table.

If I had not been so frightened for myself, I might have pitied him.

Röhm glared into my eyes as if to read the answers from my mind without bothering with words. I kept my chin up and did not blink. After a few terrifying seconds, he turned away. I sat down again.

"So he is lost," Röhm said to Rudolf. "You have lost him."

That made no sense to me. Did he mean Ernst? Or Lieutenant Lehmann?

Rudolf raised his head. He was pale, but his eyes were focused again. "I did not know of Ernst's death."

Röhm paced the room, but Rudolf and I sat as if pinned to our chairs. I did not want to call attention to myself by moving. I had no idea what Röhm and Rudolf were talking about. I was afraid to say anything lest my ignorance doom me to death.

"It has been a week, Rudolf," said Röhm in his round, southern German accent. "Seven days and my son is missing and alone. A boy of five."

A boy of five. The words echoed in my ears, but my mind could not make sense of them. Would not make sense of them.

Röhm and Rudolf walked into the bedroom. I stared at the dagger on my mother's table. A boy of five.

As if in a dream, I stood and followed them.

"I told you," Röhm yelled at Rudolf, poking him in the chest with each word, "to take care of him until I returned from Bolivia. I sent you money for his care in case I needed him. And you lost him."

Rudolf stared at him without speaking.

"I want my son," Röhm roared. "Now."

"I am here, Father," Anton said. He stepped out of the wardrobe, clutching Winnetou.

"Anton!" Röhm and I screamed simultaneously.

Anton walked to Röhm's side. "He is my father. You are my mother."

He must have crept in when I went to buy the tea. "Your father?"

The room spun around me. It was the wrong Ernst. Ernst Vogel was not his father. Ernst Röhm was. Röhm wanted neither the ring nor the letters. He wanted the only thing that mattered.

"She is not your mother." Röhm embraced Anton, lifting him like a toy. He turned to Rudolf. "What nonsense have you put in the boy's head?"

The sound of Wilhelm sobbing drifted through the front window. I could not bring myself to care.

"It is her nonsense," Rudolf said weakly, waving his thin hand at me.

I hesitated. I could produce the forged birth certificate and implicate Rudolf, but I stayed my hand. Why *had* Rudolf had it made? Perhaps Röhm had ordered him to make it, in case he needed to deny that Anton was his son.

"How long have you been caring for him?" Röhm asked me, and the moment passed.

"He appeared a few days after my brother's death. I have not cared for him long." I would not lie to Röhm if I could avoid it.

Rudolf crossed to the window.

"Nor well," Rudolf sneered, turning to face us. "The people you associate with."

He wanted to blame Anton's childhood on me. He would not want Röhm to know that his child was raised by a drug addict and a prostitute.

"I have had him only a week," I said. "No more. I am not responsible for him being raised by a boot girl from Wittenbergplatz."

Röhm rounded on Rudolf, his face furious. "A boot girl? My Elise became a boot girl?"

"It was the drug." Rudolf paced the floor. "There was nothing I could do."

"You could have told me," Röhm bit off each word. "I would have bought drugs for her myself before letting her live that kind of life. Before letting my son live it."

"I can explain"—Rudolf lifted one hand—"first—"

"You have much to answer for," Röhm said in the same quiet voice he'd used to speak to Lieutenant Lehmann. "But not in front of my son. Not here."

"Are you certain he's your son?" I glanced between them. I saw no resemblance between Röhm's strong square face and Anton's tiny pointed one. If the mother was a prostitute, any soldier might have been the father.

Röhm nodded. "I saw him often before I went to Bolivia and left him in Rudolf's care, to be hidden and cared for."

"This child?" I could barely breathe. "This one?"

"He is mine." Röhm smiled proudly. "He is a born warrior. And his existence will answer charges about matters that are becoming sticky for the party. Producing a male heir will show enough virility to stave off the current investigation."

"Investigation?" I said.

"Paragraph 175," Röhm said. "Political nonsense."

"We could find a proper mother," Rudolf said, "for the boy."

"What is wrong with my Elise? We can help her get better. There—"

"Not in front of the boy," I interjected, regaining my wits. "Ask Rudolf alone, later."

"I know nothing of his mother's whereabouts," Rudolf said.

Röhm ignored him. "Say good-bye to your aunt Hannah."

Anton cried against his father's shoulder.

"Come now." Röhm lifted Anton's chin and wiped his eyes with his stubby fingers. "It's not as bad as all that. You'll see her on holidays, perhaps."

"Where are you taking him?" My mind was slow, and I had trouble speaking.

"As soon as I can, I'll enroll him in Wahlstatt Cadet School. After that, the Royal Prussian Military Preparatory College at Potsdam. They're the finest schools in Germany."

I nodded. They were. Father had spoken of the graduates with awe in his voice. Paul von Hindenburg. Baron von Richthofen. Anton's future was now assured. He would become a warrior like his father. If the Nazis kept control of the government, he would have access to worlds that I could never give him.

I pulled the red silk handkerchief out of my satchel. "For you," I said. Tears ran down my cheeks. "To remember me by."

Anton nodded and took it. Röhm bent his head to talk to him.

Rudolf walked behind me and clamped his hand over my arm, right on the spot where he'd bruised me earlier at the paper. "Say good-bye," he whispered in my ear, and a round steel object pressed against the back of my ribs. "Let the boy go without a fuss."

I turned my head to look at him. His eyes were wild and bright. My knees collapsed, but Rudolf held me upright.

"The bullet would pass through your body and hit him," Rudolf whispered. "Or perhaps the second one would."

I did not think he would dare to take on Röhm, but I could not take a chance, not with Anton's life. I waved. "Good-bye, little Indian." My voice did not sound like my own.

Röhm did not seem to notice Rudolf pressed so closely against my back. "Good-bye, Fraulein Vogel. Thank you for caring for him."

Anton waved Winnetou's paw at me. He looked as shocked as I felt.

"Tomorrow, Rudolf," Röhm said. "Nine o'clock. At your office. I will find you if you are late, and you do not want that."

I tightened my jaw, angered that my death should be at Rudolf's hands. He did not deserve to end my life. He was not worthy of it.

Röhm walked out the door. The sound of his footsteps receded down the hall and with them my chances of surviving this encounter. I hoped that Röhm would keep Anton from seeing Lieutenant Lehmann's body if he was dead on the front steps.

Rudolf let go of my arm, and I turned. He trained the gun on my heart.

"I'll not let you destroy me," he said. "I'll come up with an explanation for the boot girl."

"We can talk about this." I stepped backward. Perhaps I could climb through the window.

"She was a prostitute when he met her. He knows that," Rudolf said, as if trying to convince himself. His nose started to bleed.

"Perhaps he won't care that she worked Wittenbergplatz." I smiled placatingly. "If he already knew she was a prostitute, why would he care what patch she worked?" If Rudolf remembered the fury in Röhm's voice when he discovered that she had become a boot girl, skilled in perversions, he would know that Röhm cared a great deal that she had worked at Wittenbergplatz.

Rudolf wiped his bleeding nose with the back of his left hand. The gun trembled in his right. "He'll care. She was a semi-pro when he knew her, working the barracks. Straight sex."

"A girl has to make a living." I was half a meter from the window. He was a coward. He'd dodged his war service. He probably did not know how to aim a gun, let alone shoot one. I knew I was trying to convince myself to lunge for the window, but I stood uncertainly. I did not believe that I would make it to the ground alive, as much as I wanted to.

"He sent her money for years." Rudolf laughed. "It wasn't much. I kept a small handling fee."

"For your hard work," I said. "Röhm will understand that."

"I did everything else as he asked," Rudolf explained. "I forged a birth certificate so that he could deny the boy's paternity if he needed to. He and Elise never had much of a relationship to begin with. Who knows if they even had sex once. Anyone could be the father."

"Why did you use my name?"

"Delivering the money was one of Ernst's jobs, and he grew fond of the boy. Ernst suggested I use his name for the father. Once I used his name, you seemed like the best candidate," he said. "Besides, I never liked you."

The bed was right behind my back. Perhaps I could circle behind it and slip through the door. But Rudolf must have seen something in my eyes.

"I've never killed anyone before." Rudolf pulled the trigger.

A wave of heat surged through my body. I fell onto Ernst's bed, covering the hole that hid the letters. Hot blood seeped out of my left side.

The gun knocked against the bed as Rudolf bent over me, smiling. "I was never responsible for your brother. You were."

Pain flashed up my body. I pressed against the bullet hole with my hand. Rudolf had won, after all.

He glanced out the window, probably looking for Röhm.

Footsteps pounded in the distance. Röhm flung open the door, Anton at his side. Röhm glanced from me to Rudolf.

Rudolf came to himself with a start and pointed the gun at Röhm.

Röhm tucked Anton under his uniform jacket as if he were a kitten and bounded to Rudolf.

The figures went out of focus, and I pushed my hands harder against my side. Pain cleared my vision. Blood leaked between my fingers.

Röhm snatched the gun from Rudolf's hand as if he were a teacher confiscating a slingshot from a naughty pupil. Rudolf paled and took a step toward the open window.

As Röhm raised the gun, Anton slipped from his grasp and ran toward me. When Röhm turned to nab him, Rudolf leaped out the window. A faraway groan told me that Rudolf had not landed well. Good.

Röhm glanced out the window with the gun drawn. He shook his head and came back to where Anton stood holding my bloody hand and Winnetou.

Sirens. *Ta-to. Ta-ta.* Someone must have called the police when Lieutenant Lehmann shot himself.

Röhm bent down and ripped through Ernst's sheet, fashioning a makeshift bandage around me.

"Field dressing," he said. "It will have to do."

The sirens grew louder.

I opened my mouth, but no sound came out.

Röhm peeled Anton's hand off mine. Anton slid the bear next to my face before Röhm hoisted him in his arms. I turned my head into the soft plush fur and listened to Röhm's footsteps fading into the distance. Winnetou's battered face was the last thing I saw.

26

Strong light shone on my eyelids. Would I see Ernst? Our parents? Walter? I was afraid to open my eyes. I took a deep breath and waited.

"Hannah," said a familiar voice. "You slept at my house often enough when we were girls for me to know when you're pretending to be asleep."

Bettina. I opened my eyes. She sat next to my bed, her knitting in her lap, and a relieved expression on her face. A soft breeze whispered through an open window nearby.

"Thank goodness," she said. "Now I can go home."

"How long?" I croaked. My throat was dry, and I cleared it. I looked around the room. I lay in a narrow bed in a small room with gleaming floors and sickly yellow walls. The smell of disinfectant mingled with the comforting vanilla scent of Bettina's perfume.

Bettina poured a glass of water from a carafe on a small table near the bed.

"Drink this." Lifting my head, she held it to my lips, as for a sick child. Swallowing hurt my ribs, but I drank the entire glass obediently. She pulled my pillow up expertly and helped me into a semi-sitting position. Pain shot up through my side, and my head throbbed. I tried to cover my eyes with my hand to shut out the sunlight.

"What day is it?"

"Monday," Bettina said, standing and drawing the curtains. "You were shot on Sunday afternoon. The bullet grazed your ribs and you cracked your head on something, but you're not badly hurt, so don't expect me to play nursemaid forever." I heard relief in her voice.

"Where am I?"

"Hospital," she said. She held up Winnetou, wrapped in my peacock-green scarf from Ernst. "Where's Anton?"

"His father took him." I noticed a speck of blood on the bear's ear. My blood.

"Ernst? Why didn't he stay to help you?" Bettina handed me the bear, and I pressed him against my face. He still smelled like kerosene, from the bath I'd given him to kill the lice. It was oddly comforting.

"Wrong Ernst," I said. "Anton's father is Ernst Röhm."

Bettina sat back down in the chair, her mouth open in shock. Voices passed by the corridor outside my room, arguing. "Tell me."

"My brother's boyfriend Rudolf is Ernst Röhm's lawyer. Röhm has been supporting Anton through him since he left for Bolivia."

"Are you certain?"

"I know nothing for certain. Röhm wants to raise Anton. He wants to send him to Wahlstatt Cadet School."

"That's fortunate for Anton." Bettina tucked a stray lock of brown hair behind her ear. "A powerful father means a good future."

"A powerful Nazi father? One who views him only as a political pawn?" I asked. "I want Anton back."

"Oh, Hannah." Bettina leaned forward and patted my hands. "Of course you do, but he's not yours. He never was."

"I have a birth certificate with my name on it as his mother." I clasped the bear.

"A forgery. Röhm probably has an authentic birth certificate with his name on it." Bettina shook her head. "You know better than this."

"I love Anton," I said, and I realized that it was true. He was strong and clever and funny, and he was part of my family, all of my family, whether Röhm was his father or not. Without him I was alone. How could I let him go? "I love him," I repeated.

"I do too," she said. "He's a dear heart. But he's not your son. He's not related to you."

There was a knock on the door, and Fritz entered, looking exhausted. Two detectives stood behind him, one fat and one thin. They stayed outside. Fritz closed the door on them before coming over to my bed.

"Bettina," I said. "Were you here all night?"

"With all of the children at home, I enjoyed the quiet," she said. "Let me find you some breakfast." She bustled out the door.

"Good morning," Fritz said. "Glad to see you awake. You're a very lucky girl."

I laughed, but it hurt my ribs and my head, and I had to stop, breathing heavily through the pain.

"Another few centimeters to the left and you wouldn't be here," said Fritz.

"Another few centimeters to the right and I'd be fine."

"I think the shooter would have taken another shot if he'd missed you entirely," Fritz said dryly.

"We were mostly worried about the blood you lost." Bettina entered the room with a tray containing a bowl of oatmeal and a cup of tea. "You have to eat and drink to get your strength back."

I took a few bites of oatmeal because I did not have the strength to argue with Bettina about it. It was cold and slimy. The tea I drank gratefully.

"Now, darling wife," Fritz said. "I'm going to ask you to be very quiet while Hannah tells her story."

"Like a mouse."

He gave her an affectionate look. "Those mice that squeak and rustle in the walls and keep me up nights?"

She put a finger to her lips and shook her head.

"Ernst is dead." I pushed aside the tray of food. "He was one of those floaters from last week."

Bettina gasped and took my hand. I could finally admit it. I sat in the bed and cried. Bettina enfolded me in her warm arms. Even without seeing her face, I knew that she was looking sternly at Fritz, cautioning him not to question me until I finished crying.

Eventually, I let go of Bettina and dried my eyes on the handkerchief she gave me. Like Fritz's handkerchief the day I'd seen Ernst's picture, it smelled of starch. Bettina smoothed my hair out of my eyes and inched her chair closer to the bed.

"So that's why you stole the picture," Fritz said.

"You knew?" I said, shocked that he had done nothing about it.

Fritz paced up and down the tiny room. "I am no fool, Hannah. I trusted that you had a good reason and that you would bring it back when you were done with it."

"Do you know who killed him?" Bettina squeezed my hand.

"Josef Lehmann," I pushed the words out, knowing that they had to be said. "Ernst Röhm's lieutenant."

"He was found shot to death at the bottom of Ernst's stairs," Bettina said, her eyes round. "What happened?"

So he had followed Röhm's orders, died the only way a soldier in disgrace could die. Ernst's murder was avenged, but I felt no joy in it.

Fritz turned to her. "Bettina, my dear, you must leave the room now."

I had never heard Fritz use that tone with her before. She pressed her lips together and left the room without a word.

"Continue," Fritz said, but before I could speak, Kommissar Lang stormed in.

"I assume command here," he said, his high-pitched voice angry. "I am in charge of this investigation."

Fritz nodded.

"You may leave the room," Kommissar Lang said. Fritz cast me a sympathetic glance before he closed the door.

Kommissar Lang poured me another glass of water. "You haven't been completely honest with me, have you, Fraulein Vogel?"

I shook my head. How much truth could I tell him?

"Shall you begin now?"

I smiled weakly. Now was the time to remember the things Mother had taught me about proper ladylike behavior. A proper lady would be fragile in my condition and a proper gentleman would want to help her.

"Tell me what happened at the apartment where you were shot. Leave nothing out."

"Rudolf von Reiche shot me." My voice quivered. I sat up in panic, looking around the room. The wound in my side hurt, and I gasped. "He'll come back for me."

Kommissar Lang smiled encouragingly. "We have two detectives outside your door. He could not get past them."

I sank back against the bed, breathing hard. Moving hurt more than I'd expected.

"What was Herr von Reiche doing at this apartment? What were you?"

"It was my brother's apartment. I was there to meet Ernst Röhm."

"Why?"

"He and my brother were . . ." I paused. "Friends."

"Why was Herr von Reiche there?"

"Is Wilhelm Lehmann being taken care of?"

"Why would you ask about him?" Kommissar Lang leaned forward solicitously.

"I heard a shot," I said. "Lieutenant Lehmman left the room most upset, and his son followed him, and I heard a shot."

"Perhaps we should begin at the beginning." Kommissar Lang placed Ernst's death photograph on my lap. "How about starting with the day that you saw this at the Hall of the Unnamed Dead and lied to me?"

"Forgive me," I said. Perhaps he could be led to believe that shame over my brother's life had kept me quiet. I dared not let him suspect that I had other reasons for remaining silent. Loaning Sarah my papers was a criminal act. I silently cursed him and his party friends for putting Sarah in danger and forcing me down this path. If I'd had my papers, I could have let the police investigate this entire affair. Aloud I said, "I was distraught. There was much about my brother that I did not want the world to know, you least of all."

Kommissar Lang looked unconvinced.

"My brother was—" My voice broke. It was a relief to talk about him in the past tense, to admit that he was dead, even to Kommissar Lang. "He loved—"

I took another sip of water and pulled myself together. Kommissar Lang sat politely, his pen poised over a notebook.

"My brother loved men." I dropped my eyes to my hands. "From the time he was a boy."

I stared at the light reflecting off the water in my glass. Kommissar Lang let the silence lengthen.

"His lover was Rudolf von Reiche, the man who shot me." I took a deep breath. It was difficult telling this to Kommissar Lang. I wished that Fritz had stayed, that someone was here who understood Ernst and trusted me. I did not tell Kommissar Lang of my brother's relationship with Röhm.

I told Kommissar Lang as much of the truth as I could. I told him that Lehmann had killed Ernst for having an affair with his son, Wilhelm. That Röhm had told Lehmann that he was a disgrace and he disappeared, and I heard a shot. That Rudolf had shot me to keep me from telling Röhm more about his son's childhood. That Röhm had taken Anton, and that he might be the boy's father, although since his mother had been a prostitute when Anton was born, anyone might be the father. I explained that Sweetie Pie was probably the mother, although I was no longer certain of anything.

Kommissar Lang listened attentively. I almost broke down a few times, but I held myself together. I needed to get through it all.

"Why were you in your brother's apartment with all of them?" Kommissar Lang asked.

"Rudolf threatened me," I said, not mentioning the Röhm letters. If I told the police about them, they would confiscate them as proof that Röhm committed the crime of sodomy and prosecute him under

Paragraph 175. But Röhm and Hitler had allies in the courts and they might destroy the letters, and Röhm would walk free. If the letters were published, their destruction would not matter. The courts would have to decide under pressure of public opinion. "He told me that Ernst had something Röhm wanted and that we were going to meet in Ernst's apartment to discuss it."

"Why didn't you call the police? Or talk to your friend Waldheim?"

"I was afraid. After what Rudolf did to my apartment I was afraid that he would kill the boy. And me." I smiled wryly. "As he almost did."

"What did Röhm want?"

"His son, although I did not know that at the time."

"What did you think it was?" Kommissar Lang raised his eyebrows.

"Something else. Anything else." I looked over at the white curtains blocking the light.

"What else could it be?"

"Where is Wilhelm?" I asked. "Was he there when your men arrived?"

Kommissar Lang nodded. "He was."

"Is someone with him? He should not be alone."

"He is protected," Kommissar Lang said. "Tell me more about his father's death."

"I know little about it. He left the room."

Kommissar Lang began his questioning again. It seemed as if hours passed. I answered the same questions, my voice hoarse from talking. I did not tell him about Sarah, the letters, or the ruby ring. About everything else I told the truth, again and again.

I retched. Kommissar Lang handed me a bowl, and resumed his questioning. So much for relying on his gentleman's background.

Eventually a doctor appeared, furious.

I lay in bed trembling, too weak to do anything else. My head pounded.

The large and reassuring doctor took my pulse and gave me two tablets. They tasted bitter.

"Is she well enough to continue?" Kommissar Lang asked.

The doctor shook his head. "She wasn't well enough to start. If I'd been here, I would have kept you from her bedside."

Kommissar Lang stood. "It is police business."

"The hospital is my business." The doctor held my wrist. "I must insist that you leave. Here, I outrank you."

Kommissar Lang tried to stare him down, but the doctor did not budge.

Kommissar Lang bent and whispered in my ear. "I hope, for your own sake, that you have told me the whole truth. I do not wish to see you in jail any more than you wish to go."

He straightened and walked out of the room.

The doctor let go of my wrist. His eyes were kind and green, like a forest in summer. "The medication is taking effect already. Rest. You must sleep for the next few days to get your strength back."

I wanted to get out of bed and float through the window to freedom. Float? What kind of medication had he given me? I tried to sit up, but could not. Unwillingly, I slept. I needed more strength to escape.

27

I awoke to the gentle light of the late afternoon. A familiar-looking doctor held my wrist, taking my pulse. He wore a white lab coat and was turned away from the door, counting out my heartbeats. His dark head turned to face me.

"Paul." I tried to sit. The room spun, and I suppressed an urge to throw up.

"You shouldn't sit in your condition, Fraulein Vogel." Paul eased me down onto the pillow.

"Why are you wearing that coat?" I asked quietly.

"There are two detectives outside." Paul's eyes darted toward the door. "No one is allowed in to see you, although there's a handsome man who's been trying all day."

"A handsome man?" I smiled. "You?"

He shook his head. "Boris. I can't stay long. I had to use all my journalistic expertise to get in here." His eyes twinkled. *Journalistic expertise* were our code words for lying. "I intercepted a letter addressed to you at the paper. It's under your pillow, with your passport."

"They made it."

He nodded. "Sarah and Tobias are in New York."

I had my papers. I could leave Berlin. I could leave Germany. Rudolf could not harm me if I was far away.

"I don't know what's going on with you," he whispered. "I don't do the crime beat, so I don't have any sources at the police station. What I do know is that the man who insisted Peter Weill be fired—"

"Rudolf von Reiche."

The fat detective glanced our way, and Paul leaned over and pried one of my eyelids farther open. He peered into my eye officiously. "He disappeared. There was a story about it this morning. Maria's been in touch with his family for quotes already. Apparently he was expected at an important dinner last night and did not appear."

I wondered if Röhm had killed him or if Rudolf was hiding out, waiting to silence me. He had more reasons to want me dead than ever before, now that I could accuse him of attempted murder. He had escaped from Röhm the night he shot me, because Röhm had tried to protect Anton from seeing me, and because Röhm had stopped to bind my wound.

"I told Boris to wait in front of the hospital for you." Paul let go of my eyelid and brushed hair off my forehead casually, but I felt his hand tremble. "That maybe you could take a walk soon. He has a black Mercedes."

I could not stay in the hospital. Rudolf would bribe someone to turn his head or give me an injection or slip something into my food. The next person who came to take my pulse could stop it. I was the only one who could link Rudolf to my shooting, except Röhm.

"You're looking much better," Paul said in a normal voice. "A few more days of rest and you'll be in tiptop shape."

"Thank you, Doctor," I said. "For everything."

I squeezed his hand. Paul took my hand between both of his, and I stared into his dark eyes. So much was left unsaid. The thin policeman started into the room. Paul dropped my hand.

"Until later, Fraulein Vogel," he said.

I nodded and watched him leave.

A few minutes after Paul left, I called for the nurse and asked to be taken to the bathroom. I washed my face and hands, listening to the sound of water outside. When I glanced through the narrow window, I saw a fountain and empty benches ahead. I was on the first floor. I had to go for a walk to see how I might get out. The disinfectant from the floors reeked. I was light-headed and dizzy.

"I wish to go outside now," I said.

The nurse looked at the detectives. The fat one sighed and stood. "We'll go with her."

Were they here to protect me from Rudolf? More likely they were here to keep me from escaping. I guess it depended on whether they thought I had shot Lieutenant Lehmann or he'd shot himself.

I felt better as soon as we got outside. The air smelled fresh and clean, and a light breeze played on my face. I stood, wondering what to do. And then I saw Boris at the edge of the front hospital lawn, leaning on his automobile. He did look handsome, as Paul had said. He wore a dark-blue three-piece suit with a burgundy tie. He looked every bit the banker.

I walked in his direction, nurse and policemen in tow.

He glanced over when he saw us coming and stood. He took a step toward us, but I turned away from him, and he stopped. Out of the corner of my eye I saw him lean back against the car again.

"Do you see that bird?" I asked the nurse, pointing to a giant fountain next to the street. I watched Boris's head move to follow my pointing finger. I only hoped he could guess that I wanted him to go there. I did not dare speak to him with the policemen around.

"I don't see it, ma'am," she said. "But my eyesight's not so good."

"I am not feeling too strong after all," I said. "Can we go back to my room?"

Sweat soaked my hospital gown by the time I lay back down.

The detectives stationed themselves outside my door again.

"I'll go get your doctor," said the nurse. "You don't look well."

"I'll be fine."

She shook her head. "I'll send your doctor by as soon as he finishes his rounds," she said before closing the door.

I slid out of bed and hurried to the bathroom, carrying a small bundle containing my scarf, my passport, a fifty-mark bill Paul had thoughtfully tucked inside it, and Winnetou. I had to get out before the doctor came. I had no idea how long Boris would wait, if he'd be there at all.

I locked the bathroom door, tossed the bundle through the window, and climbed out myself. Luckily my room was on the first floor. The way the world spun, I would not have made it down any drainpipes.

Wind blew under the thin hospital gown I wore, as I'd had no clothes in my room. I wrapped the green scarf around my shoulders. If Boris was any less clever than I hoped, I'd soon be caught and kept under such close watch that I'd never escape again. I took a deep breath, straightened my shoulders, and walked across the grass as if I was supposed to be strolling around the front of the hospital unattended.

Boris waited where I'd pointed, with his motor running. He leaned across and opened the passenger door.

I slid into the front seat and crouched on the floor clutching the bear. Boris's citrus-and-cedar scent filled the air. Comforting, like Christmas.

"This isn't what I thought would happen when the police called me last night." He pulled out into the street without glancing down at me.

"Why did they call you?" My ribs throbbed every time I took a breath, and my head spun.

"You had my card. Remember?" Boris drove calmly and confidently. "I told them I was your banker."

I laughed. "Really?"

"It is not entirely untrue," Boris said, looking down at me.

I climbed onto the seat and wrapped the scarf around myself.

"Are you cold?"

"Just feeling modest."

"In such a fetching frock?" Boris's beautiful lips smiled down at me.

I did not answer.

"Am I breaking you out of police custody?" he asked.

"Aren't you better off not knowing the answer to that, so that you can deny it later?"

"I guess that's my answer."

We drove to his house, a grand manor in Zehlendorf, on Kronprinzen Avenue. We pulled to the back door, and he draped his suit jacket around me. I wondered if it was to keep me warm or to spare the neighbors.

Boris wrapped his arm around my shoulders and helped me through his back door.

"I can walk on my own." I tried to pull away.

Boris did not let go. "If you could see how weak you look, you would save your strength for walking."

I followed his advice because he was so obviously correct. We inched up a flight of marble stairs to a bedroom. A light blue quilt covered an antique four-poster bed. Everything in the room was in perfect order and shone in the sun. Boris was a meticulous man, or a man with a meticulous housekeeper.

"You are as white as chalk." He sat me down on the bed. "Do you need anything?"

I shook my head, fighting waves of nausea. Boris left and returned with a glass of water.

When I could breathe normally again, I glanced at him. He looked worried, but also slightly amused.

"Would you like to tell me why I've broken the law?" He handed me the water.

"You broke no law." I took a sip of cool water, then another. "You picked up a woman next to the hospital."

"A suspect in a murder case, I believe." He took the glass from my hand and set it on his night table.

"Did the police tell you that?" I wondered what he knew.

He shook his head. "They said that you were found, covered in blood, in suspicious circumstances, with a dead man downstairs. They suggested that you had shot him, in self defense, and he wandered down the stairs to die. I have no idea what the truth is."

I pulled his jacket closer around myself, cold.

"I have to say that you are acting very suspiciously," Boris said. "Please tell me that I won't regret my decision."

"I cannot give advice on regret," I answered.

Boris studied me before speaking again. "Why did you need to leave the hospital?"

"I had to get away from the hospital. I am in danger." Even I could hear that I sounded like an actress in a bad movie, so I talked more quickly. "The man who shot me will try again."

Boris raised his eyebrows. "He is not dead then?"

I shook my head. "He is not dead. And I did not shoot the man who was dead, as that is probably your next question. He shot himself."

For a few seconds we sat in silence. "Do you have any clothes I could borrow?" I asked.

He left the room. A few moments he came back and handed me a simple cotton nightdress and a woman's robe. "Here you are. They're from Trudi, but I think they'll fit. I hope they will fit." He smiled his movie-star smile, his eyes twinkling. "I certainly don't want to anger you, if what the police said is true."

I thanked him and locked myself in his luxurious bathroom. The floor was marble, and a footed tub stood in the corner. A large modern mirror with a black border hung over the sink. I looked terrible. My fair skin was paler than usual and drawn tight over my cheekbones. Strangely vacant eyes, a shade too dark, stared at me from the mirror. My fingertips explored a lump on the back of my head. It was the size of a duck egg and had a thin scab running down the middle.

My breasts were smashed flat under a thick band that held a wad of gauze in place against my left side. I looked like a boy. A dirty, bloody boy. I knew it was stupid and vain, but tears trickled down my cheeks.

I'd lost a child who had never been mine to begin with. My brother was dead. A handsome man who had rescued me from police custody without a word waited outside the door, and I looked like a morphine addict freshly released from the hospital after an overdose.

I sat on the toilet seat and cried out my grief and self-pity.

Finally, I stood and washed my hair in the sink. It made me dizzy, but it also felt good to have clean, wet hair. The shampoo smelled rich and luxuriant. It probably cost more than my weekly food budget. After I washed and dressed, I felt better than I had since the shooting.

When I came out I smelled beef broth with onions. I inched down the stairs, clutching the brass railing in an effort to keep the stairs from moving.

"You're looking much better." Boris stood on the checkerboard floor of his tiny kitchen. He wore suit trousers, a white shirt, and an apron. "I made beef tea and toast for you. I wasn't sure what you would be able to keep down."

The broth was wonderful, rich and meaty. I forced myself to sip it. I wanted it to stay down.

While I ate, Boris talked about the weather, his boat, anything but what he most wanted to know.

"Thank you," I said, pushing the bowl aside at last.

"Where's Anton?" he asked, finally.

"With his father." Light from the kitchen window reflected off his thick hair and lit his dark, gold-speckled eyes.

"Is that good?"

I sighed. "Oh, Boris."

He gathered me into his arms and held me while I told him all I dared. I did not mention the ring or the letters or anything about Sarah. He too, wanted to know why I had not gone to the police when I first saw Ernst's picture, and he too, did not believe my answers, but he did not press me.

When I finished, Boris said, "You are a woman of great strength."

I shook my head. "I only do what must be done."

"There is strength in that."

I changed the subject and talked about Anton. How much I missed him. How much he loved Winnetou, the Apache brave in the Karl May stories. How he wanted to be a warrior. When I wound down, Boris said quietly, "He's not your son, Hannah; more's the pity."

"I know."

"He has a father to care for him now. A man of wealth and power."

He sounded like Bettina. "A man who left me to die," I said. "He's been back in Germany for six months, and he was content to leave his son in the care of a woman he knew was a prostitute until it became politically expedient to claim him. He does not love the boy. He might not even be his father."

"Perhaps not. But he has a stronger claim as Anton's father than you do as his mother." Boris took my hand as if I were a small child, but he aroused feelings in me that were not childlike. "And he is not all bad. He bound your wound and left before the police could cause him trouble. Maybe he knew that the police would care for you better than he could. He drove your killer away and he protected the boy. That should count for something."

I felt weary. Not the blinding exhaustion that I'd felt earlier in the day, but an unbearable weariness.

"Let it be, Hannah. It's not your fight." Boris's hand felt warm against mine. "Stay here until you are better. Until Rudolf is found. Then go on with your life."

"What life?" I said. "I have no job. No family. Nothing. No one."

He looked deep into my eyes, and I could tell that he hurt for me. "Not quite no one."

The front door opened and Trudi's voice called out, "Vati, we're home."

Boris took his arms from around me and stood. "Wait here."

I nodded.

Boris walked across the kitchen with quick strides. I heard him talking in a low voice. Trudi's higher voice answered, sounding indignant. A third voice joined in. The housekeeper?

I dropped my head on my arms on the table and drifted off to sleep. The slam of the front door woke me, and I started up, disoriented. My heart pounded. Where was I? Where was Anton? I had to retrieve the ring and the letters.

I stood and stumbled. Boris was suddenly by my side. He caught my arm, as always.

"I think you need to sleep somewhere a bit more comfortable."

"Where's Trudi?" I asked, remembering where I was.

"I sent her to her grandmother's."

Boris helped me up the stairs. He drew back the light quilt for me and helped me climb into bed. I could not remember if anyone had ever helped me go to bed before, even when I was a small child. He tucked me in between his fine linen sheets and kissed my eyelids. "Sleep, Hannah. Let me take care of you, at least for a little while."

I felt the reassuring pressure of his body sitting on the edge of the bed until I fell asleep. It was the best sleep I'd had in years.

28

Shadows of leaves danced across the ceiling in the bright morning light. I lay very still, trying to remember where I was, and why I felt so happy. My head throbbed dully and my side still hurt, but it was manageable. I glanced over at the edge of the bed and remembered Boris sitting there the night before. I ran my hand over the spot where he must have sat.

Stiffly, I climbed out of bed and smoothed the covers back into place. A simple dress of Trudi's hung on a chair next to the bed. The house was empty, but Boris had left a note on the kitchen table telling me to help myself to breakfast. A *Berliner Tageblatt* lay neatly folded in the middle of the table.

I ate a huge breakfast at the tiny table and read through the paper. Rudolf was still missing, and the police suspected foul play. I was not mentioned. There was a feature on Ernst Röhm's unification with his long-lost son, whose mother was missing. So, did they not want to admit that a former prostitute was the mother of Röhm's son, or was the true mother someone else entirely, someone who was truly missing? The picture accompanying the story showed Anton and Röhm dressed in dark-colored suits staring grimly into the camera. Anton Röhm looked like a boy who had lost his mother.

I paged to the obituaries. Josef Lehmann's obituary stressed his importance to the Nazi party and mentioned that he was survived only by a son, Wilhelm Lehmann. It did not say how he had died. His funeral was scheduled in three days. It would be a grand Nazi pageant. I imagined Wilhelm at the center of such a spectacle, alone. His father had given his life to protect Wilhelm and do his duty for the party. I wondered how Wilhelm felt about being a Nazi now.

After I dressed, I used Boris's telephone to call a taxi. It was extravagant, but I had no strength to find a bus stop or sit on a jerky train. I silently thanked Paul for the money he'd given me in the hospital. Outside it was chilly, and I grabbed Boris's jacket from the hall closet. It was another thing of his that I had to use. I added it to the list of things that I owed him.

I took the taxi to Wilhelm's house, remembering the address he'd written on the beer coaster that first night at the El Dorado. I rang his bell over and over until he opened the door, his face swollen from crying and deep circles under his eyes.

"Hannah," he said. "What more could you possibly want from me?"

"I came to see if you needed help."

He opened the door. "Help me then." The smell of alcohol on his breath was overpowering.

He led me down a narrow dark hall. The wall inside his front door had a large signed picture of Hitler. "To my dear friend, Josef, for your service to the Reich. Adolf Hitler." It was placed so that you would see it every time you entered the apartment.

I turned my back on the picture and walked to the living room. Without being invited, I sat in an austere leather chair. Wilhelm threw himself like a sack onto the sofa across from me. I glanced around at the spare furniture. Nothing hung on the walls. This was a soldier's room, spartan and simple.

"I must apologize for not helping you," Wilhelm said, after several minutes of silence. "I didn't know you were up there, bleeding."

I opened my mouth to speak, but he raised his palm to stop me.

"I'm not the kind of person who would let someone die without helping," he continued. "But my father was dying."

He bowed his head. Tears fell unheeded into his lap. Although I longed to cross the room and comfort him, I stayed put. He would not welcome my comfort.

"I didn't know." He gulped and wiped his nose on his sleeve. "You were up there, bleeding, I would have gone up to help you, if I'd known."

"I know." I believed him. Wilhelm was a good person, still. I wondered how long his goodness would last as he fought and killed with the Nazis.

"I found out when they were taking you down on a stretcher. You were soaked in blood, pale as snow. But the police said you would live, and then they took me."

"Took you?"

"They asked me how my father died. What we were doing there."

"And what did you tell them?"

"I said that we were accompanying Röhm to a meeting, but that I did not know more than that. I barely did know more than that."

"What did you say about your father?"

Wilhelm stared at his folded hands. I listened to the ticking of a clock.

"I said that he shot himself in the chest, when I was only steps away from him."

"Oh, Wilhelm."

He spoke over me. "That I held his head while he was dying, but he never said a word."

I crossed the room and sat next to him. I reached for his hand, but stopped myself.

"He loved me," Wilhelm said, his voice a whisper in the quiet room.

"Yes," I answered softly.

"Ernst. My father. Both of them loved me."

"They did."

Wilhelm sat up straighter, as if my presence reminded him that he needed to act strong. "They both did what they thought was right."

"Yes."

"And both are dead because of it. Because of me."

"You did not make your father take Ernst's life or his own." I spoke more sharply than I'd intended.

"Röhm," he spat the word out. "Röhm made him take his own life."

"Yes, but—"

"Will you defend him?" Wilhelm turned to me, his bloodshot eyes filled with rage. I feared what he might do to me.

"He left me alone in that room to die," I said at last. "He's no friend of mine."

"And he took Anton," Wilhelm said. "They left before the police came."

"He is Anton's father." I stood up and walked back to my chair. Distance seemed a better policy. "It's in the newspaper this morning."

"I haven't read it." He ran his fingers through his brassy hair.

"Anton will be raised a warrior. Like he always wanted." I took a deep breath. "As your father raised you."

"Like your father raised Ernst."

Wilhelm lurched out of the room. I realized that he was quite drunk. I had to be very careful not to anger him. He returned with a tiny object in his hand. The third lead soldier that Ernst had rescued all those years ago.

"Ernst gave this to me . . . on that last night." He held it in his outstretched palm.

"He loved you." It did not feel like enough to say, but it was all I had.

"He said it would free me from my father. He said it freed him from caring what his father thought of him." He turned the soldier over and over in his strong hands. "After my father's funeral, Röhm and Anton are going back to Munich. Röhm has a man there to take care of him. As soon as he can, he'll put Anton in boarding school. I asked after him. Even with my father dead, I hear things."

"A boarding school might be the best thing for him," I said, thinking of the life that Röhm led. The less Anton saw of it, the better.

As if reading my mind, Wilhelm said, "Röhm is having a birthday party for Anton tomorrow. At the El Dorado, at noon, before they open."

"He will be six." My heart turned over in my chest.

"I am invited," he said, picking at his cuticles till they bled.

"Will you go?" I felt a surge of hope.

Wilhelm shook his head and dropped his bleeding hand. "I don't want to see that man again."

"Won't he come to your father's funeral?"

Wilhelm sighed. "Yes."

"Take me with you." I could not disguise the desperation in my voice.

"To the party?" Wilhelm sounded surprised.

"Yes."

"No women. Röhm is very strict about such things." He picked at his cuticles again.

"No women?"

"It said so on the invitation. Men only. The storm trooper parties are often like that. They want to keep the weakening . . . err . . . civilizing effect of women away from them."

"I want to make certain that Anton is well. I want to tell him that I am alive."

Wilhelm looked at me appraisingly, then gave a quick shake of his head. "You will have to be a boy. Come by at ten and I will get you ready."

I made him tea and breakfast before calling another taxi. When I went to my apartment, I insisted that we circle the block twice so that I could look for policemen or Rudolf. After I asked the driver to wait for me, I crept up my stairs. I leaned against my door, trembling, for a full minute before I worked up the courage to go inside. Rudolf could be in there. But eventually I tired of standing in the hall like a child afraid of the dark and pushed the door open.

My beloved apartment was still in shambles from Rudolf's warning. I packed my only suitcase with my clothes, Anton's few outfits, and the smallest family pictures. I was grateful that the police had removed Mitzi's body. Had Kommissar Lang been responsible for that? There was more to him than met the eye.

When I asked the taxi driver to take me to Ernst's apartment, my voice trembled. This time I did not dare wait at the front door, because I feared that more courage would never come. I marched into the kitchen and plucked the ring from its hiding place in the stove with a pair of tongs. Our teacups sat on the table, half-empty.

I steeled myself to walk into the bedroom. My head spun. Blood soaked the mattress. My blood. I had nearly died here. My knees collapsed. A chill ran over me, and I fought down an almost overwhelming urge to flee.

My hands shook as I reached down through my dried blood and pulled the letters out of the mattress. A splash of blood stained the brown wrapping paper, but none had seeped onto the letters.

I looked around Ernst's apartment for the last time, running my fingers along his beautiful dresses. This was the last place that Anton had seen me. I hoped that Röhm had told him I still lived. Back in the kitchen, I cleared the cups and wiped down Mother's table. Then I stumbled down to the taxi in a haze of tears, the letters and ring clutched in my hands.

I had the taxi take me to Herr Klein's shop. I rapped on the door.

"Hannah," said Herr Klein, pulling me and my suitcase into the shop and closing the door. "Paul said that you were in the hospital, guarded by the police."

"I left. I do not trust the police to keep me safe," I said. "A powerful man is after me."

"Is it about the ring?"

"Strangely, no," I said. "But that is why I am here. I want you to cut it in two. Then set them in two buttons, painted black. Quickly."

He peered at me through his round spectacles. "You are asking me to butcher the Mona Lisa."

"Yes."

He took the ring out of my hand with a sigh. "Desperate times these are."

"I want to sell you all the other pieces. I need American dollars. Or gold."

He nodded. "I have the receipt. I will bring it out with the money."

He disappeared in his back room with the ruby. I leaned against the table. Exhaustion seeped into my bones and my aching head, but at least the ring was now secure in Herr Klein's safe.

Herr Klein returned with a cup of strong tea. After I'd had a few sips, he counted out bills into my hand for the jewelry.

"Thank you," I said. "But there is more."

"Isn't there always?"

I handed him the package that contained the letters. "Can you hold this for one week."

"And then?"

"If you have not heard from me, deliver it to Paul."

"And why can't you give it to Paul now?"

I hesitated before I told him the truth. "I do not trust him not to open it. It is dangerous, more so than the ring. Take special care of it."

He shook his head and took the package. "What have you stumbled into?"

"Something I must stumble out of."

Exhausted, I returned to Sarah's apartment and retrieved the extra letter that Herr Silbert had done the forgery from. I hoped I had enough energy for my last two stops: the ticket office and Tegel prison. I would need every precaution I could think of to survive another day. Even that seemed unlikely to pull me through this. Still, my wits were all I had. And a brave needs to keep his wits and his arrows sharp. I stared at the special paper I had bought, knowing that my future rested on it.

29

Tomorrow I would sneak into Röhm's party and reassure Anton that I was alive. After that, I did not know, but I was ready to do whatever was needed.

I opened Boris's iron gate and walked to his front door. If he was not home, I'd sit on his expensive front steps until his neighbors noticed and called the police to arrest me. I knocked.

"Fraulein?" A thin woman with a pinched nose opened the door, drying her hands on an immaculate white apron. It looked like the apron Boris had worn yesterday.

"Hannah," I said, not mentioning my last name. "I am here to see Herr Krause."

"I know." She looked me over with stern gray eyes set close together. "He left word that you were expected. I am his housekeeper, Frau Inge."

She showed me in and deposited me in the living room. She insisted on carrying my suitcase upstairs for me and bringing me a cup of coffee and a piece of apple cake.

"Herr Krause also asked me to buy you an afternoon paper." She looked me up and down, suddenly noticing that I wore one of Boris's jackets. She did not look pleased.

I thanked her and accepted the paper. As I savored the excellent coffee and delicious cake, I read. A formal picture of a young Rudolf von Reiche covered a quarter of the front page. He'd been handsome once, with a long elegant face and high forehead. His dark eyes looked intelligent and searching.

I tore myself away from the picture and read the article by Peter Weill, noticing with satisfaction that Maria had not captured my style. But I sobered as I read what had happened to Rudolf. He'd been brutally beaten, perhaps whipped, and thrown alive into the Spree. Unlike Ernst, he'd been alive enough to drown there. Röhm's justice. Rudolf had been whipped by someone, as Sweetie Pie had been whipped by her clients, then cast into a watery grave, as had Ernst. I noted that he had not been shot, as I had.

I felt sorrow I had not expected. I had never liked Rudolf. He had tried to kill me, would have killed me if Röhm had not intervened. But he was still a human being. Ernst had loved him, even if I would never fathom why.

I sat on Boris's sumptuous leather sofa and read until dinnertime, when a key rattled in the front door.

A twinge of pain ran down my side as I stood awkwardly and walked to the front hall.

Boris stood inside the door, taking off his gloves. When he noticed me, his eyes lit up. "Hannah," he said. "I am glad to see you here."

"I am grateful to be here."

Frau Inge appeared in the doorway to the kitchen. "Let me take those for you."

He handed her his hat and gloves. "We will need only two places at dinner, Frau Inge," he said. "Trudi is staying with her grandmother for a few days."

Frau Inge whisked away, clinking dishes against each other as she put them in the cupboards.

"Your china won't hold up to my staying here." I glanced at the wall that separated the hall from the kitchen.

"I can buy more china." He crossed the hallway and took me in his arms. It was the first time in many years it had felt right to be held by a man, and I relaxed against him. He smelled of limes, cedar and, un-expectedly, cigars.

"Do you smoke cigars?" I asked, inhaling his scent.

He laughed. "One of my clerks smokes cigars, my little detective."

I stepped back and looked up at him. For a few seconds he gazed into my eyes. His voice was thick when he said, "I did not know if I would see you again. I felt you might vanish. Like a wisp of smoke."

"Even smoke leaves a trace." I turned my head away, unable to look into his eyes. I was frightened to feel anything for him, afraid that he was correct and one of us would vanish.

He tilted my chin so that he could look into my eyes again. "That's not much of a guarantee."

"Dinner is ready," Frau Inge said in a frosty tone from the doorway.

Boris stepped back and took me by the hand. He led me to a for-mal dining room. The mahogany table shone like glass from frequent polishing. Made for large formal gatherings, it was much too big for the two antique plates sitting on it.

Frau Inge lit the candles with brisk movements.

"I will clear, Frau Inge," said Boris. "You may leave early."

"Thank you, Herr Krause. Good night." She nodded in my direc-tion. "Frau Hannah."

Boris and I ate truly marvelous sauerbraten and red cabbage with potato dumplings. Frau Inge slammed the back door midway through the meal.

"Frau Inge is not used to women in her home?"

Boris smiled. "I haven't given her opportunity. Until now."

"Ever the staid banker."

"And the busy father. I've been busy with Trudi and work for many years." Boris looked off into the distance, his eyes bitter. "Too busy."

"I know how that can be."

"I believe you do, Hannah." He took a sip of wine, his lips moist. "What is next for you?"

"I do not know." I cut a dumpling into tiny pieces. "I read today that Rudolf is dead."

"Does that make you feel safe?" Boris looked at me with serious eyes.

"Does it make you feel safe?" I asked, smiling. "Or do you think I crept out last night and murdered him?"

"I will take my chances," Boris said. "I'm a brave man, after all."

I took another bite of sauerbraten. Frau Inge was a marvelous cook, far better than I. I swallowed the meat. "I think Röhm has nothing against me. I will soon be out of your way."

"You don't have to leave." Boris reached across the table and took my hand. I watched his lips form the words. "Even when you are well."

"I could stay here, in this castle with a servant and eat delicious meals and be waited on, forever?" I laughed. The idea was ridiculous.

"Yes." He looked offended and pulled his hand back. "Perhaps."

"Boris." I stretched my arm across the polished table and stroked his arm, his muscles hard under the fine linen. "I don't know."

"No one knows anything, Hannah." Boris still sounded upset.

I stared down at my plate.

"Tell me of your other doings today." I could tell that he strained for a normal tone. "Did you go home?"

I nodded. "The police removed Mitzi's body." I took a deep breath. "The rest is smashed and filthy, but I did gather a few photographs and clothes. I also went to see Wilhelm."

"The boy whose father killed your brother?"

"Yes."

"And?" Boris pushed his plate back and took another long sip of wine.

"He is grieving for his father and for my brother."

"Does he have other family?"

"Not that I saw."

I pushed back my plate as well, and we drank expensive wine in silence. Money could buy many things, after all. Peace, a grand house, good food.

After the wine, we cleared the table together. It felt comfortable, and right. Not counting Ernst, I had not helped a man clean up since Walter, over a decade ago. This was the life I could have had, if Walter had lived, except without the housekeeper and in a much smaller house.

I began to wash a plate, but Boris caught one side of it. "Frau Inge would be mortified if we washed up. She'd take the dishes back out and rewash them."

I laughed. "You are not serious."

He stood right next to me, holding the other side of the plate, and I turned to him. "She's done it before."

Before I could answer, he leaned down and kissed me. The plate crashed on the checkerboard tile floor. I tried to pull away to gather the pieces, but Boris would not let me. I did not want to move anyway.

Like everything else about him, his kiss was deep and rich and sensual.

When he stopped I clung to him, dizzy. My lips tingled, and my heart beat out of rhythm.

"I am sorry about the plate," I whispered.

"I can always buy more china," he said in a husky voice.

He carried me to his bedroom, careful of my wounded ribs. Even Walter had not carried me. I felt like a teenage princess in a fairy tale, not a thirty-two-year-old reporter with a gunshot wound.

The bedroom was spotless, as always, and Boris set me on top of the quilt. His eyes were dark, and he inhaled sharply when I ran my fingers through his wonderful, thick hair. I slid my hands down the smooth linen of his shirt. His heart pounded under my palms.

I pulled him down onto the bed, leaving just enough room between us to unbutton his shirt. I smelled starch as I pulled it off his back and felt the warm smoothness of his skin. Boris groaned. He lifted me gently and unbuttoned the back of my dress, pulling it off me with one quick motion.

Then I felt his naked skin against my body for the first time. I longed to cut off my bandages so that there was nothing between us, but I soon forgot that anything was between us at all.

Boris was a wonderful lover, tender and careful around my wounded side and my bruised head. Never once did he hurt me. In this, as with wine, he was the connoisseur; taking his time, slow and thorough. If all men were like him, I could understand why Ernst took so many.

Afterward, I lay curled in his arms, content for the first time in years.

Boris breathed slow and even next to me. I closed my eyes and pretended that I could stay like this forever. How intoxicating it would be to give in and let this take its course. I could live in the castle, with the king. As if he read my thoughts, Boris pulled me closer to him. Frau Inge would cook and clean for me. I could find another job, without worrying about the pay. Food would never be a problem. And there would be someone there to rely on, and more. I sighed and shifted next to him. Much was at stake tomorrow.

"I've never made love to a woman with no breasts before." Boris stroked his hand over the bandage that covered my chest.

"They're there, just buried."

"Like so much else about you."

I said nothing.

"What are you doing tomorrow?" he asked. "Will you be here again when I come home from work?"

"Wilhelm said that Anton will be having a birthday party tomorrow, at noon. At the El Dorado."

"The bar?" Boris ran his fingers through my bobbed hair.

"The bar will be closed." I leaned into his hand like a cat being stroked.

"And?"

"And I intend to go."

Boris slid both his arms around me. "What will you do?"

"Tell Anton that I am alive." I shivered. "The last time he saw me I was lying in a pool of blood."

Boris tightened his arms. "He deserves to see you alive."

I lay next to him, enjoying the soft warmth of his body and his bed. I had dozed off when Boris spoke again.

"After the party, what then?"

"Bankers have to know everything, don't they?"

"Only the important things."

I pulled myself onto my right elbow and winced. I wanted to see his face.

He seemed sleepy and relaxed, but his eyes were watchful.

"I may need to leave in a hurry."

"I can take the afternoon off and wait for you. As Anton said, my automobile is as fast as the wind."

"Boris." I brushed his thick hair off his forehead. "You do not want to be involved."

"How do you know what I want?" He bent down and kissed me again, long and lingering.

It was many long moments before I spoke again. "Did you want that?"

He smiled. "I think I'll always want that."

Blood rushed to my ears, but still I wanted to warn him away. "You are no law breaker, Boris."

He sat up. "You intend to snatch the boy?"

"Perhaps."

"Kidnap the son of a top Nazi official?"

I sat up next to him and pulled the quilt to my chest. "I might."

Boris's look told me how insane my thoughts and plans were. I lay down beside him without another word. Whatever happened, we still had tonight.

The next morning, Boris's side of the bed was empty and cold. It had been the most wonderful night in my memory, and I ran over it in my mind while I washed and dressed in one of my own dresses from my suitcase. I repacked my belongings, including my green scarf and Winnetou the bear.

Frau Inge was downstairs when I came down with my suitcase.

"Good day," she said. "Herr Krause left orders that I prepare you breakfast."

The way she said orders left little doubt about how she felt about it.

I ate a quick breakfast and called a taxi. The million-dollar ruby was turning me into a profligate.

Frau Inge helped me carry my suitcase out through the yard. "Leaving so soon?"

"One never knows, Frau Inge," I said, suppressing a smile. "I might be back before you know it."

30

I took the taxi to Herr Klein's and picked up the ruby buttons. I borrowed a needle and thread to sew them on Winnetou's eyes. Herr Klein shook his head, as if not convinced that this was a safe way to transport jewels.

When I got to Wilhelm's, he looked pale and drawn, but better than the day before.

"You're glowing," he said. "There's a man." A mischievous smile crossed his haunted face.

"Is that the only reason a woman can look happy?"

"It's the only reason I could look that happy," Wilhelm said. "But keep your secrets. We have work to do."

He led me to his bathroom and made me sit on his toilet. "I'll have to cut your hair, but I think I can use some for a mustache."

"Whatever it takes." I wondered how Boris would react to me with a man's haircut. Bad enough that my breasts were bound flat.

As Wilhelm cut my hair, he groaned at my sparse eyebrows. "Mascara will help," he said. "But they're so delicate."

"I don't pluck them," I said.

"How unwomanly." He ran his hand expertly through my hair and clipped. Tufts of hair fell onto my shoulders and the floor. I tried not to think about it.

"The hair is done." He walked out the bathroom door. "Don't move and especially don't look in the mirror."

I did not want to see myself as a man, so followed his advice. This reminded me of the days when Ernst would insist on helping me with makeup before I went on dates, after Walter died. My many first dates. There were few second dates.

Wilhelm returned with a small blue pot. "Spirit gum." He dipped his hand in the paste and ran it above my upper lip. It smelled like rubber cement. He took a pinch of hair and applied it, strand by strand, sticking it into the spirit gum. When finished, he trimmed it delicately.

"Now the mirror!"

Ernst stared back at me from the mirror. Ernst as he might have looked with a more masculine haircut and a mustache. I was shorter and my features more delicate, but I could easily pass for a boy in my early twenties, except for my dress. When my eyes met Wilhelm's in the mirror, his too were full of tears.

"You look so much like him." Wilhelm straightened my hair. "I never saw it until now."

I forced a smile on my face. "Nor did I. You are a miracle worker, Wilhelm."

He coughed, and we both pulled ourselves together.

"I helped out during school productions," he said. "And Ernst taught me much about makeup, although mostly he went from boy to girl, not the other way around."

I stared at myself in disbelief. I was a man. I straightened my shoulders and grimaced at the mirror.

Wilhelm held up a black sock.

I raised my eyebrows.

"Your equipment, monsieur." He stuffed the sock with other socks and helped me tape it to the inside of my right thigh, on top of my underwear.

"I feel well endowed." I looked down at the sock. "And that sock looks happy."

"It's not all about size, you naughty boy."

He helped me tie the bandage tighter across my breasts. It hurt my wounded side, and I hoped it wouldn't bleed.

Wilhelm helped me into a thin undershirt and a too-large Nazi uniform. Even Mother would not have recognized me. It was disquieting, but also liberating.

I tucked the forged letter into my breast pocket.

We rode to the party in silence. We parked behind a familiar form in a black Mercedes watching the door to the El Dorado. Boris! My heart leaped and my eyes filled with tears as I hurried across the street to the club.

"Helmut," Wilhelm said. "Don't cry like a woman."

"Jawohl." I pushed open the club door for him.

I handed my suitcase to the coat-check boy. He did not recognize me from the other night. "Thank you, Fraulein," I said, in a deep voice.

"You are most welcome." The coat-check boy fluttered his eyelashes at me.

"Try not to talk," Wilhelm whispered out of the side of his mouth as we passed through the red curtains and into the club.

The room was full of black and brown uniforms of the Sturm Abteilung, the Schutz Staffel, and regular Nazis. I had never been in a place with so many men before. The lone woman serving drinks was probably in drag.

When Wilhelm shepherded me to the bar and ordered two whiskeys Oliver's eyes widened, but he said nothing. Did he recognize me? I turned my back to him.

"Are all these men attracted to other men?" I whispered to Wilhelm.

"I wish." He laughed. "Many of the SA men are, especially the ones clustered around Röhm. Most of the SS are not. You never know about the regular Nazis."

I took a manly gulp of whiskey and glanced around to find Anton. He sat at a small round table next to Ernst Röhm. He clutched a white

El Dorado balloon and looked thoroughly lost. I longed to sweep him up in my arms and carry him away. He sat with the military bearing drilled into the children of officers, but his eyes were far away. I did not see another child anywhere.

"Not much of a party for children," I whispered to Wilhelm.

"I'll ask Röhm to dance," Wilhelm said. "Then you can talk to Anton."

Wilhelm walked across the room to Röhm, his head held high and his face an expressionless mask.

As soon as they were safely out on the dance floor, I hurried to Anton's side. He looked as pale as the day I met him, as remote as the little boy who climbed into my wardrobe and closed the door, ready to wait quietly until his mother's workday ended.

I touched his shoulder.

"Hello, sir," he said politely. He looked up at me, but I could tell that he did not recognize me.

"Indian greetings, Anton," I whispered. "It's Hannah."

Anton gasped. "Are you dead?"

"Alive but camouflaged," I said. "I had to sneak into this encampment to see you."

He wrapped his arms around me and hugged as hard as his tiny body could. I gritted my teeth against the pain in my side and hugged him back.

"I wanted you to be alive," he said. "Winnetou saved you."

"He did," I said. I pried his wiry arms off me. "Anton, I don't have much time. Are you well?"

"My father hit me when I told him I was an Indian." Anton's lip trembled. It looked swollen. Had Röhm hit him in the face? "He says Indians are dirty."

"Do you want to stay with him?" I glanced over my shoulder at Röhm. He had not noticed us. "I would not ask like this, but I have no time, and no choice. But think it through quickly."

He shook his head immediately. "I want to go with you."

"I don't know where we're going, yet. And there may be danger."

"The brave can trust his chief." He stuck his small hand in mine. "And you are not only my chief. You are my mother too."

I opened my mouth to correct him, as I had so many times before. Instead I said, "I am your mother, in all ways that matter."

Across the room, Röhm turned toward us and beckoned to Anton. "Go to your father now."

"No." Anton's grip on my hand tightened.

"Listen carefully, these are orders," I said. "Go to your father now. As soon as he is not watching you, go out the front door, but walk slowly so no one is alarmed."

"I will not spook the deer." Anton let go of my hand and clasped his hands together in his lap.

"Do you remember Herr Krause's automobile?"

He nodded.

"It is across the street. Herr Krause is in the front seat. Get in the backseat and lie down on the floor. I will come for you."

Anton nodded.

"Now go to your father."

Wilhelm hurried over to me while Röhm lifted Anton and introduced him to a group of black-uniformed SS officers.

"You have assured him that you are well. Now go. It is not safe." Wilhelm drew a red silk handkerchief out of his breast pocket and wiped sweat from his forehead.

"I won't leave without Anton."

Wilhelm paled and tucked the handkerchief back in his pocket. "Röhm will hunt you if you take him."

"Anton wants to go."

"Nowhere in Germany will be safe."

"Anton wants to go."

Wilhelm's eyes widened, and I turned. There was Ernst Röhm, walking toward us. "You have not introduced this little pigeon, Wilhelm," he said, beaming. "A terrible oversight."

"Captain Röhm, may I present Helmut Fischer?"

Fish and fowl. "How do you do?" I kept my voice low and rough.

"Better now." Röhm took my hand and led me to the dance floor. "Do you waltz, pigeon?"

I raised my hands into position.

"Good, you know the girl's part," he said. "So many men have only learned the boy's part and we can't both be dancing that."

"I can dance many ways."

Röhm pulled me closer to him, roughly. "I bet you can."

I traced his thick pink scar with my eyes, trying not to stare at his badly mended nose. He smelled like the love letters he'd sent Ernst. I tried to imagine him dripping cologne onto the pages. Had Ernst actually loved this man?

As if reading my thoughts, he said, "You look much like someone I once knew. Someone who meant a great deal to me."

"Should I be him?" Behind his head Anton marched toward the door, looking neither right nor left.

Röhm leaned in and kissed me. His kiss was confident and cruel, and his arms tightened around me like iron bands. Pain shot down from my wound, and my knees buckled. Anton disappeared from my vision.

I shuddered in revulsion, but Röhm smiled. "You are a quick one, pigeon."

He pressed his hips against me, and I turned my leg so that he could feel my sock, glad that Wilhelm had stuffed it so tightly.

"After this dance," he said. "The dark room." He inclined his head toward the back of the room.

"As you wish." My stomach heaved. I had to get away from him, and soon.

We waltzed around the floor, and Röhm stared hypnotically into my eyes. He was an excellent dancer. Strong, in control. A natural leader.

After an eternity, the music ended. Röhm grabbed my hand and began to lead me back to the dark room. I knew what would happen in there if he found out who I was. And what would happen if he didn't.

Oliver appeared at Röhm's elbow. "You have a call, Captain," he said. "I believe it is from the Führer's office."

"Wait for me," Röhm said. I nodded and clicked my heels together, bowing the traditional soldier's farewell.

Röhm reached down and squeezed my bottom so hard I yelped. That would leave a mark. "Don't run off."

He swaggered to the bar.

"If you go to the leftmost dark room, Hannah," Oliver said quietly, "there is a back door that leads to the makeup rooms and out the back."

I was shocked into silence. Oliver recognized me. What if Röhm did too? I gulped.

"Hannah?" Oliver said. "You must hurry."

"Thank you," I said. "For everything."

Oliver smiled tightly. "I knew you would work things out. Your brother deserved that."

"When did you know he was dead?"

Oliver glanced over his shoulder at Röhm. "When he did not show up for work after the night at Wilhelm's I suspected the worst. Now go."

"I have a suitcase."

"I will tell Wilhelm to leave it by the front door. I don't know what you are planning, but leave at once. I cannot help you further. Röhm is a very dangerous man."

"Thank you," I said again.

"Your brother would have wanted me to help."

I walked to the leftmost dark room, my legs shaking. As I closed the front door, Röhm waved to me. There was no lock. In pitch darkness, I felt my way along the walls. My shoes stuck to the floor. I shuddered.

My hand found a door handle on the back wall. It was locked. I felt along the handle to see if I could unlock it from this side. My fingers were wet with sweat and slipped off the handle.

I took a deep breath to steady myself, and the front door opened.

Röhm stood silhouetted in the light. I turned quickly, door handle hidden behind my back.

Röhm lit a candle and placed it on the bench. In the flickering glow his scarred face looked almost normal. He swiftly took two steps across the room and put his palm flat against the back door. There would be no escape that way. I released the door handle.

"Come," he said. "Kneel down."

I stared at him, unable to move. If I ran, I could not get away. His men were all around us. But I had to leave soon. All of my plans depended on it.

He pulled a cape off his shoulders and spread it on the sticky floor in a practiced, courtly gesture from another era. The room was so small that the cape covered the floor.

He took my left hand and gently pulled me away from the back door. We took an awkward step, and we were standing in the middle of the cape. He knelt and pulled me down to a kneeling position next to him. Even through the cloak, the wood was hard under my knees.

"I am not a barbarian," he said softly. He leaned forward and kissed me gently. I could not think. I was paralyzed. He held my wrist loosely.

He reached one hand up and ran it across my cheek, as gentle as a butterfly's wing. "You look like someone I loved much."

"I . . . I . . . I," I stuttered, realizing too late that I had forgotten to deepen it to sound like a man.

"But you of all people know that," he said with a sad look. "Hannah."

When I tried to lean back, his fingers tightened around my left wrist. "I came only to see Anton," I said.

"To see him, or to take him?" he asked. "I saw him leave. My man watches him even now."

I bowed my head so that he would not see my tears. I would show no weakness in front of him. Even now that I had lost.

"You are merely one woman, Hannah," he said. "I command many men. There is no shame in losing to a stronger adversary."

"Anton would say that a true warrior can defeat all his enemies, no matter how strong."

"He loves you very much," he said. "He thinks you are his mother."

"I did not tell him so." Until a few minutes ago.

"A boy needs a mother," he said. "I worshipped my mother. Ernst despised yours, though, didn't he?"

I stared at him in shock. Sorrow etched his face. "I don't know how Ernst felt about our mother."

"He loved you like a mother." Röhm caressed my bottom, and his eyes glazed over. "You look so much like him."

"Let me go." I struggled to keep my voice steady. I reached behind me and removed his hand from my bottom. He let me.

Never letting go of my wrist, he moved from a kneeling to a sitting position. He ran his eyes over my face thirstily. "Do you find me repulsive?" He licked his lips, the candlelight shining off his sweaty red face.

"No," I lied. I tried to pull my wrist free, but he tightened his hand around it. I cried out in pain.

"Do you want the boy?" he asked, ignoring my cry.

I nodded. He toyed with me like a cat with a mouse. I would not give him the satisfaction of watching me struggle in vain.

"Then be his mother." Röhm smiled as if he had found the solution to all of our problems.

A chill ran down my back. "How?"

"Marry me." He hauled me into his lap, one hand under my knees, the other behind my neck. His cock was hard against the backs of my thighs. The buttons of his uniform pressed against my bandages. Hot pain shot down my side from my wound.

"You will mother the boy, live in comfort and ease, and I will have a wife, to satisfy the party. You'd make a better party wife than an ex-prostitute. And your brother would have wanted you to take care of the boy. Marrying me solves many problems."

"It might solve problems. But it also creates them." I took a deep breath. Ursula would counsel me to accept the offer. Money, power, and the boy. But also Röhm, a brutal Nazi. I would rather take my chances on my own, with the money from the ruby.

"It doesn't have to." He peppered my neck with sweaty kisses.

I struggled to get out of his arms.

"You look so much like him," he said, in a dreamy voice. "If you would consent to wear that uniform sometimes, we might even produce children."

"I consent to none of this." My arms were pinned against his chest in a lover's embrace. He was so much stronger that he seemed not to notice that I struggled. He turned me around so that my back faced his stomach. He reached around to my belt buckle. "I don't need your consent, pigeon."

I struggled against him, but he was as implacable as stone. He pulled off my belt buckle, and I felt his strong fingers on the button to my trousers. Panic filled my mind, and I screamed. Röhm clapped his hand over my mouth and nose. I could not breathe.

"This doesn't have to be unpleasant," he said. "But it can be."

One hand held my mouth and with the other he stripped off my trousers and underwear. Tears ran down my cheeks onto his fingers.

He turned me around and looked into my panicked eyes. "I will let go of your mouth if you promise not to scream."

I nodded. After he let go of my mouth I gulped a few breaths of air.

He ran his hand up and down my naked legs and lay me down on his cloak. The wool was scratchy under my bottom. He seized both my wrists with one hand and undid his belt buckle. It made a muffled *clink* when he dropped it on the floor.

I closed my eyes, trying not to feel his hands on me, his body on me. "I have the letters," I blurted out.

His arms tightened around me. I could not breathe. Shooting pains ran up my side from my wound. Lights danced across my eyes. "Where?" he asked.

"Can't . . . talk," I croaked.

He loosened his arms, and I sucked in a lungful of air. Hot pain flashed across my chest, and I gasped. I pulled the letter out of my pocket. "Here is one."

Röhm snatched it out of my hand and skimmed it. "And the others?"

"They are in a safe place. A place where they will be published if I do not contact them in one hour." It was a week, but I did not want Röhm to know that.

"You have fire, pigeon."

"And I have your career. Probably your freedom. 'Ode to Bootsie's Cock' would read well in court."

He loosened his grip on my wrists. "The rhyme scheme is well thought out."

I sat and pulled my legs up under me. I longed to cover my nakedness.

"So." He smiled, devilishly. "Where are we now?"

"Let me go with Anton." My voice was ragged. "And I will destroy the letters." It hurt me to say those words. How could I live with Sarah, or myself, if Röhm gained more power?

"Marry me first," he said. "With photographers. Then I will let you both go."

"No." I shook my head. "I do not trust you."

"But I should trust you?"

"You have thousands of men to follow me, to keep me in line. I have only myself."

"And the letters."

I shrugged.

"I need to be seen as a father, even a husband right now. I can't give that up."

"Those letters make it clear that you are not."

He put one hand on my windpipe. "With blackmailers," he said. "You pay forever."

I jerked my head back, but he tightened his grip. "You have no time to break me," I said. "The afternoon papers go to press in an hour."

"An hour can last longer than you can imagine." His eyes glittered in the flickering candlelight.

I closed my eyes.

He released my windpipe, shaking his head. "I can't hurt you if I look at your face. I see Bootsie. It's as if he's in the room with us. Sometimes in the war . . ."

I rubbed my neck.

"I loved your brother," he said. "More than you can understand. He . . ."

I said nothing. There was nothing more for me to say. It was his game, now.

"He spoke of you." Röhm ran his fingertip across my eyebrows, one after the other. "He trusted you."

"He would not want you to hurt me."

Röhm's eyes were dreamy again. He cupped his hand around the back of my head and stroked my hair with his thumb, almost unconsciously. His eyes filled with tears.

"He's gone," he said. "Just like that."

"I miss him." I shifted on the scratchy wool cloak. I longed to be dressed again.

"As do I." Röhm stared into the candle flame. "He trusted you. Said you were honest. And a bad liar."

I smiled.

Someone knocked on the door. "Telephone," a voice said. "Urgent."

Röhm rolled his eyes. "Leave," he called out. The man did not knock again.

"I will let you go today," Röhm continued. He reached one hand up and ran it through my short hair. I gritted my teeth. "With an escort. He will help you to retrieve those letters. You will marry me. You will give me one week for the photographers. I want a wedding, with a bride in a white dress. And I want a honeymoon on the North Sea. After that you may live separately from me."

I slumped.

"If I need you again, for publicity purposes, I will call, and you will come. In return, you and Anton can live where you choose."

He tilted my face and stared at me with his hard blue eyes. "If you publish those letters, you destroy all three of us. I will find you and kill you. Do I have your word?"

"You do." I pushed the words out of my mouth like vomit.

"Dress and go retrieve those letters," he said. "My men will follow you. There are more men than you know. And more than you can evade."

He leaned forward and kissed me. I knew he was wishing I was Ernst. And pretending that I was. His mouth ground against mine, and I tasted blood. His or mine. Or both.

31

I wiped Röhm's kiss off my mouth and dressed with shaking hands while he watched. He'd forgotten the ruby ring. The ruby ring that would buy me a new identity and freedom. I would not publish the letters. On that I would keep my word. But I would not marry him and chain myself and Anton to him forever. We would escape from Germany and run so far and so fast that he would never find us. I would never go back into a dark room with Röhm. Not for love, money, or safety.

My suitcase, containing two precious rubies and all of my money and clothes, rested by the front door. I picked it up and hurried across the street, hoping I was not too late. I noticed that Boris had removed the numbered plates from his car. A sensible precaution. Boris had a talent for undercover work. He had unexpected depths.

A man in SA uniform stood next to the Mercedes. I assumed he must have searched the suitcase and found the train tickets to Hamburg I'd purchased earlier in the day. I hoped he'd been worried enough about me finding out that he'd repacked everything carefully.

He tipped his hat at me. "Fraulein Vogel," he said. "I am to follow you and bring you back."

I nodded to him.

I checked to see that Anton was lying safely across the backseat before I slid into the front seat. Boris looked at me in shock. I remembered that I was dressed as a boy.

"Thank you for coming," I said through lips swollen from Röhm's kiss.

"You are full of surprises." Boris put the automobile in gear. He drove for a moment before saying, "Maybe someday we can drive somewhere like normal people."

"We will be followed." I looked out the back window. "By the man who was standing next to the car."

Boris looked in his rearview mirror. "Two of them," he said. "But their car is not as powerful as mine."

I kept watch as Boris accelerated. "They are still following us."

"No one follows me." Boris began to speed in earnest. The car engine groaned with delight at being let loose to run. Anton laughed in the backseat. I closed my eyes.

Boris cut the wheel sharply to the right and careened the wrong way down a one-way street. A car honked at us, but Boris drove up onto the sidewalk. Metal screeched on the bottom of the car. I held on to the dash and hoped that we escaped our pursuers before we ran into something or someone.

I looked back. The other car was having trouble maneuvering around the car that had honked at us.

Boris yanked the wheel to the left. I feared the car might roll over. I gasped when my wounded side slammed against the door.

Anton's head popped up out of the back. "Stay down, Anton," I said, and he disappeared behind the seat.

Boris accelerated and made for a main road. I glanced back. Our pursuers were no longer in sight.

"They're gone," I said.

"Let's put a little more distance between us." Boris shot past a white-gloved policeman, who waved his hands and blew his whistle at us.

Anton glanced back at the policeman. He and Boris laughed together.

"You are enjoying this," I said to Boris.

"What's wrong with that?" Boris asked. "I've never had a chance to enjoy this car as much as I should."

"Faster!" screamed Anton, and Boris obliged.

I ripped off my Nazi shirt, emptied the pockets, and flung the shirt out the window. I rubbed spirit gum and hair off my upper lip.

Boris slowed. "I think we are not being followed anymore."

I pulled off my trousers and threw them after the shirt.

"Somehow, this isn't how I thought I'd see you naked again." Boris looked down at me with a grin.

"We haven't much time."

Boris raised an eyebrow. "You have another appointment?"

"I'd hoped not." I bit my lip. "But I do."

"What's our destination?"

I gave him Sarah's address while pulling on a dress and stockings from my suitcase, glad to be a woman again. As I'd hoped, my suitcase had been rifled through. I'd known what Röhm's men would do the instant Röhm said my name in the dark room. They knew the suitcase contained a set of tickets to Hamburg. I smiled, thinking of them staking out the train station.

At Sarah's apartment I retrieved a set of plane tickets, a forged visa for England, and two forged passports from her mailbox where I had hidden them earlier that day. I checked the clock in Sarah's apartment. We barely had enough time to get where we needed to go.

Again Boris drove like a madman, and not much later we parked at Tempelhof Airport.

"Thank you." My hand stroked my suitcase. Inside were false papers I'd had created at Tegel prison that morning, for twenty packs of cigarettes and three gold pieces. No one knew about them but me and Herr Silbert, the forger. Anton and I would have to leave England before Röhm found us there. I was not certain where we would go.

Röhm would not think I had money for plane fare. I hoped that he would waste time looking in Hamburg because of the tickets I'd planted in the suitcase. I'd known his men would search it.

Boris reached in the backseat and brought back a cloche hat. "It's Trudi's, but I know she won't miss it. Your hair looks terrible."

"I thought it rather dashing." I put the hat on and looked in the mirror. I looked like a woman again. A woman with no breasts.

"Maybe if I were that sort." Boris's lips smiled, but his brown eyes were sad.

I ran my hand along his close-shaven jaw. "I am grateful you're not."

"Call me when you arrive, so I know you're safe." He paused and nervously licked his lips. I leaned over and kissed him once, lightly. I did not dare kiss him too long, because I could not be tempted to stay. "I'll be in London in August, for a finance conference."

"I could meet you, if we're there." My heart sunk. We would not stay long in London.

"If you're not there, I'll be at another conference in New York in December."

I smiled. "You are a world traveler."

Boris reached an arm around the nape of my neck and kissed me slowly and gently. It hurt, because of the damage that Röhm had done to my mouth, but I did not want him to stop. "Hannah," Boris said in surprise. "Your lips are bleeding."

I looked into his worried eyes. "It's a long story."

Anton climbed into the front seat. "I like stories."

Boris moved over to his side of the seat.

I handed Anton Winnetou the bear. "He missed you."

Anton grabbed the bear and hugged him. "What is wrong with his eyes?"

"They see magical things," I told him. "Take good care of them."

Anton nodded gravely.

Boris looked down at Anton, who held the bear and stared at us suspiciously. "I have a gift for you, brave little man." He pulled a brown-wrapped parcel from the backseat. "I'd hoped you could open it at my house."

I bit my lip, and Boris cleared his throat. "Open it on the plane," I said. "We do not have time to open it now."

We trotted across the tarmac, Boris on one side, holding my hand and my suitcase, and Anton on the other, clutching my free hand. How I wished that I could hold on to both of them. I squeezed Boris's hand, the one that I would have to let go of.

"Do you need money?" Boris asked. "For traveling?"

I shook my head. "We are well provided for."

When we reached the stairs that led to the plane Boris kissed me for the last time, long and slow, blotting out any trace of Röhm. I never wanted him to stop, but eventually I pulled back.

He ran one hand down my cheek.

"If things had been different." I traced my finger across his lips. "I would have stayed."

"If things had been different," he answered. "I would have insisted."

"But things are not different."

"Will you ever be able to come back to Germany?"

"I suspect Röhm won't give up on his son easily."

Boris nodded. "I could not give up on my child easily either."

I stepped out of his arms. "Nor can I."

Boris sighed. "I don't expect you to."

"Excuse me, miss," said a burly man in coveralls. "I have to roll away the stairs now. You must get on if you're taking this flight."

I nodded and turned toward the stairs so that Boris would not see me cry. I clutched the handrail and climbed the stairs. I had to get through this.

At the top of the stairs, I turned around. Boris lifted one hand. I waved back through eyes blurred with tears. I might very well never see him again, and there was no chance that we would ever have a life together. It felt like losing Walter all over again.

Anton jumped up and down and waved his red silk handkerchief. "Until our trails cross again," he called.

Wind tore the handkerchief out of Anton's hand, and he cried out.

"It's gone," I said, as he turned to go down the stairs.

"But it's the last thing you gave me, before—"

"It won't be the last thing anymore, I promise."

Anton looked uncertain as I pulled him into the plane. "You are safe now," I told him. "We are safe, and we will have many years together."

As the door to the plane closed, I hoped that I had told him the truth.

The engine noise changed to a high-pitched whine, and I realized, for the first time, that I was afraid of flying. I clutched the arms of my seat. Soon I would be leaving the ground. I would be leaving behind all that was familiar in my life with a small boy I barely knew.

Anton, unaware, plastered his face against the window to watch the ground rushing by. We rose into the clouds, away from Berlin, away from Boris and the life I might have had with him, and away from Röhm, at least for now. I wondered how long we could stay ahead of Röhm, if he tried to find us.

After a few minutes of watching clouds, Anton unwrapped his gift from Boris. All three volumes of the Winnetou series by Karl May. I covered our laps with my peacock-green scarf and settled down to read him the first volume, the one he knew by heart.

Glossary

Abitur. German equivalent of a high school diploma.

absinthe. Bitter alcoholic drink made with wormwood that was banned in Europe and the United States because it was said to cause insanity. It is now legal again in some parts of the United States and Europe.

Alexanderplatz. Central police station for Berlin through World War II. Also called the Alex.

Bahnhof. Train station or subway station.

Berliner weisse. Pale wheat beer made in Berlin. It is usually mixed with a shot of raspberry or woodruff syrup.

Berolina. Tour company in Berlin.

El Dorado. Gay bar in Berlin that was popular during the 1920s and early 1930s, closed by the Nazis, and reopened in the 1990s.

Ernst Röhm. Early member of the National Socialist party and close friend to Adolf Hitler, often credited with being the man most responsible for bringing Hitler to power in the early days. Openly gay.

Hall of the Unnamed Dead. Hall in the Alexanderplatz police station that showed framed photographs of unidentified bodies found by the police.

Horst Wessel. Young Nazi turned into a martyr by the Nazi party after being killed by a Communist. A song he wrote, "The Horst Wessel Song," became the Nazi party anthem.

jawohl. Emphatic form of yes.

Kaiser. Leader of Germany before the founding of the Weimar Republic. After World War I, the last Kaiser, Wilhelm II, abdicated his throne and fled to the Netherlands.

Kinder, Küche, Kirche. Children, kitchen, church. Policy of the Nazi party on where women belonged.

Kölnisch Wasser. Popular German cologne created in the early 1700s. Literally translated as "water from Cologne" in English and "eau de cologne" in French. Still sold today.

Kommissar. Rank in the police department similar to a lieutenant.

loden green. Grayish green color usually found in traditional Bavarian wool clothing.

Mosse House. Building that housed the *Berliner Tageblatt,* where Hannah Vogel worked. It was damaged during the Spartacus Uprising in Berlin in 1918 and restored by Erich Mendelsohn, a famous German architect. The building was again damaged during World War II and restored in 1990.

National Socialist German Workers party (Nazi party). Party led by Adolf Hitler that eventually assumed control of Germany.

Paragraph 175. Paragraph of the German penal code that made homosexuality a crime. Paragraph 175 was in place from 1871 to 1994. Under the Nazis, people convicted of Paragraph 175 offenses, which did not need to include physical contact, were sent to concentration camps, where many of them died.

Peter Kürten. Serial killer from Düsseldorf. He was arrested, tried, and guillotined shortly before the novel takes place. Hannah Vogel would have covered his sensational trial.

pfennigs. Similar to pennies. There were 100 pfennigs in a Reichsmark.

Reichsmark. Currency used by Germany from 1924 to 1948. The previous currency, the Papiermark, became worthless in 1923 due to hyperinflation. On January 1, 1923, one American dollar was worth nine thousand Reichsmarks. By November 1923, one American dollar was worth a little more than four trillion Reichsmarks. Fortunes were wiped out overnight. In 1924, the currency was revalued and remained fairly stable until the Wall Street crash in the United States in 1929. When the novel takes place, one American dollar was worth 4.23 Reichsmarks.

Reichstag. Elected legislative assembly representing the people of Germany.

Schultheiss pilsner. Pale lager brewed at the Schultheiss factory in Berlin.

Schutz Staffel (SS or Blackshirts). Nazi paramilitary organization founded as an elite force to be used as Hitler's personal bodyguards. Led by Heinrich Himmler.

Sturm Abteilung (SA, Brownshirts, or storm troopers). Nazi paramilitary organization that helped intimidate Hitler's opponents. Led by Ernst Röhm.

Tempelhof Airport. Famous airport in Berlin. It was remodeled under the Nazis, used in World War II, and became the central airport for the Berlin Airlift of 1948. It is currently slated to be shut down.

Wannsee. Both a borough in Berlin and a pair of linked lakes. It is a well-known swimming and recreation spot in Berlin, with one of the largest inland beaches in Europe. Wannsee, however, is best known because it was at a villa on this lake that senior Nazi officials came up with the "final solution to the Jewish problem" (i.e., the murder of all of the Jews in Europe) on January 20, 1942.

Weimar Republic. Name given to the German government from the end of World War I until the Nazi takeover (1919–1933).

Wertheim department store. Large department store chain in Germany. The store in the novel was one of the largest department stores in Berlin at the time. The Nazis later seized the business, as the Wertheims were Jewish. In 2006, Wertheim's heirs successfully sued another department store chain that purchased the store after World War II. The property in the settlement is now valued at 350 million dollars.

Zehlendorf. Wealthy borough in Berlin. Boris's house is on Kronprinzen Avenue in this borough, later renamed Clayallee to honor General Clay, the American general who ordered the Berlin airlift in 1948.

Author's Note

A Trace of Smoke is set in Berlin in 1931, the year Germany was lost to the Nazis. Although the characters are mostly fictional, their world is based on meticulous research. When I lived in Berlin for three years in the mid- and late 1980s, I became fascinated by the city, its history, and the German language. I graduated from high school and finished a semester of college there. When I chose 1930s Germany as the topic for my senior history thesis at Carnegie Mellon University, I remembered the city I loved, and a pink triangle I'd seen at the Dachau concentration camp that showed gays were imprisoned there. In 1989, I began to research what had happened to them. It was difficult, as not much had been written about it. When I returned to the topic years later to write this novel, I was pleased to discover a wealth of useful primary and secondary sources.

Many places in the novel existed as I described them. The novel opens with the main character viewing her dead brother's picture in the Hall of the Unnamed Dead. This hall in the basement of the Berlin police station at Alexanderplatz where pictures of unidentified corpses were displayed was hauntingly described in a 1923 newspaper article by novelist Joseph Roth, in *What I Saw: Reports from Berlin 1920–1933*.

The newspapers Hannah longs to hide behind, and many other visual details, appear in the movie *Berlin: Symphony of a City*. This 1927 documentary shows a day in the life of Berlin, filming everyday Berliners going about their business from early in the morning until late in the night. The newspaper she works for, the *Berliner Tageblatt*, was published by the Mosse House, which looks as I described. I don't know if they carried details from the trial of the Vampire of Düsseldorf, one of the earliest documented serial killers, but many German newspapers in mid-1931 covered this trial.

Hannah's apartment is similar to the mother's in the opening scenes of Fritz Lang's movie *M*, which was released shortly before my story starts. I saw comparable apartments while visiting student friends in Kreuzberg, a neighborhood in Berlin, in the late 1980s.

The gay club where her brother sings, the El Dorado, existed in 1931, became a Nazi political headquarters in 1933, and is currently a gay bar again. I first came across it while doing research for my history thesis. Numerous pictures of its exterior exist on the Internet, and Mel Gordon's *Voluptuous Panic: The Erotic World of Weimar Berlin* contains photographs of the interior, as well as pictures of dancers and letters from the time, describing the activities there.

When I lived in Berlin, I often shopped at the Wertheim department store, but wasn't aware of its complicated history until I decided to send my main character there to face the Nazis. There are numerous pictures available of the department store on Leipziger Strasse. Its fascinating history—it was stolen from its Jewish owners by the Nazis, ended up being owned by the Communists in East Germany, and was recently the subject of a court battle by Wertheim's heirs—is documented online and in newspaper articles.

Ernst Röhm really did exist. He helped Hitler come to power and was one of his closest friends. A charismatic soldier decorated several times in World War I, he expanded the Sturm Abteilung (the storm troopers) in three years from eighty thousand men to over four million. He was unashamedly gay and was prosecuted for it in 1932, on the basis of sexually explicit letters similar to those in the novel, although less graphic. These letters were leaked to the press during his trial for offenses against Paragraph 175 and were published in the *Munich Post* in 1931 and 1932. He was acquitted. I was lucky enough to find and study one of the original copies of his 1928 autobiography at Berkeley's Doe Library. I don't think it's ever been translated into English or even published using modern German fonts. His tendency to staff his offices with attractive young men was commented on by socialite and journalist Bella Fromm in *Blood and Banquets* and a visit he made to the El Dorado is described in Sefton Delmer's autobiography, *The Counterfeit Spy*. There is no evidence that he fathered a child. All of the encounters he has in the novel are fictitious.

I found many old maps and photographs, including a subway map from the summer of 1931 that the main character might have carried around in her pocket and pictures of her office building, Wertheim, Wittenbergplatz subway station, the Kaiser Wilhelm Memorial Church, and the gay club where her brother sings. All of the films, newspapers, and magazines in the novel existed at that time. Most of the consumer products mentioned by name, such as Elbeo stockings or Ravenklau cigarettes, were advertised in the *Berlin Illustrierte Zeitung* magazine in 1931.

While the boy in the novel is not based on a real person, I borrowed his manner of speaking from a minor character in the movie *Emil and the Detectives* filmed and released in Berlin in 1931. Karl May, the boy's favorite author, was the bestselling German writer of all time. His books set in the American West are very well known and were admired by Albert Einstein, Ernst Röhm, Adolf Hitler, and many other German schoolchildren from the 1890s through today.

General background information also came from primary sources I haven't already mentioned, including the diaries of Harry Kessler and William Shirer and a 1931 collection of the *Berlin Illustrierte Zeitung*. Additional secondary sources included *The Rise and Fall of the Third Reich* by William Shirer; *When Biology Became Destiny: Women in Weimar and Nazi Germany* by Renate Bridenthal, Anita Grossman, and Marion Kaplan; *Weimar Culture: The Outsider as Insider* by Peter Gay; *The Weimar Republic Sourcebook* by Anton Kaes,

Martin Jay, and Edward Dimendberg; *Weimar: A Cultural History 1918–1933* by Walter Laqueur; *Before the Deluge* by Otto Friedrich; *Marlene Dietrich* by Maria Riva; and *Lenya: A Life* by Donald Spoto.

I read many wonderful novels set in Berlin, from Christopher Isherwood's *Berlin Stories* to Philip Kerr's *Berlin Noir* trilogy and *The One from the Other*, to Joseph Kanon's *The Good German*.

Read on for an excerpt from
Rebecca Cantrell's new novel

A Night of Long Knives

available in hardcover in June 2010 from Forge Books

1

Wind rustled in grass browned by the drought plaguing Europe. Unseasonable heat and a parched smell invaded the gondola. The Graf Zeppelin's massive shadow stole over tidy Swiss houses, streets, and fields. I wiped my palms on my thin cotton dress, sweating as much from fear as heat. I had not been so near Germany since I fled three years before, after kidnapping the purported only son of Ernst Röhm.

Röhm was chief of staff of the storm troopers and commanded thirty times more men than Hindenburg, the president of Germany. And yet reports of homosexuality dogged him. Doubts that could be squashed by the small boy squirming in front of me. Anton provided final proof of Röhm's virility.

"Good day, Frau Zinsli," said Señor Santana. Like everyone else in the past three years, he used the name on my forged Swiss passport. I had left my real name, Hannah Vogel, behind. Except for brief visits to London to meet my lover, Boris, I had not had a true conversation with an adult I trusted in more than one thousand days.

"Good day." I looked out the window again. We were nearing a large lake. The zeppelin was scheduled to land in Zürich, Switzerland, but I could not remember any lakes near Zürich.

"How is the young man of the house?" Señor Santana nodded to Anton and snapped his fingers for Dieter, the waiter. Twice. "Bring me a cup of that excellent coffee!"

"Yes, sir." Dieter's gray eyes searched in vain for the beautiful Señora Santana.

"Have I told you that my plantation supplies the coffee for the zeppelin line?" asked Señor Santana.

"You have." Several times.

"Wonderful harvest this year." Señor Santana produced two sheets of stationery from the pocket of his cream-colored linen suit. Even at its hottest, Europe was no match for South America in temperature, and he always looked crisp and fresh.

"Will you show me a new plane?" Anton asked. "Please? Please?"

"Do not beg." I tousled his short blond hair. Without turning, he removed my hand. Too old for that, at nine?

"My husband loves being begged for his silly planes." Señora Santana, a former flamenco dancer, made her entrance. She paused at the edge of the viewing area, as if expecting applause, then patted her sleek black hair and dropped gracefully into a chair. Spicy perfume drifted over me, and I coughed.

Anton ran to her, hand out.

"That counts as begging." We had left Pernambuco, Brazil, five days ago and his manners had already deteriorated.

Señora Santana laughed and dropped a chocolate-covered ball of shredded coconut into his palm.

"*Gracias,*" he said, around the sweet.

"Thank you," I said as well. The Santanas seemed harmless. They were traveling to Hamburg to visit his warehouses. Fashion interested her more than politics, he spoke only of the coffee business, and neither was outwardly pro-Nazi.

I turned to the window just as we floated north over the midnight blue mass of the lake. Cool air dried the sweat on my arms and raised goose bumps. The only lake this large in Switzerland was Lake Constance. Its depths were frigid in both winter and summer. But on the northern edge of Lake Constance lay Germany.

Dieter set Señor Santana's drink next to him and he took a large sip. He handed a sheet of paper to Anton with trembling fingers. Nervous energy, or too much of his own product?

"A drink, Frau Santana?" Dieter was besotted with the glamorous Bolivian and rarely let her out of sight. His fingers fidgeted with brass buttons on his jacket.

"Please." Her accent gave the German words an alluring lilt. "A cold lemonade."

I rubbed my palms along my cold arms, fighting to stay calm while we flew north. It was probably a sightseeing diversion. No need to worry.

Anton drew a feather, his Indian symbol, and scribbled his first name inside it. He loved Karl May's popular Westerns and wanted to become an Apache brave like Winnetou. He had invented an Indian communication system, complete with symbols, twigs, and smoke signals.

"Can you show me a new design?" Anton asked. "A plane I never saw before?"

Señor Santana tapped the sheet with his bitten fingernails. "Perhaps you have seen them all."

He and his wife exchanged a smile as Anton looked stricken. Watching him squirm was part of their game.

The northern edge of the lake came into view. Fishing boats dotted the beach, and dark pines surrounded a German seaside town. I stared down, heart racing.

"Maybe one more." I barely heard his words, but I knew that behind me Señor Santana folded a new plane, fingers quick and dexterous, and Anton copied each movement, tongue peeking out of the corner of his mouth as he concentrated.

"Always straight creases," he said, before Señor Santana could remind him. I nodded in agreement without moving from the window.

The pines were beneath us now. We were in German airspace. I inhaled sharply.

"What's wrong?" Anton's voice sounded worried.

"I do not know yet." I never lied to him, although it would be easier. "But we are off course."

"Probably nothing." Señor Santana patted my arm. "A course correction. No danger. Zeppelins are very safe."

"Indeed." Did he know how easily the zeppelin's hydrogen-filled envelope could ignite? We might as well be riding a bomb. Into Germany. But at least we were not descending. Yet.

Señora Santana fanned herself with a painted black fan, nails flashing crimson. "Where is that boy with my lemonade?"

"A side trip could be an interesting diversion, don't you think?" Señor Santana set his airplane next to his empty coffee cup.

"I have an important appointment in Switzerland. Not Germany."

"Germany!" Anton gave me a worried look before tossing his new airplane out the viewing window. The greetings he sent to each country we visited spiraled down toward our homeland.

After we lost sight of the plane's white form, he waved to people below, as he always did. When we flew low over South America, everyone waved back: men waved tanned arms, housewives waved aprons, children waved handkerchiefs or leaves, babies waved sticky fists.

But in Germany only children waved. Adults scuttled into houses or under trees.

In spite of Hitler's rhetoric, Germany was at peace with her neighbors. What had its citizens to fear from the sky? I had more to fear from the land now that Nazis ruled it. If I landed in Germany, Röhm's men would kill me and snatch Anton.

I cursed the day I had accepted the assignment of chronicling the zeppelin's voyage from the Swiss magazine where I worked, under a pseudonym, as a travel writer. I had almost turned it down. But I longed to return to Europe. I wanted to see Boris. I missed him. I missed the feel of his body next to mine, his smell, the sound of his laugh, his tenderness with Anton, and his solidity. He was the only tie to my old self, and the one person I dared to trust. On the sultry streets of Rio de Janeiro, the danger of Germany had seemed very far away. Like a fool, I had agreed to go.

"We're docking," Anton shouted.

The zeppelin's motors had changed pitch. He was correct.

"Could you please keep an eye on him?" I asked the Santanas. "I must fetch my hat."

"But of course." Señora Santana laid her arm possessively across Anton's shoulders. "The boys will make more airplanes."

"Wait here, Anton. Until I come for you."

He nodded, and a grim look that should have belonged to an adult crossed his face. I trusted him to stay, brave but worried, until I returned. He caught my eye and winked. I touched my left eyebrow, our secret farewell gesture.

I walked out of the viewing room at a measured pace, but as soon as I was out of sight, I sprinted down the opulent corridor to our cabin. The carpeted floor swayed beneath me and I staggered.

When I opened our door, the scent of Argentinian roses enveloped me. Every day the steward replaced the bouquet. Just the kind of lovely and extravagant gesture my flamboyant brother had adored in the years before his murder. He hd been dead for three years; I grieved still.

The cabin looked in order: beds folded flush to the wall, neatly packed suitcases lined up by the door, camp stool covered with my contraband newspapers. Since suspending freedom of the press, along with most other freedoms, a prison sentence awaited anyone bringing foreign newspapers into Germany.

I glanced at the *Berlin Illustrierte Zeitung* from June 24, 1934. The Führer and Il Duce shook gloved hands. Mussolini wore a black hat set straight across his head, a well-tailored uniform, and the air of confidence that befits the fascist dictator of an entire country. Hitler carried his homburg half crumpled in his hand. He wore a baggy raincoat belted too high and an aggrieved expression. *Someday*, Hitler's insecure smile seemed to say, *I too will sweep away the last vestiges of freedom and own my land as you do yours; remember that when you deal with me*. Mussolini smiled back, unimpressed.

What had really happened at that meeting? The world might never

know, with most once powerful political journalists dead, in concentration camps, or in hiding. If I had not fled Germany, I would be
among their ranks and, while I was grateful for my freedom and the
time with Anton, I felt guilty for not exposing Germany's sad and
dangerous story to the world.

On top of the newspaper rested a twig with one bend in it, a secret
Indian message that Anton had last stood here alone. One bend, one
person. I slipped the twig into my dress pocket.

I scooped up the newspapers and dumped them on the floor at the
end of the corridor. No point in going to prison for those, assuming
I evaded prison for kidnapping. I grabbed our suitcases and hurried
to the control room.

Captain Schmelling stood in front of the spoked wheel, gauges
ranged on both sides. Struts angled off either end of the dash. Anton
adored the captain and had spent every moment that he could in the
control room, the top of his head barely level with the chrome com-
pass. He even flew the zeppelin for a moment. After deeming the quietly anti-Nazi captain unlikely to have connections to Röhm's SA, I
had felt safe enough to let Anton enjoy his time in the male world of
zeppelin officers. I regretted it. Who had alerted Röhm?

Although it was strictly forbidden, I turned the round doorknob
and entered. Captain Schmelling spared me a quick look. "Women
are not permitted on the bridge." He gestured to his first mate.

"Why are we landing in Germany?" I sidestepped the mate.

"Engine trouble." Captain Schmelling looked straight ahead. "We
must make minor repairs at the main hangar in Friedrichshafen. All
passengers are to disembark."

He nodded again to his first mate, who grabbed my arm and pro-
pelled me out of the control room.

"Have a cool drink at the lounge. The delay is regrettable, but un-
avoidable." The mate noticed my suitcases. "You won't need those."

I pulled my elbow out of his grip and ran back to Anton. Engine
trouble. I could not make myself believe it. In our lives, nothing was
accidental.

What would Röhm expect? For us to assume that we had landed in Switzerland and walk off with the other passengers? He would station men by the ladder. Hide? He would ransack the zeppelin.

That left running. And he was a canny old soldier. He would position men at the exits.

A hot breeze from the land streamed through the gondola windows and against my face, replacing the cool breezes from the lake. All around the gondola, windows stood open to keep the passengers cool. He might not have foreseen that. What if we climbed out a window at the rear of the zeppelin and exited out the back of the hangar? At two hundred thirty-six meters, the zeppelin was big enough to hide the Reichstag building. More than big enough to conceal us while we made our escape.

I hoped.

The landing looked typical. Men raced across the withered field to catch ropes dropped from the sides of the zeppelin. No sign of brownshirted storm troopers.

I placed our suitcases outside the viewing area so that the other passengers would not see them. Anton stood between the Santanas, his arm pointing out the window.

"Anton." I touched his bony shoulder. "You did not pack your bag. Come."

He raised his delicate eyebrows in surprise, as he always packed his bag perfectly, but he said nothing. He knew that I would not tell a lie about his bags without a good reason. I longed to tousle his hair, grateful for the trust between us. It had kept us alive so far.

"Excuse us," I said to the Santanas.

"You must do your chores properly," Señor Santana said. "Especially since you are the man of the house and must take care of your mother."

"I will always take care of her."

"Such a serious boy!" Señora Santana fanned herself again. "He needs more fun in his life."

"He is a little man," her husband argued. "Fun is only for small boys."

"Fun is for everyone." I wished that Anton had more of it.

He followed me to the hall.

"We are not going out the front," I said when we were alone.

"Why?" His voice dropped to a whisper.

Our lives together had been too filled with secrets. "I think there are men here for us."

During the voyage I had scouted the passages and rooms. We made a detour to a supply closet to snag a coil of rope I had seen there. After I draped the heavy rope over my shoulder, we hurried toward the rear. The interior grew more and more utilitarian until we teetered along a metal catwalk.

The floor jerked, and I stumbled. They had tied off to the mooring mast. Next we would be towed backward into the massive hangar. That meant we had only minutes until the passengers climbed down the long wooden ladder to the ground.

Together we ran to the back window. I measured with my hands. Barely large enough. My size did not help in a fight, but it was an asset while running. I glanced at the concrete floor, four meters below, then tied the rope to the frame that separated two windows. I yanked. The frame held firm. Good German engineering.

Anton's eyes shone. He loved adventure, and it had been so long since we had been in immediate danger that he had almost forgotten it was no game. That was just as well. It would do no good to have him too terrified to think. When danger threatened, let him keep his head clear and be strong like Winnetou.

"As soon as we stop," I said, "I will throw our bags out the window, then drop the rope. On my signal, climb down as fast as you can. Run to the wall and wait."

If we hurried, we might get out of the hangar and around to the front of the airport before the storm troopers noticed that we were not among the other passengers.

The zeppelin slipped inside the hangar. Everything darkened. He clutched my hand. A brave nine year old, but he still had limits.

The zeppelin stopped. We bobbed in place. I dropped the suitcases and rope to the hangar floor. A gray comma of rope curled on the far-away concrete.

I hoisted him out the window. Rope burned against my palms as I slid down after. The hard floor jolted my ankles, but I snatched up the suitcases and sprinted toward the back wall. His white singlet flitted ahead of me like a moth.

At the start of the trip, the captain had informed us that the hangar was so immense that it had its own weather patterns. Sometimes clouds and rain formed inside. Right now it was clear and too hot, the same as outside. I hefted the suitcases and sprinted, winded. The singlet stopped. He had reached the wall.

"Come along," I whispered. Vast emptiness swallowed my voice. I peeked over my shoulder at the rippling silver surface of the zeppelin. My gaze rose to the huge swastikas painted on the tail fins. How had this happened to my country, the land of Goethe and Schiller?

Anton grabbed the handle of his suitcase and we skirted the wall, heading for the back exit. The sunset outlined the front of the hangar in orange, but little light penetrated this far.

My ragged breathing pricked my nerves. Stealth and speed were our only weapons.

An arm encircled my neck. A hard muscle pressed against my throat. Anton cried out, but I could not see him.

"Shut your trap," breathed a squeaky voice in my ear. A cold blade pressed against my ribs. "I can let some air into you. We only need the boy."

I nodded my chin against his arm. The knife retreated, but the man held my neck fast. His sweat smelled of vinegar.

"Put her out," said a voice with a Swiss accent.

The honey odor of chloroform suffused the air. I held my breath. Too late. My captor gripped me so tightly I did not fall.

2

I drifted awake, slung over the back of a storm trooper who smelled as if he had not bathed since before the zeppelin left South America. To my left, Anton lay as lifeless as a rag doll in the arms of another massive storm trooper. Was Anton still breathing? I struggled toward wakefulness. I could not move toward him.

"You give him too much, Mouse?" asked the man on my right. He spoke like a man in command. He had excellent diction and a light Swiss accent, like the actor Emil Jannings.

Mouse bent his head to Anton's chest, and I flopped around on his shoulder. "He's breathing good." I recognized the squeak. The man who had held the knife to my ribs. And, from the sound of his accent, he was from Berlin. A traitorous voice from home.

Grass crackled underfoot when we marched onto the field. The first passengers milled out of the hangar, silhouetted against the sunset. I thought I recognized Señor and Señora Santana at the front of the pack. They always rushed onto the field.

Because explosive hydrogen filled the zeppelin, smoking was forbidden there and in the hangar. They spent the entire trip snapping chewing gum and dashing off every time we docked to grab a quick smoke. Twin matches flared and illuminated their faces. Surely they must see us. Red embers glowed at the tips of their cigarettes, and the smell of cigarette smoke wafted across the field.

I opened my mouth to call out, but instead I floated away again.

This time I came to in the backseat of an automobile, jammed between Mouse and the storm trooper who had carried Anton. I assumed that Jannings must be the driver but would not know unless he talked.

Anton lay across my lap. I breathed to clear my aching head. He twitched and I squeezed his hand.

The automobile shot forward through the twilight. We must still be near Friedrichshafen, where the zeppelin had docked. Not far from Switzerland.

Flight was our best alternative.

I shifted so that my shoes rested against the floor. When we jumped I would need to push against something solid. Anton tensed. The men on either side of us seemed not to notice.

I counted a few breaths, then cautiously cracked open an eye. Dark trees flashed by the window, illuminated by the last gray light of evening. We traveled about forty kilometers an hour, so perhaps we were in a town with a tree-lined street, full of friendly houses. Did such a thing exist in Germany anymore? I must hope so. It was unlikely that this would work, but we had to escape as soon as we could.

I grasped Anton's hand. *Be ready*, I thought. *One, two, three.*

I lunged to the left, swinging my elbow at Mouse's trachea. Unfortunately, his muscle-bound shoulders surrounded his neck, so the target was small. I missed, but scrabbled for the door lever anyway, right hand clasped in Anton's.

Mouse grabbed my arms and tossed me back against the seat. For good measure, he slammed his elbow into my left side. My breath whooshed out. The man on the right yanked Anton across the seat.

Jannings's hands stayed relaxed on the steering wheel. "Keep her quiet, but don't—"

Mouse grabbed the back of my head and slammed my face into the front seat. My nose struck the wooden top. Blood dripped onto the black leather upholstery.

Anton struggled in the other man's arms. He boxed Anton's ear.

Mouse yanked me upright. Springs squeaked in protest. I struggled to inhale. Blood ran from my nose.

"Mind her face, you stupid bastard," said Jannings. "We're not to damage it."

Mouse grimaced, obviously used to causing pain but unused to keeping faces pristine while doing it.

He drew his palm across the blood from my nose and wiped it on the automobile seat, leaving a dark streak on the leather. My eyes watered.

"It ain't broken." He released me and I slumped against the seat.

Air returned to my lungs in painful, shuddering breaths. Each one sent a dagger of fire down my side, but my body craved oxygen.

Anton bit his assailant on the thumb. He grabbed Anton by the scruff of the neck and squeezed. I could not speak to tell Anton to let go, that they would hurt him. Mouse wrenched Anton off the other man's hand. Beads of scarlet blood dotted his thumb. With an ease born of long practice, Mouse twisted Anton's arms behind his back. He yelped.

"Easy on the little one," said Jannings. "He's not to be harmed."

"He bites." Mouse did not let go of his arms.

"He's a child," said Jannings. "Should I hold him while you drive? We could switch, if you're not up to the task."

Mouse swore under his breath, and Anton swore back at him. I looked at him, shocked. I had not heard such language from him in years. But he remembered everything, even the vocabulary of his early years being raised by a prostitute.

I gritted my teeth and drew in a long breath. "Where," I gasped, "are you taking us?"

"Where we're told," said Jannings. "And no harm will come to you unless you fight us."

"We will comply. Release the boy."

"Do it," Jannings said.

Mouse let go of Anton's arms. Anton rubbed his wrists and glared.

"Respect your Uncle Mouse."

"You're not my uncle." Anton looked ready to attack. "I don't have any uncles."

I studied Anton. His emphasis on the word "uncle" gave me pause. Before I took him in, an uncle in his world was a pimp. Was Mouse a pimp? Did Anton recognize him? I held his hands to calm him down.

"Winnetou stalks the deer." I hoped that he would know what I meant. Winnetou knew that stalking meant waiting for your moment, quietly. Anton nodded and some tension drained out of his shoulders.

Then I turned toward Jannings. "We are Adelheid and Anton Zinsli. Swiss citizens. I demand to be brought to our embassy." I said it more because it was what a Swiss citizen would say than because I expected results.

"I'm sure it will get sorted out." Jannings's eyes met mine in the rearview mirror. "Fraulein Hannah Vogel."

Anton gasped, and I cursed inwardly. "I have no idea to whom you are referring."

"You will," Jannings answered. "In good time."

Anton fumed next to me. Bruises bloomed on the pale skin of his arms. I fought down a rush of blind rage at Mouse. He would pay for hurting Anton.

After the anger subsided and my nose stopped bleeding, I had time to become afraid.

We drove north and east, probably toward Munich. But Röhm should be in Berlin. Or Venice. I thought of the pictures of Hitler and Mussolini in the newspaper, Röhm absent from them. Since we left Germany in 1931 he had stood on Hitler's right in almost every photograph I had seen. His absence was unexpected. I hated the unexpected.

"He'll be glad it went off so well," said Anton's assailant. I named him Santer, after the villain in the Winnetou books. His breath reeked so strongly of beer that I smelled it even through the metallic scent of blood in my nose.

"It's not over yet." Mouse ran a scarred hand through his greasy blond hair, revealing gray streaks at his temples. His pale blue eyes had more cunning than I expected.

"Will be soon." Santer flexed his fist. "They won't give us any more trouble."

Santer in the books died most painfully, I reminded myself. I fingered my side. It hurt every time I inhaled. I breathed shallowly to lessen the pain. Every so often I endured a deep breath to keep from getting dizzy.

"How's your side?" Mouse asked. "I don't reckon I cracked more than one rib. Just enough to keep you quiet."

No accident then. He had known just what he was doing. Breaking ribs was probably his trademark.

"Thank you for your restraint." Sarcasm dripped from my words, and he smiled.

"Feisty one, ain't you?" He wound a strand of my hair, the same shade of blond as his own, around his index finger.

I yanked my head away.

"None of that." Jannings watched in the rearview mirror. "The boss has his own plans for her."

Mouse shrugged. "Maybe after."

I sucked in a deep breath and winced. Anton shot Mouse a murderous look. I grabbed Anton's arm.

"Cracked rib," I told him, thinking back to my nursing training during the Great War. "Nothing serious." I did not add that it might be serious and was always painful. Instead I smiled, but he looked unconvinced.

"Where are we going?" I asked again.

No one bothered to answer. Mouse tipped his uniform hat over his eyes and started to snore.

Santer reached across me. I gasped when he pressed on my rib. He thumped Mouse on the chest. Mouse snorted and turned to the side.

Silence reigned.

Even with the windows down, it was too hot jammed between

Mouse and Santer. I hugged Anton's small form. Under normal circumstances he never would have allowed it, but he was as frightened as I.

We looked out the window. Dark fields streamed by. If houses existed out there, all were unlit.

"This is Germany," Anton whispered. "I was born here."

I ran my fingers down the bridge of my nose. It did not feel broken. "It was a different country then." I did not try to keep anger and bitterness from my voice.

"It's a better country now," Jannings said. "Stronger."

"Stronger does not always mean better," I answered.

"It does." Jannings kept his eyes on the road. "You'd do well to remember that."

Santer fell asleep. I thought of attempting another escape, but the automobile traveled at least eighty kilometers per hour. Even if we landed uninjured, we had nowhere to hide. I twisted around. The round hump of the trunk was where we might end up if we tried to flee again.

Anton sat as alert as an Indian scout, waiting for his chance. I was proud of him, but furious with myself. How could I have accepted the zeppelin assignment? Switzerland was too close to Germany.

We approached the outskirts of a large city; Jannings slowed. House windows glowed yellow on either side of us. Perhaps someone would hide us, or come to our defense.

"Almost there." Jannings handed Mouse a brown bottle. He withdrew the glass stopper. The odor of chloroform filled the car. I kicked at his hand. If the bottle broke everyone might go down. But Mouse was too strong and had no qualms about leaning on my rib.

Anton struggled against Santer, cursing.

Mouse smashed a damp cloth against my throbbing nose. A sticky sweetness filled my mouth. Air shimmered, moved, and then it was dark.

I woke stretched flat on a bed, my clothing stuck to me. How long had I been unconscious? My head pounded, my nose ached, and my side burned. Moaning, I rolled onto my injured rib. We told our patients to lie so, to let them inflate the uninjured lung fully. Now that it was my own rib, I regretted how blithely I gave that instruction to wounded soldiers almost twenty years ago, surprised none had taken me to task for dispensing such painful and probably useless information. I lay still, breathing shallowly, afraid to open my eyes. Was I in a concentration camp?

I forced open my eyelids. Dark wainscoting clad the walls to waist height, flocked yellow wallpaper above. My suitcase rested next to a waxed pine Biedermeier wardrobe, near the front door as if deposited by a friendly bellhop. Heavy curtains covered the windows, blocking out all light. A green-shaded lamp shone on the night table next to my bed. Next to the table stood a solid wooden chair.

Seated in the chair was Ernst Röhm.